The Guest Book

Also by Mae Marvel

Everyone I Kissed Since You Got Famous

If I Told You, I'd Have to Kiss You

The Guest Book

A Novel

MAE MARVEL

ST. MARTIN'S GRIFFIN
NEW YORK

This is a work of fiction. All of the names, characters, organizations, places, and events portrayed in this work are either products of the author's imagination or used fictitiously.

First published in the United States by St. Martin's Griffin, an imprint of St. Martin's Publishing Group

EU Representative: Macmillan Publishers Ireland Ltd, 1st Floor, The Liffey Trust Centre, 117–126 Sheriff Street Upper, Dublin 1, D01 YC43

www.stmartins.com

Designed by Meryl Sussman Levavi

The Library of Congress Cataloging-in-Publication Data is available upon request.

ISBN 978-1-250-39208-4 (trade paperback)
ISBN 978-1-250-39209-1 (ebook)

First Edition: 2026

10 9 8 7 6 5 4 3 2 1

For our queer, neurodivergent, late-blooming, too-much-too-soon-or-too-late soul siblings who hear "not like that" and somehow find the courage to do it *just* like that even harder. We make the world bigger for everyone else.

The Guest Book

Chapter One

"Once upon a time"—Cosima Frank swept the rain from her curls with a sigh—"lawyers knew how to manage an estate with a bit of flourish."

She pressed her trench coat into Duncan's outstretched hands and shook out her umbrella, spattering rain onto the marble floor.

"Is that so?" Ever the gentleman, he carefully hung up her coat for her in the alcove off the foyer.

"Haven't you seen the movies? They're supposed to gather the mourners together for a reading of the will where dark secrets come to light. Perhaps an elegant young woman faints. That sort of thing."

"Your meeting with the attorneys didn't go how you expected?" Duncan offered her his fond, paternal smile, which Cosima made an effort to return. All the small muscles of her face that made it possible to smile had grown stiff with disuse.

"At one point, I wasn't sure if the gentleman from the title company was describing the Venice Beach lot Mother bought in the seventies or if he was casting a spell," she said. "Although I did learn that her various waterfront investments have appreciated nicely. No one can say Phoebe wasn't savvy with her money."

Duncan glanced toward the center of the foyer, where a three-story-tall pink marble fountain of an elephant, complete with gold saddle, dominated the space. "At times," he said diplomatically.

Duncan was always diplomatic.

She followed him to her mother's study, where they had been meeting in the afternoons. The routine had settled on the pair of them in the quiet of the massive Beverly Hills estate that Cosima's mother had liked to call "the Castle." Without its queen, there wasn't the bustle of staff making rooms ready for guests anymore. There weren't caterers, or a bartender coming to the back entrance to set up in one of the lounges for a gathering. There weren't deliveries of flowers or dresses. No architects or moneymen or agents or managers or glittering, famous, beautiful people here, admiring a new painting or antique.

It turned out the Castle was only the Castle because of Phoebe. Without her, it was a collection of empty rooms.

The smallest one was this study, where Cosima and Duncan could still smell a thin vapor of her perfume and survey the chaos piled on her desk, feeling as though she would walk in at any moment to kiss Duncan on the neck.

They settled into their chairs, a wingback by the tiled fireplace for Duncan and an Eames that could take all of Cosima's long legs without making her back sore.

"Were there many photographers at the gate?" He reached down and pulled two seltzers from a concealed fridge in the study's breakfront.

"Fewer. The rain's so bad today."

The weather for the funeral had been obediently sunny, seventy degrees, and clear as crystal—Los Angeles obeying Phoebe's whims, as usual. But it had been raining ever since, for three weeks straight. The drumming of the rain became a constant in the background while Cosima sat to be interviewed about her mother, the Queen of Hollywood, and how nothing in the world would be the same without her.

The tears of the world would end, she assumed, whenever the rain did. On the first sunny day, the planet would start to spin again, and with it Phoebe's legacy, which Cosima had inherited so she could preserve it forever.

She was the Castle's princess, after all.

Duncan placed his seltzer bottle on the edge of the overflowing desk, centering it on a silver coaster. He pulled out his phone and a pair of tortoiseshell-rimmed glasses that made a distinguished contrast to his salt-and-pepper hair and beard. When he leaned back, his shirt settled into a drape worthy of Robert Redford. "Are you ready?"

Cosima took a deep breath through her nose. She counted to four before exhaling over a slow eight counts to settle her tight stomach. She'd had a number of doctor's visits and tests attempting to get to the bottom of her sharp stomach pain, only to have a kind physician suggest that she consider developing a mindfulness practice and try deep breathing. It didn't work—her stomach still managed to twist itself into a pinching knot—but she figured the extra dose of oxygen would assist with the next set of tasks at hand. "What do we have today?"

Duncan tapped his phone. "I'm sending you a file with terms from the public library for their display of Phoebe's papers."

Cosima retrieved her tablet from her bag and swiped it awake. "Got it."

"I already had the attorneys review them, and I accepted their edits. You just need to sign."

Nodding, Cosima dragged the papers into her project organizer. "Next?"

"There's an issue with the release of the budget for the endowed theater chair at UCLA. When I talked to the foundation CFO, she said what's needed is a phone call to the bank, but you're the only one authorized to talk to them."

"Right." Cosima made a note, adding it to the list for her assistant to schedule an appointment. She took another slow breath.

Duncan leaned back in his chair and fiddled with his heavy gold wristwatch. Her belly cramped again, this time because he was stalling, and she knew why.

"You've seen the stock reports," he said.

This wasn't a question. In her Burbank office, a high-definition wall-mounted monitor displayed the vagaries of the global market in real time. She had a phone and a tablet and a laptop, all of them connected to the internet. In addition, Cosima received a crisp butter-yellow cardstock folder every morning with her breakfast. It, too, contained a market update, among other briefings essential to the operations of Phoebe Frank Studios, better known as PFS. It was the same folder her mother used to review while eating her own breakfast.

"Power vacuums make the market nervous." Her voice sounded far away.

"They do. On the upside, that means the market will settle out once a new CEO has been named."

Once you name the new CEO, he meant.

Cosima's mother had built PFS into an empire on the shoulders of her first project, *Ship of the Cosmos*, a low-budget film that she wrote, directed, and starred in as Captain Astra Saturnine. *Ship of the Cosmos* went on to become one of the biggest film franchises of all time. It spawned sequels and prequels, limited-series spin-offs and animated versions, comic books and novelizations, action figures, fast-food toy tie-ins, and conventions. For three decades, PFS had been synonymous with *Ship of the Cosmos*, even as the studio's scope grew to constitute a significant portion of Hollywood's continued output.

And yet Phoebe Frank, in what was possibly her first misstep, had not named a successor. Instead, she had charged Cosima with the knighting. Phoebe had called this a "compromise." Cosima considered it a punishment, since it had come after she made it clear that she could not—or, in her mother's view, *would* not—succeed Phoebe.

That last, horrible, monthslong argument with her mother was the first time Cosima had refused to do what Phoebe wanted.

It surprised them both.

Cosima often thought of her life as Phoebe's daughter in terms of *before* and *after*. From her birth and appearance on the cover of *People*—swaddled in lace, cradled in her loving mother's arms—until her graduation with a niche degree in the arts, her life had been a public performance of what it was to be the daughter of a famous creative. After the whirlwind of finals and graduation, Cosima had traveled, experimented, and dreamed of making something of her own. Then she'd come home to rest and regroup, only to be told that Phoebe needed her. Cosima's advice was required. Her *unique* knowledge of Phoebe Frank Studios. How well she could anticipate what her mother would want done. How good she was at doing things Phoebe's way.

It worked out well for Phoebe. For the stockholders, too—until Phoebe was gone.

Now, the global entertainment industry, the markets, the PFS licensing and franchise partners, the media, and even the internet cinephiles looked to Cosima for a decision that she'd already taken too long to make. They had expected her to deliver it like a puff of white smoke from the Vatican, perhaps. Or they'd looked for the name of the annointed to float from the Castle on the exhale of her mother's last breath.

Duncan watched her for a long, quiet moment.

Her stomach pressed against her heart, her throat, and locked her voice up tight.

He sighed at the screen of his phone. "Do you want to talk about the garden project instead?"

She did not. She took a sip of seltzer, hoping it would remind her stomach to be a stomach rather than a bag of knives. "Of course. That sounds perfect."

When he looked up from his phone, it was to smile at her with sympathy.

Duncan was wonderful. He'd always been wonderful, ever since Cosima's mother met him on a jet boat in the French Riviera, where he had at least six heiresses and models fighting over him—but naturally he chose Phoebe, with her long legs and curly hair and big eyes. At that time, Phoebe's fame was wildfire, but, telling the story, she'd liked to portray herself as though she were an awkward girl reading on the beach, noticed by a handsome rake.

Cosima had her own memories of that trip. She'd been four years old, just beginning to understand that there was a difference between her mother when she was being her mother and her mother when she was being "Phoebe Frank." Cosima had liked it when her mother took her into the cold sea, holding her hand. She'd liked this tall man with his fascinating Scottish accent. He found a gold coin behind her ear and gave it to her, and he said it was real gold. She could still remember the way he crouched down, putting his kind eyes right at her level. He buckled her into a bright pink life jacket he'd bought for her in a beachside shop. It pressed underneath her chin when she sat down on his boat.

Duncan set his phone on the arm of the chair and removed his glasses. "Maybe we can reconvene in the morning. You've already had a long day putting out fires."

Cosima looked out the window of her mother's study at the sprawling landscape of native plants and quiet, flower-filled paths to the pool. The gardens had been Duncan's intervention. A casual gardener in the way many Europeans were, Duncan had decided to cultivate plants and flowers as a way to cultivate his relationship with Cosima. The first time Cosima and Duncan's gardens had been photographed for a magazine, she was sixteen. There had been several more features over the years, the product of writers and editors charmed by the duo and the oasis of California native plants they'd created.

At the height of Cosima and Phoebe's arguments about the future of PFS, Duncan had used the garden to broker a ceasefire. He'd suggested to Phoebe that Cosima's desire to build something of her own was equal to Phoebe's but not identical. Perhaps a few calls could be made to support Cosima's passions. Audiences might be interested in a new kind of gardening show, a stylish one filmed at the Castle. Many an empire began with a single audience, as Phoebe well knew. Cosima simply needed her *own* audience. If this grew into a younger, leaner sister studio to PFS? Well. It wouldn't be surprising.

And so, the blow to Phoebe thus softened, Cosima came to be in charge of two projects. First, she was to handle the peaceful transition of power and the initiation of a new era for PFS so that everything might be done just the way Phoebe would want. Then, a few weeks from now, she would begin filming the pilot of *An American Castle's Garden*.

PFS had already inked multiple streaming contracts and a global distribution deal for the new gardening show, somewhat losing sight of the "leaner" sister studio that had initially been imagined. *Cosima's* studio now employed dozens of people who depended on her new passion and vision.

She missed gardening. It would have been nice to be out there, her knees and hands in the dirt, alone with her feelings.

"I'm fine, Duncan. Truly," she said. "I do need to find a paper, since we're here in Mother's office." She rose to her feet. Her arches hurt. "One of our producers wants it, something she said Mother put aside for her in her desk. A note from Scorsese he wrote after he saw *Ship of the Cosmos*."

Her mother's desk was a disaster, though Phoebe had always claimed to have a "system." No one had been permitted to touch the teetering piles on top of it—not even Cosima. She didn't know where to find a note from Scorsese, even if she'd had the urge to search for it. She trailed her fingers across the stacks of paper and wished it were the end of the day so she could take off her shoes and curl up in her bed like a small, soft animal.

Instead, she started taking apart the piles, flipping each item over, one by one. There were papers falling off the desk, sliding under it, drifting onto her mother's desk chair. Duncan rose to his feet. "I'll just give you a hand."

"I've got it." She reached out to steady a stack before it collapsed but miscalculated, sending it tumbling to the floor. "Shit."

A sheet of her mother's canary-yellow stationery fluttered to the carpet between her feet. Cosima crouched down to retrieve it, her arches throbbing.

Her hand stilled over the paper.

"What is it?" Duncan asked.

It was a list. One she'd written down for her mother, who dictated the items to her when the doctors made it clear Phoebe was intractably ill despite her efforts to hide it.

"Mother's au revoir list." She tried to keep her voice neutral as she picked the paper up. If she sounded distressed, Duncan would try to help. If Duncan tried to help, Cosima would end up with one more thing to do.

This list of her mother's was the reason why Cosima had stayed the night at the Getty, curled up in a sleeping bag in the dark beside Phoebe with a laughing Rembrandt looking down at them. Why she'd skydived, buckled to an instructor who smelled like cold air, the wind impossibly loud in her ears. They'd met a "nose" in Paris, who bottled a scent for the two of them. One by one, they'd drawn a line through each of the items, until the time came when her mother needed to rest and be taken care of.

Because it was *Phoebe's* list, it also included her wish for the Castle to be converted from their private home to a center for the performing arts. Who could deny her such a generous bequest? The Castle, of course, had never been for Cosima or Duncan. It was a decadent showpiece, Phoebe's homage to Hollywood. *Phoebe's*.

Cosima was surprised to see an item left on the list. She'd forgotten about it.

Stay at Gregory Place, it said.

An inn, located in a tiny village in England. A long time ago, in the 1980s, it was where Phoebe met and fell in love with Cosima's father, a dashing Formula One driver who died in a race when Cosima was in preschool. Phoebe had wanted to have the "full-circle experience" of visiting the inn together with Cosima. She'd said Gregory Place was "magic."

Duncan cleared his throat. "It was such a lovely thing for the two of you to share."

Was it? Cosima bit back the comment, feeling awful for even having the thought.

Duncan read the list over her shoulder. "Ah. A trip over the pond would be a pleasant escape for you once you've made your announcement to the stockholders and we've wrapped up filming season one. I was already planning on opening my estate in Dundee for a visit. You could tick this off the list, then come up and breathe clean Scottish air and put pen to paper for ideas for season two."

"Yep." Cosima rubbed her thumb over the paper. Her lungs were too tight. Her stomach roared into her throat. "Good idea."

"Are you all right, darling?"

She closed her eyes, annoyed she'd let her tone be short. "Yes, I'm sorry. The day was too long for these shoes. You're hearing my arches and pinky toe, not me." She gave him a practiced smile.

But she wasn't half the actress her mother had been. When Duncan quickly turned his head toward the dark window, she witnessed his mask slip, his mouth bracketing with grief. All at once, her vision telescoped, framing Duncan's face at the pinpoint end of a long black tunnel. Cosima shook her head, trying to make the tunnel disappear, but his faraway face didn't change. From here, she could hear the water in the elephant fountain. She could smell the familiar pompelmo fragrance her mother liked to infuse into the air.

She had never known any other home but the Castle.

Cosima didn't know why it was still so important—always and forever the most important thing—to make her mother happy.

Her mother was dead.

Duncan turned toward her again. His fond smile had been restored. "We're both knackered." He started out of the office, but before he went through the doorway, he squeezed her shoulders. "Breakfast at Lulu's?"

She nodded, or she didn't. She couldn't meet his eyes.

Eventually, with a final pat, he left.

Cosima came back into her body enough to notice her feet hurt too much to stand. In that, at least, she had been truthful with Duncan. She collapsed onto the Eames ottoman, staring at the mess she'd made of her mother's desk. Her phone and tablet buzzed and chimed with notifications while her eyes started to burn with the tears she would not shed.

When her stomach cramped, hard, taking her breath away so completely she couldn't even gasp, she dropped the list in her lap and picked up her phone. She watched one notification after another slide up the screen while her hand vibrated.

She opened the phone's browser.

With a fingertip, she filled the boxes with the required information at each step. Her payment confirmed with another notification. Shucked-off heels in hand, she walked barefoot past the elephant fountain, up two flights of stairs, and came back down with luggage she'd packed in the dark, her heart alternately pounding and freezing in place, her stomach so tight it felt numb.

The last thing she did was strike through the final item on her mother's list and set the paper down on Duncan's chair.

Then she ran from the Castle. Escaped, really—a princess dashing through the pouring rain into the night.

Not to find magic. Magic didn't exist anymore.

Chapter Two

Edie sighed over her map in frustration until the innkeeper sighed back.

"If you're set on seeing a hedgehog, I suppose there's the road past Baroness Rachel's manse. She puts hedgehog houses in her garden, so you might look there." Morag Beveridge retied the strings of her apron. She shoved a dripping collection of branches, leaves, flowers, and possibly mosses—lichen?—into a large jar and then poked at it. Edie guessed it would end up being one of the innkeeper's "arrangements" for the lobby.

Edie squinted at the map with renewed enthusiasm. The phone plan she'd bought before her trip here didn't work, and she spent a lot of her time wishing she'd learned how to properly read maps in school. "The road past Baroness Rachel's—is that Church Street?"

"Where it loops up the hill and runs into Rectory Street." Morag stuck a fake bird on a stick into her arrangement. At least, Edie hoped it was a fake bird and not a taxidermied bird.

Or what it actually looked like, which was an alive bird that had been rendered immobile by a spell but kept on a stick for a hundred years.

"Loops up the hill?"

Morag looked at Edie over her glasses. "We're on Gregory Close."

"Yes."

"Go out the front door, turn—"

"Left!"

Morag blinked at the interruption. She was still getting used to Edie. "Yes, left. Walk all the way to the high street."

"Then I turn right on High Street." Edie put her finger on the map, trying to follow along. "Oh, I see. I can take that to Church and turn right and go to the top of the loop!" She put the map down. "But what is the road that Baroness Rachel's manse is on?"

"A lane that spins off the loop where it meets Church Street."

"Called?"

Morag gazed at one of the beams in the ceiling of the inn's lounge. "Can't recall."

Edie laughed. "You've lived here your entire life!"

"Eighty-six years." One of Morag's long white braids slid over her shoulder when she nodded. She was a lively, active eighty-six, favoring a uniform of sturdy jeans and wool sweaters with her apron. "I think it's had more than one name, and that's why I can't remember."

Edie folded her map and collapsed back into the dusty mauve-and-cream striped upholstered armchair that she'd adopted as her own in the eight days since she arrived at Gregory Place. She rolled her head to look out the wavy glass of the lounge windows. "It's raining again. Do hedgehogs come out of their garden houses in the rain?"

“Why would I know that?” Morag pulled a tea bag out of a mug, added soy milk and sugar, and brought it around the reception desk to hand to Edie with a packet of what had become her favorite biscuit, bourbon creams. “Here you are, love.”

“Thank you.” Edie put the biscuit packet on the arm of the chair and pulled her legs up beneath her before wrapping her hands around the hot mug. She studied the room as she waited for her tea to cool enough to sip.

The lounge at Gregory Place had textured mauve-on-brown wallpaper and at least six mirrored occasional tables that Edie could not seem to keep fixed in her field of vision no matter how hard she tried. The flesh around her knees had acquired a number of spectacular bruises. The décor reminded Edie of her grandmother’s house in Fond du Lac, Wisconsin, which had last been decorated when Edie’s mom graduated high school and moved out in the early nineties.

When Edie first got here, the contrast between this room and the inn’s spare stone exterior had kind of blown her mind. The slate-roofed building promised fireplaces big enough to roast venison, or maybe a suit of armor gleaming in the hallway. The plaque at the inn’s door said that Gregory Place dated to 1758—older than the Declaration of Independence!

A lot of England was like that, it turned out. Historic, but lived in by not-historic people in a completely ordinary and ever-so-slightly disappointing way.

Of course, she had only been to this one tiny corner of England, Harlaxton village, but she’d read a lot of tourist brochures in the lounge and gathered there were places she could visit that were even older and looked less disappointing. She would if she had the money for one of those limitless train passes. She did not.

Edie's room was clean and serviceable, but dust furred nearly every surface of the lounge. Some of the stacks of magazines featured the wedding of Princess Diana, and they were not collectibles. There was a spot where the mauve carpet crunched if you walked on it. She doubted Morag could keep up with the details of the inn at this stage of her life. The innkeeper didn't have any employees, as far as Edie had been able to tell.

It was not lost on her that these were the same reasons she'd been able to afford such an extended stay at Gregory Place on her limited budget. Age. Infirmity. Lack of better options.

Though it was a little surprising, now that she was here, that Gregory Place hadn't successfully kept up with the times. Harlaxton received a steady stream of tourists to visit the massive Harlaxton Manor, which had appeared in movies and beloved BBC series. The village was so pretty, it sometimes made Edie's eyes cross in pleasure, and it was lousy with the kind of plaque-bearing buildings and structures that dads on vacation liked to take pictures of.

But if you wanted to stay overnight at Gregory Place, you'd better enjoy bedsheets on the unpleasant verge of damp, a cranky innkeeper who might be scratching sigils into the dirt to keep people away, and the noise of what had to be a hundred foxes screaming in the overgrown garden at night—a sound that Edie had been certain, on her first night, was a bloody, stabbing murder happening right outside her window.

The food was fucking amazing, however. And Edie knew food.

"Maybe I could help you with something?" she suggested.

Morag, who now sat in a rocker by the windows opposite the lounge, took a noisy sip of her tea. "Like what?"

Edie tried to think of a diplomatic way to put it. The problem was that she was not a diplomatic person. "I do have an entire culinary arts certification from the finest vocational school in Green Bay, Wisconsin."

"You're not to step foot in my kitchen." Morag said this mildly, but she had said it much less mildly several times prior when Edie had attempted to get a closer look at the space.

One would think, given that Edie had just lost the love of her life—her own place to feed people, which she'd made with her own two hands—that she would be wary of kitchens and all of their beautiful promises.

If only.

"Your great loss," she said. "Well, okay. You obviously have stacks of paperwork to catch up on." The stacks in question, located behind the reception desk, were tall enough to be visible from where Edie sat. "I have had so many jobs. It's true most of them were in the weeds of food service, but I can file. I can toil at the hot fires of a paper shredder."

"Stay away from my papers."

She sighed and looked at the ceiling. "I am a hard worker, Morag. I love to do things. Put me to work. Use my body and what many might consider my talent for divergent thinking."

"I can plainly see you can't sit still." Morag raised an eyebrow at Edie. "You want the English experience? Take a walk. Complain the season's coming too early or too late while you trudge through the same rainy weather we have in all seasons."

"I could tidy the lounge." Edie opened her biscuit packet, watching for Morag's reaction to this salvo.

She scoffed. "Needs more than a tidy."

"It needs a shovel and a pressure washer, but for today, I could dust and haul these ancient magazines and newspapers to recycling." Edie popped a whole biscuit in her mouth.

"And what would be the point of that, lovey? Gregory Place isn't in any guidebook. No one's beating down these doors. It's just you and me and—" Morag pointed above her head.

The other guest, she meant.

Edie hadn't gotten a look at her. She didn't come downstairs for Morag's modified-vegan-for-Edie full English breakfasts, even though the mushroom bacon was extraordinary. Instead, Morag left a tray in front of the guest's door for every meal, and the guest put the empty tray outside of it when she was done. She didn't go for walks, or for excursions, and she hadn't left her room to sit in the lounge or stroll over to the manor, even though it was genuinely massive and had been built by an English madman named Gregory Gregory.

Edie hadn't been there, either. She was saving the madman's manor house tour for a special occasion. The special occasion being free third Thursdays.

She had inspected the neat line of mysterious skin care products on the guest's shelf in the bathroom. Their labels looked like they were made by a calligrapher working under a rainbow while angels sang, and they smelled so good when Edie guiltily twisted off their heavy lids that her eyes rolled into the back of her head.

"I've already taken too many walks in the rain," she said. "I have a lot of energy, and I'm here for weeks yet. Let me organize something. Or clean it. I love vacuuming."

Morag pointed a digestive biscuit at her. "Don't touch my Hoover. It's temperamental."

"Please," Edie begged. "You don't have a television. I don't have a computer, and my phone's a brick. All of the books in the library are by Barbara Cartland."

"A genius if there ever was one."

"You won't let me read the guest book." Edie looked with longing toward the inn's enormous, olive-green, leather-bound guest book where it sat closed on top of the reception desk. It looked as old as the building. She was starting to feel desperate to flip back the cover and see if the first entry had been written in the crabbed hand of an Elizabethan scribe, possibly in rhyming verse.

It had been raining *so much* since she got here.

Morag set her mug down on the table at her elbow with a decisive thump. “You want something to do?”

“I do, Morag. I really, really do. It’s not a good idea for me to have any time to think at all.”

This was a spectacular understatement.

Morag smiled and started rocking in her chair. “Then go wake up the princess.”

Edie’s mug froze halfway to her lips. The entire time she had been here, Morag had emphasized how critical it was to stay quiet in the inn during the daytime so that “the princess” could rest. Edie had, of course, asked Morag nearly one hundred thousand times why she called the mysterious guest by the nickname—if it was because she knew this guest or something about her, or if it was a joke, a dig, an insult—but Morag wouldn’t say. Edie had gotten the impression that this woman was perhaps ill, or maybe not a paying guest but someone Morag was sheltering for an unknown, Gothic reason.

Edie had even wondered if the guest *was* a princess.

This was England. They had them here.

Without hesitation, she stood, walked across the lounge, and put her mug and packet wrapper on the reception desk. Then she brushed her hands together. “I will do that. I will go wake up the princess.” Edie smiled at Morag’s surprised expression. “You didn’t think I would.”

“I don’t know what to think about you, to be quite honest.”

This response did not bother Edie. It was not an uncommon reaction to her existence. Her mom liked to say that if she hadn't been at the birth, she wouldn't know where Edie came from. *Certainly not Wisconsin*, she liked to add.

"I will walk up those stairs, knock on her door, and ask her if she wants to go to the lane off Church Street where it meets the Rectory Street loop and see a hedgehog, so put a pair of extra wellies by the door."

"You think that's the way to go about it?"

"I think it's worth a shot. Maybe we'll become best friends. Maybe we'll take the bus into Grantham and have a fancy dinner while you sit here by yourself and crack into one of those romance novels."

"Maybe. Who knows?"

Edie paused, one foot hovering over the first step on the staircase that led to the inn's guest rooms. "What's her name?"

Her belly fluttered at her question. It felt like knowing this name would conjure something up. Open a kingdom.

Morag smiled. "Cosima."

As Edie climbed the narrow staircase, she practiced the name under her breath. *KAH-sih-ma*, it sounded like. She'd never known anyone with that name. She'd never heard of it. She wondered how it was spelled and if it was a name associated with a region or country or culture. Her mom had named her after the band Edie Brickell and New Bohemians. She'd had their song "What I Am" on heavy rotation during the pregnancy, when she was going through a neo-hippie phase.

Edie passed her own room. She'd left her door open to keep the air moving. The room gathered a bit of a mildew smell if it was shut up all day.

The other guest's door was at the end of the hall. The breakfast tray sat outside, demolished. Nothing was left but a smear of egg yolk on a plate. If this woman was convalescing from a mysterious illness, it didn't affect her appetite. Edie made a mental note to carry the breakfast tray downstairs so Morag didn't have to.

Before she knocked, she softly pressed her ear against the door.

Silence.

She knocked—three firm knocks. Her heart knocked as many times and, it felt like, louder.

"I don't need any housekeeping today! Thanks!"

The woman was American. Or maybe Canadian. She didn't sound sick. She *did* sound annoyed. Maybe even annoyed-plus. For sure, she had just dismissed whoever was knocking on her door, which in the woman's experience could only be Morag, but Edie wasn't Morag, so she should identify herself. Otherwise it was probably weird.

"Um. It's not Morag." Edie bit her lip and listened. Nothing. "Hello?"

The door swung open so fast, she nearly fell into the room.

"What?"

The voice was much more annoyed than annoyed-plus.

Edie took a few steps back, carefully avoiding the breakfast tray. The woman framed in the doorway surprised her. For starters, she was a lot younger than Edie had assumed she would be, though Edie didn't know why she'd assumed the hidden stranger would be old. Maybe because the only person she'd been talking to for a week was Morag. This woman was in her twenties or maybe early thirties, somewhere in the same general zone as Edie's twenty-eight.

Also, she was tall, which always surprised Edie, whose people were not. Her people were Wisconsin sturdy. While Edie had escaped the tanklike silhouette of her two brothers, she was short and had a body her mom called "comfortable." One of

Edie's girlfriends had called it "a body for sex and being fed grapes," which she secretly liked.

Additionally, this woman was a *mess*.

Edie guessed her pale brown hair was probably curly, but right now it was more nest-y, at least on one side of her head. She wore a pretty cream-colored short silk robe, but it had something that Edie guessed—hoped—might be HP Sauce dribbled down the front. Her full lips were chapped. Her eyes were the kind of eyes that turned down at the corners, and they were big, with long, dark lashes, and a color that a driver's license would describe as blue, but they weren't. They weren't gray, either. They were lovely. Familiar, too, somehow? With purple-dark circles underneath them, but Edie assumed those were temporary.

"So, hello! I'm Edie. Edie Whitelock."

The woman widened her eyes in a way that was unmistakably aggressive and communicated, *Tell me why you are standing there right this second or I am slamming this door.*

"I'm your neighbor." Edie pointed down the hall. "Just right there. We share a bathroom! Kind of weird, actually. I've never stayed somewhere I had to do that, but my mom told me to expect it before I left, because it's common here. In England. Europe. She was a Phishhead, following the band around. Not here, London. But she got pregnant with me and had to go home. So my dad was technically English. *Is* English. He's not why I'm here, though, before you think this is a lost-dad reunion sort of situation. He doesn't live here anymore. He lives in Florida with his wife and four kids. I've met him a few times. But my mom always said I should come here, you know, I guess because I was made here?"

The woman gave her another expressive look that Edie could only translate as *You have ten seconds or less.*

"Sorry! I'm not giving you a good first impression, I know." Edie was giving her a very accurate first impression, in fact. "The thing is, I'm going for a walk to check out some hedgehogs that live in bitty little houses in Baroness Rachel's garden. I mean, I don't know Baroness Rachel, but Morag does. She says it's fine to go into the garden to look. I have a map. You should come with." Edie, to her horror, did a couple of finger guns at her hips with a shimmy, as though she were one of her mom's friends who'd come to pick her mom up for wine bar night.

The woman blinked. It was a long, slow blink. Then, her eyebrows, which were perfect wings of the sort only achieved in TikTok videos, furrowed into a frown that Edie genuinely felt in her soul.

"Listen." Edie's voice now matched the other woman's annoyed-plus-plus energy. "No one else is here but you, me, and Morag. There is not any social action taking place in this inn that can conceal deeply antisocial behavior. I won't lie—Morag and I have been talking about you. Not *you*-you, but about this situation."

Cosima closed her eyes. They stayed closed for what seemed like a long time. Then her shoulders, which Edie hadn't realized were up around her ears, dropped down and rounded her back in defeat.

"Fine," she said. "I'll look at the hedgehogs." Her voice was low and sharp. Like a broadsword.

She didn't slam the door, but she did close it very firmly.

Edie stared at the heavy wooden door for a moment. Then she bent down, grabbed the tray, and slowly walked downstairs with it, trying to form a thought.

She had been successful, yes. But also, she hadn't thought she had been *convincing*. Yet the princess was getting ready to walk with her to Baroness Rachel's garden.

"Had you already talked to her?"

Edie asked this question of Morag on her way past. She was headed for the stony cavern that was the kitchen to put the tray on the huge wooden prep table, which Edie was certain had been made sometime around the Norman Invasion.

"Is she going for a nice walk with you?" Morag sat knitting in her rocking chair. That was what she did in the margins of bustling about the inn. There was an overflowing bin by the back door of wool hats, scarves, and mittens for guests, all of them slightly misshapen and in odd colors. The conversation Edie had tried to have with Morag about how much one's knitting should be expected to improve over forty years hadn't gone well.

"She agreed in words if not in spirit." Edie bustled into the kitchen and turned on the taps to do the dishes on the tray before Morag could tell her not to.

"Back off." Morag appeared suddenly in the cased opening to the kitchen, making Edie jump. She elbowed Edie aside and took over the washing. "Go get your jacket and wellies on. I already put hers by the door."

Edie could not believe she'd gotten herself into this. She'd promised hedgehogs to a tall, wild-haired stranger with terrifying eyebrows who'd disliked her on sight, and she stood only a meager chance of delivering them.

She had literally never seen a hedgehog.

But still, *still*, there was an unmistakable electric buzz at the base of her spine. It was similar to the feeling she'd had as a child standing with her toes curled around the edge of the high dive, and many times since, when she stood right on the cusp of doing something that would change her life and likely end in humiliating failure.

Probably it was just that she hadn't talked to anyone but

an eighty-six-year-old innkeeper for more than a week. She was getting an extrovert's social engagement high from simply speaking to a stranger.

She stood by the back door, staring down at a pair of brand-new Hunter wellies in sleek black. Edie wore the scuffed green, inn-supplied ones that were a half-size too big and had gotten stuck in the mud, then come off more than once. She did have a rain jacket that she'd borrowed from her brother, also too big. Morag claimed its bright lime color "burned her eyes," but it kept Edie dry.

The other woman's wellies looked like they belonged in one of the fashion spreads in Morag's crumbling magazines, on the feet of a model whose outfit was described in a caption that mentioned Harrods and quoted an improbably high price.

And then there she was. The princess.

She'd gathered her hair into a bun on top of her head that looked like an expensive, intentional mess. Her jeans were trim, her jacket a deep plum wool plaid with a series of plackets and collars that laid perfectly along her shoulders and front. Edie had never seen a jacket like that. She didn't even know if it was called a jacket, or if it had some other sartorial name only known to people who spent two hundred dollars on rubber boots and had three kinds of face cream.

The woman bent over and slid her feet into the boots. The shafts snugged over her calves without a hitch. This improbable person looked at her, one of those eyebrows lifting. "Are we going?"

And then Edie made a mistake. She couldn't have known it was a mistake, of course—that was how mistakes worked—but she would've appreciated a hint about this one.

It was just that she'd suddenly recognized why this woman's

eyes looked familiar. She had seen those eyes for the first time when she was five years old, sitting next to her mom on their red sofa in the Jackson Street apartment watching *Ship of the Cosmos* on DVD, mesmerized by Captain Astra Saturnine, a girl hero.

But this woman was not Phoebe Frank, who played Captain Astra in four movies and two epilogues.

Which meant she must be the person occasionally photographed *with* Phoebe Frank, usually in a magazine that had dressed them alike.

Edie had never been someone who followed pop culture closely. She was more likely to develop a single obsession with a show or music artist or movie every couple of years or so, such that she would learn everything about it to the exclusion of all other interests. And in the last few months, Edie had paid attention to virtually nothing but her own increasingly snowballing problems. However, *Phoebe* Frank and Captain Astra and *Ship of the Cosmos* were famous in the way the president was famous. Or the Princess of Wales.

Edie spoke without thinking, excited to have figured it out. "You're Cosima Frank." She pronounced the name the way she'd always said it to herself or heard her friends say it, *Coe-SEE-ma*—a pronunciation so wrong that it turned out Edie hadn't even recognized the *real* name when she heard it.

Cosima. Cosima *Frank*.

Cosima Frank. She had promised hedgehogs to *Cosima* fucking *Frank*. Who was staying at Gregory Place? The inn that came up first upon typing "cheapest place to stay in England" in a Google search?

"Not to you," Cosima Frank said and strode out into the rain, letting the heavy door bang shut behind her.

Edie winced. "Fuck."

Morag appeared, holding out a hat for Edie that looked like a fistful of wet moss.

"You might have mentioned who she was," Edie said. "Saved me looking like an ass."

"You did that all by yourself." Morag adjusted her glasses to peer after her guest. "I'm surprised she agreed to the walk. It's really coming down." Cosima was already halfway to the first turn. Her legs were incredibly long. She hadn't looked back even one time. Morag shook the hat at Edie. "Go on and make nice before she gets lost and carried off by the foxes."

Edie understood, then, that *this* was to be her project. Morag was turning over responsibility for this tall, angry, celebrity-adjacent person, who should not have been staying at Gregory Place and was not behaving as she ought.

Because Cosima Frank was undeniably having a breakdown.

It was a state Edie knew well. She'd been through the pressure cooker of friends and family trying to get her to cheerfully scale her crisis to what would make them more comfortable, which was somewhere around the level of, say, Kwik Trip running out of her favorite doughnuts. Tears were unwelcome. Yelling was off the table. Rude behavior prompted swift correction.

But sometimes it just felt good to fall apart.

She yanked the hat onto her head and opened the door, her boots immediately slipping on the rain-slick stone step. "Thank you. For real." Then she started jogging after her reluctant companion.

"Hey!" she yelled, afraid to use Cosima's name again. "Hold up!"

Cosima stopped and turned around. She put her hands on her hips, stomped her expensively shod foot, and yelled back, "*You dragged me out here! You keep up!*"

With nothing on her agenda and a very desperate need to be distracted, Edie was more than happy to keep up.

If Cosima Frank required someone to make space so she could throw a party for her enormous crisis, breakdown, or mess of her own making, Edie Whitelock was her girl.

Chapter Three

Cosima didn't want to slow her pace to accommodate this short woman in her appalling green coat and preposterous hat, but her upbringing overwhelmed her irritation—with being caught mid-wallow by a stranger, with the rain, with Morag's meddling—and stopped her in her tracks.

She didn't like standing still. Standing still meant she had to contemplate that she'd been mean for no reason. Was *being* mean for no reason, she mentally corrected, because she had no intention of stopping.

Even though it wasn't Edie's fault she'd recognized her. It would have been more strange if she hadn't. Cosima had been in the media a great deal lately.

It would have been infuriating if she had pretended *not* to recognize her. Cosima hated that. Not only was it disingenuous, but it meant a stranger was acting based on their assumptions about how *Cosima* felt about being recognized. Without asking.

This woman had recognized her all at once, in surprise, after

Cosima had shucked out of the robe she'd been wearing since yesterday evening and got herself into real clothes, tinted sunscreen, and blusher.

She put her shoulders back and spread her toes in her boots as she started walking through the rain again, slowly now, feeling her unused muscles trying to figure out if it was good to be out of her room, outside, moving, or if she'd rather be in bed with a Toffee Crisp reading one of the thrillers with cracked spines from the shelf in her room until she fell back asleep.

Her life felt suspended. Dreamlike.

Or it had, until this woman knocked on her door.

On the airplane, Cosima had hunkered down into her first-class pod by the window. She'd accepted a soda and a dish of warmed nuts and then been overwhelmed by the sensation that the floor of the plane underneath her had dissolved, and she was suspended above the night sky, barely holding on but not falling.

On the airplane, she couldn't remember the names of any of the board members. It was only her body, hurtling through the night sky.

She'd landed and hired a private car and gave them the address to Gregory Place. She'd slept the entire way. When she arrived, she passed her credit card to Morag and told her that she didn't want to be disturbed, to which Morag had said, *Of course not*, which was how she knew Morag knew who she was. Then Morag took her to her room with multiple framed portraits of her mother, the plaque that said *Phoebe Frank Slept Here*, and Cosima was certain the innkeeper had the full picture.

For two days, she slept, refusing everything except water, heavily creamed and sugared tea that she hadn't ordered, and then a mysterious juice Morag put on her tray that she said through the door would "build her up."

After she drank the juice, she ventured from the room to take a bath at the end of the hall, draining the enormous tub and adding more hot water until her skin was as saturated as a newt's.

Then she ate. And ate. She ate for two days. Eggs, bacon, fried mushrooms, toast, grilled tomatoes, sausage, sweet buns, roast, gravy, pudding, potatoes that were clouds on the inside and crisp with heat and fat on the outside. She took baths. She imagined she was dry ground, and the food and baths were constant rain. She was a four-acre fungus, swelling and swelling, shooting up round, white mushrooms in the dark.

When Edie knocked on her door, it was after a week of online shopping and pacing her room. She'd pulled down her mother's pictures (all signed) and stacked them in the closet. She'd silenced every notification on her phone and turned off the red numbers in the corners of the apps so she didn't have to see them. She'd stomped around.

The anger felt good. Cosima never got to be angry in the Castle.

She wasn't sure who or what she was angry with or about, but so far, every person and part of her life that she thought about made her angry. Phoebe. Duncan. The Castle. The construction equipment in the gardens. The stock market. PFS stockholders. California. England.

Then Edie knocked. Her hair was long, dark, and shiny. She had a fast smile. She was nervous, but she was also there—there like a boulder in a national park. There like air was always there to breathe. Her selfness was so extremely, very *there* that Cosima became aware of her own body for the first time since the Castle. She realized her belly was full from breakfast. She could feel how dry her skin was from so many baths. She could smell

Edie, like lemony cut grass. She came back inside of her body in stages, until she could really hear what Edie was asking her.

To leave her room.

The last thing she became aware of was that she wore nothing but a dirty robe (easier to go to and from a hot bath if you never dressed). That was when she firmly shut her door.

"God," Edie Whitelock panted, catching up. "You can cover a lot of ground in not a lot of steps."

"You should see if Morag has one of those little personal scooters. Or a golf cart. It must take you all day to get to the post office, and this village isn't even a mile wide." Cosima shoved her hands deep into the pockets of the shooting jacket she'd bought online, which Morag had delivered in its box outside her door, along with all the other boxes.

Before Cosima could feel badly for her unfair and sharp comment, Edie laughed. "Ha, ha. You know I'm not even that short? Five three. The average height of a woman in the United States is five four."

"That's the *average*," Cosima said.

Edie's voice was an alto's. Those borrowed wellies were too big for her feet and too tight for her calves. When they squelched in the mud, she had to pull her boot back on where it was undoubtedly slipping off her heel. It bothered Cosima. Things that didn't fit tended to bother her.

She stomped in a puddle.

"What do you mean, 'That's the average'?" Edie was good at mimicry.

Cosima took a deep breath. The outside air was so *outside*. "I mean, if you add together all the heights and then divide them by the number of people, you get five foot four."

Edie laughed again. "I know what an average is. I don't

know what you mean by saying 'that's the average' in an imperious tone."

Cosima, for the first time in eleven days, felt herself want to smile.

Something about Edie's thick dark hair with its part down the middle, concealed now by that hideous hat, and her thousands of multicolored freckles and her smirky mouth made Cosima feel like this was a person who could take on the towering wave of her meanest emotions and then tell Cosima to fuck off.

She walked a little faster to see if Edie would try to keep up. "I meant that it takes a lot of short people and a lot of tall people to compose that average, but five four being the average does *not* mean there are necessarily a lot of people who *are* five four, nor does it mean that it's normal you're only an inch below this arbitrary number."

She snuck a look at Edie and glimpsed a dimple appearing, then disappearing from her cheek. The dimple was an affront.

"Fair. You might've let me have it, though. My life at five foot three inches is hard. For example, I look absurd in dress pants. Like a painting of a Victorian baby that's dressed in grown-up clothes, except the cuffs are dragging on the floor and have mud on them." Edie mimicked this vision, arching her back and hiking up imaginary pants, pretending to trip on a cuff. It was inane.

"What's hard about *your* life?" Cosima put a snap in her question. The so-called pants Edie wore were very tight jeans, probably stretchy. They were absolutely correct for someone with a figure like that to wear, because why try to disguise it? *She* wouldn't. Cosima had to get pleats tailored into her real pants so it looked like there was any figure at all under her clothes, and Edie got a good ass for free.

"Well. Interesting question." Edie tapped a finger against her lips. They had come up to High Street, which ran along a low stone wall. Cosima hadn't been back to see it since she passed it in the car that had taken her to the inn. It felt different walking beside it, seeing all the little plants shaking off the rain. "Let's play a game."

"No. I've already agreed to this walk. I won't agree to anything else."

Cosima did not know where her refusal came from, but snapping that "no" at Edie felt like taking off slingback stilettos at the end of a fourteen-hour day.

But she said it to the air, because she'd lost Edie. She turned around.

Edie had stopped. There was a huge orange cat sitting on the stone wall, blinking slowly. Cosima watched as Edie made a little whispery sound, *spspspsps*. The cat stood, arching its back, and then bumped its head against Edie's hand. She stroked the cat and scratched around its head. The cat's tail rose up in the air, flicking at the tip.

"Suit yourself," Edie said, petting the cat. "But we're staying in the same inn at the same time in a country neither of us live in, and you've been hiding in your room. If you don't want Morag to keep siccing me on you, you'll have to come out occasionally. Might as well have some fun."

"I don't want to have fun." When Cosima said it, she imagined she was tipping over a table full of toys and screaming.

Edie leaned against the wall. *Her* hair didn't curl in the damp. It remained straight. The moisture caused it to separate into dozens of dark ribbons that slid against the horrific, noisy nylon of her jacket. Her nose was red. Cosima had no way of predicting what this woman would do, but whatever she did, Cosima wanted to force the opposite until she felt like she had never been anything but a contrary hermit who snarled at the entrance of her cave.

"Then don't have fun," Edie said. "It was only a suggestion. My game can be played with the intention to lance psychic boils. Plus, I'll go back to Wisconsin at the end of the month, and you'll go back to . . . ?"

"Los Angeles."

"Los Angeles. Which is far, far away from Green Bay, in more ways than one. I didn't mean to come at you by recognizing you like that, I'm sorry, but also, it's proof our lives couldn't be more different."

"How do I know that? You could be the heiress of some kind of Midwest dairy conglomerate."

"We have those! Dairy money, department store money, paper money, cannery money. Green Bay Packers money. But I am not one of those. I am the daughter of a single mother with two younger brothers who I shared a room with. My mom's got a three-bedroom now, but she had to be pretty crafty when I was growing up."

"So what's your game?" Cosima stepped toward the cat cautiously, and when Edie drew her hand away, she gave it an experimental stroke down its back. The cat's fur was soft, its body hot underneath the fur. The cat pushed up into her fingers and surprised Cosima with its positive reaction to her touch. It was purring so loud, it sounded like it might hurt something inside of itself.

"We figure out whose life is worse," Edie said. "Don't call it a game, call it an ice-breaking activity. We already started. I told you I can't wear real pants and that I grew up in Green Bay, which, depending on which polls you're looking at, is either one of the nicest places to live in America or the most racist and the drunkest."

"I can't tell you about myself. You could call any tabloid, especially right now, and they would pay you for the information."

Edie grinned. "See? That sucks. You're already great at this game. What the hell do you even talk about if you can never talk about yourself or anyone you care about? The weather?" The orange cat bumped his head into Edie's bright green too-big coat, and she scratched beneath its chin.

"Money," Cosima said. "Mostly. There are a lot of ways to talk about money."

Edie laughed. Her laugh came so readily. "I'll bet. Here's mine. Back home, I'm called by my nickname more than my actual name."

"Which is?" Cosima watched as Edie picked up the cat and snuggled him against her chest. It made her throat tight. The sun had come out from behind a cloud, and shafts of improbable golden light made the ordinary stone and brick buildings of the village seem to glow. She felt restless without the weather matching her mood.

"Frog." Edie raised an eyebrow at Cosima.

Cosima could admit that Edie, in her green coat, hat, and boots, seemed to be leaning into the name, but she couldn't think of a less *fair* thing to call this woman. "Why?"

"Because I'm short and round, and my face is covered in multicolored polka dots." Edie indicated her freckles. "Also, my eyes are green, and when I was in middle school I had to wear headgear to move my teeth and jaw." Edie mimed an apparatus around her head and pulled her mouth into a grimace in a way that did recall a frog.

"Freckles are chic right now. And green eyes are the most rare. Almost no one has green eyes. There is, I'm sure you're aware, nothing wrong with your body."

Edie set the cat back onto the wall. It started on its way as though it were late for an important appointment. "Well. Thank you. To be clear, I'm not hung up on how I look. It was always obvious how much smarter I was than my brothers, who are ding-dongs, so it didn't get in too deep. But the nickname persists. One of my brothers has kids who call me 'Auntie Frog.'"

"Auntie Frog is objectively charming. No points for you. How does one *win* this game?"

Edie glanced over at Cosima with an expression so drawn and tired, it slowed Cosima's stride in surprise. "Oh, we'll know when one of us wins." Now Edie's laugh was dark. "The discomfort and social embarrassment will come over us like a black cloud."

Cosima pulled her hands out of the pocket of her shooting coat and shook out her hands. She stretched her arms over her head. It was as if her body had already decided to tell Edie whatever she wanted to know, and so it needed to warm up first. "Here's mine. I got my period in front of Harry Styles at a pool party."

"Jesus Christ."

"I was sixteen. I had just gotten home for the summer from boarding school with a few of my classmates, and—"

"Wait. *Boarding* school?"

She hadn't expected that to be the part of her story that tripped Edie up, but she should have. Edie was right. Their lives were different. Phoebe had made sure Cosima's life was safe. Exclusive.

"Yes. Ecole d'Humanité, in Switzerland. For high school only. My mother couldn't stand having me gone before then."

"Obviously. Carry on."

Cosima did not linger on that *obviously*. She had told this story before, at brunches or in VIP lounges with cocktails, but this time, she decided to tell it straight, without euphemisms or edits. "My mother had a pool party to celebrate the summer vacation. She got somewhat carried away."

Edie snorted. "Don't spare the details on my account."

She walked faster in retaliation. "There was a tent with a facialist and hot stone massage. Of course, One Direction performed."

"Of course," Edie said, breathing hard but keeping up with squishy stomps of her ill-fitting boots. "It would've been embarrassing to have someone like Maroon 5, my god."

"I wore a bikini. It was—"

"—white," Edie interrupted. "It was white, wasn't it?"

"Yes. It was." Cosima could feel her cheeks burning, even now. "And I was sitting on a cabana chair that was upholstered in white canvas, and Duncan—"

"Who's Duncan?"

Just like that, Cosima felt the ground slip under her boots. Like when the plane's cabin had opened up beneath her.

"No one. Duncan is no one."

As soon as she said this, the knives came back, sinking into her middle, sharp and deep. The road in front of them had a slight uphill grade. She tried stomping her way up it to feel the pain of her feet against the earth instead. *Here, here, here.*

But she couldn't get the ground back underneath her. She didn't want to play this game anymore.

Edie didn't ask her to finish her story. Why would she? It was a foolish story, a story Cosima told because almost one hundred percent of the anecdotes she could tell at a brunch or in a VIP room were about her mother, and this one was only *secondarily* about her mother.

And it was humiliating. A humiliation impossible without her mother's fame.

"I've had eight jobs in ten years," Edie said in the silence. Her voice was still cheerful in its husky, laughing way, but there was something else there, too. Something that hurt.

She stopped at an intersection, looked around, and made a turn.

"I'll tell you about the last, worst job," Edie continued. "But I'm going to warn you, this is where the discomfiting cloud of doom settles over us, and it becomes clear we've shared too much."

"It won't. That would mean you've won, and I won't let you." Maybe it wasn't healthy to want to win at who was the most fucked-up, but Cosima did. She wanted someone else to see it and acknowledge it and back away from her like she was terrifying.

Then maybe the knives would go away.

"My training is in culinary arts. When I was twelve, I became a vegetarian after a teacher showed our class one of those slaughterhouse videos about the horrors of factory farming." Edie shrugged at Cosima's shocked look. "Wisconsin is very hardcore in very uneven ways. It affected me deeply, and my mom was someone who thought chicken was vegetarian, so I got into cooking. Like, really into it. I wasn't great at school. I was never diagnosed with anything—my mom is apparently 'not into labels,' either—but I struggled with putting concepts together, staying organized, knowing when and how to start something."

"Executive function."

"Yes! That's it. But when I was cooking, I didn't have any problems. I could keep in my head all the prep and how everything would come together and what had to be finished when.

My sophomore year, I started a vocational path at my high school. I graduated with a diploma and a culinary arts certificate, went on for more training at the technical college, and then there were the years marked by the sorts of failure I think a person is supposed to learn from, and then there was Fauxmage."

The trees pressed in on a narrow lane that separated the front gardens of much bigger homes made of stone with Victorian flourishes and wrought iron gates.

"It was a vegan creamery. I made fine plant-based cheeses, hard cheese, soft cheese, aged, blue. I sold it by the pound or on bespoke cheese boards. Plus pastries, crackers, and breads to serve with cheese—I bought those—and shortbread I made. I had a storefront on Broadway on the west side of Green Bay. Even though my real estate agent told me the lease was a steal for a commercial space with a permitted kitchen, I was terrified. I did everything myself."

Cosima didn't understand the flat, heavy tone in Edie's voice. "My favorite vegan creamery in LA is Su Lin's. She makes a smoked vegan gouda that apples should be grown to eat with."

"Mm-hmm." Edie crossed her arms, even though the sun shafting onto the lane had chased the chill out of the air. "Su Lin's was one of my exemplars in the deck I presented to my banker for the business loan. Well, I should say, to my banker, and then to loan officers at six other banks before I found one gullible enough to take me on."

Cosima wasn't getting something. "Why gullible?"

"A cheese store that doesn't sell cheese? What's next, a butcher shop that makes everything out of tofu?"

The bitterness in her voice was unmistakable. "I'm a fan of the Knifeless Butcher in Culver City," Cosima said.

Edie looked up at the dripping canopy of trees. "Tell that to my family and friends and their helpful unsolicited feedback. 'If you hate it here so much, why don't you leave?' 'You can't make cheese out of nuts and mushrooms and vegetables.' 'I don't get it. It's not cheese.' 'Forty-five dollars a pound! For what, a salad compressed into a cube?' 'What do you pair with the cheese, no-booze wine?'" Edie kicked an acorn. "And yes. I did. I didn't have a liquor license."

"It exists, right? Fauxmage? You found a bank and made the sign. You told me what you sell. So who cares about the critics? Or your so-called friends and family? They can stuff their heckling mouths with Kraft singles." Cosima was starting to worry Edie would win this game.

"That's the thing. They were right." Edie smiled. It was her first obviously, identifiably not-real smile. "Four months. That was how long I had my dream. It started coming apart after the first quarter. The amount of money I needed to make in that fourth month to stay open was more than I'd made in the three months prior. I tried so many different kinds of things—social media ads, newspaper coverage, interviews with the Chamber, bids to serve the lactose intolerant—for it all to end with a sad closing party and an article in the paper headlined 'No Mo Faux.'" Edie gave Cosima another two-dimensional smile. "Did the cloud come? Is it weird now between us?"

Cosima pressed her hand against her tight stomach. "No. You don't win. The pool party wasn't my worst. I just haven't said it myself because you already know my worst."

Edie's brows furrowed. "I do?"

Cosima looked into Edie's face and realized she was perfectly serious. How could that be?

Except Edie had just told her how—working hard, trying to revive a failing business, then being here. She hadn't caught up to the news. Or she didn't want the news, in the aftermath of what had happened to her, and was avoiding it.

They were both here, after all—strangers on a damp lane, thousands of miles from home—on the promise of seeing a hedgehog.

"My mother died."

"Fuck me, Phoebe Frank *died*?" Edie's eyes were wide with shock.

No one had believed Phoebe was mortal. No one seemed to have contemplated any possibility other than Phoebe on earth forever, taking audiences far beyond it in film after film, appearing in interviews with only the smallest of character creases around her famous eyes and glamorous threads of silver snaking through her curls.

Only Cosima and Duncan weren't shocked.

But there had been surprises even between the two of them. Cosima had seen tears in Duncan's eyes before—at the end of her ballet recitals, at her graduations, when she held her parakeet George in her hands as she rested him on a bed of coneflowers in a grave Duncan had dug—but she'd never seen him weep. She'd never heard his heart break like crystal. Not until her mother died, defying everyone. Taking life's deal like anyone else, without negotiation.

Cosima had not cried. Her mother had told her not to.

But here, in this no-place far away from shock or broken hearts, confronted with one small woman's simple shock and watery eyes, Cosima felt for a moment like a daughter, a girl, a very tired woman, who'd always thought Phoebe was in charge of the world, and who was angry that her mother had left her.

"God, Cosima." Edie had both hands plastered to her cheeks. "I am so, so, so sorry."

"You didn't know her." She shook her head, seized with a vicious impulse to yell, *I ran away! From everything! All of it!* "You don't know me."

Edie frowned, gathering her hair from her shoulders and twisting it like the tar-covered rope of a tall ship over her shoulder. "I don't. I didn't. But even if it's complicated, it's not anything you want to happen to anyone."

"It's not *complicated*." Cosima bit the inside of her cheek until it hurt the same amount as her stomach. "It's private."

But even as she chose the word, *private*, the lie gave a twisting pinch to her lungs.

It wasn't complicated, and it wasn't private. Secrets weren't the same as privacy.

Edie's enormous green eyes contemplated her expression. Cosima let her look. She lifted an eyebrow and imagined a sledgehammer smashing apart the hot lump of grief in her throat.

"Okay, then." Edie shoved her hand into one of the kangaroo pockets of her gargantuan green raincoat and pulled out a crumpled pink and yellow bag. "Rhubarb custard?" She unfolded the top of the bag. "I'll be honest, they're not what I expected when I bought them from a shop at Heathrow. Morag calls them 'boiled sweets' like she's in a three-hundred-year-old play *about* British people instead of a British person of this century, though I suppose she straddles the centuries. I think you need sugar." Edie shook the bag and held it out to Cosima.

"I know what rhubarb custards are." Cosima took one. The rough and sour surface of the candy—the way it flooded her mouth with sweetness when she rolled it between her teeth—chased away the sharpness in her throat and made one more survivable moment. Like her hot baths, how they stung, then surrounded her. Like the first bite of Morag's butter-soaked toast after a night of bad dreams.

They stood in the lane, sucking on candy. For as much as Edie talked, she seemed to know when to be quiet. An occasional breeze rattled rain from the leaves of the trees overhead. Everything smelled muddy and green, spiked with the wet mineral scent of weak sun hitting the graveled lane.

Cosima didn't know how long they had been standing still and silent when she noticed a movement and soft, rustling noises coming from the beautiful garden behind a fence that faced the lane. She looked toward the movement. Water shook off a big, floppy bergenia leaf.

A hedgehog ambled into view.

"Holy shit," Edie said. "That's one of Baroness Rachel's hedgehogs. Morag was not kidding."

The hedgehog paused in the lane, pointing its sniffing nose into the breeze, no doubt smelling their candy breath.

"My mother said the inn was magic." The hedgehog's back leg rose, and it furiously and comically scratched behind its ear.

"Phoebe Frank said that, for real?"

"You can't say her whole name every time you talk about her. 'Phoebe' is fine." Cosima crunched the candy. "It was in the eighties. She met my dad here."

"You came here to be close to her?"

Cosima blinked at the unexpected question. Had she?

"What I'm doing here remains to be seen," she said.

"Same, girl, same." Edie shifted in her boots, somehow not startling the hedgehog, who only looked at her and adorably yawned, showing off rows of pointy little teeth.

They watched it sniff the ground, then amble away, disappearing behind a fence.

After it had gone, they started to walk back from where they came, saying nothing all down High Street. They were nearly to the inn when Cosima broke the silence, surprising herself. "Have you seen the garden? At Gregory Place?"

"I've *heard* the garden. The foxes are hard to ignore. But I haven't looked at it yet. I do want to. I want to see where Morag is getting her weird hex bouquets."

"I can see into it from my windows. It's a mess."

"I'm guessing it's hard for Morag to do that kind of work anymore. She tells me she's eighty-six, but I think that's just her human glamour's age. She dates back to the druids at least."

"It looks like it was cared for once."

One night, before Edie arrived, Cosima hadn't been able to sleep. She finally gave up around five in the morning. She'd pulled on clothes and tiptoed down the stairs, leaving out the back door. It felt like a dream. She followed a path to a gate set into a stone wall. It took a great heave on the handle to budge the creaking iron.

She made her way around the perimeter first. In some places, she could walk along a path. In others, overgrowth blocked her way. She estimated the fenced area was two acres.

The lot the Castle sat on was considered parklike at eight-tenths of an acre, about thirty-five thousand square feet, but the first-floor footprint of the Castle took up ten thousand square feet of that. After the pool, cabana, tennis court, and garage were accounted for, the gardens Cosima and Duncan had cultivated weren't even fifteen thousand square feet.

Two acres was almost *ninety thousand* square feet of rough and neglected stone walls, follies, ponds, beds, greenhouse, orchard, and copses. At one time, this was a garden that would have offered tours. It would have bred new varieties of roses and narcissi in its greenhouse. Its gardener would have had a display at the Chelsea Flower Show.

Cosima spent the last few hours of that moonlit night

roaming around, mentally cataloging what she found, digging emerging perennials from fallen leaves, and guessing at the slope and where the garden was dry, where it was wet. She came across a hedgehog then, too, in a den under a stone bench, blinking at her while it gobbled a grub.

It was clear no one had gardened at Gregory Place since at least as long ago as the interior of the inn was kept up, but perennials carried on even without tending. Someday, a gardener would know Gregory Place again. Cosima's envy of this unknown, imagined, faceless gardener was breathtakingly sharp and unexpected.

When she had finally gone inside, Morag had made her breakfast tray. Cosima took it from her wordlessly and floated back into her room, where she ate her breakfast and was finally able to sleep. She'd had her first good dream since she came here, of herself and Duncan, planning a new flower bed. Her mother was there, cutting flowers in a big hat. Phoebe told them to plant a garden in the shape of an elephant, and then Duncan tried to come up with a list of plants that would look gray or silver in the California sun.

"If someone *was* taking care of that garden," Edie broke into her musing, "they weren't doing it by themselves. Same with the inn. The way Morag is running it, she couldn't handle much more than the two of us. For the inn to make real money, it would need a staff around the clock. It would have to exist on the map, and that takes people."

They returned to the inn in silence that should have been more awkward. Cosima climbed the stairs. She took a shower, not a bath—progress—but then got back into her bed, a pile of crisps and candy bars at her elbow and a stack of gardening magazines she'd grabbed off an end table in the lounge.

She wondered who had won their game.

Mentally, she awarded the point to Edie. What Edie had lost was something she had made herself, from her own dreams.

Cosima told herself it was ridiculous to feel sad about the inn's dark and moldering garden. She had plenty else to feel sad about if that was what she wanted.

Was that what she wanted?

Chapter Four

Edie sat straight up in bed, clutching the duvet to her chest, her heart pounding.

Where was she? She looked into the shadows of the room, fitting them together until her brain relaxed marginally.

England. Harlaxton. Gregory Place. The noise of the storm had yanked her out of a restless sleep.

The rain started up again after dinner, and it had been pummeling Harlaxton village ever since. Thunder periodically rattled the windows in their stone sills. Lightning strikes lit the interior of the inn in startling strobes that followed the booms.

The slow leak from between the beams in Edie's room added to the cacophony. Under the drip was a copper stockpot big enough to cook down an ox. It looked like it was older than Morag, who had heaved it up the stairs at bedtime. The *ping!* of water drops in that pot had made their way into Edie's nightmares.

Edie eased back down against the pillows, and then the thunder clapped again, followed by a wicked streak of lightning.

"Fuck this." She threw off the duvet and slid to the edge of the bed, her feet searching for and then finding her slippers. Surely this was an emergency that would override the ban on entering Morag's kitchen. Edie wouldn't be put out into the storm for making herself some tea and searching for a package of bourbon creams.

She crept down the stairs, their usual creaking obscured by the roar of rain against the old glass windows and a roll of thunder. Of course, it was only in this moment—the first in all of her time in this primordial inn—that Edie remembered ghosts.

She took another step down, coaching herself to breathe normally. Ghosts were not real. Probably. Yes, this inn had been built in 1758, and that was an older-than-the-United States number of years for people to have been dying inside its walls. Some of them would have died badly, or with unfinished business, or maybe even brutally at the hands of a psychopath.

She made it to the bottom of the stairs, scanning the dark lounge for any signs of danger, supernatural or otherwise, when a flash of lightning lit the room all at once, revealing a *figure* in one of the wing chairs.

Edie screamed.

The figure screamed back, and so Edie put her hands over her eyes—she didn't want to see herself get ax murdered—and then one of the lounge lamps clicked on, and someone was extremely angry.

"Fuck me, Edie! Why are you creeping down the stairs like that?"

Edie dropped her hands to see Cosima wrapped in a different robe, her curly hair in a loose braid, her hands on her hips and shiny purple gel patches under her eyes. "Why are you sitting down here in the dark?" Edie whisper-yelled at Cosima. "You have never sat down here before!"

“The storm woke me up!” Cosima hissed back.

“The storm woke *me* up!” Edie yanked up her sweatpants, which were much too big and tended to creep downward. “I was getting a cup of tea, not *lurking*.”

“Well, I was sitting.” Cosima crossed her arms. “Also not lurking.”

Edie had known she would eventually talk to Cosima again, though she had imagined something less terrifying, even if it was Cosima. Since their walk two days ago, the princess had returned to her lair at the end of the hall. She *had* begun retrieving her own meals from the kitchen, taking them up to her room on her tray, but the only words Edie had heard her speak were when she told Morag she didn't need to make a separate non-vegan menu on her account. Cosima could eat the same as the “other guests.”

She meant Edie. The other guest. Singular.

Edie approached her. Now that the light was on, it seemed laughable that she had been thinking about ghosts and murderers. Everything was still untidily mauve, dusty, and tired, not remotely creepy. Even the long row of garish porcelain figures on the piano, which Morag called her “Stoke-on-Trent Ladies,” looked less demented than they did in the light of day. “You were sitting in the dark.”

Cosima picked up a closed laptop from the chair, shook it at Edie, and put it down again. “I was watching a movie on my computer, but the battery died.”

“Sure.” Edie made herself sound skeptical, but she couldn't hold on to the anger that had been fired by the jump scare. “You have internet? Movies?”

“I make a hot spot with my phone. Not ideal, but it works.” Cosima wrapped her robe around her legs.

Edie cautiously took the chair opposite, tugging down her

T-shirt, which was from high school, and so a little short and tight. "I could never get the international plan I bought for my phone to work."

If Cosima were someone regular, Edie would have volunteered to fetch her charger so they could watch her movie together. But even in under-eye patches, she was not an approachable person.

Sometimes over the past two days, Edie had heard the door to the inn open and close, but she was never fast enough to catch Cosima on her way out or in. When she had seen her at mealtimes, she was always dressed—no more stained robe and nest-hair—but her wardrobe didn't resemble Edie's collection of jeans and faded hoodies. She always looked like one of those Instagram ads for a clothing brand with a one-word name like "Neure" that sold four-hundred-dollar sweaters made from organic yak yarn and perfectly neutral slacks that skimmed over the models' legs in a waterfall before breaking over mysteriously shaped leather shoes with soles made from cork.

Cosima was, Edie had come to understand, the actual *archetype* of the kind of woman she had avoided having a crush on for several years now. Edie had learned how to avoid this kind of woman the hard way, because of *course* Edie adored tall and elegant women who were a little mean and emotionally messy but who still somehow made life unfold before themselves effortlessly. Women like this were obviously such a good choice for someone like her, eager as she was to mask her actual personality in the hope of inspiring sweetness from a girlfriend who forgot her birthday and slept with other people.

Edie hadn't been avoiding Cosima, exactly, but learning about Phoebe Frank's death changed things. Cosima was mourning the loss of her mother. The whole world must be mourning along with her, though Edie had missed it in her obsession with her personal litany of disasters. When Cosima told her that her mother had died, Edie had wanted to offer something more than a rhubarb custard, but they were strangers.

"Edie," Cosima barked. "You're staring at me."

"Not staring. Thinking." The pool of lamplight was too low for Cosima to see the hot blush Edie knew must be racing up her neck.

"About?" Cosima lifted her aristocratic brows until they resembled a Venetian canal bridge, curved and built around a perfect ratio.

You, Edie answered with her mind. "Tea. Biscuits. How I'm not going to be able to go back to sleep. What to—"

An earsplitting thunderclap all but slammed into the inn, shaking the windows and making both of them jump.

"My god," Cosima whispered. "I'd rather deal with earthquakes."

"Wisconsin sometimes has storms like this. When I was little, I used to love when the storm sirens came on and Mom took us into the basement. She'd get out our old board games and set them up, and my brothers would be nice to me for an hour."

"Good *lord*, Whitelock. Are we still playing the game?"

"No." Edie curled up in the chair, twisting the waistband of her pants to match the new position of her body. "My therapist, if I still had one because I could still pay the premiums on my insurance, would not approve."

One side of Cosima's mouth curled up in something that might be the beginning of a smile. "You *are* playing the game."

She was. Not because she wanted to win, but because she liked talking, and she couldn't resist the opportunity to find out more about this compelling woman. "Speaking of discovering my joy while hiding in the basement during a storm siren, did I tell you I had a party?" She hooked her leg over the arm of the chair. Like many queer, neurodivergent people, she was incapable of sitting in a chair normally.

"A party?"

"The last day Fauxmage was open. After closing, all these people came to eat the rest of the stock and cheer me up. It was amazing. I had such a good time. Everyone ate every last bite of cheese I had, the baked goods and homemade crackers, and drank my stock of nonalcoholic wine. People told stories that made me sound amazing. We toasted my doomed adventure into artisanal culinary offerings."

"That sounds nice. What's the catch?"

"The catch"—Edie recrossed her legs, studying the beams on the ceiling—"is that once the last person had gone, I looked around at what I had made from my own heart and talent, and I couldn't figure out where the fuck all of those people had been for the past four months."

For a long moment, they both listened to the rain pelt against the glass in their circle of lamplight. Edie discovered that telling the story here, in the dark, to Cosima, made it hurt a little less than it had when she left Wisconsin.

"I ran away," Cosima said. "One minute I was meeting with Duncan to go over what we most urgently needed to accomplish, and the next I was booking a plane ticket. I didn't tell him I was leaving. He's probably up to his ears in extra work, but I don't know that for certain because I haven't been checking my phone."

"Duncan was your mom's boyfriend?" Edie tried to keep her tone light. Crushy feelings aside, she liked this woman. She wanted to give her the space she needed to deal with how her life had been upended. From the self-recrimination in her tone, it sounded like her life had been upended a lot.

Cosima pulled the gels from underneath her eyes, then

leaned back and looked out the window. "'Companion,' everyone says, though they ought to say 'fiancé.' There was a press release after he gave her the engagement ring, a beautiful emerald, and she said yes. She wore it for years and years. But she didn't marry him."

"Is that what he wanted?"

"I don't know."

"But it's not what *you* wanted," Edie guessed.

Cosima's lack of response was an answer in itself. Edie knew a little something about yearning for a family even when everyone said you already had one.

"My Duncan's name was Mike," she offered. "He had a mustache that I thought was horrifying, but I would've cried if he shaved it off."

Cosima didn't look away from the window. Edie couldn't tell if she wanted to hear more, but she was definitely the sort of person who'd stop Edie's talking if it got to be too much.

"I was fourteen, which is the worst age to be alive," Edie continued. "I fought with my mom constantly. We're way too much alike. But Mike understood that I needed to be doing something all the time. He'd take me to the garage where he worked and show me how to change the oil in a car, or the tire. He taught me to drive manual transmission, even though I didn't have a permit. He piled up pillows on the driver's seat and zip-tied a chunk of two-by-four to each of the pedals, and we'd bomb around the back roads. He fostered animals with me from the shelter. My mom and him never got married, but I wouldn't have survived sophomore and junior year without Mike."

Cosima pulled her long, shiny legs underneath her, her forget-me-not eyes serious. "What happened to him?"

"My mom and him broke up when she met another guy at

work. This was the same month I was graduating from high school. Mike tried to stay close, but he'd turned down an opportunity to manage a factory in Pennsylvania several years in a row so he could be there for us, and then he didn't have to be."

"He didn't *have* to be."

Edie could guess why Cosima picked at her fingernail when she repeated this phrase. She would be thinking of Duncan, who was not her father. She would be wondering whether it was only her mother he'd stayed around for.

Edie knew. She *knew* what it was like when a Mike walked away, and no matter how spiky and imperious Cosima was, she should get to keep her Mike. "What happened to your dad?" she asked.

"He died when I was three. Phoebe always said he was the love of her life, and maybe that's true. What I remember about him is that I was always a little . . . scared isn't the right word. Is there a word for feeling both anxious and exhilarated at the same time? I remember he would pick me up and hold me up high above his head and spin around."

"Your body remembers him."

"I suppose." Cosima picked at a hole in the upholstery of the chair. "He's why I'm here, in a way. My mom had a list. Things she wanted to do with me. She called it her 'au revoir list.' The only thing we didn't do on her list was stay at Gregory Place. This inn is where my parents met."

Phoebe Frank's bucket list. That was why Cosima had come here.

On the surface, it made a nice fairy tale—the daughter helps a mother with a terrible diagnosis see her last dreams through—but Edie strongly felt that kind of thing was not really what daughters were *for*.

It had long been a point of contention with her own mom.

Edie only wanted to be loved and wildly approved of without qualification. She wanted the freedom to love her mom in all of her own weathers. She wanted to be able to shop for grown-up things with her mom, things like a car or a mattress, and also to stay at her mom's house after a breakup and sleep in her bed while her mom played with her hair. Tanya Hoberg loved her—Edie didn't doubt it—but she did seem to feel that her children were there to take care of *her*, and watch out for and manage *her* moods.

It was impossible for a child to really know what their parent needed and to fulfill that need.

But that did not mean the child wouldn't try.

"I'm sorry—" Edie began, her thoughts racing as she attempted to piece together a way to say this that met the bare minimum of courtesy.

"No." Cosima laughed. "No, never mind. Obviously I'm trying to win your game again."

"Good. Keeps me on my toes." It was a banal thing to say, but she'd been caught off guard by Cosima's quick reversal, and by hearing her laugh. Her laugh wasn't refined. It matched her wild hair and her mean little tricks, like walking too fast for Edie to keep up with. Like changing the subject and claiming to be trying to win the game. "I was coming down to make myself tea. Do you want some? A package of biscuits? I'm afraid to make anything more. Morag will know, and then I'll find a jar under my pillow filled with nails and crow beaks."

"Yes. I could go for some Jammie Dodgers." Cosima lifted that one corner of her mouth again, almost smiling.

Edie tried not to oversubscribe her heart to that half smile. "Just the cookies? No tea?"

"Maybe a glass of water."

Edie stood up. "I'm on it."

Cosima stood, too, and made a slow circle. She took in the piano heaped with figurines, the stacks of magazines and newspapers, the three pale-pink wing chairs and two mauve love seats and five small mirrored tables. Her gaze stopped on the reception area. Edie watched her take note of the forbidden guest book—the one in olive-colored leather, as big as the surface of a school desk.

Before Edie could take in what was happening, Cosima crossed the room in four quick strides and grabbed the forbidden book with both hands.

"Cosima!" Edie yell-whispered.

She sat down with it in the wing chair Edie had just vacated. The heavily gilded book took up the entirety of her lap. *"What?"*

"You can't have that. Morag says." Edie shuffled back into the lounge and reached for the book.

"Morag isn't here. She's sleeping. When I was watching my movie earlier, I could hear her snoring, even though her apartment is all the way at the back of the kitchen. Also, right here, it says 'GUEST BOOK.' I'm a guest."

Edie glanced toward the entrance to the kitchen. She tried to listen for the sound of Morag snoring, but she couldn't hear over the rain and rumbles of thunder.

"Are you afraid you'll get in trouble?" Cosima creaked open the front cover. Edie saw marbled paper. A black-and-white photograph. Her heart was *racing*.

"No! But am I afraid Morag will hex me? Yes. Yes, I am. She could live another three hundred years if she bound me to this place and drank my youthful blood." She stepped closer to Cosima. "Seriously, though, that guest book is important to her. She won't say why, but before you and I met and decided to be best friends forever, I tried everything I could think of to get her to let me look at it. I mean, it's obvious I *need* this guest book. I need to have a very cheap English Experience where I sit by a fire and thumb through the pages of the past. Otherwise, what memories do I have to take back with me to the factory floors of northeast Wisconsin?"

"You didn't try using me as your excuse. You might have suggested to Morag that we should look at it because it's likely my mother's stay is documented in this book. One might say I have a *right* to open it."

Cosima raised one eyebrow and turned another page without glancing at it. She was making a compelling argument in favor of breaking Morag's rule. Her point overruled the part of Edie's moral compass that suggested Morag might have a good reason to keep the guest book private.

Edie peeked at the page Cosima opened to. She spotted something that looked like a poem.

She'd read a magazine article once about the Victorian scrapbooking craze, with girls trading their kid-leather-bound scrapbooks back and forth, painting watercolor floral arrangements onto rag paper to express sapphic longing in flower language. That article had made Edie feel like she was born in the wrong century. In the wrong country. To the wrong life.

She felt that way a lot.

"What does it say?" She swallowed.

"Do you want me to read it to you? Would that keep you safe from Morag, or is even knowing what's inside enough to get you demerits? Maybe I should take it up to my room and peruse it privately. Remove the temptation." Cosima laid her hand flat over the first page.

"Why is it that the only time you've come down to the lounge, it's to be mean to me?" Edie sidled even closer to where Cosima was sitting.

"I came down because I couldn't sleep and wanted to watch a movie." Cosima turned another page, but she tipped up the cover so Edie couldn't see.

Craning for a better view, Edie bonked her hip into the end table next to Cosima's chair. "Fuck!" She rubbed the spot on her hip. "Listen, I have been exceedingly patient with your"—Edie waved her hand in a circle around Cosima—"needs, but—"

Cosima shut the guest book. "Needs? You've been patient with *my* needs?"

"I have. Look, I get that you are mourning your mom, but if you and I were the type of people to know what to do with our feelings, we wouldn't be on an English vacation, *here*, in *February*. Maybe we can help each other."

Cosima's mouth firmed, and the architectural feathers of her brows furrowed. "Is that so."

"That's so, princess."

Edie would not have guessed it was possible for Cosima to sit up even straighter, but she did. Her hands gripped the sides of the guest book as though she might lift it over her head and cudgel Edie with it. "You can't call me that."

"Princess?" She stepped closer. "Princess. Princess. *Prin*"—Edie pointed—"*cess*."

Cosima narrowed her eyes, and at that moment, lightning shot across the sky and lit her face up and made her pale irises seem like they were piercing Edie's soul.

"You don't scare me," Edie said. It was a lie, but also, there was no particular reason why Cosima *should* scare Edie. She was just a woman. A very hot, rich, prickly woman, but also, hedgehogs were prickly, with pointy little teeth, and all those quills and teeth were for one thing and one thing only. To keep everything they were scared of away.

"I *should* scare you," Cosima said. She made a sound in her throat.

"Did you growl at me?" Edie stepped to another lamp and turned it on to better peer at Cosima, whose face was stormier than the weather.

Cosima smacked the cover of the guest book. "I don't fucking know! I have plenty of reasons to be angry. What of it?"

"You can growl because you're angry," Edie said, leaning in to study Cosima more minutely. "But I don't think you *are* angry."

"Because you're so empathetic and went to therapy when you had insurance for ten minutes?"

Ha! Edie could not be insulted with her own confessions. She was her worst enemy. Always had been. "Because, *because*, princess, you haven't left. You're still here, and you could have gone at any point—like, for instance, when I came down the stairs and we screamed, and I bothered you, you might have excused yourself to your rooms."

"Room."

"But you didn't. You stayed here and crossed swords with me, and we shared a few things. Now I know you're at this inn because of your mom's list, for starters. But the list is just what got you here, not why you stayed. There's something you want from this place, or need, that you don't have yet." Edie snatched at her pants before they could finish slithering to the floor. "You know what I think? You want to play. You're afraid I'm going to ruin your fun."

"Aren't you?" Cosima was gripping the guest book so hard that her knuckles had turned white.

"I'm not. We're going to get up, and we're going to sneak, very quietly, to the dining room, and we're going to spend this dark and stormy night looking at that guest book. Maybe it will only be a bunch of names. Or maybe it will turn out to be where Morag writes down her spells, and we can disenchant this inn and find out it's actually a clean, not-leaky, fucking *painting* of an English inn. Either way."

"Will you still make the tea first? I want some now. This feels like a moment for tea and biscuits."

Edie didn't feel as brave as she had about that, now that she knew Morag slept in an apartment on the other side of the kitchen. But if she paid close enough attention, she could lift the kettle before it started to whistle. "Um. Yes."

"And could I have two packets of Jammie Dodgers?"

"As long as you leave my bourbon creams alone, also yes."

Cosima rose to her feet with the grace of an aristocratic virgin performing a Viennese waltz. "We have a deal."

She passed the guest book to Edie. It weighed even more than she'd imagined, and it smelled like the antique mall off the interstate that she always badgered her mom to stop at on the way home from Appleton.

They snapped off the lights in the lounge and snuck into the dining room, only turning on a small fake candle in the middle of the table.

Edie made the tea, wincing at every noise, waiting in between noises to see if Morag's snores were interrupted. She tiptoed back into the dining room with two mugs on saucers, the biscuits gripped to her side by her elbow. "You haven't peeked?"

"No. I have integrity."

Edie sat down next to Cosima and slid the book between them. The rain hadn't let up, but the thunder seemed farther away, and the lightning only touched the outsides of the windows while the inside of the inn remained dark. "Are you ready?"

Cosima nodded. "Open it."

She said it as solemnly as a girl swearing a blood oath on the playground. Edie felt her soul go still, charged with the gravity of this shared moment. They looked at each other for a breathless heartbeat. Then Cosima smiled.

Her smile wrinkled the bridge of her nose. Devastating.

Edie focused on the book.

The leather creaked when Cosima lifted the cover. The marble endpaper was olive and pink swirled together, and the first page had an illustrated picture frame, in the middle of which was a photograph of a beautiful square-jawed woman with dark braids, a straw hat, an apron, and a cigarette.

"Oh my god, that's Morag," Edie said.

Cosima gently pulled the photo from the slits in the paper that held it down and turned it over. In spidery and faded ink was the innkeeper's name, Morag Tourmaline Beveridge, and a date.

"This was taken almost fifty years ago." Cosima handed the picture to Edie. "Imagine doing the same thing for fifty years."

Edie studied the picture. "That's the goddamned dream, isn't it? All that time to make something real, something that will outlast you. It's not always the same, it's fifty years of different things that add up to a legacy."

Cosima turned in her chair. "You're serious."

"Cosima Frank, I opened a *vegan cheese shop* in Green Bay, Wisconsin, a city—and I'm just now realizing you might not know this—where tens of thousands of football fans wear foam cheese wedges on their heads. And there wasn't a single moment, until the end, that I didn't believe in what I'd built and want it to still be there a hundred years after I was gone."

To her relief, Cosima didn't laugh. Her eyebrows were pensive. "I do know something about legacy," she said.

Right. That made sense. Edie gave her back the picture. "I imagine you must. And I also have to guess you might have different feelings about it than I do, because, after all, you're here."

Cosima nodded, her lips a tight line.

"Should we dig in?"

Cosima touched her finger to the range of dates on the page with the photograph. "If this guest book starts as long ago as this, my parents will be in here."

"Then we *have* to dig in. It's what Phoebe Frank wanted."

"Stop calling her 'Phoebe Frank.'" Cosima sounded distracted, trailing her finger down the edge of the paper. She turned to the first page, revealing a long column of signatures on one side. There were pairs of printed lines on the facing page for guests to write something to the proprietor or for future guests to read.

"Let's find out why *Phoebe* thought this inn was magic." Edie leaned in and moved the battery-operated candle closer, lighting up the page.

Her shoulder touched Cosima's, and she didn't move away.

She tried to resist the protective feeling that came over her with the lowering of Cosima's walls, but it was useless. As her mother liked to say, Edie had to be Edie.

If Cosima needed to drop her guard to let a little magic in, Edie would keep her safe. It wasn't the smartest impulse to follow. Edie was no longer able to deny that she *had* manifested an unfortunate crush on Phoebe Frank's daughter, despite her best intentions. But she could keep a lid on it. They could spend what was left of this dark and stormy night traveling through the pages of this guest book together. Cosima could play.

Edie would worry about her relentlessly optimistic heart in the morning.

Chapter Five

"Wait, did it say the one with the crook or the shepherdess?" Cosima sat on the piano bench in the lounge, holding a dusty Royal Doulton bone china figurine in each hand so that she could compare them more closely. One had a wide-brimmed hat and held a big shepherd's crook, and the other sported a bonnet and cradled a lamb in her arms.

"It doesn't say. It just says, 'Gregory's blushing shepherdess keeps a secret.'" Edie was reading off the Notes app on Cosima's phone, where Cosima had translated the message they found in the guest book.

Her mother's message.

It had been easy enough to find the record of Phoebe's visit. The guest book entries were in chronological order, and even if they hadn't been, at some point Morag had protected Phoebe's signature with a long strip of clear tape over the top of it.

In the two lines for guest messages, her mother had written a message in the code she'd taught Cosima when she was a girl so they could leave notes to each other without the staff leaking their whereabouts or plans. She called it "Phoebe language," but Cosima had later learned that it was a simple Caesar cipher, with each letter of the alphabet substituted by the one that came six letters before it.

Because my name has six letters, she'd told Cosima. *And so does yours.*

Edie had pointed out that the existence of this code, and particularly the reason for its existence, gave Cosima a solid point in their game. Cosima had laughed and told her that she and her mother and Duncan all enjoyed codes. Duncan's mother had been a codebreaker in the Second World War, and he'd taught her and Phoebe quite a few of the tricks he'd learned as a child.

Cosima only realized after she'd finished speaking that this was a personal detail she'd never told a stranger before.

Edie came up closer to her, blocking the light with her body in a way that rendered Cosima's attempt at inspection pointless. "So I guess either one of these figurines could be the shepherdess?"

A little irritated, she shoved the two porcelains back onto the piano top. "*Both* of these have red cheeks. *Both* have the accessories of a shepherd. You've wandered around this inn much more than I have, so you tell me, is there anything else that could be a shepherdess? A painting? A statue?"

The blunt ends of Edie's dark hair brushed her bare waist where her miniscule EAST DANCE TEAM tee didn't meet the waistband of her sweatpants.

"I've been everywhere except Morag's kitchen and your room," Edie said. "As far as I know, you're holding the only sheep-related items in the place. Which one has a secret? No idea."

Cosima shook them one at a time near her ear. Nothing.

"So the secret isn't that your mom filled one of them with diamonds."

"She thought diamonds were tacky. Her style was more about aggressively buying controlling shares in unwitting companies." Cosima inspected the statues for any cracks or hidden openings. "And real estate. So much real estate."

Edie sat down next to Cosima on the piano bench, holding out her hand to take one of the figurines. In the last hour that they'd spent decoding Phoebe's entry, Cosima had grown more accustomed to Edie's physical closeness. It wasn't what she was used to. At the Castle, everyone maintained a bubble of personal space. There were air-kisses. Side-by-side strolls with her mother in the gardens—some of their best times together—or planting out a perennial bed with Duncan while they knelt in the dirt in happy silence, several feet apart.

Cosima couldn't remember the last time she'd had casual human contact with anyone. In LA, everything was so vast, the margins wide, the rooms and boardrooms capacious and minimally furnished. They were places to breeze in and out of.

There were people who'd made it plain that Cosima could have all the human contact she wanted from them, but the prospect had never appealed. She didn't want the person who met her eyes at a restaurant to touch her. She couldn't imagine any of the people who'd pursued her wrapping their arms around her, or putting their mouth on hers in a kiss, or pulling her into bed, skin to skin. Her friends were not people who held hands or piled into cars and brunch booths. They didn't try on each other's clothes or braid each other's hair.

It wasn't that Cosima didn't *want*. She did. But hers was a nonspecific yearning that pulled at her chest and sometimes throbbed between her legs. It felt personal. Quiet. And it had never been called up by her connection *to* any other person.

But Gregory Place was emphatically not the Castle. This inn was an intimate warren of furniture and tight hallways. Every chair and mattress swallowed a person up in cushioning and featherdown.

Here, there wasn't anywhere for Edie to be *but* close.

At first, the incidental brushes of Edie's shoulder against hers as they bent their heads over the guest book hit as bright as the lightning, briefly fuzzing Cosima's senses with too much input at once—but then the sensual static broke up into clear impressions. She recognized the almost lemony, cut-grass smell of Edie's skin from the amber bars of Pears soap that the inn provided for free. Even with her middle exposed, that skin was warm where her arm pressed against the heavy silk of Cosima's robe sleeve and along her thigh.

Some bit of Edie was always moving, shifting, or fidgeting. Cosima liked it. It gave her plenty of ongoing information about where Edie's body ended and began, and if she was likely to talk or be quiet or take a sip of her boiling-hot, sugar-sweet green tea.

Edie turned the figurine around in her hands. "It has a hole in the bottom where it came out of the mold." She skimmed the pad of her finger around it, then held up the figurine, closing one eye, and tried to look inside. "I can't tell if there's anything in here."

"If there were, you'd think it would have fallen out. Or that you could hear it rattle." Cosima lifted her own shepherdess to look in the hole made by the slipcast funnel, but it made her feel faintly ridiculous, closing one eye and squinting as Edie had.

"Use your phone flashlight."

Cosima turned it on and aimed it into the hollow space of the figurine, Edie leaning against her to look, too. "I don't see anything."

"I think there's a spider. Do you see her? Or it could be a bit of dirt."

Cosima handed the phone to Edie. "Look inside yours."

Edie pointed the light as the thunder found a bass-note rumble that gave Cosima goose bumps all over.

"Holy smokes," Edie whispered.

"What?" She leaned over to look and spotted the edge of what looked like canary-yellow paper. The hairs on the back of Cosima's neck stood on end. "Oh! That's the color of my mother's stationery."

Edie's smile was so wide that Cosima could see a tiny divot on her otherwise smooth incisor where there must have been a bracket for braces. It was perfectly kitty-corner to a deep brown freckle on her lip line. Probably Edie had hundreds of constellations like this, all over her body.

"Can you get it out?" Cosima asked.

Edie angled the tip of her finger into the hole, but it only rustled the paper. Then she turned back to Cosima, reached up, and slid out one of the hairpins that kept the shorter curls near Cosima's face from falling out of her braid. "I'm going to borrow this."

Cosima touched the place where the hairpin had been. She watched Edie slide the pin onto the edge of the paper, tugging it closer to the hole. She tried to use her finger again to ease it out.

Knocked loose by Edie's fingertip, the hairpin pinged onto the floor, and the paper curled away.

"Fuck." Edie bent over and grabbed the pin. She held it up with a laugh. "Despite what it looks like, I'm not trying to pick you up."

Cosima's brain glitched. "Pardon?"

"You know. I dropped a hairpin." Edie's cheeks had gone pink.

"I don't understand the relevance."

"It's an old-fashioned signal. You see a girl you fancy, and you drop one of your hairpins. If she picks it up, then she's—" Edie wrinkled her nose and brows like Cosima had suddenly gone out of focus.

"Gay?" Cosima guessed. She'd never heard of this.

"Yep. I like to learn about that kind of thing. Queer life in history. I love looking at antique pictures of sapphic couples that everyone thought were roommates." Edie pushed the hairpin inside the statue again, clearly distracted now. "I have this book, *Eye to Eye: Portraits of Lesbians*, by a lesbian photographer who called herself JEB. She published it in 1979, and it's probably my favorite book." She darted a quick, unguarded glance at Cosima. "I love all of the layers of meaning and code and elaborate Easter eggs that queer women and girls got up to. How they figured out to do that so they could make lives for themselves that felt bigger than what the world was willing to let them have. I think about how amazing it would've felt to receive an acrostic ring from a girl you were desperately crushing on, you know, spelling out A-D-O-R-E with an amethyst, diamond, opal, ruby, and emerald, and then wearing it to your history lecture so she would see it. I'm glad no one will put me in an asylum for being a lesbian anymore, probably, but I do wish there was something with a little more depth and meaning than swiping right on a phone screen."

Cosima blinked. Her eyes stung, which was absurd. Who *was* this woman who made gourmet vegan food and dreamed about romantic history while wearing what were obviously her brother's castoff pants for pajamas? How had someone so singular and imaginative not found a place better than a foam-hat cheesehead town that made fun of her for not being the same as everyone else?

"I can see what you mean." Cosima didn't know what else to say. Most of what came to mind risked swerving them into a deeper involvement than made sense while they were both guests at an inn, distracting themselves from their lives.

The storm *hadn't* woken her up. It had been an anxious, throat-closing dream about Duncan weeping, accusing her of throwing him away. Her mother wasn't in the dream, though Cosima looked for her while Duncan was yelling. When she woke up, she texted him for the second time since she'd come here. The first had only been to confirm where she was staying, because she didn't want the world looking for her. She trusted Duncan to keep that from happening.

When she woke up from her nightmare, though, she texted to tell him that she was resting. Eating good food and taking walks. It was a scenario Duncan would approve of, though she imagined it wouldn't be long before he tactfully asked for her return date.

Her mother's company remained headless. The specter of the market loomed. A small city's worth of people depended on her to keep it aloft so they remained employed. Even if Duncan stalled and rescheduled whatever he could for their soon-to-be-filming show, she guessed they were already losing thousands a day.

She thought of Edie's story about her mother's boyfriend. How he'd left when he no longer had a reason to stay. But Duncan wasn't leaving. He had put something in motion that meant that he genuinely needed Cosima for years to come. Even worse—even from here—she could sense the pressure Duncan felt to do right by Phoebe by making their gardening show and the studio it spawned successful.

Because he loved Cosima. He loved Phoebe.

Duncan's love was easy to return. Cosima only had to follow the directions.

He'd texted back immediately to communicate his cheer that she was resting, but what he didn't say was what Cosima heard the loudest. Nothing about the board. The CEO appointment. Their television show. The omissions meant Duncan knew there was something very wrong, and that he'd decided to handle the situation with care.

Cosima didn't want to feel wrong. She didn't want to be handled. But the points of the daggers pressed against her ribs anyway.

She had come downstairs into the lounge and watched a movie, dialing up the sound in her earphones until it was loud enough to drown out her guilt and indecision.

"Give me that." Cosima held out her hand for the shepherdess.

Edie gave it to her. "You want to try with the hairpin?"

"No. You can tuck it in your reticule."

Edie snorted as Cosima set the first shepherdess back on top of the piano. Then she rose and walked out of the lounge to the clear area of traffic-polished flagstones in front of the reception desk.

When the next rumble of thunder had built to a crescendo, she dropped the secret-keeping shepherdess on the floor.

The fine bone china exploded like a bomb.

"Jesus *Pete*, Cosima!" Edie whispered.

Cosima surveyed the destruction. "I may have miscalculated."

"You fucking think? Morag's going to kill us. Actually kill us. Put us in a cage, fatten us with candy, and roast us in that monster of an Aga she's got." Edie sighed. "I wish she'd let me use it. I would love to cycle sourdough boules through that mother."

"I'm not worried about *Morag*, I just forgot I wasn't wearing shoes or slippers, and now I'm trapped by china shards in bare feet." She bent over and snatched up the rolled-up piece of stationery the figurine had been hiding. "I got it!"

"Don't read it yet. Wait there while I find a dustpan and broom." Edie hustled past her and disappeared into the kitchen. She reappeared with a broom and carefully swept up every speck of china, one fist gripping her pants at her hip, then pulled out a pair of Morag-knitted wool socks from her side pocket and handed them to Cosima. "Do you think you can slide your feet into those? I think I got everything, but in case I didn't, I'd rather you had socks." Edie stepped next to her. "You can hold on to my shoulder."

Cosima placed her hand on Edie's shoulder, balancing on one foot as she slid a sock onto the other. She didn't know when she'd last been offered such a simple act of caretaking. Edie's skin was warm through her T-shirt, round and firm with muscle. Cosima had to surrender to the other woman so that she wouldn't be hurt, and the simple trust plus Edie's body under her hand, kneeling at her feet, made her ache unbearably.

She didn't want the ache to stop. Far from it. She wanted to sink into this trust and unobligated caretaking like a hot bath. It hurt *good*.

Cosima switched hands on Edie's shoulder and tugged on the second sock, her cheeks hot.

Edie set the dustpan and broom against the wall. "Now we can read it."

By silent mutual agreement, they took the paper to the dining table and sat back down with the guest book. Cosima unrolled the stationery—the paper stiff and dry with age, but verifiably from her mother's stationer.

"It says, 'Look, Listen, and Love.'" Cosima let the paper go on the table, where it rolled back up. "So helpful. Thanks, Mother."

"Wait, though." Edie put her hand on Cosima's forearm. "My brain is doing something."

"What is it doing? Don't break it."

"Shh." Edie closed her eyes.

"Should I get another cup of tea? Will this take a while?"

Edie opened her eyes. "Now is not the time for our charming banter. I actually have to focus when an unformed thought wiggles its way in. Be quiet before it wiggles back out and I start thinking about frosting recipes."

As Cosima waited, she looked for more constellations on Edie's face, visually tracing a path from a tiny moon-shaped scar above the corner of her left eye to a trio of freckles on her cheekbone, then discovering a pale freckle that surrounded another darker freckle like a miniature Saturn. Then Edie opened her eyes.

"I got it! Come on." She jumped out of the dining room chair and ran back toward the lounge, Cosima following in the slippery wool socks. Instead of going all the way into the lounge, Edie took the hallway next to the stairs, behind the reception desk, and led Cosima into what Morag called "the library." It was a medium-sized room that opened to the garden. Its walls were lined with unremarkable bookshelves housing hundreds of paperbacks. Edie stood on a stool to skim her finger down a row of titles. She tipped a book off the shelf. Cosima caught a glimpse of a couple, the woman wearing a voluminous pink gown. "*Look, Listen, and Love*! It's the title of a Barbara Cartland novel!"

"I'm not reading that," Cosima said. "It's already almost four in the morning."

Edie flipped through the pages with her thumb before turning the book spine-side-up and shaking it. Another piece of Phoebe's yellow stationery fluttered out. "We don't have to!"

"How did you know about that book?" She bent down to pick up the paper.

"Cosima, god love you, but I *told* you my phone's bricked, Morag doesn't have TV or the internet, I don't have money for a train pass, and I've been here ten days. Walking in the rain and memorizing this library have been my primary pastimes, other than fantasizing about cooking in Morag's kitchen or looking for her furniture polish."

Cosima was chagrined. "Right. Of course. Lucky us, in this case."

"What does it say?" Edie sat down on a love seat with mauve and baby-blue stripes. Cosima could have taken the rocking chair across from her, but she didn't. She sat on the other side of the love seat and held up the note so Edie could see it, too.

When Cosima read it, she couldn't help her fond huff of laughter. Her mother must have been so pleased with herself when she wrote this clue. "It says, 'Rosemare.'"

Edie's brow wrinkled. "Do you know what that means?"

"I do. My mother was the kind of person that loved the meanings behind names—the literal meanings, the cultural ones, the stories. If you met her, it wasn't unusual for her to translate your name or tell you something about it. Like 'Whitelock.' It refers to a white field or meadow."

"I've read that somewhere. What does 'Rosemare' mean?"

"Literally, it just means 'a pink mare' or a pink horse. The wallpaper in my room is pink, with rows of prancing horses."

"I have been dying to see your room." Edie surged to her

feet, then fumbled for a hold on her sweatpants, whose attempted escape revealed three inches of purple cotton underwear patterned all over with tiny white hearts.

Cosima averted her eyes as she got up. "You could've asked," she said, following Edie from the room.

"I could've asked the resident Hollywood depressive to have a look at her giant suite?" When Edie reached the stairs, she stopped and turned around. "Yeah? When? Should I have had my meals sent up to your room so we could chat over them together for a change in scenery?"

"Fair, but remember, my mother's dead."

And then Cosima couldn't believe she'd said it. Said it like *that*. Like a little jab in a bout of what Edie called their "charming banter."

Frozen in place, Edie put her hand over her mouth, and—maybe because she'd been studying Edie's face at close range—Cosima understood she was holding back laughter.

That was what made Cosima laugh. It felt strange enough to her throat and chest that she mainly choked, but then Edie was giggling madly, and it turned out her genuine laughter was infectious, so Cosima laughed more while Edie shushed them and laughed, and they stumbled up the stairs bent double.

Cosima flung open the door to her room. It must have been nice once. The large bed was flanked by original Lane dressers and a small dining set centered on quite a lovely ivory cut-pile wool rug that needed cleaning.

"You weren't kidding about the pink. This is outrageous." Edie crossed to where there was a big, darker pink square on the wall opposite the bed. "Looks like there was art up once."

Cosima walked to the closet to retrieve the stack of framed pictures of her mother. She laid them out on the table with a flourish. "I wouldn't call it art."

Edie put her hand over her mouth again. "Morag decorated this room after your mother's stay as a tribute to Phoebe Frank?"

"It seems she did. Well, not *decorated*, but the pictures, the plaque, the binder of *Ship of the Cosmos* trivia questions in the bedside dresser, and the decoupage roses around where Mother *signed* the wallpaper"—Cosima pointed to the spot—"do give the room a certain air of homage."

"Grieving or not, I wouldn't want to sleep in a room with that many pictures of my mom peering at me from the walls. Why would she sign the wallpaper? Obviously, Morag embellished the signature with the roses, but is that because she discovered the signature afterward? Or did she ask your mom to literally autograph the room?"

Cosima looked more carefully, then leaned close and slid her nail under a long, thin cut in the pink paper. "I'm going to guess she signed it as a kind of 'X marks the spot.' I'm ripping it off."

"That's fine," Edie said. "But, for accounting purposes, let the record show that *you* broke the shepherdess and ripped the wallpaper. I can't afford surcharges."

Smiling, Cosima carefully followed the cut with her fingernail, lifting and tearing off the paper until it revealed a corner of yellow stationery, which she pulled out. "Here we go. Oh, there's a lot of writing on this one." It slowed her heart down to see it. Her stomach clenched.

Edie must have sensed the shift in mood, because she eased away, putting space around Cosima to afford her greater privacy. "Take your time reading it. It will give me a chance to snoop." She clasped her hands behind her back in a show of *I won't touch anything.*

While Edie looked around the room, Cosima sat on the edge of the bed. Her eyes instantly adjusted to her mother's heavily slanted, dramatic script.

My love,

I don't yet know who you are, but I do know that you will exist. I knew you would exist not three days from the moment I met your father, a man I haven't even made love to yet.

I met him walking from Gregory Place to the manor when I was overcome by a small herd of sheep. He was as much a tourist as I am, but he herded them away for me, laughing at how ineffectual he was at the task, and after walking together for only an hour, he changed his booking from a hotel in Grantham to Gregory Place.

Federico Russo is a man I would not have looked at twice in California, but such is the magic of this inn. Here, there is the quiet necessary to listen. I can eat real food. The weather makes my decisions for me—if I will go out or stay in. If I will read or warm up with tea. It means I could hear your father's dry wit instead of missing it in the fray. I don't feel as though I am losing time or money or the public's interest if I do nothing but lie in his arms and stare at the clouds. He's a race car driver, of all things, absurdly Italian, who has shown me that a man's eyes can genuinely sparkle.

He had no idea who Phoebe Frank was, but he came to know me in such a short time. Tonight, I told him I would marry him, very firm, and he put down the novel you found a clue in and said, "Of course. I will buy you an aquamarine to match your eyes."

I also told him that when we had a child, I would never be romantic enough, not in Hollywood, not ever as Phoebe Frank, to tell them about how I fell in love for the first and only time, and he told me, "Tesoro, you can tell them. You can sing our love to them. You can write it in a book or act it in a play."

It was important to me that you would know about this

love. He calls me Tesoro, "treasure," and so I came up with this silly idea to create a treasure hunt for you. One day I will bring you here, or ask you to go, when the time is right. I'll tell you to find my name in the guest book and see if you can take it from there.

I love you. Right now, you're made only of stars and hopes I didn't know I had, but I love you just the same, because it's almost as if my love for your father means the two of us can't contain it. We already need you to hold more.

Your mother (!!!)

Phoebe

Cosima put the letter down in her lap. Outside, weak morning light was beginning to gather under the dark clouds.

Her mother sounded different in the letter. She sounded young, and hopeful, and excited for the unknown future.

Cosima thought of Duncan's kind gray eyes. The future this letter imagined didn't include him.

She thought of the way the light looked in Phoebe's office, slanting through a crystal highball glass and illuminating the amber color of the bourbon her mother liked to drink neat, chasing it with a razor-thin slice of lemon. How she would claim, after the third or fourth drink, that she needed time by herself to think, and send Cosima away.

Phoebe Frank was good at everything she did. She was the best alcoholic Cosima had ever met.

How strange it was to be sitting in the same room where her mother wrote these words. Alive, when she wasn't.

When everything and nothing had turned out as Phoebe Frank expected it to.

"What's next?" Edie asked, sitting down on the other chair around the table.

"There isn't a next." Cosima laid her hand on the letter. "This is what I was supposed to find."

"You, specifically? But you weren't even—"

"Born. Or conceived. My mother had to make that clear." Cosima's throat closed, and before she could stop it, her face, her neck, were wet with tears that came as fast as the rain had fallen. "I'm not crying," she said.

Edie scooted her chair over until her knees touched Cosima's. "Of course you're not crying." She made a *pffft* noise. "Who would ever even cry if they found a letter their late mother left them years before they were conceived on the off chance an elderly innkeeper would never redecorate, just to say—and I'm spitballing, here—'I love you'? Absurd. *Crying* is for kitten videos and when you're tempering chocolate and it breaks. *These* are tears more like having your period in front of Harry Styles. Completely involuntary."

Cosima felt her throat choke her again, and she shocked herself with a laugh. "My period."

"Perfectly natural. However, it doesn't mean that you don't need a hug? Only to soothe the discomfort of this period your brain is having. Not because you're *sad*."

Cosima wiped her face with her hands. "Maybe." At the corner of Edie's eye, the curve of her eyelashes made a question mark with a freckle for the dot. "Yes. I will take a hug."

Edie wrapped her arms around Cosima's shoulders. She put her palms flat against her back. Her hot cheek and sleek hair brushed against Cosima's cheek. Slowly, awkwardly, Cosima put her arms around Edie's middle. She could feel the other woman's ribs rise and fall with breath. She was surrounded by the smell of Pears soap and green tea, and her eyes burned, but there weren't any more tears.

After a while, she realized Edie wasn't going to let go first, and that made her think of Edie on her knees, sweeping up every shard of china around Cosima's bare feet.

About Edie knocking on her door and asking her to look for hedgehogs.

They'd found one, too. She supposed hedgehogs would forever remind her of Edie now.

When Cosima pulled away, Edie let her go immediately. "We need to get the guest book back before Morag wakes up," Cosima said.

Edie's eyes went wide. "Fuck me, yeah we do. For a few days, I tried to beat her to being awake, but I found her creeping around the kitchen at ten past five in the morning and gave it up."

They raced quietly down the stairs, the rooms dark, and went to the guest book, still open on the dining table with the battery-operated candle flickering away. Edie closed it and picked it up to head to the reception desk, but then a long red ribbon slipped out and fluttered to the floor.

"I've got it," Cosima whispered. "Where did it come from? It looks like it was part of the binding."

Edie set the book down on the table again. "This page. I had my fingers between the pages, and that ribbon slipped past them." She opened the book. There was a bit of crusty glue at the top of the binding where the ribbon had been attached for a bookmark.

Cosima smoothed it into place, then stopped. "Look at this." She pointed to a guest's signature and message from 1977.

Edie craned to see it over Cosima's shoulder. "Are those little *symbols* on the message line?"

She reached around Cosima's body and pinched the bottom of the page between her fingers. Only when Edie had nearly finished folding the page did Cosima see the crease. It went right through the middle of the page. It had been there already. The bottom of the page neatly met the top, and then Cosima could make out where there were tiny holes cut out, framing the symbols perfectly, with more symbols written on a blank signature line on the folded-up page. Edie moved it back and forth. "For serious, Cosima, I think this *is* a code!"

"A cipher. That's what you'd call it. Not a code." Cosima sat down. She wished she had a pen and paper.

Edie flopped bonelessly into the chair beside her. "No wonder Morag wouldn't let us look inside. This book is filled with sinister English secrets."

"So are you two ladies going to hunt for the treasure?"

Cosima and Edie screamed as Morag appeared in the dining room. She wore an ankle-length white linen nightgown. Her loose hair streamed nearly to her waist in silver ripples, and she held a collection of dripping hellebore in one hand. *Lenten rose*, Cosima thought automatically.

"Swear to god, Morag," Edie panted. "I'm going to make you wear a bell."

"What treasure?" Cosima asked.

"Agatha Llewellyn's treasure."

"The *novelist*?"

Morag ignored this question. "She put the first clue there in the book. I've never let anyone see it because the treasure's meant for someone else. No guest of mine."

Edie made a noise like a muffled squeak.

"So why would *we* hunt for it?" Cosima narrowed her eyes at Morag. There was something more complicated going on here than the modest legacy left by her mother. Agatha Llewellyn was a well-known Welsh author. Why didn't she have a plaque of her own?

The old woman walked to the reception desk and placed the burgundy Lenten roses in a very fine blue-glazed Qing vase that

Duncan would have coveted desperately. “I’ve never had guests here who did nothing but hang about,” she said darkly. “The place needs an airing out from all the poverty and melancholy.” Her smile was just as dark. “And I have reasons of my own to think this would be a good way for the two of you to spend your time.”

Edie looked over, her face so nakedly pleading, Cosima nearly laughed.

“We’ll talk about it after breakfast,” she said diplomatically.

But she thought about *Tesoro*, and the Castle, and Duncan’s careful reply to her text.

Her stomach hadn’t hurt, not for more than a minute, since Edie came into the lounge.

Maybe a treasure hunt was exactly the kind of rest a princess needed.

Chapter Six

Edie put her head down on the table in a fruitless attempt to settle down her restless body. She watched Cosima flip the bottom of the guest book page up and then down again while mumbling to herself and writing in a Gregory Place–branded spiral-top notepad that Morag had produced from the reception desk.

She had not counted on the amount of time required for code-breaking. Or on how little Cosima enjoyed being interrupted when she was trying to concentrate.

"Is the washing finished?" Edie asked Morag, visible through the open door to the kitchen. She was mixing up a quick bread with shredded carrots and raisins that she often served on the side with lunch. Edie had asked for the recipe a dozen times and been denied.

"Already have it on the drying rack by the radiator in the back. Your jacket must be dry." Morag tipped the bowl toward her body when she noticed Edie was watching too closely, trying to guess the recipe.

"Don't bother. I have a jacket for you in my room," Cosima said.

"I will not fit into any of your jackets." Edie sat up and stretched. The storm had stopped hours ago. It looked like the sun was out for the first time in a long time, but she didn't want to leave Cosima to the guest book alone. She had already hogged it, working on Agatha Llewellyn's cipher even as she refused to formally, officially commit to the treasure hunt.

"Of course you won't. Why trade one ill-fitting jacket for another? It's a jacket that will fit *you*."

"That you discovered in Morag's lost and found? Because I've been through that box, and there were not any size-fourteen extra-short jackets with plenty of room in the bust."

"I ordered it." Cosima put her pencil down.

"You bought me a jacket? You don't even eat meals with me. You walked me down a village lane, disappeared for days, and then reappeared to be Indiana Jones with me after several arguments in the middle of the night. I'm supposed to believe you bought me a jacket?"

"Yours doesn't fit." Cosima said this with one of her Arch of Hadrian eyebrows lifted, as if it were an answer rather than the kind of statement that inspired countless questions.

Edie felt a strange, fluttery buzz directly under her sternum.

"I realized I hadn't returned the courtesy of asking you for a walk." Cosima's posture was perfectly straight, her shoulders back.

"That is true." Edie bit her lip to hold back the impulse to tease Cosima, whose perfect posture was a warning.

"However, when I thought to ask you, I remembered your jacket."

"My brother's rain jacket. The green one."

"No color green I've ever seen." Morag contributed this

from the kitchen, folding parchment into her baking tins. "I started needing my glasses when I drive after seeing that jacket."

"Yes," Cosima confirmed. "It's terrible, and you look terrible in it." She folded her hands on top of the open guest book and gazed at Edie with a frank, unperturbed expression. This was the way Cosima looked at Edie when she'd said something she considered outrageous.

Edie had no intention of calling Cosima out. The jacket *was* terrible, and she did look terrible in it. Hearing these facts spoken aloud did not bother her. She was more interested in knowing why her looking unsightly in a jacket was a problem Cosima had decided to solve.

"So you thought about walking with me, but then you remembered you'd have to walk with me wearing my jacket, and the horror sent you straight to curvy girls jackets dot com."

Cosima cast her eyes at the ceiling. "To Paul Smith's, but yes."

"Oh, *quite* posh," Morag called out cheerfully.

"And so you took it upon yourself—"

"—to fix it. Yes. To make you look as you should look."

"According to . . . ?" She knew the answer. She just wanted to hear Cosima say it.

"Me." Cosima crossed her arms. "But not *me*. It's about you. A grown woman. You're a chef. You've owned a business. You're an intelligent and attractive woman with dramatic features. You don't have to wear it." She added this last statement as she started to grow pink. "But no one like you should have to wear a hand-me-down poorly fitting windbreaker from their brother. Unless you want to."

Edie bit back her smile. "Unless I want to."

Cosima gave a very tiny nod.

"Take the jacket, lovey!" Morag shouted. "It's a Paul Smith. Pawn it when you get back to Wisconsin for a bit of seed money."

Edie studied her companion at the table, still trying to work out all the pieces of this puzzle. Cosima looked perfect, of course, in a starchy rose-colored linen shirt and high-waisted pants. She wore her hair parted down the middle, slicked into two tortoise-shell barrettes clipped above her ears, her curls smoothed into long coils. But Edie didn't feel at all lesser in her jeans (which were the really-let's-call-them-leggings kind) and Northeast Wisconsin Technical College sweatshirt.

Cosima didn't work like that. Cosima was very much *for* herself. She wasn't Cosima *at* anyone.

What Edie found herself hung up on was Cosima saying *no one like you* and *an intelligent and attractive woman with dramatic features*. Edie had never had anyone suggest she deserved more. Or even that she wear clothes that fit her, or weren't cast-offs or from Kohl's.

"I haven't said I wouldn't wear it." Edie smiled. "Is it a shooting jacket?"

"No. The shoulders of a shooting jacket wouldn't properly frame the line of your bust. It's a walking jacket." Her cheeks lit with slashes of red across the cheekbones.

"It's good you've considered my assets." Edie bit her lip, watching the slashes go maroon. "And what color is it?"

"Oh, for heaven's sake." Cosima closed her eyes. "It's only a jacket."

"A Paul Smith!" Morag called.

"It's green, all right? Green. The green of your eyes."

"Thank you, princess," she said, her voice a little rough. "I'm excited to wear it."

Cosima's brow furrowed, a ripple across its mirror pond, but then she smiled, politely, looking down at the guest book. She cleared her throat. "I think I know what to do with this. The cipher Agatha made. If you're interested."

Edie glanced through the door that led to the kitchen, but Morag had bustled out of view.

Edie and Cosima had compared notes on what they knew about Agatha Llewellyn. She had written about a dozen moody, gory mystery and thriller novels in the seventies and eighties that were runaway bestsellers but that no one read much anymore. She was rumored to be a recluse, and her fans complained about her failure to complete the last story in her best-known series. What had brought her to Gregory Place or made her decide to pen a cipher in the guest book in 1977 was a mystery.

"You have to pay attention when I explain." Cosima put her hand over the page with the cipher, frowning at Edie.

"I will try my hardest if you ignore my distracting stimming behaviors." Edie stood up to change her position at the table.

"I don't mind your squirming and wiggling."

Cosima's eyes went wide, and Edie laughed. She slid onto the pew bench next to Cosima. "What have we got?"

"Do you know about the Cistercian monks? The medieval sect. They broke off from the Benedictines around the twelfth century."

"Oh. I only know about the *other* Cistercian sects. Not the medieval one."

"I can't tell if you're being serious." Cosima wrinkled her nose.

"These are the guys into manual labor and who invented their own math, isn't that right?" Morag had appeared out of nowhere, making Edie jump. She sat down where Edie had been with a large mug of tea.

"Good god, announce yourself, old woman."

"Yes," Cosima said to Morag, ignoring Edie's comment, "though they didn't so much invent their own math as their own numbering system. They used variations on a vertical line to represent every number between one and nine thousand nine hundred and ninety-nine." Cosima pointed at the symbols they had noticed on the message portion of Agatha's signature.

"Those are Cistercian numbers?" Edie inspected the long row of lines. They looked like dozens of number ones, except each had a little appendage in a different place. Some looked like flags. Some like a stick figure with no head. "What's the number?"

Cosima folded up the page, and the squares cut out of the paper each framed a Cistercian number. Now, next to every tiny window, there was a letter. "You can see how this is assigning letters to go with the Cistercian numbers."

"Yes."

"First, I had to write down what letter in the alphabet each Cistercian number went with." Cosima flipped to a page in the notepad and showed it to Edie. "Then it was simply a matter of looking up what Cistercian number corresponds to what Arabic number, and then assigning *those* numbers to the alpha order letters. You'll see that the reference cipher gives us three is A, six is Z, and so on."

"Indeed simple. Ridiculously so."

"Edie." Cosima said this with a warning in her voice.

"Quite clever, lovey," Morag said, taking a long sip of tea. "You won't need sudoku to keep you sharp like I do."

Edie took a deep breath. "*Could you tell us what it says, Cosima?*" she asked in a rush, holding her hands clasped as though begging.

"But I haven't shown you how I cross-referenced both alphanumerical reference codes to crack what Agatha wrote." Cosima flipped through several more pages.

Edie gently placed her hand over Cosima's holding the notebook. "I do have limits."

Cosima sighed. "Demeter mundum vastat sine filia Proserpinae, quam Hermione in saxum vertit, donec Perdita redit."

"What it? Reddit?"

"I caught 'Demeter' and 'Persephone,'" Morag said. "Is this about the myth?"

"Oh!" Edie raised her hand. "I do know that myth! The supplier I bought grape leaves from was called Demeter's, and there was the entire story on their label. Demeter is the goddess of agriculture—"

"Well, actually—" Cosima interrupted.

"*Shhht.*" Edie cut her off. "Let me have this, nerd. And her daughter Persephone hooked up with Hades, the god of the underworld, and he took her away, so Demeter made the lands barren, big problem, and that made him give her back, and Demeter returned fertility, but he also tricked Persephone into eating pomegranate seeds, which meant she still had to live with him part of the year, and this is how we get the seasons. You know, harvest versus growing."

"I will allow it," Cosima said. "But this Latin isn't referring to the myth."

"God*dammit.*" Edie slumped. "Ugh."

"Hermione!" Morag had been leaning over to read the Latin in Cosima's notebook. Now, she clunked her mug down on the table. "This is about Shakespeare's *A Winter's Tale*!"

"Very good!" Cosima said.

"Wait, I didn't get a 'very good,' and I told you about the Latin story."

"Greek myth," Cosima corrected. "Translated, this passage says, 'Demeter lays the world to waste without her daughter Persephone as Hermione turns to stone until Perdita returns.'"

"Mm-hmm." Morag nodded.

"Don't mm-hmm." Edie glared at Morag. "You didn't know. Don't act like the star pupil." Then, her brain lit up in a white-hot flash before going dark, like it was a lightbulb that snapped its filament after the switch was hit. She stood up. "Wait. Wait. Wait. Wait."

"For what?" Cosima asked.

"For my mind to change the lightbulb and illuminate the thought I had."

Cosima sighed. "How long will this take?"

"Better question," Morag said, "how many innkeepers does it take to change Edie's lightbulb?" She wheezed out a laugh.

"Don't quit your day job," Edie said. "The map. Walking."

"What about them?" Cosima rubbed her temples. "Honestly, Edie, I have six whole pages in this notepad about interpretations of this speech in *A Winter's Tale* that could point us in the right direction. I think we should get started on that."

"When you ghosted me after our one and only walk, I *also* was thinking about how to make another walk happen, but I was somewhat deterred by my inability to navigate a mile-wide village in rural England without a working phone in my hand. So I studied the map. Like, I cut out a little person and walked it about the map to try to lay it down in my head. One of the places my little person walked to was Hermione's Stile."

Morag toasted Edie with her mug. "There you go."

"There I go!" Edie held her hands in the air. "Wait! There *we* go! Get my fancy jacket, woman! We're going on a walk to see a stile! What's a stile?"

Cosima closed her notebook and smoothed out the page in the guest book. "It's a set of stairs in a fence, usually a stone fence, so that people can go over it but animals can't."

"Animals can't use stairs? That can't be right."

"Of course some animals can use stairs. Cats. Probably dogs." Cosima looked like she wasn't sure about that one. "Definitely monkeys."

"The English keep monkeys in their fields?" Edie could feel helpless laughter beginning to gather. "I have not seen one monkey, Cosima."

"Ugh! What I obviously mean is that cows and sheep can't use stairs! Regular field animals!" Cosima's cheeks were pink again, but in a way that looked nearly like she was having at least a little fun.

"I feel like they could," Edie said. "Maybe it's more that English farmers don't teach them how to use stairs, which seems cruel. I'm glad I'm vegan."

"For heaven's sake." Cosima gusted out an exasperated breath and stood up. "Come up to my room and get your jacket, and let's go find Hermione's Stile."

"Yes. But take some pictures of the cipher, too, so you can show your Duncan."

Cosima met Edie's eyes for a long moment, and they moved over Edie's face like they were reading her. Like Edie was a code.

She wasn't. She'd just learned from when she was small how to give other people what they needed without making them feel they owed her anything in return.

"I could do that," Cosima said. "Thank you."

"You bet."

"Before you go up." Morag looked at Cosima, and Edie felt the tiniest shift in mood whistle through the room. "I am wondering if this is, indeed, how you want to be spending your time at this moment. Rather than applying yourself to a certain decision?"

Morag asked the question the way Edie's mom would ask her, right before she was determined to do something unhinged, if it "was what she really wanted to do." What did Morag know about Cosima that Edie did not?

Cosima's mouth firmed. "At this moment," she said, "what I want to do is go to Hermione's Stile."

Morag only nodded. Cosima made her way up the stairs, and Edie followed. "I'm pretty excited about this walk," she said to lighten the mood. "One, I've been in this inn too long. I've named the spider in the corner of my room. Two, I can wear my new jacket. Three, I can see a stile close-up and in person for the first time. And four, treasure. Should we bring a shovel?"

"What on earth would we need a shovel for?"

"For the treasure, of course!"

Cosima's laugh was like a peal of church bells, and Edie's heart felt as though it might burst in breathless anticipation. The light through the inn's antique windows outlined the silhouette of Cosima's legs through her elegant pants and lit up every color in the patterned wool carpet runner. It made Green Bay and Fauxmage feel far away and long ago, like they'd happened to someone else.

She waited for that feeling to make her sad, but it didn't.

It was true that this was how she'd felt after she signed the lease to her store and used her brand-new bank money to go to Ace Hardware and buy paint and brushes and a broom. Probably this kind of zealous excitement was not an emotion Edie should strictly trust.

But *god* did it feel good.

Better than anything else.

Chapter Seven

As she let Edie into her room, Cosima tried to compare the brand-new and confusing emotions detonating inside of her body to any other feelings she had ever had before.

She failed so miserably that she reverted to her adolescent self, leaning in the doorway with her phone while she pretended to be cool and unbothered.

“There’s the box,” she said. “I need to send a few texts.” She leaned in a manner she hoped seemed insouciant.

“That’s too bad, because I was going to ask you to film the unboxing for me. Oh! Too late, I’m in.” Edie dug through the tissue paper.

With a deep breath through her nose, Cosima did as Edie had suggested and sent off a quick explanation about the guest book to Duncan, with pictures of the coded page and her notebook.

He wrote back immediately, though it was ungodly early in California.

Fascinating! Your thinking of the Cistercian monks was absolutely brill. You have your mother's luck with vacations, my love. Enjoy the magic.

Duncan's text made her throat go tight. With love. With guilt inspired by Morag's not-so-veiled question. Cosima was the shepherdess, smashed apart, looking for what part of her mother was inside of her to tell her what to do. She was an adventurer, trying to solve puzzles and ciphers and needing Duncan to tell her it was okay.

"Oof."

She looked up from her phone at Edie's muffled grunt. It took a long moment to process the sight of Edie pulling her oversized, faded sweatshirt over her head, revealing a ribbed tank that bunched up over her belly. She had a pierced navel with glittery jewelry.

"I don't think these sleeves will fit into the jacket," she said by way of explanation. Her long hair lifted in static in some places and poured over her now-bare shoulders and between her breasts in others.

Edie took the jacket out of its tissue paper and slid her arms into the soft, gray-green hemp tweed. Cosima would have gotten wool, but she knew Edie was vegan. It fit perfectly, darted in the right places, pockets at the hip, the collar framing her face as Cosima had imagined.

Without thinking, she crossed the room, stepped behind Edie, and swept her hand under her nape to free the long ribbons of her hair from the jacket. When she tugged them out, the sensation was silk-on-silk against her hands. She smoothed the long, dark length of indulgently soft hair down Edie's back.

Edie shuddered. Probably anyone would at the feel of their

hair being lifted and pulled at their nape. But the small shudder shook Cosima . . . *awake*.

Edie turned around and smoothed her hands down the front of her jacket. "Well, I know I haven't ever worn anything so pretty. I'm so glad I asked you to take a walk."

This would be the moment to tell her that the jacket wasn't transactional. That she'd felt a lot of pleasure shopping for it. Buying it. That she was glad Edie was here.

And so, of course, Cosima grabbed her own jacket from the end of the bed. "Are you ready?"

Edie grinned, and, for now, the too-big feelings dissipated in the excitement.

Cosima was glad to be in the big outside, tromping and squelching their way across this field. Soft, wet spring grass soaked the cuffs of her jacket when she reached down to touch it. The sky was low over the softly rolling hills, the grass at mid-calf, the weather perfectly cool and sunny.

Another world from Los Angeles. A different life.

But she didn't hate it.

"It makes sense that we'd have to go through fields to find a stile." Edie's voice broke through the almost frantic layers of birdsong. "But don't you think there's been *a lot* of walking through fields? If I had walked this far through any field in Wisconsin, I would've already been shot. Or at least barked at by a poorly trained dog."

Cosima stumbled over a stone. "I can never tell if you're serious."

"Why? You live in America. Be careful, there's a lot of those big stones now that the grass is thicker. Also, does it smell like sheep? Is it this jacket?"

"Of course not, it's—"

"—holy fucking shit!"

Edie went down in the grass, and then there was an enormous flurry of movement and an improbable, complaining *baaa-aaa-aa*.

"Edie!" Cosima parted the grass in front of her with her hands.

A black-faced sheep looked up balefully from its position on its side next to Edie, who was on her ass on the ground, trying to avoid being kicked by the sheep as it attempted to right itself. "It just came up on me! Right against my hip! Goddammit!"

Edie hiked herself to her feet just as the sheep hopped up, and then it turned and butted her in the stomach.

"Hey! Hey!" She backed up. "I did *nothing*. This is your field, right? Look where you're going!"

The sheep backed up again, pawing at the ground with one of its front hooves, and put its head down. Cosima grabbed her arm. "Run, Edie! Run!"

She dragged Edie beside her, stumbling over the wet, stony earth through grass that grabbed and tangled at their wellies. The sheep tramped along behind them, neither slow nor fast but huffing alarmingly, udders swaying. Cosima was just beginning to wonder if the combined strength of two American women who were not at the peak of fitness would be sufficient to outlast one nettled English ewe when she heard a long, low whistle.

Turning toward it, she spotted a shape arrowing at them through the grass.

It burst into view, a black-and-white sheepdog circling the ewe to come to a stop in the space between them, where it got low to the ground and laid its ears flat.

Cosima heard another whistle. The dog feinted toward the ewe. She ran away, bleating with irritation.

A woman appeared, walking toward them from the direction the dog had come from. She gave them a jocular wave. "Don't mind her!" she shouted. "She's been a bit terrible since having her lambs."

The person was as tall as Cosima, with salt-and-pepper hair cut blunt along her chin. Her fossil of a blue sweater had darned elbows. She put her pinkies in her mouth and let out another sharp whistle. "Linda!"

Another disturbance in the grass signaled the dog's return, and then there Linda was, dropping to the ground and putting her head between her paws at the feet of the woman.

"That was amazing," Edie said, still out of breath from running. "What a great dog!"

"Oh, well. Linda does all right. Her mum, now, Linda Senior, was something else. Swear she read my mind." The woman put her hands on her hips. "You two must be Morag's guests. I'm Thorberta Fernsby, but everyone calls me Bert, of course."

"Of course," Cosima found herself whispering. Edie had moved half a step in front of her. Whether this choice was due to Edie's extroversion or an attempt to prevent Cosima from being recognized, she couldn't be sure.

"Sorry I crashed into your sheep," Edie said. "I didn't even see her!"

Bert laughed, crossing her arms and bending over as if Edie had the wit of the ages.

"Bert, I hope we're not trespassing." Cosima stepped beside Edie, extending her hand and being rewarded with the brief clasp of Bert's firm, powerful grip. "I'm Cosima Frank, and this is Edie Whitelock. You're correct, we're guests at Gregory Place. Morag assured us it was permitted to walk through the fields."

"Oh, that's right, isn't it?" Bert didn't react in any way to Cosima's name. "These fields belong to the sheep, as you found out for yourself. Won't be long before they can't sneak about in the grass with their lambs. They'll have it grazed down, and summer will have begun in earnest, poppies crimson and showy in the ditches like ribbons along the roads." Bert let out a short, happy sigh. "Lincolnshire at her finest."

Neither Cosima nor Edie had a ready response to this unexpected poetical reverie, but Bert seemed satisfied to listen to the birdsong and enjoy the light breeze for a moment. Both of them jumped when she suddenly clapped her hands together. "You'll be looking for Hermione's Stile."

"How did you know that?!" Edie exclaimed. "Who told you?"

Bert only crossed her arms and threw her a broad wink.

Cosima wondered if it made her a bad person that she'd so quickly had her fill of Bert. She wanted to get back to the part of this day that was just her and Edie and the open countryside. "Would you be able to point us in the correct direction?"

"The map wasn't exactly specific," Edie added. "There was one of those tiny rulers to measure the space and convert it to how many miles to go, but I don't really understand how to measure the distance for yourself once you're in the place and not using the map. I think we've been walking across this field for a half mile-ish."

"Edie's navigating has been quite helpful," Cosima said, because she didn't want Bert to get the wrong impression. "I think we only need a last point to get us there."

Bert's smile showed off the glint of gold crowns. "In the end, you might need a bit more than a point. That's what I think. But I reckon you'll find quite a bit of what you're looking for, and maybe more than you can believe possible."

"Do you mean the treasure?" Edie stage-whispered. She gazed up at Bert with eyes that had gone so green, they matched the grass.

"For heaven's sake." Cosima pressed both of her palms to her temples. "Hermione's Stile?"

Bert gestured to a wide-limbed tree hulking over a low dip in the field some fifty yards away. "You'll have seen that on your map. Harrington's oak, it's called."

"We're close!" Edie exclaimed. "On the map, the stile is only one length of the tiny ruler past the tree!"

"About that," Bert agreed. "Lucky for you, the weather will be nice and clear all day in the event you may need to venture a bit farther."

"We should go, then," Cosima said. "Bert, it was lovely meeting you. Thank you for your help."

Linda stood up and gave herself a shake as if Cosima's words meant the same to her as to her mistress. Bert beamed. "Watch your feet heading down the hill. It's slippery from the rain. I will see you two by and by."

Bert whistled at Linda, and they took off in the direction they'd come from, Bert in long strides and Linda only visible as she parted the grass in front of her. "By and by," Cosima said. "Good lord."

"Wasn't that the best thing that has ever happened to anyone on earth?" Edie's eyes were wide when she turned to Cosima. The sun had brought color up in her cheeks and the blunt tip of her nose. The breeze was picking up her hair and sending it in piecey bits, like she had walked out of a Ralph Lauren ad. "Obviously, if having a nice conversation in a pasture with a boomer and her dog is the best thing that has ever happened to me, I'm still winning at our game, but I can *pretend* it's magical."

Cosima couldn't help it—she snorted and started walking toward the tree. "You're not winning. Not by a long shot. My life has been so repressed, for example, that it never occurred to me I could text Duncan about something trivial, like the cipher. I felt I couldn't, not without giving him a reasonable explanation for why I've abandoned my post and am developing a dust allergy in England."

"Hmm." Edie reached down and picked a long strand of grass to twirl. "You definitely get points for that. Though, get ready for my next observation."

"Which is?" Cosima couldn't be sure if she was ready, but everything she wasn't ready for was another turn of the key, winding everything up, pushing her forward. Was that good or bad? Did she want to be awake?

"I didn't know it was so nice to have clothes that fit." Edie ran her hand over the sleeve of her jacket. "I've never done anything but make do when it comes to clothes. I feel like an entirely different person wearing this jacket."

Oh, she certainly had *not* been ready, and now Cosima wasn't sure what to do with her hot cheeks. "Who do you feel like?"

Edie gave her a one-sided, crooked, self-effacing smile that pinched Cosima's heart. "Myself, I think. Who knows? Turns out I've hardly met her."

"Yes." Cosima turned away from that smile, which was beginning to feel emotionally lethal. "You do get game points for reaching the ripe age of twenty-eight before owning a properly fitted garment."

"Do I get extra points if the reason I own it is because you're the first person who's paid attention?" Edie knocked Cosima with her shoulder, soft against her arm. It made her want to close her eyes and see if it would happen again.

The first person who'd paid attention. What world had ignored Edie Whitelock? Her appeals were so conspicuous. The jacket simply made Edie *more* Edie.

Edie in her green jacket was, to Cosima, as correct as the

perennial beds at the Castle, shape-shifting through the high season from one glorious bloom to the next.

She supposed it was how her mother felt, making movies.

It was a feeling Cosima wanted more of for herself.

They reached the tree, which was dripping with rain under its branches. Edie held her hands up to the water. "Do you know what this is called? Fog drip. This tree is so huge, it's nearly storming under here."

And this woman had called *her* a nerd. "The hill is steep." Cosima walked around the trunk of the oak, brushing rainwater from her arms and hair while looking dubiously down the rain-flattened grass of the hillside. "Maybe we should find a way to walk around."

"Let me see." Edie came up beside her. "Cosima! Look! There's the stile! It's just—"

And that was when Edie fell down the hill. On her ass. Like it was a slide at the carnival.

"For fuck's sake!" Cosima looked around for a different approach, but there was nothing for it. She sighed heavily, sat down on the grass, and gave herself a shove.

It was terrible. The ground was saturated and surprisingly cold. The uncontrollable speed of her slide meant she would never be able to wear these trousers again. Edie had started laughing so hard she was tipped over, slipping down the hill curled up like an armadillo. Or a hedgehog.

Cosima came to a stop beside her, hip deep in a puddle, Edie still choking on laughter, every part of her wet. "Didn't you hear me when I said we should find a way around?"

"I—I diiid," Edie coughed out, holding her sides. "I totally did, but then I was ass over fucking teakettle." She unfolded herself and starfished on the ground, looking up at the sky racing with fat, bright white clouds. "I lost my boot halfway down."

"Naturally." She injected the word with skepticism, but in truth, Cosima wanted to laugh. She got up and looked behind her, scanning the hillside for it. Once she spotted the boot, she looked around on the ground until she located a good stone. She closed one eye and got the boot lined up and then sharply flung the fist-shaped stone at the boot, knocking over its shaft and sending it skittering down toward them.

"Holy fuck, Cosima." Edie hauled herself up as the boot came to a stop at the bottom of the hill. "I'm positive I've never seen anything sexier in all of my life than you hauling off with that giant goddamned rock."

"I did shot put." Cosima brushed her hands off and handed Edie the boot, locking down any thoughts that wanted to make themselves known along the lines of *If you knew how to be sexy for Edie Whitelock, you wouldn't stop.* "At boarding school," she said, needlessly.

"Of course you fucking did." Edie yanked on her boot, her smile guileless. She batted her eyelashes. "Be in my zombie shelter?"

Cosima snorted, appallingly flattered. "Let's look at this stile."

They walked up to the crumbling wall of huge, blond stones. There were narrow stone steps built into it, allowing someone to climb up and over the barrier easily. Judging from the graffiti carved into it, the wall had long been a destination for local kids.

"Oh, look! There's one of those interpretative signs." Edie stood by a small wooden post with a green sign, and Cosima joined her to look at it. "That is a truly enormous dong." Edie pointed at the Sharpie vandalism over the prim lettering Hermione's Stile.

"You needn't have mentioned it. Ghastly thing."

Edie snorted. "Seriously, though, I'm glad the English are so good at their signage. I love that wherever you go, everything is labeled with a little contextual information. 'Hermione's Stile was constructed of local sandstone at or around 1688.' 1688!" She knocked her shoulder into Cosima again, and Cosima tried not to be pleased. "Unreal. How do they even know? 'Its name most likely refers to Hermione Blackwood, notable for running the local livestock market, though she was a single woman.'—*though she was a single woman?* Now I wish I had a Sharpie." Edie flicked the sign with her fingertip. "There are corrections to be made here."

"What do you think we're looking for?" Cosima studied the fifteen feet of crumbling wall with the slender double staircase, up one side and down the other. "There's not much wall left here, but enough that it could take ages to find a clue if it's small. Add to that the graffiti, and I wouldn't know where to begin."

Edie had approached the wall and hunkered down to examine the penknife-carved defacements. "This one's from 1803. V plus M. With a heart." She traced the heart with her finger. Always hands-on, this woman. Tactile. Kinetic. "It reminds me of this time that Mike took us to Ohio. His sister lived there, in the Hocking Hills. It was so pretty. There's a cave there called Old Man's Cave with a waterfall, and there's graffiti like this on the walls. I thought it was so amazing to think about how all these people from history were just regular people, you know?" Edie stood up and leaned against the wall.

"In Pompeii, there's graffiti on what would've been the wall of a bar between two men fighting over a woman named Iris. It ends with something like 'and you're just jealous and also suck.'

One third of Neanderthal graffiti boils down to, basically, 'I fucked your mom.'"

"Cosima!" Edie screeched.

"What? Have you *seen* a Roman vase? They drew phalluses on everything. There's thirty-five-hundred-year-old graffiti from a Chinese teenager in Egypt complaining about his vacation to the pyramids. Most of the graffiti in medieval pubs in England is some variation on 'the Pope puts stuff in his butt.'"

Edie clapped her hands, grinning madly. She did a little bounce from her tiptoes to her heels. "I could really listen to you talk about this all day."

"People are just people," Cosima said. "You're completely right about that. A good reason not to listen to your brothers."

"Ah." Edie's smile dimmed. "You've turned a discussion of dirty graffiti into a small lecture."

Cosima mentally winced. She'd been thinking for days about the things Edie had said about how she grew up. "It's only that it's bothered me what you've said about . . . well, what they say."

Edie adjusted her body against the wall with an unconscious fluidity that Cosima recognized as a sign she was thinking. She waited, looking around at the dips and rises of the landscape, irregular fields bordered by old stands of trees.

Lincolnshire really was beautiful.

"I was excited when my mom told me I was going to have a little brother or sister," Edie finally said. "*So* excited. I was in the second grade. It wasn't going well. Constant behavior interventions. I refused to learn to read. This girl Amber had smashed me in the mouth with a tetherball, and one of my front teeth turned gray." Edie tapped on a tooth that was as white as the others now, then closed her mouth, and Cosima could see the old gesture, as clear as day, of a little girl trying to hide her tooth. "The bullying was intense, is what I'm saying."

“I’m sorry.”

“I’m sorry, too. All of that hangs around inside for a long time, it turns out. Maybe forever. So the idea of a little sibling, someone who would be born loving me and who I would love from the beginning? It was the most amazing thing I could imagine. And it *was* amazing, for a while.”

“What happened?”

“My brother Ethan’s dad left. He was a nice enough guy, I guess, but I think even then he was having some trouble with gambling at the casino. Ethan was in Head Start, and, like me, a lot to deal with. By then, I’m in fifth grade, and it’s actually worse, because this is where the orthodontia starts to come into play, and the burgeoning figure you are enjoying today was somewhat less appreciated by the preteen set.”

Cosima touched the now-soft letter in her pocket, hoping the ink hadn’t run in her fall down the wet hill. Even before she was born or conceived, Phoebe had wanted her to know she was absolutely precious. Created from love. She’d named Cosima after all of existence—*cosmos*.

It was difficult to think that the woman who wrote the letter she’d found behind the wallpaper was the same one who built an enormous, walled empire. She was starting to think that there really were two different Phoebe Franks. Would the young woman who wrote the letter really have wanted her daughter to spend her life tied to the stock price of the company *Phoebe* made?

Why had Phoebe wanted her to come here? Who did she want her to be?

Edie kicked a pebble away from the base of the wall, pulling Cosima’s attention away from her own unproductive navel-gazing.

“My mom was with Andy by then,” Edie said. “She’d just had

Chris. That's my little brother. The pregnancy was hard on her. She struggled with postpartum depression. I was old enough to babysit. So—"

"You couldn't have been old enough to babysit. At ten? Eleven?"

"But I'd been helping with Ethan since he was born. I loved that little potato. If I was less excited about Chris, it was only because my mom was having a rough time, and Andy was kind of a dick. Chris had colic. He cried so much until we figured out he needed special formula, but by then Andy was out. He couldn't deal. Mom was sad. I had freakishly strong arms for a child and could hold and bounce him endlessly, which was the only thing that worked." Edie flexed a muscle for Cosima, but her smile had gone back to the not-real one.

"I'd think your brothers would adore you, given all of that."

"See, that's how I know you're an only child. No boy is going to adore his weird older sister who has the authority to get him in trouble because she half raised him. Especially once they were in school and knew how the other kids felt about me. I can't blame them for wanting to fit in, you know?"

"I do. I blame them. You're not weird. You're not a frog. You shouldn't have to take your brother's raincoat to England because, why? He tossed it at you and told you not to get wet? And you received this as affection?"

Cosima could tell from Edie's expression she'd hit close to the mark. Her stomach twisted, making her swallow against the unexpected pain.

"*Anyway*," Edie said after an awkward silence. "Probably everything I just blurted about my formative years sounds like I'm trying to win the game, but I'm actually humbled by how good my ass looks wearing this." She turned around to look over her shoulder at Cosima. Her smile almost a real one.

"Your ass looks very nice." The words felt wrong in her mouth. Cosima couldn't pretend to flirt like Edie and not have it mean something.

"Thank you. I'll take it, even if I forced the compliment." Edie fiddled with one of the buttons on the jacket. "But you need to be mean for the rest of the day so I don't fall in love and end up demanding you cuddle me to sleep."

With that, Edie turned away to inspect the rest of the wall, leaving Cosima madly extrapolating from the sensation of Edie's shoulder bumping into hers what it would feel like to hold her in her arms in bed.

"Cosima!"

She sucked in air. "Yeah?"

"From where you're standing, you can see the whole stile from above, right?

"I can."

"Did you bring your nerdy little notepad?"

Cosima patted herself down and felt the spiral of the notepad in her inner pocket. It hadn't fallen out in their adventures. "Yes. What do you see?"

"Am I wrong, or do the wall and the two staircases make a cross? Like a Christian cross?"

Cosima looked. "Yes. I don't even have to squint."

"This may be a super long shot, but I remember in the guest book message that the first number looked like a cross, too."

Cosima got out the notebook and flipped through it. "You're right. That's twenty-two."

"Okay. But what could that mean? I could be grasping at straws here."

"It could be a coincidence."

Edie climbed up one set of the stairs and sat down on top of the wall. "It probably is." She leaned back. "It's such a beautiful day, and the code worked so perfectly, like a fairy tale. But it's been fifty years. Probably the next clue's been destroyed by now, right?"

Cosima made herself think. She had helped to run an empire for one of the most particular women in the world. If she couldn't sort through a handful of data points left behind in a guest book by a Welsh novelist, she should be ashamed.

Then she remembered something. A data point. "Give me your map."

Edie unbuttoned her jacket, briefly scrambling Cosima's brain with a view of her corrupt tank top. She reached into the inner pocket. "What do you need it for?"

"Can you look at when it was made, or a copyright? I know it's a new map, but I mean the original drawing, which looks like it was hand-drawn."

Edie inspected the map. "Here! Nineteen sixty-seven, by the Harlaxton tourism office."

"If I'm remembering right, it has numbers on one side and letters on the other, creating a grid, so the inn is like location C-12?"

"Yes."

"What's location D-22? Twenty-two was the cross in the Cistercian numbers, and D is the letter associated with twenty-two in the guest book. It's worth a shot, right?"

Edie looked up at her, eyes wide, coat unbuttoned, hair damp, clearly absolutely admiring of Cosima, and it was the best compliment she'd ever received.

Then she looked down at the map. "Fuck me!"

"What?" Cosima's heart was racing.

"D-22! It's the church! A cross! D-22! All of it! You're amazing!"

"It could still be wrong. We could be missing something."

But Cosima's stomach untwisted and filled with butterflies.

"We could always be wrong." Edie shrugged. "If we are, we start over, or we find something else to do. There's no failed treasure hunt police. It's just you and me, and the sun's finally shining, and Morag is making jacket potatoes for lunch. We've already won!"

Cosima could only grin back, her hand over her mouth to hide just how big her smile was, swallowing over the first tears she'd felt for weeks and weeks that weren't sad ones.

She would worry about how very fucked she was when it came to Edie Whitelock later.

Chapter Eight

Edie followed the direction of Cosima's finger, pointing up at one of the carvings on the exterior of the church. "There's the flea," Cosima said.

Edie spotted the crouching, rough-bodied stone flea. A church volunteer named Greer Burton-Bailey had told them about the High Gothic church in passionate detail, breathlessly spilling tea about the church architecture drama of the twelfth century, including the habits of famous medieval stone carvers.

"John Oakham was here." Edie was careful to keep the defeat out of her voice, lest she infect her treasure-hunting partner with it.

"Yes." Cosima tipped her head. "Though it looks more like—"

"A frog." Edie nodded. "Definitely a frog. I have a question."

"How could you possibly have a question about this church after that woman's endless presentation? I've never known as much about a crypt in all of my life."

"Closing in on my point. There is a lot to know about this church. A lot of nooks. A lot of crannies. A lot of carvings. Places up high and down low. I looked very carefully during our girl Greer's tour, but I didn't see a carving with a giant X or an arrow labeled 'treasure here.'"

"Perhaps the church *is* the treasure," Cosima said, with a wry smile Edie hadn't seen yet. "It is a Grade I listed building."

"That's not the kind of pessimism my burning thigh muscles and growling stomach are interested in hearing." Edie sighed. "Should we go back indoors?"

Cosima's jacket hung open, and her pants were wrinkled beyond recognition, ballooning over the tops of her wellies. Her smooth hair was long gone, replaced by a nest that she'd clipped up with her two barrettes. Her perfect posture hadn't flagged, however. If anything, she looked more imperious than usual.

But something had shifted between them at the bottom of the wet hill, at Hermione's Stile. Edie knew she was in danger.

She didn't want to risk her worst impulses on such a genuinely lovely person. That was why she needed to take a step back and tell her heart not to beat so fucking fast when she stood close to Cosima. She was old and wise enough now not to hurt this woman, but she probably never would be old and smart enough not to hurt herself.

And her heart was already broken. Wasn't that why she was here, in this tiny town in a part of England she previously could not have pointed to on a map—to nurse the pieces of her heart until they could be fit back together again?

She had no business letting the shattered mess in her chest be softened by a tall, pretty-eyed princess with a three-cornered jawline and a smile that was hard to earn, even if the mess in her heart was begging *Please, please, please. Just this once.* Her heart was in no way trustworthy.

"If we go back inside, it should be with a plan," Cosima said. "Unless we want to—"

"There you girls are!" Greer Burton-Bailey whipped around the corner of the building in her chair, motoring it to full speed in their direction with her pointed chin pressed hard against the Permobil joystick. She came to a stop in front of them, the bright pink topknot of her hair releasing a few more fine strands to join the others blowing around her face. "You found the flea!"

"We did," Edie said. "Though we think it looks more like a frog."

"That it does!" Greer readily agreed. "I came to find you because it occurred to me that if you're interested in everything Agatha got up to, you might want access to some of the church records."

"What church records?" Cosima asked.

"Such a good question." Greer maneuvered closer. "After your tour, I remembered that the retired vicar, Dorna Rhodes, our first woman vicar, liked to tell stories about notable folks who've worshipped at the church, and that Agatha was one of them, during her stay. Even if a person's only come around once, they still sign our register, and we try to get a donation from them. Someone who's regular for a time might have left a bit more behind than that."

"Agatha would have signed the register personally?"

The interested snap to Cosima's question pulled Edie's attention back to their search. "Who knows?" Greer laughed. "Once, an investigator from London came to have a look at the records and solved a murder, so a clue to a scavenger hunt set up by an author is more than a bit likely."

Edie looked at Cosima for cues as to what to do next, and then followed her when Cosima told Greer to lead the way. They ended up at a cottage within the low stone wall of the church. Greer took the ramp to the curved-top wooden door, where she used her lanyard to activate a scan pad that unlocked it. "This used to be the rectory, but now we use it for archives, storage, two offices, and meetings. I'll orient you, then leave you to it. Help yourself to the electric kettle in the kitchen to make tea if you like."

Greer led them to a large room in the back of the cottage ringed with cabinets and showed them the filing system.

Once she had gone, Cosima sat down at the small round table in the middle of the room and pulled off her coat. Her linen top had crumpled spectacularly. "Where do you think we should start?"

Edie's throat was tight. "Can I be honest? Standing in this room gives me hives. Greer could have explained the filing system from now until the sun consumes the earth without my understanding it. Is there a medieval trapdoor somewhere in this house that I could chuck myself into?"

Cosima nodded, her eyes big and perfectly blue-gray and sympathetic.

Ugh. "I know it's pathetic." Old hurt rolled up from her chest, and Edie pinched the end of her nose to stop it. A big part of her was ready to simply walk back to the inn, eat lunch, and hide in the library with a stack of vintage romances. This day—this adventure, the clues, the sense of purpose, the mystery—all of it should have been a dream come true. This was something Edie *had* dreamed about, in fact. But now that it was happening to her, Edie couldn't make herself *stay* here. It felt like she was watching herself from above, lost and uncomfortable in damp socks and too-big wellies.

She forced herself to fake it. “Maybe you can get us started and remind me how Greer explained what’s where? Or I can take notes. I don’t take great notes. They’re more like quarter notes. Get it? My junior year English teacher made that joke. God.” She was panicking. “I think I just need to eat.” She hitched out a laugh that sounded strange coming out of her throat and looked at the timber-and-plaster ceiling.

“Edie.” Cosima’s tone promised comfort, understanding, but Edie needed the snappish Cosima back.

“I’m okay.” She unbuttoned her jacket and slid it off. She caught goose bumps and shivered when the cold air of the cottage hit her arms, but that was good. It reminded her she was a clumsy Wisconsin girl who wore stretchy jeans and Old Navy tank tops, not the woman who’d felt Cosima’s fingertips against the nape of her neck, tugging the hair from her collar.

“Maybe I’ll make some tea,” Edie said. “I think tea would be good. And if you think looking for something in these archives would help, I’m down to help how I can. If you think you’d rather go back to the inn for reheated jacket potatoes, that works, too.”

Cosima didn’t respond, so Edie left the archives room and stepped into the galley kitchen, where she spotted a pour-over carafe and a canister of nice coffee. She mentally thanked whatever church worker was a coffee snob while she went through the ritual of making coffee, her hands and her body comforted while her brain spun in circles at three thousand revolutions per second, not landing on anything.

She was dysregulated. She hadn’t slept enough, and she’d had a fantastically exciting morning followed by hours of physical activity. Her tender, vulnerable heart was getting a workout. None of which would be a problem if she and Cosima’s adventure hadn't suddenly reached a point at which there was no clear direction—the state of affairs Edie was least capable of handling. Her strong preference, always and forever, was to find a way to throw herself all-in at *something* while her feelings of overwhelm ran themselves down in the background. The only shortcoming to this approach was that as soon as there was nothing to throw herself at, Edie's overwhelm came rushing back to take over her body.

She needed this treasure hunt to keep moving. Ideally, it would move her all the way back to Green Bay before she had to think about how much she did not want to be there.

She used the time she spent making the coffee to take deep breaths, one after the next.

"Surprise." She walked back into the room with two big mugs of coffee. "Better than tea."

"Give that to me immediately." Cosima reached her hands out over a small file box with pastel-colored notecards spread over the table. When Edie handed the mug over, Cosima brought it to her lips to take a long drink. Her eyes rolled back, her eyelids fluttered down, and her cheeks went rosy as she swallowed.

Edie's heart ached. It had been a while since she fed someone something perfect.

She sat down and took a drink of her own coffee. "Why the fuck doesn't Morag serve coffee? My entire soul is singing in harmony."

"I'll demand it. Tell her to charge me a premium. English people don't *only* drink tea."

"Maybe they do in Harlaxton," Edie said. "Nothing has changed here in fifty years."

"On that subject, I think I might have something."

Edie pulled a random notecard toward her. It had been written on in sticky blue ballpoint ink, the handwriting a cramped cursive.

"Nothing changes here," Cosima said. "When we had the tour, I noticed a bulletin board where visitors and congregants can tack up notecards. They use it to write requests for prayers, or say something they particularly enjoyed about a church event."

"Okay."

"When they take the notes down, they keep them." Cosima picked up a short stack of cards and flipped through them, then put three in front of Edie. Edie picked them up.

"So these are from—"

"—when Agatha was in Harlaxton. 1977. On a hunch, I found the box from the year she was here, thinking she might have left her own."

There were two pastel pink cards and a yellow one. The cards were written in the same handwriting from the guest book, in soft-tipped pencil. Edie read the yellow card first.

> Personal blessing for us with a lovely, knowing prayer. Very unexpected grace that would not have come from my own parish church. All our love, A. B. Llewellyn.

Edie held it up. "This is the kind of thing my mom would say in church. Something that sounds like a eulogy she wrote when she was drunk."

Cosima gave her a small smile. "I was more interested in the other two."

Edie read the first one.

> The rat carving on the east-facing stone panel of the font is much more darling than I would've guessed given its accountability for the plague!

"It wasn't the fault of the rats, really," Edie said. "It was the fleas."

"Yes. Read the other one."

Edie pulled it forward.

You could drop a pocket watch into one of the nostrils of the green man poppyhead, and no one would discover it for a thousand years, if not longer.

"That is an exceedingly weird observation to pin to a bulletin board. Have you read her novels? Are they this weird?"

"Yes. Did you notice the green man poppyhead? Greer told us about how every medieval church had a green man, remember? She showed it to us."

Edie had enjoyed that part of Greer's lecture, actually. "Hmm. Did she? Was it green?"

"No. They aren't green, or at least, they don't have to be. They're pagan symbols of the natural world, with foliage carved all around their faces and—" Cosima stopped. "You're teasing me. You remember."

"I do."

"And you remember the poppyheads?" Cosima narrowed her eyes.

"The carvings on top of the skinny plinths at the beginning of each pew, yes. I paid attention. No quiz necessary."

"So you know what Agatha's talking about on that card."

"The giant man-head with leaves sprouting from his face who has nostrils the size of shooter marbles? Again, yes, and I had a similar thought about how many things I would have tried to shove in his nose had I gone to this church."

"When you were a child."

"Obviously"—Edie smiled—"at any time in my life."

Cosima took an imperious sip of her coffee. Edie was glad. Imperious Cosima with eyebrows that could hook a trout was a woman she could relax around. "I thought that perhaps we could check the font and the green man."

"You want to pick the green man's nose." Edie nodded solemnly. "You should've just said."

Cosima wrinkled *her* nose, then tidied up the cards and put them back in their box. "I'll clean up after the coffee and meet you outside."

Edie had been dismissed, but it was okay. The caffeine had dusted away the gloomy thoughts that had been working hard to keep her down. She was on *vacation*.

She was hunting *treasure*.

Outside the vicarage, she took a deep breath of the outside air, cooler than it had been at midday but holding clear. From here, she could see a wide slice of this place. The fields were the softest green, still mixed with the browns of late winter, and embroidered with huge trees and stone fences. Everything felt like a storybook, a little unreal.

Edie took a deep breath, and Cosima appeared at her side. She'd buttoned up her jacket again and refastened her hair. "Let's go see the green man."

"After we fish around in his nose, do you think we should walk the mile to the Gregory Arms? Morag has probably given up on us for lunch. I've only gone to the pub one other time, but it's nice. They fry their chips in peanut oil and bring vinegar to the table. It's the vegan lunch of champions. Only two pounds forty pence, also."

Cosima pulled open the church door. "If you like."

Her voice was nice and sharp. It released the last vestiges of panic from Edie's chest.

They found the green man halfway down the aisle, the

poppyhead slightly bigger than the others on its row of pews. The head of the wooden carving was about the size of a grapefruit. Its nostrils were worn smooth at the edges, suggesting that generations of children had been sticking their fingers in his nose.

"Do you want to do the honors?" Edie asked.

"Hmm." Cosima reached a hand up, then crossed her arms, tucking her hands into her elbows. "Hmm."

Edie laughed. "You don't."

"It seems unseemly."

"I'll do it!" Edie fished her finger into the green man's left nostril, wiggling as she went. She twisted her finger around. Nothing but smooth, polished wood. "No gold."

"Ew."

"I meant gold-*gold*, not boogers. Lord. California girls are prissy. I'm going into the right." Edie slid her finger into the other, slightly larger nostril, again wiggling her finger around like a wormy scope. She was just about to give up when the edge of her fingernail caught something hard that wasn't wood. "Oh."

"What?" Cosima stepped closer. "What is it?"

"I don't know. I can't quite get it." Edie switched to her middle finger.

"Aarrgh." Cosima looked away, toward the altar.

"Really?" Edie stood in the aisle, her middle finger up to her knuckle in the carving's nose. "It was my using my middle finger that tipped this over into indignity for you? It's *longer*, Cosima."

"I know! I just. I can't. I can't look at it."

Edie gazed at the soaring ceilings and fished around again, directing her fingertip to where she'd felt the anomaly. "It's a coin."

"Can you get it out?"

"It's hard to get my fingertip to grip it. Hold on." Edie pulled her finger out and shoved her hand down the front pocket of her jeans. "Trident." She unwrapped the gum and stuck it in her mouth. "I remembered I put the last piece from a pack I bought at the airport in my jeans this morning. Give me a minute."

Cosima watched Edie chew her gum. "What if the gum gets stuck in there?"

"It might." Edie blew a bubble. "I'm actually surprised there wasn't *more* gum down there. Do you think there's a volunteer whose job it is to clean gum out of the nose of the green man?"

Cosima's nose wrinkled again.

"Did anyone ever tell you your face is going to freeze like that?"

"All the time." Cosima sighed. "Followed by a lecture on why I should never get filler, because they don't rigorously test injectables."

Edie blew another bubble, then popped it with her middle finger, leaving the skin of gum over her fingertip. "Here I go."

She carefully dipped her finger into the nose, not wanting to stick the gum anywhere but to the coin, then pressed her finger on the edge of it. "Okay. I stuck it to my finger. I'm going to pull out."

Cosima's choking laugh echoed through the empty church. "Maybe I *am* prissy."

Edie was smiling as she slowly slid the coin out, watching it emerge until she had it grasped between two fingers. She held it triumphantly in the air. "It's fifty pence! Twenty percent off my chips!"

Cosima grabbed her wrist. "Let me see! You didn't even look at it."

Her fingers circled Edie's wrist in a firm grip, and Edie

resisted without thinking, palming the coin and dropping her arm so she could bury her fist against the softest part of her stomach. She hunched over it. "No! Don't take it! I *will* look, but not until you stop grabbing at me!"

"What are you doing? Why are you bent over like that? I'm not going to *take* it from you!"

"I have two brothers, and they're both taller than me." Edie straightened, but she pushed her arm behind her to rest at the small of her back. "This is how short people protect their resources."

Cosima's ears had gone pink around the rims. She was breathing fast, closer than Edie had realized, with her fingers at Edie's elbow.

"Promise you're not planning to swipe it out of my hand the instant I let down my guard?" The question came out a little too husky. Edie took a step back, and then Cosima did, too. She still had her fingers curled around the coin, hot and sticky with gum.

Maybe she could chalk this up to jet lag. Could jet lag come for you eleven days later and make you embarrassed and horny at the same time?

"I would never," Cosima said. "I thought we were in this together."

"We are definitely in this together. Possibly, I might be dealing with a certain amount of trauma around protecting a prize." Edie swallowed. "Please forgive me, and also completely forget that ever happened."

"I will remember it until I die. I'm going to write about how unhinged your reaction was in my journal. But if we don't look at that coin and confirm it's *only* a fifty-pence coin in the next literal moment, I will in fact knock you over and pin you to the ground. I went to an all-girls' boarding school. I played rugby. Lacrosse. Field hockey. I could take both of your brothers."

"That is absolutely hot. I'm tempted not to show you this coin, just to see what would happen, but I will submit." Edie held her hand up, palm flat between them.

"There's a lion on it." The coin was silver, with an image of a woman beside the lion. It wasn't circular. Edie counted seven sides while Cosima breathed onto the palm of her hand. "I assume that's Brittania with the lion. Is this the current fifty-pence coin?"

"No clue. We should flip it to heads." Edie moved the coin to sit on top of her thumbnail and then flipped it. "Ow! Moth-er*fucker*. British coins are heavy!" The coin spun on the aisle carpet, then settled flat.

They both crouched down, the tops of their heads nearly touching, and gasped.

"There's an engraving!" Cosima breathed.

"You were right about the notecards. Good job! Your attention to detail is god-tier."

Cosima looked up, grinning. Her real smile made wrinkles at the corners of her eyes and over the top of both cheeks. It was really, really good. "Your mom was right, too," Edie said without thinking. "Don't ever get fillers." Cosima's brows folded into a confused tangle that rippled the skin on her forehead. Edie felt a blush coming on, so she grabbed the coin from the floor and stood back up. "I'm going to read it, even though you're the one who found it." The coin had the type of engraving normally found on a locket or pocket watch. "It says, *And Now for a Piece of Cake.*"

"What?" Cosima squeaked. "What does that mean?"

Edie felt the swarm of excited bees low in her belly before she even had the answer fully formed, so excited was she to have the experiences of her life add up in such a perfect way. "She means an actual cake." She permitted herself to take Cosima's elbow. "Greer said that the stone carvings in the interior of the church were done sometime between the eleven and fourteen hundreds, right?"

"That's right."

She led Cosima to the front of the church, where the stone carvings outlined the nave.

"I might not know history, but I do know cake. At that time, the cake everybody was baking on this side of the pond was a simnel cake." Edie guided her to a carving she'd noticed on Greer's tour.

"Simnel cake?"

"It's a yeasted cake. If I made it for you now, you'd think it was more like bread. It was round, one layer, baked with a domed top because of how the yeast rose the dough out of the tin. It was studded with whatever the baker had on hand that was sweet—berries, dried fruit, nuts, chunks of apple or quince or handfuls of currants. Sometimes even cheese."

Edie put her hand on the dome-topped carving, with its little stubs all over it. The round cake was carved to look like it rested on a linen.

"Oh! That's a cake!"

"It's a cake." Edie ran her fingernail under the top of the carving. "And the other thing I noticed when I, of course, identified this as a carving of a cake, is that this isn't just a carving. It's a tabernacle. Thank you, casual Catholic upbringing." With a soft grind of stone on stone, Edie carefully lifted off the top of the cake.

"A tabernacle?"

"Where the priest keeps the sacrament. The bread. The crackers. The wafers. Or, in this case"—Edie reached into the shallow stone tabernacle, and her hand found a thick envelope and pulled it out, dust raining from it—"a treasure. Or the next clue to one."

She handed the heavy cream envelope to Cosima. Her entire body had been overtaken by a shimmering, incredible feeling.

She'd been right. Edie Ashlynn Whitelock was *right*.

As Cosima ran her finger under the flap, Edie pressed her eyes shut hard enough to see colors behind her eyelids. She heard Cosima's sharp inhale, the sound of paper sliding against paper, the unfolding rustle of something substantial. She had never wanted anything more than she wanted to be able to run up to herself *as* herself, the kid version of herself, and tap her own arm and say *freeze tag*, stopping time.

Because what came after this kind of shimmering, incredible feeling was always bad.

"It's a map," Cosima said. "Oh, wow, Edie. It's a map!"

It was the most joyous she'd ever heard Cosima be. The sound of it cracked open Edie's eyes. Cosima had opened up a map, the kind on a big piece of paper, folded in half and then into rectangles. She held it cradled in her arms in order to see it all at once.

"What does it . . ." Edie almost didn't want to know.

"There's England. And *Europe*. All of the countries are sketched in black and white pencil, except England, France, and Spain. Those are more detailed, and in color. They have illustrated frames around them and little details. Like a square around each of those countries with what to pay attention to. The details are tiny sketches"—Cosima turned the map to show Edie—"and could be puzzles. Or hints, maybe. At a glance, it's not obvious what order one would go to these places, or exactly which places one would go." Cosima shook her head, then turned the map around, smiling. "You found a genuine treasure map."

The map was handmade, in watercolors, annotated in the same handwriting as on the notecards, but with more flourish, using a fancy pen.

France. Spain. A dotted red line indicating a trip over the English Channel. She touched the paper with the tips of her fingers.

"It will be such an amazing trip. A real adventure." Edie did her best to smile at Cosima without letting her eyes burn with tears. Her shoulders were so tight, they made her arms ache right down to the elbows. "Now"—she pointed at Cosima to match her faux-stern voice—"you'll have to write me a postcard at every stop you make along the way. Or help me unbrick my phone! Phoebe Frank would be so excited that you were doing this. You'll have to tell Duncan all about it." She took a stealth, quick breath, a trick she'd learned so she wouldn't lose it in front of her brothers. "Epic. Truly."

Confusion folded Cosima's forehead. "I don't understand."

"You don't?" A tiny fire of anger lit in Edie's heart. She was tired of not being understood. "Remember Fauxmage, and why I'm here, and why a big day is seeing a hedgehog, and my hideous borrowed coat? You live in a castle. In Beverly Hills. There's a fountain with pink elephants, which I know because I saw pictures in a magazine at the twelve-dollar haircut place where I still go, sometimes with my mom. I used to play with an action figure of *your* mother."

Edie pressed her hand to her sternum. She'd had no idea her heart could race this fast. She wasn't being fair. She didn't actually resent Cosima. She didn't want Cosima's life.

But she had never figured out how to get the life she wanted and keep it.

"I'm sorry. I am. It's just that by the end of the month I'll be standing in the test kitchen of A Presto! Pizza Crust Factory, the closest I'll ever be to Italy, figuring out if I can get ten more grams of semolina flour out of the recipe in order to save the company half a million dollars a year. And that's if I don't get fired from this job, a job my mother is leveraging her own job to get me. It's decent union money. She tells me if I'm careful it should be enough to get me a two-bedroom with a pool and a nice used SUV. Maybe when I'm forty, if the world hasn't burned down yet, I'll have enough saved to mortgage a ranch home with a bar top in the basement for my friends to hang out and watch the Packers."

Cosima folded the map in half. "Stop it."

"Stop what? Telling the truth? Look, this has been fun, but—"

"I said *stop*." Cosima was being rough with the map, folding it in the wrong directions, causing it to crumple.

Edie took another short, sharp breath. It didn't help. "Cosima."

"You don't know what you really are." She said this almost in a whisper, but she was angry. Not sad, not annoyed, not annoyed-plus. Furious.

Good. "You don't know who I am either." Edie worked to keep her voice even. "You've already told me who you think I am. You said on the first day we met when I recognized you, when I realized you were Cosima Frank, you said—"

"Not to you." Cosima's lips were white, her famous blue-gray eyes iridescent. "I said I wasn't Cosima Frank to *you*."

"You're not," Edie said. "You were correct about that. Because Gregory Place is magic, right? For a little while, I can be friends with a princess. I can adventure across the countryside, across the world." She crossed her arms, her breath getting shorter and shorter. "But then my time runs out with the last of my money, and Gregory Place turns out to be just a musty, leaking inn in a place everyone else in England has forgotten about. I'm guessing your mom didn't stay long enough to figure that out."

She unbuttoned her jacket and slid it off, her throat caught in a vise of self-recrimination and hopeless, unanswered anger that was too familiar.

Grandiosity. Her mother liked to say that Green Bay *wasn't good enough* for Edie, but this place was too good for her.

None of this—the stone carvings and tall women with pretty eyes and European treasure hunts—was for her. She was a cut-rate tourist on a self-pity vacation. She handed the jacket to Cosima. "I don't want this. It's too nice of a gift."

"I don't want it either."

She folded the jacket and set it down on the floor. "I'm just going to walk back, okay?"

Edie didn't wait to hear whatever Cosima might say. She stomped away in a fugue of unnecessary drama and unregulated feelings like one of the foxes she'd seen, its winter coat coming off in rags, its ears and tail low, trotting away as though a woman on a walk might attack it.

Or, truly, more like a startled frog escaping into a pond with a messy splash.

Chapter Nine

Cosima stabbed the chicken curry with her fork, taking a huge bite. The curry was wasted on her. Her mouth couldn't taste anything but the last words she'd said to Edie.

I don't want it either.

She looked at Edie's green jacket, folded up beneath hers on the pub bench.

"Anything else, duck?" The Gregory Arms publican had a circlet of salt-and-ginger hair orbiting his head. His shoulders looked like they could toss full wine barrels. He'd attended her the moment she sat down in the scrupulously clean pub, giving her three specials to choose from and a surprisingly long list of nonalcoholic drink options, and after he'd served her meal steaming hot, he hadn't returned until the moment she'd scraped up her last bite.

Cosima liked him for his predictable efficiency.

"A bourbon, neat," she said. "With a slice of lemon."

He nodded while taking up her plate and pint glass. "A square of the sticky toffee pudding alongside?"

"Yes."

"Jug of custard?"

"Yes."

"Right back."

He disappeared just as a large party came into the other dining room, laughing as they'd been caught in the rain.

The rain was why Cosima was here and not at the inn, though she had half a mind to hire a ride to pick her up from this pub and rush her to the airport, full of just enough suppressed anger and curry to keep the tears at bay.

She would, too, if she knew what she would say to the agent at the airport ticketing desk when they asked where she wanted to go.

Cosima pulled her phone from the pocket of her jacket. There were four notifications on the screen, all from Duncan. His were the only notifications she still allowed to push. She opened the first one.

> Had lunch with Corrine Lake, and it was a balm. I told her about your decoding and treasure hunt adventures. She was delighted.

> Turned the corner on the east patio this morning with my coffee and was completely taken by the show your mother's row of camellia was putting on.

So bright pink, the color of the sky and grass was glowing around them. I imagined it was Phoebe saying hello.

Remember when you and I put those in for your mother's birthday? You were nine and so serious about sprinkling the rooting powder into each planting hole.

Cosima turned the phone over, her chest tight. Not a word about PFS. The impatient board. The stock price. *I used to play with an action figure of your mother*, Edie had said, but Phoebe's oversized legacy was absent from these texts.

She and Duncan never said what they meant.

The publican appeared with a tray and arranged her whiskey, dish of lemon, plate of cake, and custard jug, along with a fresh set of cutlery. "There you are. My name's Tam, if I haven't said. Settle up or put in another order at the bar, duck."

"Do you have vegan food?" Cosima blurted. She wrapped a hand around the whiskey glass. "I'm sorry, never mind."

Tam shoved his hands in the pockets at the front of his apron. "You're a friend of the Edie girl staying up there at Gregory's Place with Morag, then."

Cosima shook her head back and forth. *No*. "Yes."

That made Tam smile. "Haven't figured it out yet?"

"I don't know." Cosima looked down at the bourbon. She wasn't sure why she'd ordered it. She didn't often drink. Duncan didn't, either. The idea of bringing the edge of the glass to her lips was a horrible one.

Tam put his meaty hand on the back of the chair across from her. "Do you mind if I take a load off?"

Cosima shook her head. Her stomach hurt, really hurt, the way it had before she came here.

"No use pretending I don't know who you are," he said once he'd settled in. "Everyone in the village does, of course, and I've loved Phoebe Frank's movies since I can remember. Me and me mum both. We remember when she was here, you know, with the race car driver, your da." Tam smiled. "All of us were starstruck at first, but Phoebe put everyone at ease right off. Encouraged me to try for a part in the community theater up in Grantham, and I've tread the boards in a production every season since. I'd never told anyone but Miss Frank I was a secret thespian, and she treated it serious. I met my husband in a production of *Epsom Downs*, so I owe not a little of my happiness to her. I'm sorry for your great loss."

Gravity gave up its grip on Cosima's heart, and it tumbled into her throat, triggering tears so sudden that she found herself letting out a laugh. "God, I'm sorry." She shook her head as she wiped at her face. "Thank you, is what I want to say. Thank you for telling me about your experience with my mother. I don't get to hear many truly personal stories about her."

Tam waved his hand. "No, duck, I'm sorry for springing it on you like that. Too much for over cake."

"No. It's not. I'm glad to know. I think her stay here really meant something to her." Cosima thought again of the audacious love and confidence of her mother's letter and the clues she'd left for Cosima to find it.

The mother Cosima knew had been a woman who made magic, but not someone who believed in it.

She touched the whiskey glass. She wasn't sure when it happened that her mother could only find respite in a bottle. Even now, only Cosima and Duncan and her mother's doctors knew it had killed her.

Grief, and addiction, and obsessive work. All of it a monster.

Maybe that's why Cosima didn't want to please the board and the stocks by feeding it. Maybe she thought it would starve and never eat anyone else again.

Maybe a person could make something so big it eventually ate them.

She didn't know. But it did feel right that Phoebe had put this place on her list so Cosima might learn something *different* about her mother. That once upon a time, Phoebe had been a girl who met a reckless boy in an English lane with an easy smile.

Cosima slid the bourbon in Tam's direction. "On me? I don't know why I ordered it. Duncan would be shocked." Cosima didn't need to explain who Duncan was. Tam would know. "Edie might say it was because I want to feel close to her. To my mother."

Tam picked up the whiskey and toasted Cosima. "To Miss Frank. And her companion, Duncan, god protect him." He took a drink and put the glass down. "Now, you've mentioned Edie twice."

"We're both staying at Gregory Place." Cosima heard her tone go tart.

"You're both looking for Agatha's treasure is what you're doing."

Bert had been aware of their agenda, too. "Is there a Facebook group? How does everyone know?"

"Morag's been crouched over that guest book like a dragon for years. Every time likely candidates stay up at her inn, we all hold our breath hoping she'll release it from her grasp, but this is the first time she's let go. Don't know if it's because she's decided to be afraid of dying or if she believes you're the two to get to the bottom of this business once and for all. Seems like you got pretty far today. A map! What a thing."

"How did you know we—"

"Greer." Tam's eyes twinkled.

Of course. Greer would have been nearby when they had found the map. She would have witnessed them stealing it from the church. Though, if Greer knew what they were looking for, was it stealing? Cosima reached over to her jacket on the velvet-cushioned bench and pressed the pocket where the map reassuringly crinkled.

Greer must also have witnessed the argument between her and Edie.

Pulling her jacket closer, she retrieved the map. "This is it." She held it up for Tam to see, then laid it on the table between them. "You can look if you want to."

Tam raised his eyebrows, but then he put the bourbon down and rubbed his hands together before picking up the map. He tipped it at her. "You sure? This is your treasure to find, but I'm as curious as a ginger cat to take a look. To think it's been in the church all this time."

When Cosima nodded, he carefully opened the map and leaned back. Cosima took a few breaths. With the benefit of food and her clothes mostly dry, she felt the guilt that was always stalking her, hunched in a dark corner of her brain.

Tam furrowed his hedgelike brows at her. "The curry not sitting well, duck?"

"Dinner was excellent. That noise was my feelings escaping from my body."

Tam set the map down and leaned forward. "Now, perhaps an aging gay publican wasn't what you had in mind to receive your troubles, but standing behind that bar for most of my life surely gives me some part of a therapist's credential."

Cosima felt her shoulders start to soften in Tam's empathetic gaze. "Edie," she said.

"I've had the honor. Rare to meet a person who can talk so much and actually be interesting. Or someone who puts their worst and best right out there like it might help all of us learn to do better."

"That's a good summation." Though it wasn't a summary that captured Edie's husky voice, or the dozens of discrete patterns of her freckles, or her moody green eyes and dark, satiny hair.

"What about her?" Tam took a sip of his whiskey.

"She's different. For me."

Cosima wasn't an actress. She couldn't do what her mother could with her expression or her eyes when she said a simple line from a script that made an audience weep. But she *could* hear what her heart meant when she said those four words out loud to Tam. *She's different. For me.*

Tam held his chin, looking away. He had a small gold hoop in his ear, and a charm with the letter *K* dangled from it. She wondered what name the initial stood for. The name of his husband? She watched the charm wink in the low light of the pub and realized she would do the same. If she had someone who was hers, she would wear their initial, their picture in a locket, their name tattooed on her thigh.

She had never had a thought like that in her life.

"Let me narrow this down," Tam said. "Different from—"

"Everyone," Cosima said. "You know, my mother wrote me a letter that she left here for me to find. I'm staying at Gregory Place because she put it on a list we were working our way through before she died, and of course, when I came here, she had something for me to do. Find this letter and read it. Maybe she thought I would learn where I came from. Or what I was for."

"A director in more ways than one."

"I don't remember that my mother ever, not even once, made a rule. Not a curfew, not a single reminder not to run through the halls. I wasn't grounded. She never yelled."

"But there *were* rules, I'm guessing."

Cosima closed her eyes. "I have never, ever *not* known what Phoebe Frank wanted me to do. In any given moment of my life. Even this moment. After she's died."

Tam shifted his body in the chair, making it creak. "Baby."

"Baby?" Cosima was *mostly* certain Tam hadn't addressed her by a pet name, but not entirely.

"My great big tuxedo tom. Oh, he was the worst. Fat as a steer at market, but agile enough to cause trouble. He'd leave me a row of headless mice at my doorstep every night like a ghoul, then settle down in my lap in front of the fire as sweet as any creature could possibly be. He slept curled up at my feet. If I moved even a little, his needle teeth would sink into my toes. He hissed at children. Swiped at dogs. The vet fixed him, but somehow he got my neighbor's prize Persian pregnant. That was a right mess."

Tam's grin was more of a grimace. His voice had been getting rougher as he told her this, making her heart beat fast.

"The day he died, in my arms, at the old vet's, I wept so long, his fur was sopping. I carried him home in a blanket, and I didn't sleep until I had made him a resting place. It was spring. I lined the hole with tulips and hyacinth, and placed him in. Took me ages to cover him over with earth, because then it would be final, you see? I'd never be able to hold him again. I'd never feel his fat full stone of weight on my lap or hear him thundering down the stairs. There's been a Baby-shaped hole in my life ever since. I closed the pub for a week and couldn't leave the house. Lost my voice from crying."

"*Tam.*"

"Yeah. Yeah." He leaned forward. "Wasn't a year later my dad died. I was with him when he went, taking a shift for my sister. He had mostly slept for days, had already refused to eat, would have only small sips of water. Told us he saw our mum, and I believe he did, even if I never saw him do more than give my mum orders from behind the bar and glare at her when he thought she was too slow getting food out. My mum would've come if my dying dad wanted her to, because he was good about them unspoken rules, as well."

"Oh." Cosima understood this. People so powerful they could summon a ghost to do their bidding.

"My mum begged me not to tell him I was gay," Tam said. "But I was in love. I guess I thought, or wished, that he loved me enough to accept one thing in his life he didn't understand. Funny, because ninety-five percent of my life looked exactly like his. I'd just be going about *one* thing different. And not even that different! I loved Killian, and my dad had six children with my mum, so I figured he must know something about love."

"He didn't understand." Cosima's cheeks and ears felt too hot, but her stomach was a little lighter, less painful. She tried to trust it.

"I don't know if he did." Tam ran his finger along the lip of his glass. "He didn't say one word about it. I told him, he turned around and pulled a bitter and put it on the bar for me to take to a table. Message received."

Cosima shook her head, thinking about wordless messages and how much power they'd had in her own life. She grabbed the map off the table and held it up. "Phoebe was like this. She gave me a map showing every place I was supposed to go and what I was supposed to do once I got there. But what I'm realizing is that there was no destination. She wrote to me in that letter about how she had fallen in love with my father, how she loved him so much, it was overdetermined that I would someday exist. But did it never occur to her to tell me, once I was here, where I was going? Was I simply supposed to follow her so that she could see every option up ahead and choose for me?"

"What do you think?"

Cosima cut off a big bite of her sticky toffee pudding. It was perfect sweetness. The perfect foil to this horrible, amazing, confusing day. "I think maybe when my father died, she changed. She was happy to tackle the risks and pitfalls of Hollywood and come out on top, but once she'd loved and lost, that was her limit. I think every time she came close to any kind of risk with Duncan or me, she pulled back. More silence took over, and less was said."

"You're describing someone incredibly powerful."

"Incredibly complicated."

He sighed. "That's why I told you about Baby and my dad. When Baby died, oh, but it was pure, pitch-black grief. I knew what he was, I knew every bit, so I knew what I had lost, and I knew what part of my heart I'd lost with him. When my dad died, duck, well. Do you know how surprised I was when there was so much I *didn't* lose, but gained? Acceptance, just to start. I felt so much better without him. That's complicated. Relief, the freedom of an open life, but the ability to still imagine everything we might have said and didn't? I would have rather pitched myself off a cliff. I'd have rather felt ten times the grief of when Baby died. It would have meant the love was pure, wouldn't it? The hurt and pain would have come from something I understood, instead of a hundred things I had to learn in the years he's been gone."

"So what the fuck, Tam?" Cosima had another bite of pudding. "I've got more than an English pub's worth of a legacy to tend to, as I'm sure you can imagine."

"You'll find yourself stopped short, again and again, with having to figure something out. You'll make something up, and it will work, or it won't. Either way, you'll learn something about yourself. It's just that." Tam finished the bourbon.

Cosima poured custard over the pudding she had left, and she and Tam let their conversation settle over them while she thought of nothing but rich sponge and vanilla custard.

"You know I've never had a romantic relationship?" Cosima drew her fork through custard and crumbs. "And you'd think, after everything we've just talked about, the reason would be that Phoebe didn't want me to. But that wasn't it. I'm not sure she noticed, actually."

Tam laughed. "You did start this conversation talking about Edie." He lifted his huge, bushy brows, but Cosima ignored the knowing look.

"It wasn't about Phoebe, for a change. There was simply a moment when I realized I didn't want to. I've always loved romantic movies and books and music, but there has been this empty space I didn't understand when it came to *me* and romance. *Me* and sex." She glanced at Tam. He didn't seem embarrassed by the intimacy of her confession. "There was never anything I needed or wanted from anyone I ever met."

"Folks know more about that now. The ace spectrum, it's called. You find it?"

Cosima made a design in the custard with the tines of her fork. "Yes. But identifying myself on that spectrum has been the *only* thing I've been able to do. There's never been a hard click. With anything or anyone."

"And I say again, you started us here with Edie."

"I did." Cosima put her hand on her stomach. It didn't twist. It didn't tighten.

"Any clicks?"

"Here's my problem. If there *are* clicks, what could be done? There could be a castanet band of clicking, but"—Cosima put her fingers in her ears—"la-la-la-la. I live in LA. Edie lives in Wisconsin. Our time here is limited. I don't know how much Edie told you about what she's been through, but she's dealing with a lot. I am also dealing with a lot, and I'll have more to deal with the moment I touch down at home. Years' worth of more. And, of course, she has given me no indication whatsoever that there is even a teeny, tiny click for her. In fact, we spend a lot of our time together arguing. Bickering." Their charming banter.

Tam folded his hands on the scarred table. "So it begins. The great Cosima Frank experiment."

"But I don't want to experiment with Edie. She should have something big. Something no one else would give her."

Tam lifted the map from the table with a raised eyebrow.

"Yes. That. But the treasure is the least of what she should have—*no*, what she should *expect* someone to give her. If a world existed where she could be mine, I'd spend the rest of my life raising her expectations."

Tam's face said it all, but he wisely didn't do more than nod.

Cosima adjusted her posture to create a bit of distance between herself and that confession. "She was so excited. I saw it in her face, before she counted herself out. She wants to go where the map tells her to go and find what it asks her to find." She pulled it back across the table toward herself and ran her finger along the soft edge of the paper. "Personally? I'm not looking for instructions from the past life of some Welsh novelist. But wherever this could take Edie, I'd like to go along."

"Interesting that you see this"—Tam tapped the map—"as

simply going along and not something that could change your own direction."

"That's enough therapy for tonight, Tam." Cosima softened her stern tone with a smile. "But if I could ask you for one more thing, could you take a look at the map and tell me everything that you notice? I'm hoping a local might see a few things that we"—Cosima shot a look at Tam, whose knowing grin was entirely too self-satisfied—"might otherwise miss."

"Will do. And, look, the rain's let up. I'll have a peek at this and call Killian. He's upstairs settled in with reality TV and his chocolate, I'm certain, but I'd like to have him drive you back to Gregory Place. It will take him a bit to get shoes on and come down, so I'll have a moment to study this while we wait."

Cosima let herself lean back into the upholstery. Her gaze caught Edie's jacket. She brushed her hand over the soft fabric, imagining she could smell the grass-and-lemon smell of Pears soap mixed up with the old incense and candle wax of the church, the apple blossoms that had been everywhere today, and just a little bit of sheep.

She had no doubt she could convince Edie Whitelock to find this treasure with her. The thought made it easy for Cosima to understand why, when she was on the plane over the Atlantic Ocean, she'd felt like there was absolutely nothing under her feet and she was hurtling unmoored through space.

Because she was.

Chapter Ten

Edie jumped when the kitchen door of the inn banged open.

"It's not what it looks like!" she shouted in her panic that it would be Morag, while throwing a tea towel over a bowl of flour and the plant butter she'd just cubed.

"It looks like you're baking." Cosima shut the door behind her.

Edie pressed her hands against her chest. "Jesus HC in a bike basket, you don't knock?"

"On the kitchen door? Where's Morag?"

"She's in Grantham picking up the linens from the laundry, but she said she'd be late because she has dinner with the East Midlands Tourist Board. If that is a real organization. But she said 'late.' What time is late to an eighty-six-year-old? What time is it now?" Edie pulled the tea towel off the bowl and scooped up the cubes of butter. She dumped them into the sifted flour and started cutting the butter in with her fingers double-time. "Ignore what I'm doing. You saw nothing."

"It's eight." Cosima pulled off her jacket and put it on a chair by the pantry. Her linen shirt and trousers had dried into a web of wrinkles, the muddy hems of her pants were stuffed into even more muddy boots, and her hair had frizzed magnificently around her head. She looked beautiful. And disconcertingly soft-eyed.

Edie concentrated on rolling pea-sized crumbs off her fingertips. The humiliation and frustration of their argument hadn't faded. "Eight feels late. I should've started earlier, but I had to nerve myself up."

"To do what?"

"Shortbread." Edie made finer and finer crumbs gravel through her fingers, realizing that her decision to mix up shortbread had been a bad mistake. She made amazing, award-winning shortbread, but also, she had made shortbread every day for Fauxmage. Taking her body through the motions of this task had quickly turned into genuine psychological torture that she'd only identified when Cosima burst into the kitchen. She felt dreadful, like a creature that dwelled at the bottom of a well.

Cosima sat down at the work table, folding her hands. "And you're making shortbread because?"

"Because I wanted to make shortbread. If you're going to sit there when it's getting late enough that I'm going to be caught and then thrown out and have to sleep in the greenhouse, then you could make yourself useful and zest that lemon."

Cosima surveyed the work table. "This lemon?"

"Any lemon." Edie blew out a breath. "But yes, that one, because I washed it."

"I don't know how to do what you're asking."

The admission somewhat deflated Edie's effort to keep this conversation brisk and far, far away from her feelings. She took her hands out of the bowl and pushed the Microplane grater across the space between them. "I'm asking you to zest."

Cosima picked up the plane, the tool in one hand, lemon in the other. "And zesting is?"

Edie sighed—sighed out all of the air in her lungs—and brushed off her hands into the bowl. She walked around the football-pitch-sized table and arrived at Cosima's side, where she took the lemon and the grater from her, then stroked the lemon a few times over the plane, making a teaspoon's worth of fluffy zest fall onto the table. "Removing the zest. Just the yellow part, none of the pith, the white part. Move the lemon around and go in one direction."

"Thank you." Cosima held out her hands for the plane and the lemon. When Edie gave them to her, she made an experimental stroke with the lemon. "Oh! Look at that!" She pointed at the twenty-five flakes of zest she'd made.

"Well-done, chef."

Edie returned to her station. She dripped coconut milk into her mixture and started folding it with her hands, and when it was three or four folds from being ready, she glanced across the table at Cosima. "I'm ready for your zest."

Cosima held up a tea saucer with a perfect pyramid of yellow flakes. She stood up on the rungs of her stool and bent over the table, holding out the saucer until Edie could grasp it. Which she did, for a moment—before it slipped through her buttery fingers to break on the edge of the bowl.

Saucer shards rained down into her shortbread dough, ruining it.

"Very seriously fuck this in so many different directions." She put her head down on her arms on the work table and smelled lemon zest and butter, a sensory reminder of a full year of hope and failure.

"Sit down," Cosima said. "Give yourself a moment."

"No. I have to hide the evidence."

"Just let me," Cosima said. "Morag won't suspect a thing. Essentially all I did for my mother was clean up messes."

It was a comment that struck Edie as not entirely aligned with how Cosima had spoken of her life before. What kind of messes had she been cleaning up?

She watched Cosima roll up her sleeves and pick up the pieces of the saucer to make a stack. She found a bench scraper next to the bowl. "I've seen chefs during events use these to clean the area?"

"Go for it."

Cosima scraped the counter, then pulled a paper grocery bag from the recycling to dump crumbs and zest into. She wiped down the coconut milk carton and wrung out a rag over and over with hot water to clean the table until there was nothing left but a folded-up bag of Edie's crimes and clean dishes on the draining board.

"What *is* it that you do?" Edie accepted the glass of Ribena that Cosima poured for her. "And forgive me if it's rude to presume you do anything."

Cosima dried the bowl and nested it with others on a shelf. "I'm the acting board chair for Phoebe Frank Studios."

"What does the board chair do?"

"I make a decision about anything that anyone thinks my mother would have had an opinion on. Before, I didn't have an official title, I just did whatever she didn't want to, and kept people from doing things that she wouldn't like or that would make her upset."

Cosima folded the tea towel in a perfect square and put it on the table before pouring her own glass of juice. Her voice had gone flat.

What Cosima had just described—that wasn't a job description. That *was* a mess, probably toxic, definitely treacherous. Somewhere in what Cosima was saying and not saying, Edie guessed, was the secret she'd gotten angry with Morag about. Edie wasn't sure she wanted to know what it was.

That was a lie. She wanted to know desperately.

"So do you like being a board chair? What do you go to college for to do that?"

Cosima's smile was distantly polite. "At Bennington, we developed our own course of study. My degree was a kind of blend of taxonomy with art history."

"That doesn't sound like a straight path to sitting around a conference table."

"The straight path to my job was being born Cosima Frank."

Edie accepted the smackdown. Should've expected it. Her muscles felt shaky. She'd taken a shower when she got back to the inn, soaked through with cold rain, and after she was dry and comfortable and her stomach was full with Morag's genuinely incredible take on pasta ca' muddica, she'd refused to answer Morag's questions until Morag had to leave, and then she'd paced between the dining room, where the guest book still was, and the kitchen, until she was thinking too much about everything that had happened and she started making shortbread.

She had wanted, by the next time Cosima saw her, to have repaired the tumble in her brain enough to smooth over her meltdown at the church and then joke her way out of the treasure hunt, out of spending any more time together, out of everything but endless walks in the English countryside and meals Edie had decided she would start taking in her room.

Her heart hurt. She kept thinking of the map, wishing she

really had been able to freeze time, to drag out that moment when they'd found it for longer, standing next to Cosima, teasing and laughing, elated.

"I suppose I'm not someone who could possibly understand what it is you're responsible for," she said.

Cosima shook her head, her golden-ratio eyebrows furrowed in gentle concern that made Edie's heart feel too tender. "Edie, listen—"

"It's okay, truly."

"No. You were disappointed," Cosima said. "By finding the map."

"I was disappointed I couldn't go to any of the places *on* the map."

Cosima was studying Edie with the same frown between her eyebrows that she'd had bent over her notebook, working through the cipher. "And you know I could pay your way, and would be glad to, but you wouldn't ask me to because . . ."

"I not only wouldn't ask, if you offered I wouldn't accept. A jacket is one thing—it was a kind of inside joke between us. I had already bought you a hedgehog pencil set, for example, at the tourist center's gift shop."

"You had?"

"Yes. But a European vacation is not a pencil set."

"I once spent thirty-one thousand dollars on an Hermès Birkin bag because I spilled olive oil on my purse when I was in Dubai with my mother."

"*Jesus* HC rises again, Cosima! Don't tell me things like that. I'll re-Catholic and take vows of poverty in defense against my shock."

But Edie laughed, for the first time in hours.

Cosima laughed, too, and then—probably because of the lack of calories and sore heart and possibly because Cosima was so fucking pretty it was starting to burn Edie's eyes—they were laughing together, but not at anything, really. They were just laughing like children who'd needed to go to bed hours ago.

"Let *me* send you." Morag's voice made both Cosima and Edie scream.

"Why do you do that, woman?" Edie gasped. "Do I need to put up mirrors so I can see in all directions at the same time? Would I even see you in the mirrors if I did?"

Morag ignored Edie's questions. She'd pinned her braids up, and she wore a plain wool peacoat with a hammered silver stag's head brooch on the lapel. "First of all, stay out of my kitchen. This is your last warning. Second, I'm aware you don't want to let Cosima pay your way. To be clear, *I* would let her. She wouldn't miss it."

"I wouldn't," Cosima confirmed. "I would make it back in interest by the time I'd Venmo'ed it to you."

"Don't be vulgar," Morag chided. She turned back to Edie. "*I* will pay you to go on this treasure hunt."

"And then what, I give you the treasure? What labor or goods are you getting in return?"

Something passed over Morag's face that made Edie's heart skip a beat. It was something sad, and she had never before seen Morag be sad. Morag, as far as Edie was concerned, should not ever *be* sad. She should only and always be as scary and self-satisfied as she'd appeared in the smoking-hot photograph they'd found in the guest book, and should not ever die, additionally.

It was possible Edie had attached herself to Morag.

"I can admit this place could use a facelift," Morag said. "No, that's too drastic a statement. More like a bit of tasteful Botox."

"You're not making sense," Edie told her. "Do you need to sit down? Or a cracker?" But there was a flutter in Edie's belly. A good flutter.

"For heaven's sake. In exchange for your travel money, I'd like a menu update, within a few parameters, and a new vision for the lounge."

"God! Morag! Are you being serious right now?" Edie had a thousand thoughts at once. "You know, if we're getting into the lounge, I have an idea for—"

"*Just* the menu and the lounge. There have been developers sniffing around for years. I spoke to a man at the tourism board meeting. It's time I sold, and with your updates, the inn will fetch a better price."

Edie's flutter stilled, leaving a vaguely sick feeling behind. "What kind of developer?"

Morag's mouth turned down at the corners. "An outfit that does real estate holdings. Avista? Avessa?"

"Avissa," Cosima said with a tight nod. "They'll be most interested in the land, not the hotel. Is the building listed on the National Register?"

"Grade II. He said it's likely as not they'll leave the inn to sit and build around it, but if it's up to a 'modern aesthetic standard' he may be able to convince his management to put in a higher bid, perhaps even start off a bit of an auction."

I was only kidding. That was what Edie wanted to say—that she hadn't meant it when she'd asked Morag to put her to work, that she didn't know how to clean out and redecorate the lounge, that she had no ideas for the menu and hadn't been prowling all over this inn thinking up a hundred different ways to apply elbow grease and make it shine.

Edie *liked* this inn, but she didn't like it for Avissa, a name that sounded like a snake's hiss. She'd set herself up to be disappointed again. She'd imagined too many things that could never be true.

At least with Cosima she'd known her imagination had gotten away from her. Her feelings about the inn had snuck up on her. "Listen, Morag . . ." Her mouth was so dry. She felt a little sick.

"Please do it." Cosima cleared her throat. "Let Morag hire you. I want to go, and it's likely not *recommended* to treasure hunt alone. There were plenty of clues today we needed both of us to solve, not to mention what might have happened if you'd been alone with that ewe."

"What ewe?" Morag interjected. "Did Bert's sheep get after you girls?"

Edie wrapped her arms around herself. She knew what Cosima was doing. Cosima was a good person, fundamentally, who believed Edie wouldn't disappoint her if she could help it, so Cosima was pretending to need Edie so that Edie could go.

Thank goodness Edie was also impulsive.

"Okay."

Cosima looked at Morag, who raised her eyebrows. "Okay? As in, yes, we're setting off tomorrow?"

"It looks like it."

Cosima grinned. It was one of her genuine smiles, the kind that made creases at the downturned corners of her eyes, and Edie's inconvenient flutter moved inconveniently lower and became more like a heavy pulse.

But she could ignore that. She could. She could politely refuse to think about what it would be like to rub her bottom lip against Cosima's grin and how her curls would feel against her cheek while she was softly biting Cosima's neck. She was a grown-up. Ish. She would figure out how to go on this treasure hunt and be around Cosima and not let it turn into reckless hope.

Cosima turned in her stool to face Morag. "There are a few matters to arrange and clarify."

"Oh?" Morag had slipped her arms out of her wool coat and hung it on a tree by the door. Now, she moved to the Aga to retrieve the kettle and carry it to the sink.

"Yes. We've paid you room and board to stay here. You will be transferring a portion of Edie's paid stay, of course, to apply to accommodations on this trip, with any overages taken care of by Edie using her expertise on behalf of the inn. However, in my case, I would be paying my own way on this hunt."

"I can arrange for a refund." Morag's eyes were actually twinkling.

"No. There's something I want in exchange for my unused room and board."

"Which is?"

"Access to the garden and greenhouse. And an account at the garden center in Grantham." Cosima crossed her arms.

"You've already been stomping about in my garden." Morag said 'my garden' like it was a patch of zinnias and a few herbs instead of a vast, walled space of sentient botanical monsters.

"As a guest I have, but I want real access. Pruning and digging and repairing access."

"Fine. Don't move the roses or use power tools during quiet hours."

Cosima bit back a smile, her teeth sinking into her bottom lip in a way that confirmed for Edie that her casual questions about Morag's garden on the day they went on their hedgehog walk had not been casual at all. Cosima had a thing for gardens. She was a garden person, and if she'd come far enough to convert her yearning to poke at Morag's crumbling relic of a garden into a formal request, it meant that she was feeling better than the version of Cosima in an HP Sauce–stained robe whom Edie had been so determined to help.

And Edie was *so glad*.

This gladness was incredibly dangerous. These were feelings. *Like*-her feelings. Sudden-recall-of-the-way-Cosima-had-looked-at-her-at-the-stile feelings. Soft skin, shuddering breath, gripping hands, psychic elation feelings.

When she'd found Gregory Place on the internet and did the mental no-money math, she had imagined a small respite of a hermitage from which she would emerge practical. These feelings were not practical. They were precisely what she'd been trying to avoid.

"I have some conditions, too." Edie crossed her arms. She didn't know what her conditions were, but she was ready to improvise.

"Which are?" Cosima's tone was back to imperious.

"We should have the same budget." Edie tried to match Cosima's tone. "It's not fair if your money means we can buy our way to every clue or bribe someone."

Cosima made a noise like a sharp bark. "I would never!"

"You don't think you would, but I bet your threshold of using money to solve a problem is much lower than mine. Also, if we manage to make our way to the places on the map like France or Italy, I want to see more than the inside of the Four Seasons."

"I'm not *actually* a princess. I don't have a rider for my accommodations wherever I go."

"But do you agree?"

"Of course," Cosima said through her teeth.

"My second condition is that we come up with a system for resolving disagreements. If you believe the answer to a clue or the next action is one thing and I'm inclined toward another solution, we're not going to have time to fight about it and then wait a week for you to emerge from your rooms. My time here is up at the end of the month."

Suddenly, the four weeks Edie had carved out to heal felt like a pinch of sand in an hourglass.

"We'll resolve it like we do in business," Cosima said. "We take the dilemma to a third party to decide after we present both of our cases. Whatever this third party says goes. We can alternate choosing a third party."

Edie smiled. "I accept. Finally, we have to agree on what to do with the treasure. If we find it."

"What do you think it is?" Morag asked with a noisy sip of tea in a tone that was too jokey. In addition to being falsely bright, it struck Edie as . . . nervous.

Edie narrowed her eyes at the older woman. "What do *you* think it is? A grimoire? Flying potion for your broomstick?"

"I don't need more riches." Cosima's voice was prim.

"*Ugh*. You know that makes you sound *more* Mary Sue. And I don't want you handing them over to little old me. Your head would explode with gratified charity."

"You know what?" Cosima pointed at Edie, her cheeks a little pink. "Fine. We split it. If it is remotely splittable, that's what we do. Fifty-fifty. And I'll call my personal lawyer to draw up the contract."

"And I'll call my half sister Meadow, who is a lawyer, to talk to *your* lawyer." Meadow was an attorney for a school district in Florida, not really a treasure contracts kind of lawyer, but she was also free and had drawn up Edie's LLC for Fauxmage perfectly well.

"Fifteen percent," Morag said. "No. Make that twenty."

"What?" Edie and Cosima's outraged exclamations were perfectly matched.

"It's my guest book."

"Fine," Edie said, at the same time Cosima said, "Seventeen."

"Seventeen and a half." Morag nodded. "But if I die before I spend it, my will's not to be contested by you lot."

Cosima held out her hand to Morag. "Deal."

"What is this?" Edie gestured between the two of them. "Cosima is not the CEO of this treasure hunt."

"She is as far as I'm concerned," Morag said. "I'm not worried if you sic someone named Meadow on me, but Cosima likely owns an entire firm of lawyers."

"We start tomorrow," Cosima said. "Eight AM." She stood up and literally sailed from the kitchen.

Edie was not sure she had balanced the scales sufficiently. "You need to brace yourself for some changes around here," she told the innkeeper. "Who knows? Maybe you'll love my updates so much that you decide not to sell to a soulless real estate outfit!"

Morag made a chuffing sound that Edie couldn't quite categorize. "Warn me the day you pull up the carpet in the lounge. I'm allergic to dust." She removed herself from the kitchen.

Edie had definitely not managed to balance the power. In fact, the more she thought about it, walking up the stairs to her room, brushing her teeth to get ready for bed, the more she wondered if she might have been had.

But she couldn't stop grinning into her pillow as she fell asleep.

Chapter Eleven

Cosima took a few steps back when Adina Bidderscombe crossed her arms over her baby-blue kitten sweatshirt.

Apparently, Morag had attended primary school with Adina, who was the housekeeper of the massive Harlaxton Manor. Before placing the phone call that ensured Cosima and Edie this jaundiced welcome at the manor, Morag had announced, darkly, that making this request would place her in Adina's debt, which she had not been in since 1981.

Having now met Adina, Cosima did feel a certain amount of pressure not to put Morag in a bad position. Ridiculous, her increasing interest in the politics of this vanishingly small English village.

"Morag called up here and told me what you two were up to," Adina said, "but I won't have you disturbing the students. Their British Studies presentations are next week. I've been near scraping them off the ceiling, they're so stressed." She delivered every word like she was snapping a sheet off a clothesline.

The manor, built by Gregory Gregory in 1837, had been used by US colleges as the site of enchanting study abroad experiences since the 1960s. Prior to its current incarnation, the manor had served as a Royal Air Force base in World War II and a Jesuit residence after Gregory Gregory's heirs petered out in the 1930s.

Cosima knew all of this courtesy of a lecture she'd received during her walk to the manor with Edie, who had absorbed a great deal from the brochures stuffed into dusty racks in Gregory Place's reception area.

"We completely understand that the students' needs come first." Edie smiled at the housekeeper. "I promise we will keep to empty rooms as much as possible."

Adina was not unmoved by Edie's rosy cheeks and freckles. This was fortunate, because she had neatly dismissed Cosima with a look that made it clear she was not impressed by American celebrity. Cosima wondered if she'd directed the very same look at Phoebe decades ago. Her mother may have made an enemy of this woman. Phoebe's general policy was that there could only be one queen, and Adina was not to be usurped.

Now, Adina's lean hands clenched and unclenched, her wrists no more than knobs of bone exiting the voluminous sweatshirt's cuffs. "You represent Morag. If there is a breath of trouble, I will go directly to her and hold her accountable."

"Absolutely," Edie said. "We're so appreciative."

Adina put her hand into the pocket of her dark green slacks and pulled out a gold pocket watch. She snapped it open. "Ninety minutes, no more. Two hours puts you too close to lunch, when the students will be headed to the commissary."

"Starting?" Edie asked.

"Now. Go on. Don't touch anything."

Cosima turned from the foyer, with its multistory, almost gothic fireplace, and followed Edie to the big room beyond, on the threshold of which—despite having lived in a castle of her own—Cosima stopped short with a breathless gasp.

"Holy chevre," whispered Edie.

Dozens of feet above them, the ceiling was gridded with dark polished wood beams framing squares of snow-white relief sculpture. The tidy grid matched one made of multicolored marble on the floor. Dark wood pillars ringed the room, topped by full-sized marble sculptures of the gods, their stone expressions frozen in grimaces as though burdened by the weight of the ceiling.

"*This* is the Grand Hall?" Cosima reached out and pulled Edie's brochure from her jacket pocket. "I thought the solid mile of turrets guarded by stone lions on the way up the drive had prepared me, but apparently not."

Edie shook her head, her green eyes wide. The freckles glittered over her face caught in a sunbeam from a leaded glass window. "This is going to be like finding a needle in a massive mansion where I am already lost. How did we get to this room? Was it through those mile-tall doors? Was there a portal?"

Cosima opened the brochure with a snap. "College students live here. We're smarter than a bunch of twenty-year-olds."

"I don't know about that." Edie's smile made a previously unmapped dimple appear above the left corner of her mouth.

The sight of that secret dimple compelled Cosima to take a step closer before she could think about why she wanted to. She attempted to distract herself with the open brochure. "Let's go to this famous cedar staircase, which is pretty central, and figure out the clue from the treasure map."

Edie moved even closer to look. There was nothing to do

but take in the shine of her soft hair and the smell of grass and lemon. Cosima had not once imagined herself with a partner, kissing someone, yearning for someone. She had touched herself and luxuriated in orgasms but never fantasized about getting help with them. She had read enough about the ace spectrum to understand that she was somewhere on it but hadn't explored further, so her connection to her queerness on that spectrum remained theoretical. Until now. When she could suddenly think of nothing else but Edie's bare skin against hers.

Gliding her mouth everywhere on Edie's body she could find.

What Edie's bottom lip would feel like against her tongue.

What the hollow of her inner thigh would taste like.

An erotic and desperate kaleidoscope of images filled in the answers to questions Cosima had never bothered with nor cared about. She couldn't help thinking about Edie's body, her skin, her mouth, how much of her shiny hair she could get in her fist. And it wasn't only that. It was where all of those thoughts came from. Not between her legs, even if that part of her now beat with the same rhythm as her heart. They had come from Edie. In some particular way, they were *hers*.

Everything clicked into place so utterly and so neatly, like the hushed snaps of jigsaw pieces. This was what it felt like—for her, for Cosima Frank—to fall in love. It felt like opening the door to her room at the inn and finding the first person she thought was interesting in years. It felt like not knowing if she should avoid her or figure out how to be around her all the time. It felt like feeling her body relax when Edie restlessly changed position, fidgeted, and stimmed beside her.

Falling in love was a sleeper cell of interconnected feelings in her heart and brain and sexual self, and Edie had activated it by simply being Edie.

"Cosima?" Edie's voice sounded far away.

Demisexuality was the part of the aro and ace spectrum that Cosima had learned and wondered about but decided she wouldn't be able to completely know, for herself, until and if she got there.

She had gotten here.

Here she was.

She had gotten here utterly, and getting here validated everything she had learned about herself, showed her even more, and instantly created a personal disaster the likes of which would more than likely lead to heartbreak.

"Cosima, are you okay?"

She cleared her throat. "Yes."

"Where'd you go?" Edie took the brochure from Cosima's hands. She had been clutching it, crumpling its edges.

"I'm here." Cosima desperately wanted to cover her eyes with both hands, drop to the floor, and sink into the center of the earth, where her feelings would be concealed from everyone, including herself. "Lots to look at, and I got distracted by you . . . what I mean is, by your idea to head to the staircase."

"That was your idea." Edie had a tiny wrinkle between her eyebrows, a wrinkle that was trying to understand why Cosima had suddenly exploded into three hundred pieces of herself. "You sure you're okay?"

Oh, I know I'm not okay. With this thought, Cosima closed her eyes, but it only made the questions louder and the mental images more vivid. What if she rubbed her bottom lip against Edie's forehead wrinkle? Would it smooth out? Would Edie rise up on her tiptoes and pull Cosima down to her lips?

She forced herself to take a steadying breath. "Let's head to the staircase," she rasped. "What direction?"

"This way." Edie led the way across the marble floor,

unbuttoning her jacket as she walked to reveal the first item of clothing Cosima had seen from her wardrobe that looked like *Edie*. It was a navy cotton blouse with clever darts for her bustline that kept the row of red buttons from gaping. The collar was round but not twee, and Cosima had watched Edie roll up the long, fitted sleeves at Morag's breakfast table, rapt as she secured and buttoned them at the elbow with sleeve tabs. Close up, instead of a staid Swiss dot or diamond woven into the cloth, there were small red mice.

Cosima felt feral about this blouse of Edie's. She had a lot of sudden, feral feelings about Edie, competing with the terrifying domesticated ones involving Cosima bringing Edie tea and curling up by her feet.

Fucked. She was fucked. Transformed, enlightened, reborn, and doomed.

"Oh my god," Edie said with a laugh when the staircase came into view. "Gregory Gregory is something else. The landing is bigger than my mom's entire house." She looked up the massive, carved wooden staircase, each tread longer than two park benches together, covered in miles of fine woolen runner. "It literally leads to *heaven*." She pointed.

Indeed, the ceiling at the top of the staircase, at least a hundred feet above them, had been painted as though the skies opened up above the highest floor, framed in carved marble life-sized drapery. "Gregory Gregory seems to have had a very specific sort of taste."

"What he had is *a lot* of taste," Edie said, sitting down on one of the lower stairs. "Did he have good taste? Bad taste? I'm from Green Bay, so I have no idea, but this man did have a large *amount* of taste."

Cosima sat next to her, carefully in case bending a body so full of sudden want would break it in half.

Edie put the brochure down on her lap, frowning again. “For real, what is wrong with you?”

I found an unexplored realm, a whole secret garden of my sexuality overgrown with roses that smell like Pears soap.

“There’s nothing wrong with me.”

Edie tipped her head. “I feel like I’m losing you.”

Don’t say that, don’t say that, even if it’s true.

“I shouldn’t have convinced Morag to get out her coffee maker. I’ve had a lot of coffee.”

Cosima looked away from Edie to the ceiling, desperate to pull herself together, but it was difficult to find an anchor to reality with Gregory Gregory’s fantastical heaven soaring above them. “You know what it is?” she asked.

You love her, her heart answered.

Cosima coughed. This was actually dire.

“There’s over a thousand unread messages in my text app, just since I arrived,” she said. “Twice that many in my inbox, and all of them carrying with them a certain amount of worry that I, personally, will end the world.”

“What?”

Cosima still was not looking at Edie, but she could hear her confusion. She trained her eyes on a marble ceiling goddess.

“I’m the person who selects the next head of Phoebe Frank Studios. Because I wouldn’t ascend to my mother’s throne, I have to choose who sits there. At a certain level in the movie business, money and power metamorphose into emotions. Dark magic. Fortune-telling. It’s dangerous if there’s a vacuum. Guys in suits start reading signs and wonders like an astrological chart, and I wouldn’t care, Edie. I wouldn’t care at all, except there are good people, regular humans, who simply *work* at PFS. They feed their families with paychecks that bear a facsimile of my mother’s signature.”

"But you haven't done it," Edie said. "That's not a dig. I probably wouldn't have done it either. I'm having secondhand decision paralysis listening to you."

Cosima risked a look at Edie, who smiled a small but kind smile that made Cosima feel as if a marble ceiling's worth of psychic burden had been removed from her body.

"Yes. I should have done it. As soon as the funeral was over, I should have selected this person from an array of preapproved candidates, any of whom would fill the vacuum, but instead I got on a plane and came here. Duncan isn't mentioning any of it. He's assuming I'm having a polite meltdown but that I will definitely return and do my job before any harm has been done."

"But what's the harm? If you take the time you need to grieve your mother before you decide what's next, why is that a problem?" Edie's expression of distaste made her skepticism clear.

Cosima unbuttoned her jacket, welcoming the air on her neck, her sternum. "The longer I take, the lower the PFS stock price falls. I probably lost the company ten times more money this morning over breakfast than you borrowed and lost for Fauxmage."

Edie put her hand on her shoulder and squeezed it, raising goose bumps on her skin. "Cosima."

She had to look at the ceiling again, touching her throat, trying to believe she could breathe. "And I already know what's next. Of course that's been decided. When I was disappointing my mother by refusing to take the reins of her company, Duncan rescued us. He reminded Phoebe that *my* passion was gardening—something I did with him, learned from him—and that I obviously wanted to make and grow something that was mine. He suggested he and I star in a gardening series." She framed out the title in the air in front of her. "*An American*

Castle's Garden. We start filming on the grounds at the Castle in a few weeks. And when I say 'we,' I mean Cosmos, the film studio I've just started with PFS money. *My* staff. My mother actually loved this idea. It made her happy. It made Duncan happy. I should be happy. Right now, I should be in LA, working on my show, reassuring the dozens of people that Duncan and I hired that they have work."

"I knew you were a gardener." Edie smiled.

Cosima exhaled, shaky. "You did?"

"I put it together. I also put together you were dealing with something big. This happened around the time Morag was forcing her scary telepathic powers on you about whatever it was." Edie picked up and squeezed Cosima's hand. "My only question, princess, is if you're trying to run your points up in the game just because I pulled ahead with my tantrum in the church yesterday?"

Edie had turned her body toward Cosima. Their eyes met fully, but Cosima couldn't let herself stare into Edie Whitelock's caring green eyes, so she studied a constellation of blond freckles under her eyebrow in the shape of Orion's Belt. "I will take my points," she said, stiff enough to guard her feelings.

"We're a pair, huh?" Edie asked. "It might be hard to believe, but if I don't take my recipe technologist job at A Presto! Pizza at the end of this month, the world will also end. It's true that I'm the only mouth that needs to be fed in my scenario, but I'm twenty-eight years old. I am conscripted by capitalism to make money for another forty or fifty years so I can have nice things like shelter and transportation. Save up to see the doctor. You know. Luxuries. Like you, it's all been decided already, and there's something about a lack of choice that really has a way of breaking your heart, doesn't it?"

Cosima smiled in an attempt to hold her tears at bay but felt them race down the sides of her nose anyway. "Are you saying we're rebelling?"

"Hmm. More like we're putting on a show similar to my four-year-old niece's when I start filling the bathtub. Suddenly, the *Bluey* episode she's seen seventy thousand times has depths she hasn't mined that are vital to her continued existence. Then she's hungry. Then she has to poop. Her free will demands encore after encore while reality gets more annoyed. We're in our encore era." Edie looked around them at the magnificent staircase. "You have to admit it's pretty fucking good. We really know how to stall, you and me."

Edie pulled one of her legs out from the knot she'd folded them in, bent it over both Cosima's legs, and gathered her close for a hug.

Her forearms pressed against Cosima's shoulder blades. Her cheek against Cosima's ear.

The hug thawed her on the inside, leaving behind the mess of a garden in spring—unregulated, terrified, and so thrilled, it made her nauseated.

Edie started to pull away.

No.

Cosima dragged her hands up and around Edie's body, and before she knew it she was *crushing* her. She had to fist one of her hands to keep it from palming the nape of Edie's neck and pulling her face closer.

"Oof." Edie squeezed back. "Easy, tiger."

Cosima accepted this correction but could not make herself let go. "Sorry."

Edie pulled her arms away and leaned back, holding on to Cosima's forearms, which were nearly around Edie's neck. Her face was inches away, her eyes too many different shades of green to name.

"I'm sorry. I know you must be using your giant brain to try to figure out how to fix your situation, or to feel more responsible about it than you should." Edie's voice was low, almost whispering, probably because her face was so close. Cosima's body had gone simultaneously syrupy with desire and stony with restraint and hot with feelings.

"I am responsible, as it happens." She sounded like she'd screamed all night at a concert and tried to talk the next day. Or screamed all night doing something else.

Stop. Stop. Stop.

Edie's breath smelled like cinnamon toothpaste, which she would never forget, so precisely could she imagine sucking on Edie's tongue.

"I don't think your mom was fair to you." Edie took a deep breath. "I've thought this before, about the list she made. Her bucket list. In principle, it sounds nice. It sounds like the kind of story in one of those weepy internet videos your friend sends you in the middle of the night when they're on their period. But if I had to guess, Phoebe Frank gave you that list, all made out, without warning, and without any possibility of dissent?"

Cosima looked at the wool rug covering the step beneath her. "She dictated it to me. She'd put a meeting on my shared calendar for the purpose."

"Okay. Somewhat worse than I imagined, then. My point is, that kind of thing has to be mutual. It has to mean a great deal to *both* people. Otherwise, it's your mom dictating the terms of her good-bye because she has enough power in your relationship to do that. If she had this list for herself, to do for herself, and you *chose* to help her or join her"—Edie paused, and Cosima looked up—"do you see how that's different?"

Cosima did. She had seen it for a long time, but no one ever said it out loud.

Dictating the terms, avoiding anger or denial, preventing real communication—these moves were the core of how her mother managed her life with Cosima and Duncan.

"She loved me," Cosima said. "But the way she knew how to love me was to keep me safe. Anger and hard conversations aren't safe."

"I believe she loved you," Edie said softly. "My mom loves me, and in a different way she does the same thing. She tears down anything she thinks isn't safe or will disappoint me, and sometimes that means tearing down *me*."

"But you can't believe what she says." Cosima's voice was still rough. "Why are you taking a job in a pizza crust factory when you want so much more?"

"I tried, Cosima. For once, I decided to believe in me. I had my big chance. It didn't work."

"No one gets just *one* chance, though."

"And no *one* person is responsible for another person's legacy. In fact, the only real legacy your mom has right now is a daughter who ran away and a widowed 'companion' she wouldn't permit to be her partner or your father."

Cosima sucked in a breath.

"I'm sorry." Edie's voice was gentle. "It's just, I'm looking at this magnificent pile of a building, and it didn't keep Gregory Gregory alive, did it?"

Cosima studied the ceiling, too, and noticed another bearded, robed marble god, holding up a scroll under the bright-blue false sky. "Just his name."

Then they looked at each other, solemn, and Cosima lost track of the edges of her body again, dissolving into the space between the two of them.

Edie's leg was still around hers on the step. They were still within hugging distance. The words finished settling between them, like snow in a globe, and she saw Edie so clearly.

Slowly, Cosima leaned forward. When she closed her eyes, she heard Edie inhale with surprise, which made her smile as she kissed her on her cheek.

Just one soft, smiling press of her lips against Edie's skin, and then a moment when she lingered instead of pulling away—lingered so she could breathe in Edie's scent, because this wasn't a kiss for a friend.

But it wasn't a kiss with a future, either.

Edie slid her hand around the back of Cosima's neck just as she retreated a reluctant millimeter. "Wait. Let me—"

"Um. I basically need to use the stairs?"

They turned their heads together toward the voice. It belonged to a young person, a student, with faded purple hair shaved at the sides. The student wore a crop top that said PROTECT TRANS KIDS.

"Pardon us," Cosima said. "We're sorry."

She wasn't sorry.

"Don't tell Goody Bidderscombe," Edie said.

"What?" The student tipped her purple head like a bird.

"We were just figuring out where to go," Edie explained. "We have this set of clues, and the second one is here somewhere, but probably not obvious because the clues are from the seventies. It's got to be something that's been here for a long time, though, because the clues are so old, and whoever made them couldn't know when someone would be searching. Maybe it's a statue. How many statues are there?"

The student shrugged, unperturbed by this rapid stream of context-free speech. "If you're looking for something that's been here a long time, I'd try the library. Not the university library. Like, Gregory's. They have a bunch of stuff he left behind in displays in there."

The student bounced up the stairs.

The library.

"Get out Agatha's map." Cosima could hear her own frustration. She hadn't gotten to find out what happened after Edie asked her not to move away, and she'd really, really wanted to.

"Already on it." Edie's voice didn't sound regular, either. She unfolded her jacket and pulled the envelope with the map out of it, then opened it carefully. "Okay, so you and Tam worked out that the starting point on the map was here."

"The manor." Cosima put her finger on the sketch of the manor at the bottom left corner. "Yes, because underneath it, Agatha wrote 'The game's afoot,' which is the epigraph from Sir Arthur Conan Doyle that she put at the beginning of her first book."

"And these other sketches are probably hints to the places we have to go in each country, but we don't know the order to visit them. Presumably, something here will tell us where to go next, or one of these small drawings we already decided were part of the clues."

"It has to be something that was here when Agatha was here. I think the student had a good idea."

Edie stared at the map for several moments, her hair curtaining her face. "Cosima."

"Yes?"

"I think so, too. You know why?"

"*Why*? Don't be coy, it's rude."

Edie's quick smile made dimples appear in both cheeks. "I don't even know what coy looks like. Look at the decoration she sketched in the border around the manor illustration."

Cosima looked. "It's a ladder? With wheels?"

"Yes!"

"Follow me."

This time, Cosima managed to make her voice sound the way she wanted it to, which was, as Edie liked to say, imperious. She needed that little bit of distance between them again to survive. Just a small space without a bridge so she could breathe without thinking about lemons and cut grass and small red mice.

"Anywhere," Edie told her.

I wish we could follow each other anywhere. Everywhere.

She grimaced back at the god on the ceiling.

Chapter Twelve

Edie yanked on the handle of yet another heavily decorated double wooden door that she very much hoped was the door to Gregory Gregory's library.

It felt like they had walked through miles of hallways, ducking into one unbelievable, gilded, paneled, muraled, carved room after another, but there hadn't been the usual number of wry comments and observations from the princess. Just like there hadn't been the usual number of teasing remarks and non sequiturs from her.

A bit of heady, awkward silence was probably to be expected after you both almost went up in flames over a kiss on the cheek that was hotter than a lot of kisses Edie had experienced in dark rooms with her clothes off.

The double doors creaked open to reveal a room lined with books and dark furniture. "Library. Thank Moses."

"I thought you'd been dying to tour this place." Cosima trailed into the room behind her, her jacket over her arm, her bra tastefully visible through the creamy silk of her blouse tucked into the first pair of jeans Edie had ever seen her wear. They were a soft, pale, broken-in pair. The high yoked waist was cinched with a belt that buckled with gold double letters.

Edie had not, in all of her life, seen someone wear a silk blouse with expensively destroyed blue jeans and a designer belt. She had not borne witness to the inside of an English manor, with skies painted on the ceilings and truckloads of Italian marble carved to look like curtains. The library smelled like things she didn't *know* about—expensive pastes and waxes that servants used to clean silver and wood, cinders in massive fireplaces, paper of vellum and ink made from gall. She'd read about rooms like this in romance novels the same way she read about the minutiae of queer history, not once believing any of it was real or applied to her.

But here she was. With Cosima Frank.

"Edie?"

When she looked up, Cosima was close again, her head tipped and her golden-flocked eyebrows furrowed. "Yeah?"

"I found it."

Edie hadn't even started looking. "What? How? How do you know?"

"We go to Tattershall Castle next." Cosima indicated one of the nearby bookshelves, and Edie walked over to see.

The bookshelf was sealed with plexiglass. On it sat a chessboard, set up as if it had been abandoned in the middle of a game.

"White just castled," Cosima said, tapping the plastic with her fingertip.

"I don't know what that means." She peered at the pieces. "I've never played chess."

"Assuming this has been set up like this since Agatha was

here—and I'm guessing it must have, because I can see dusty museum wax poking out from under the pieces—then Tattershall Castle is next. Plus, this shelf is right by the ladder, which has been locked in place, and the rook in this chess set looks exactly like the sketch of Tattershall on our map. It even has carved stones like the castle, and windows where there are windows in the sketch."

The princess was right. They were going to a castle.

Cosima started out of the room, already on her phone. "I'm going to figure out a ride to the train station and buy the tickets."

As Edie followed her out, she could hear the voices of college students filling the previously hushed hallways. She would've loved doing something like this when she was in college. Nothing like this had been offered to her, but that didn't mean it had been out of her reach. She'd seen in the Harlaxton Manor booklet that one of the colleges that used this site for a study abroad experience was a community college. Edie had gone to a community college.

Too late now. But no matter what, Edie could have this treasure hunt with this woman. She could even have her outsize crush and its private buzz. It was hard to remember, after losing so much, what she could have, but it wasn't nothing. Sometimes magic intervened, at least a little, on reality.

She hoped Cosima felt the same way about this adventure. Edie looked forward to learning much, much more about gardening while wistfully watching *An American Castle's Garden* and thinking about the way Cosima Frank's lips had felt on her skin.

They went back through to the foyer with its terrifying stone fireplace, then stepped out into the pea-gravel drive. "You called a Lyft?" Edie asked. "Do they have that here?"

"I don't know. I don't do Lyft. I called Killian, Tam's husband. He brought me back to the inn last night and said he was happy to drive me anywhere I needed to go." The sun hit the golden sandstone of the manor, making the air glow, framing Cosima's incomparable face against turrets and stone lions and the blue English sky.

Edie smiled at her, withholding nothing, and Cosima smiled back. They both looked away at the same time like they were bashful fawns in an old cartoon, but right now, in Edie's life, that was a little spicy, honestly.

While they waited, they had time to walk around. Cosima found the enormous glass conservatory on one side of the building and looked in at the plants longingly before Killian drove up in a red Toyota Yaris. He was a big, bald, handsome man with a personality that filled the entire space of the car with animated chatter, and when he arrived at the train station, he gave them directions on how best to get to Tattershall, along with his good wishes for finding the treasure.

After the rush from Killian's car, tickets, and locating the right platform, they located empty seats on the overheated train. Edie couldn't make herself take off her jacket and lean back. She was having that restless, nothing's-quite-right feeling that made her brain start to manufacture reasons for it—reasons that were all equally anxious lies, but also felt definitely true.

"Why are you not talking?" Cosima lifted up the armrest and turned toward her.

"I don't talk *all* the time."

"You do."

"You just haven't known me long enough to enjoy my quiet moments."

Cosima crossed her arms. "I'm worried it's because I kissed you on the stairs."

"On the cheek." Edie cleared her throat and turned her head lest she witness Cosima's reaction to her strategic avoidance.

"Edie Whitelock." There was forgiving amusement in Cosima's tone.

"It's not you. I keep thinking about how I never fit." Edie hadn't known she would share this thought until she spoke it aloud. "My whole life, everyone's said that, or things like it. But no one ever suggested, 'Hey, Edie, maybe there's somewhere else where you *would* fit.' I was just supposed to figure out how to shave off all the inconvenient bits of myself until I could cram myself into the mold."

She ran her finger along the edge of Cosima's upholstered train seat, fuzzy, in shades of blue with a pattern of abstract red circles. It was difficult to keep hold of her thoughts. Cosima didn't rush in with a lot of questions, though. She sat still, her body relaxed. It had the effect of slowing down Edie's heart rate and settling her jumpy muscles.

"My dad is English," Edie said. "I mean, you wouldn't notice his Englishness right away, particularly, because he's lived in Tampa a long time, and he's obsessed with golf and playing the penny slots, but he's still responsible for half my genes. I could've done a study abroad year."

"But you didn't."

"I didn't. If I didn't fit in Wisconsin, why use my second passport and find out I didn't fit here either? An entire other country I should feel comfortable in but maybe wouldn't. Even if sometimes it's been difficult, I'm grateful that I could never have *not* been gay. I briefly attempted stealth lesbianism. The Converse and compulsion to wear too many rings gave me away. That, and I was constantly following girls around and telling them how pretty they were. But everything else about me was on the table to be Green Bay-ified."

"I think I've actually known you long enough to understand what that means." Cosima smiled her private, reserved smile.

"It doesn't take a lot of deep background. But maybe I'm less chaotic and all over the place than I had led myself to believe, and happiness would be more possible if I hadn't decided everyone was right about what I deserved."

Cosima's crescent moon brows found two wrinkles in the middle of her forehead. "I like it better when you talk instead of being so quiet. Continue."

"If my phone worked, I would pull it out and make you record that, so I could play it back later when you complained about me."

"When have I complained about you? You've talked plenty, and I've never told you to be quiet. You wiggle around like you're actually plugged in, but this doesn't bother me at all. What else could I complain about? That you're kind? Charming? Maybe that your esoteric knowledge goes surprisingly deep?"

"My raincoat. You complained about that."

"And I solved my own problem by replacing it. Nothing to do with you, actually."

"You complained that I—" Edie tried to remember. Had Cosima complained about her? As in *her*, Edie, the essential Edie Ashlynn Whitelock? "Hmm."

"Exactly." Cosima nodded with only the point of her chin, like a royal. "I have not. Also, you can be assured that if I do have a complaint about you, it will be one hundred percent correct. Like the jacket."

Edie was in new territory. The princess took her seriously.

More than seriously. She hadn't presented Edie with an ounce of skepticism or jokes about Fauxmage, even as Edie tried to beat her to the put-downs.

Cosima blamed *Green Bay* for the failure of Fauxmage. She had no trouble believing that Edie was meant to do something creative and special, and the existence of the pizza crust factory job seemed to offend her. And—not to beat a dead sartorial metaphor—there was the jacket. The Paul Smith jacket was the jacket of a serious woman.

She had no trouble imagining Cosima personally rounding up patrons from the brew pubs and sports bars and Targets back home and escorting them to Fauxmage until Edie had to expand to meet the demand. In no time at all, Cosima Frank had become a friend and probably the best, most loyal champion Edie had ever had.

It was the kind of friendship that, if Edie was careful with it, would mean that she lost the "whose life is the worst" game forever, just for having such a friend.

She met Cosima's big blue eyes, which at some point had become *Cosima's* eyes, not Phoebe Frank's. Cosima's were more interesting. Stormier. Right now, they were obviously trying to figure Edie out, probably because Edie was staring at them while her stomach plummeted like she was flying down the first drop on a roller coaster.

This woman was *difficult*—so difficult that her difficulty established a scale that balanced Edie's personality and made her somehow *not* difficult. Made her fit. Did Edie want to be anywhere else on earth right now than inside of this tête-à-tête with Cosima Frank on a Lincolnshire train? No, she did not. No other place would feel correct. She *liked* this feeling of fitting somewhere that was exactly right.

Cosima gave Edie a sly, subtle look that somehow communicated she was taking a break from their mutually intense eye contact before someone got too horny and kissed the other on the forehead. She adjusted her position, gracefully reclining with her arms crossed and one booted foot perched on her knee. "I could tell you something that I wasn't going to tell you. I was planning to maintain a polite silence about it." She bit her lip.

"I think my life might be better if I stopped with things like polite silence."

"That sounds like a secret." Edie's heart rate kicked up.

"I don't think so. It's not something I've known long enough that it qualifies as a secret, and I think you've already guessed it. But it might not be something you want to know for sure, out loud, sitting beside me inside a steel box with no escape."

"You must have really killed at girls' boarding school." Edie narrowed her eyes. "I bet you sat on gossip like a fat dragon on doubloons."

"I'd like to kiss you." Above the ivory silk drape of her blouse, Cosima's throat went red, making Edie's vision tunnel at the same time her heart stopped. "What I mean is, I've started thinking about kissing you, and I'm having a difficult time stopping myself from thinking about it. Keep in mind that I'm not planning on doing anything about this. They are only thoughts. Intrusive, near constant, but *thoughts*."

Edie wondered, very sincerely, if her native language was English. She had never been without words, but at this moment, she doubted that her consciousness was comprised of anything more than bright shooting lights, a racing pulse, and gay panic the like of which she hadn't experienced since she was at a seventh-grade sleepover and Britnee Cordan spent the entirety of a movie braiding and re-braiding her hair.

"Say something." Cosima made this request with her mouth. Her mouth that had picked up the blush bleeding over her cheeks and made her lips look swollen. Her mouth that would like to kiss Edie's, wanted it so much it was sending *intrusive thoughts* to Cosima's brain. Constantly. Constant, muscled, insistent kissing thoughts everywhere in her mind. About Edie.

Cosima wanted to know what Edie *tasted* like and *felt* like and how she would respond to being kissed.

"I can't say something."

"Why?"

"My friendship plan." Edie was regretting their purchase of express tickets. She needed the train to stop so she could suck in some outdoors air or lay down on the platform.

"How does what I said—what I shared very vulnerably, I might add—disrupt your friendship plan? Which you haven't mentioned to me, let's be clear."

"I don't have a friendship plan. I just said it impulsively because I'd already told you that I can't say something, and so I briefly tried something out that seemed vaguely adult. You can't just tell a person something like that." Edie had nothing. Nothing. She was rifling through a pile of disorganized boxes labeled *how not to say anything stupid*, and they were empty.

"Like what? I can't tell the person I want to kiss that I want to kiss her? Or did I tell it wrong? I wasn't under the impression there was a script."

"You said that you'd *like* to," Edie protested weakly. "That you were thinking about it. Not that you *want* to."

Cosima shoved herself against her seatback with a huff. "Semantics. Honestly. I have no words."

"*You* have no words? Now you're copying me." Edie didn't realize how loud her screech was until the older man across the aisle turned to frown at her American lack of comportment. She lowered her voice to a harsh whisper. "Look, Cosima, how am I supposed to respond to something like that?"

"Not at all, if you're going to offer up a lot of rationalization. Besides, I'm pretty sure if I'm thinking about it, it's because you're thinking about it, too. As much as I continue to enjoy our charming banter, I'd rather you gracefully receive my admission or tell me, of course, that you want to kiss *me*."

Without stopping, interjected Edie's crush demon. *Tell her you want to kiss her without stopping.*

"Seriously?" Edie tried to cool her face with the backs of her hands. "Who wouldn't want to kiss you, woman?"

That was what her mouth decided to go with. For fuck's sake. She looked at the annoyed British man to see if he was hearing this, too. He was. He seemed disappointed in her. Same. "With the hair and the blue, blue eyes and the legs? You must know that your cold, imperious reserve only makes what you have on offer hotter."

Cosima leaned forward and wrapped her hands around Edie's wrists to tug them away from her face. She was so close, smelling as edibly expensive as a pastel pink buttercream rose on a two-thousand-dollar wedding cake.

Go wake up the princess. That was what Morag had said.

Now the princess was awake—very, very awake—and Edie seemed to remember there were a lot of rules about awake princesses and kissing.

"I want to kiss you." Cosima's voice emerged honey-smooth from her throat. "I don't think it's vacation, or grief, or the treasure hunt, or *friendship*. I want to kiss *you*, Edie Whitelock." Cosima shook her head as though amazed at herself before she continued. "I've never had anything like this to tell anyone. In fact, other than a revolting handful of minutes at a party where I was compelled by a game to kiss Leland Cronkite until an ice cube from the champagne bucket melted in my hand, I haven't kissed anyone, and I haven't wanted to, and I have always been content. Until now."

Just when Edie had thought Cosima couldn't layer on any more stakes, she'd frosted the entire situation with pastel swoops of demisexuality. Edie did not have the defenses. She would be stuck dreaming forever, trying not to beg for what she wanted most.

Which meant she couldn't feint. Or lie. She only had to exercise some self-restraint, for the first time ever. "I mean, yes. Yeah. Of course I want to kiss you. Obviously." Edie's voice cracked like a twelve-year-old boy's.

When Cosima smiled, her upper lip caught ever so slightly on an incisor, and Edie ached in such a delicious way that she could not think.

Cosima came closer, her hair brushing Edie's cheek, her famous eyes searching. Edie's heart kicked hard inside her chest. Cosima *didn't* kiss her, but Edie's mouth could feel how little space had been between their lips before Cosima brushed past them and put them against Edie's ear.

"Thank you," she whispered. "I look forward to it."

Then she pulled back, letting the warm air inside the train fill in the space between them. Edie's heart still hadn't found a rhythm when Cosima looked away, leaving Edie with at least a dozen more questions.

But the moment to ask them had dissolved—or hadn't come yet, if it ever would.

A recorded voice told them their next stop was Sleaford, where they would transfer to the train that would take them to their castle.

Chapter Thirteen

Cosima watched as Edie shifted her weight from one foot to the other, wrapped her arms around herself, and twisted at the waist. With the exception of a small child who had just finished trying to use a chocolate Flake bar as a lipstick and hadn't stayed in the lines, Edie was the only person in their group fidgeting to such a degree.

Cosima sympathized. She was having a hard time attending to the tour herself.

"The castle had fallen on harder times by the nineteenth century, when the Fortescue family allowed it to decline to near ruin. The stones you stand on were used as a cowshed." Barnabus Dankworth, their volunteer tour guide, stroked his gray chinstrap with long fingers. "Then they sold out to an American syndicate, which had the castle's magnificent fireplaces dismantled and shipped to London to be transported overseas. If you'll please follow me to the next room, I'll tell you the rest of that story about the heroics of Lord Curzon, who rescued the fireplaces and launched a preservation movement."

"Maybe they could light a fire in it and we wouldn't freeze to death while we stood around learning about fireplaces," Edie whispered.

"I'd think you were warm enough from all the moving around you're doing." It was bitterly cold inside of Tattershall Castle. Since the castle was a National Trust landmark, not an occupied dwelling, that was to be expected.

Edie pressed close to Cosima's side—a different kind of torture. "The Mars Cheese Castle in Kenosha back home is at least as impressive as this place, and it doesn't cost twelve pounds just to get through the door. In fact, there are so many samples, you wouldn't have to even buy a cheese to stay warm and well fed."

"I thought you were vegan."

"Not at Mars Cheese Castle."

She tried not to laugh and snorted instead, which meant Edie grinned into her hand. After Cosima had nearly self-immolated on the train, she was having trouble with the smiles. And the wordless looks. The shiny hair. The tight jeans. All of it.

"Cosima." Edie was on her tiptoes, whispering under the drone of Barnabus talking about Ralph, Third Baron Cromwell and King Henry VI's Lord Treasurer, who'd built the castle. She curled her hand over Cosima's shoulder to aid her balance.

"What?" She put a bit of steel in her voice so Edie couldn't tell that she was annihilated with tenderness.

"We have to ditch. We *have* to. It's going to take hours to work out what clue we're supposed to pay attention to in this pile. I'd rather visit every city in Italy, France, and Wales in alphabetical order than stay in this tour group and hope this guy will point out something that tells us where to go next."

Cosima looked around until she spotted a sign pointing to the toilets. She offered an apologetic wave to Barnabus and gestured at the sign. He gave her an irritated nod without missing a single word of his speech.

"Follow me."

They found themselves in a hall, where Edie immediately took charge. "We have to go up, I think. This castle has nothing to look at but the fireplaces and the stained-glass windows, so let's do that."

Cosima followed Edie up a flight of stairs, mentally cataloging the glossy swish of her hair across the back of her jacket, the heart shape of her ass, trim ankles in Converse. Every detail in sharp focus, precious enough to seal with wax inside an envelope and lock into the fastness of a keep.

It was dizzying to notice this much. Feel this much. How did people survive this? Had her mother built an empire and felt this way at the same time? How did Duncan focus on golf or the eight-hundred-page novels he enjoyed? A colleague had gotten married a few months ago, a contracts attorney. Could a person read fine print and be in love at the same time? Cosima was having a hard time not tripping up the stairs.

Edie stopped at the landing and leaned against the sill of a keyhole-shaped window, clutching her middle and breathing hard. "I hate stairs. Are you dying?" She looked over her shoulder out the window at the rolling hills and collection of white and gray clouds moving fast over the sky, casting shadows on the landscape.

Yes. Cosima was dying.

They mutually settled into silence.

This had been happening since they left the platform in Sleaford and took the shuttle to the castle. It had been a relief when they joined the tour group and Barnabus launched into his droning lecture, giving them an excuse not to try to talk to each other. Cosima knew that a certain amount of awkwardness was likely called for in the wake of her confession, but she didn't like it.

"Should we find another bank of these stained-glass windows to try to interpret?" Edie mused. "I don't understand why the map doesn't have an illustration like the ladder to give us a hint. Did we miss something on the chessboard at Harlaxton Manor that would have told us what to look for?"

"I took a picture of the rook. We can see if we missed something."

"Let's do that on the next story after we check out the windows." They finished the climb and arrived at a new room in the tower where they could hear Barnabus's voice again.

"They beat us up here." The tour guide was already hailing them. Cosima wanted to growl with frustration.

"There you ladies are! Lucky you've rejoined us, as I'm just about to discuss the tapestries."

"Smashing," Edie said.

Barnabus began his lecture. Cosima held her phone at waist height, hiding it from him as she attempted to zoom in on the rook she'd taken a picture of in the manor's library.

"As you've no doubt noticed, these rather glorious tapestries are in theme with the room, which would have been a private room, one of the bedchambers, perhaps, used by Lord Cromwell and his lady wife. But of course none of the original furnishings or appointments remain. The tapestries date to Lord Curzon, who had them made to honor Lord Cromwell's significant connection to Joan of Arc. You'll see her just there." The tour guide pointed. "That's her trial in Rouen, in Normandy, which Lord Cromwell attended in person. She was found guilty of heresy, you'll recall, and burned at the stake, though the tapestry leaves that off."

"Wait!" Edie's voice was loud in the stone-walled room. She had her hand up, waving. "You mean Lord Cromwell, the one who built this entire castle, was known—like, very, *very* known—to have traveled all the way to Normandy, which is in France, right?"

Barnabus sniffed. "Indeed."

"To Rouen, France, to go to Joan of Arc's trial. Joan of Arc, who is a famous person?"

"Again, indeed."

Edie grabbed on to Cosima's shoulder again to whisper in her ear while Barnabus stared daggers at the both of them. "We didn't even have to come all the way here! If we had known Tattershall was freaking built by a guy who went to France—the France we already know Agatha wants us to go to, which she drew on the map with a sword on it, the kind of sword, say, a teenage general would wield, with a big ol' Christian cross on it—we could be in the Chunnel right this minute instead of freezing our toes off with these fine people."

Cosima took a deep breath of cut grass and lemons. "Indeed."

Grinning, Edie gave her attention back to the tour while Cosima silently counted to herself. It was fifteen seconds of fidgeting before Edie's voice rang out again. "We've got to bounce, Dankworth! Thanks for everything."

She grabbed Cosima's hand, and against every instinct her mother had implanted inside her, Cosima "bounced" and rudely left a planned event.

The little girl's voice followed them down the stairs. "Can we go, too, Mummy?"

Soon enough, they were outside on the grounds of the castle.

"Where's Normandy, then?" Edie walked backward in front of Cosima. "Besides France. I know I mentioned the Chunnel, but I actually have no idea. If this place shares a border with Germany, maybe we'll have to fly?"

"We can take the Chunnel. Normandy's close to England. Remember World War II? Storming the beaches?"

"Yes! Right. Rouen." She pronounced the word with an exaggerated French accent. "It *sounds* like it will be more exciting than Tattershall." They looked back at the castle. "I'm going to need to visit another castle to feel like I visited a castle."

Cosima studied the map she'd brought up on her phone. "Rouen is a ninety-minute train from Paris. It might be better to rent a car in case we need to travel around."

"What do we do first? Get to London, I guess. Do we buy Eurostar tickets there? How does it work? I probably shouldn't assume you know, but I assume you know."

"We're going to have to go back to Gregory Place to pack a bag, minimally. We should eat. If we sit down to eat first, we can plan, *then* go to Gregory Place. At that point we'll probably want to wait until morning to start out."

Cosima sounded like a schoolteacher. It felt a little unreal to be talking about going to a medieval French city with no advance planning. All the travel Cosima had done in the past had been arranged down to the type of pastry that appeared on her breakfast tray.

"Boo." Edie tipped her head at Cosima. "We have our passports. Morag suggested it, just in case."

Cosima had wondered, at the time, what "just in case" was supposed to mean. Just in case they were abducted? Suddenly deported? "I do have my passport, but I never thought we'd go to France with only the clothes on our backs."

"They have underwear in France, famously good underwear, and toothpaste, probably in flavors I've never tried. We're not going for so long that we couldn't just *go*, right? I took a year of Spanish—actually, maybe it was a semester—and I got a C, not the point, but do you happen to speak French?"

"Bien sûr que je parle français." Cosima made her accent very extra.

"Then let's *go*, princess." Edie grabbed her hand, and Cosima reminded her lungs to breathe. The nickname had officially gone from annoying to goose bump–inducing.

Though, had it ever been *entirely* annoying?

They went. An old-fashioned cab returned them to the station in Ruskington, and from there the journey went by in a rush of Edie talking, gesturing, and asking questions as she handed Cosima snacks. Changing trains at Sleaford, they had prawn crisps for Cosima and ready salted crisps for Edie. When they changed again in Peterborough, Edie found a vending machine and secured them boiling-hot paper cups of weak tea.

At a newsstand at King's Cross, there were vegan Cadbury bars, and Edie gazed up at the vaulted, latticed ceiling of the famous depot. Cosima waited while Edie traded a handful of hoarded pound coins for a magnet in the shape of a red double-decker tourist bus to give her mother, as well as a copy of the *London A to Z* with maps she wanted to "practice reading" for another visit to London someday.

It was difficult for Cosima not to think *next time, next time*, as they rushed through all of these ordinary travelers' milestones. Next time she and Edie were in London, they'd take one of the red double-decker tourist buses. Next time, they'd stay in a boutique hotel in Grosvenor Square that Edie would love.

She firmed her jaw against *never again*.

They had walked forever, winding around people, queues,

strollers, shop stands, and signs, finally arriving at the Eurostar ticket office at St. Pancras International, when they ran into their first problem.

"We have a rule," Edie insisted. "And I would never pay for a first-class ticket. There's a dining car. We don't need to have dinner delivered to our seats like we're the Princess of Wales."

Cosima pulled Edie by the elbow to the back of the ticketing queue, *again*, so they could continue their argument. "We haven't stopped all day. We're exhausted. Premier tickets will give us more space to stretch out and more comfortable seats. We could sleep. We're going to need it. As it is, I think we'll have to spend the night in Paris."

Edie looked at the ceiling of the station in frustration. "It won't be so late that we have to stay in Paris. There's a hostel in Rouen."

"I will not stay in a hostel."

"That's a shame, princess, because I've already made a reservation."

"A reservation for the hostel that only has six bedrooms, and padlocks for the lockers are extra." Cosima tried to block out the overwhelming noise of the station, the smell of ozone and urine and frying food. Her silk blouse, which she would never have traveled in given the option, felt damp under her arms and at the small of her back. "I cannot do that."

"You can't exist under the roof of a hostel?" Edie somehow looked entirely fresh, her navy and red mice shirt impossibly adorable, her tight jeans unmarred, her hair still shiny and long and so attention-getting that Cosima had begun glaring at people who gave her appreciative double takes.

"I cannot. I will absolutely dissolve into the ether. And, what's more, we agreed that we would travel equitably, not that we would travel like nineteen-year-old boys who hook water bottles onto their backpacks."

They both glanced over at one such boy standing in the queue beside theirs, who chose that moment to graphically adjust his crotch.

Edie wrinkled her nose. "I will agree to Standard Premier, which has bigger seats and dinner. I think we can *both* continue to draw breath without access to champagne and a chef-designed meal."

"Thank you."

"And I'd like to assess how we're feeling once we arrive in Paris before we stay the night."

"Only if you cancel the hostel in Rouen."

"I made the reservation on your phone, so you can do it yourself."

Their argument ended in sync with their arrival at the head of the queue, and then, following a long series of walking, passing through gates, waiting, scanning various codes, and dodging people, they were finally collapsed side by side in their leather seats, where Cosima planned to sleep for a thousand years.

"Traveling light does have advantages," Edie said. "Although there are the extra questions from scary border officials about why you don't have luggage, accompanied by a bomb dog's nose in your butt."

"Unpleasant," Cosima said, closing her eyes. "I was afraid when you got goosed that you would confess we're going to France to find a treasure."

"Of course not. We don't need henchmen following us through Europe, ready to tie us up and steal our spoils. Although I'm not sure what kind of spoils I should be anticipating. How much do gold bars weigh?"

Cosima listened to Edie talk with her eyes closed while the

train moved out of the station. She fell asleep in the dark cabin as the car settled into its smooth hum, racing overland on its way to the channel.

She couldn't tell what made her wake up—if it was a door opening or the sound of clinking glasses—but she knew she didn't *want* to. After hours of travel grime and sore legs and threatening headaches, she was surrounded by a soft smell that reminded her of the lemon zest she'd piled onto the saucer. Every muscle in her body had gone lax, her limbs tucked into or surrounded by eye-rollingly beautiful softness. The tension in her eyes and neck had been chased away by the delicious half dreams of her nap.

"Cosima."

She burrowed herself deeper into the lovely, soft nap place.

"Princess." Edie's voice was close, but maybe she was dreaming that. If she *was* dreaming about Edie, she wondered if she could initiate a meditation that would allow her to *really* dream about Edie. To hold her the way she wanted to and practice kissing Dream Edie until it got as good as she hoped it could be.

"The drinks service is coming through. It's possible you might want to, um. Find your way to your seat."

Edie's voice vibrated against Cosima's cheek. It was nice. "Am in my seat."

"Part of you is in your seat. And part of you is in my seat. On me."

Cosima opened her eyes. She went to adjust herself and then fully appreciated why Edie had interrupted her nap.

Her leg was wrapped around Edie's thigh, for starters. And, as she sheepishly slid her leg away, she discovered her forearm snuggled between Edie's breasts, her hand along Edie's jaw, and her other arm—once those two disobedient limbs had been extricated—wrapped around Edie's shoulders, her fingers cupping the nape of Edie's neck.

She rubbed her face and felt the impression of the collar of Edie's shirt pressed into her skin. She had been sleeping on her like a koala in its handler's arms, possibly with even less shame.

Embarrassing. Yes. Incredibly so. But agony to separate herself.

"You could have shoved me back into my own space," she finally said. "I am mortified."

Edie's smile made a dimple appear beneath her eye, like a shooting star. "There was no moving you. At one point I tried a bit of polite shoehorning, but you growled."

"Oh, no."

"Did you know"—Edie raised her eyebrows—"that you talk in your sleep?"

The horror hit Cosima like a splash of cold water. "What?"

"I couldn't make everything out. I had to stop listening once you were comparing my breath to the sweet perfume of June lilacs." Edie bit her lip.

"You're making that up."

"I am." Edie had a new cluster of forehead freckles from today's walks in the sun. There were six wedge-shaped flashes of gold in her left eye that Cosima hadn't noticed before. She studied them, full of slow, sleepy longing. "No talking. Just a little snoring." Edie's voice was low and husky. "The porter's holding our dinner. It's on a tray, like an airplane meal. I can push the call button, and she'll bring it."

"I'm not hungry." The Eurostar was a blanket of soft white noise, the lights low. There was nothing out the windows, only the occasional glimpse of a concrete wall to indicate they were passing beneath the English Channel. No one had been seated opposite them. They were nowhere, alone and unobserved.

“We’re in international waters,” she said. Her pulse skyrocketed in response to her own audacity, but Edie only looked confused.

“Yeah?”

More humiliation. Cosima ignored it. She had to, or else live the rest of her days without knowing how Edie’s lips would feel against hers. “I’m suggesting that the laws are different out here. The rules.”

“Do you want to pirate the other passengers? I don’t think that’s a great idea after Pierre le Pooch made such a close inspection of me.”

Cosima wanted to laugh. Here she was, with no hands-on, practical experience of this kind of thing, and Edie couldn’t tell how many rules she was willing to break on this train, in this hour before they’d be on the streets of Paris, where everything would be hemmed in by reality again. Cosima had tried innuendo and failed miserably.

But then the skin on Edie’s cheeks flooded pink, and the green of her eyes was edged out by her pupils widening. A much more than adequate reward for the risk Cosima had taken.

“Edie.” She hadn’t known her voice could sound this knowing, except that every part of her was so sensitized to the knowledge of this woman, how couldn’t it?

“I’m trying to think of a more terrible idea,” Edie whispered. “Are you sure you wouldn’t rather do some piracy?”

“Would you?” Cosima made herself keep her eyes on Edie’s, exhilarating herself with the illicit feeling of extended eye contact, which her body knew was a prelude to intimacy, and so initiated luxurious, thudding pressure in her throat, her wrists, the palms of her hands, between her legs.

“Would I what?” Edie sounded thrillingly distracted. Cosima had done that. She’d distracted Edie with her desire.

"What if I only want to know what it's like?" she asked. "What if we don't do it, and I *never* know what it's like?"

They weren't even touching, but Edie might as well be licking her neck while her hand squeezed Cosima's naked hip because this—this *almost*—was the most erotic thing that had ever happened to her.

"I want to." Edie blinked, slow, before closing her eyes, and Cosima's gaze dropped to her mouth, then her neck, where she could see her pulse at the hollow of her throat. "It's just that I've made this mistake before, at the end of a long day like this, or when something complicated is happening in my life, to seek out . . . an escape. Someone who pulls me out of my head and puts me back inside my body. I don't want to do that to you."

Cosima wasn't surprised. She wasn't hurt. "I will say that I am very badly disappointed." The declaration came out a bit more snappish than she'd meant it to.

Edie made an almost inaudible sound that fed whatever hot wolfishness was caged at the base of Cosima's spine, begging her to take this woman's clothes off on a train. Because Edie *liked* it when Cosima snapped at her. She liked being bossed, argued with, and taken seriously. She liked to feel competent, to be helpful, to be part of something exclusive and amazing.

Like this. Edie liked everything about this adventure. She didn't want to make a mistake and mess it up for her.

For a long moment, they didn't say anything. Cosima thought about Edie screaming on the stairs as lightning flashed outside, her giant green raincoat, how she teased Morag. The first days Edie was at the inn, even before she met her, Cosima had been aware of her. She sang in the shower in the bathroom down the hall and squeezed her toothpaste carefully up from the seam at the bottom—probably a habit taught by a mother who had to pay attention to how much toothpaste her kids were using.

Cosima didn't *just* want to kiss her. She wanted to taste her lemon shortbread and her cheese. She wanted to know how she would decorate the lounge. She wanted to notice when Edie needed another bar of soap or tube of toothpaste and add them to a market list.

And that meant Edie was right to pull away.

Cosima wanted a great deal that wasn't fair to ask for. A great deal more than she had any right to, considering their circumstances.

She shifted in her seat, allowing the breath of distance between them to widen a few inches, and reached for Edie's hand. She was gratified when Edie's fingers wrapped around hers.

This woman wanted legacy and roots. She wanted to make something good. Even if she agreed to take Cosima's money (doubtful) and move to Los Angeles (extremely unlikely), what would she do there, plant herself in the shadow of Cosima's secondhand fame? A life like that—a life in many ways like Duncan's—would not be soil in which Edie could thrive.

Cosima hadn't. She'd spent the years since college nurturing the legacy of a mother who had never asked what she wanted. That was what she'd run away from—the impossibility of growing into her own life when all of her resources went to Captain Astra and her empire of projects.

It wasn't fair of Cosima to imply to Edie that all she wanted was to practice kissing. But it also wasn't fair to *her*.

Edie's shoulder pressed into Cosima's upper arm as she reached abruptly overhead to press the call button. "Dinner," she said, without looking at Cosima. "I'm still hungry. Sorry."

By the time they had trays of food in front of them, the train had emerged from beneath the water and was rocketing through the dark countryside, the windows streaked with rain. Cosima tried to remember if she'd seen this view before, what it looked like in the sunlight, but she couldn't. The last time she'd been to France was after a visit to Duncan's relatives in Scotland. Her mother was doing reshoots on location in Egypt for a film she'd directed and starred in. It had dragged on, the budget bloated, investors nervous, and Phoebe was spiky with them both, plagued by migraines. Duncan had taken Cosima away. She remembered, in France, a clear stream they'd visited. He'd rolled up his trouser legs and guided her into the water, the rocks slippery with moss, tiny creatures darting across the surface of the water when they crouched down and kept still.

"I've never been to France." Edie broke a cold pita roll in half and piled a bite of the bread with falafel and hummus. "Probably that goes without saying, but I wanted to tell you I'm glad to be here." She put her knife down. Her hair slipped from behind her ear to frame the curve of her cheek.

"I'm glad to be here with you," Cosima replied.

It would be their last tender moment before shoving through the crowds and waiting in ground transportation lines with other grumpy, tired travelers. It helped that they didn't have luggage to contend with, but the prospect of another hour in clothes she'd put on at seven that morning made Cosima want to scream, and, what's more, it was colder in Paris. Lincolnshire, in southern England with a large run of coast, had been feeling springlike, especially during the day, with flushes of the early season colors of white and purple blending with pale green.

Paris was dark, bitter, smelly, and loud.

"What are you doing?" Cosima watched Edie step up behind the man in front of them in the Sixt queue, moving directly in front of Cosima.

"Getting ready to rent the car," Edie said.

"I'm renting the car."

Edie looked over her shoulder. "You're tired. I'll rent it and drive us to Rouen."

"You will not." The ice in her tone caught the attention of a kid sitting on top of a piece of rolling luggage, holding an American Girl doll and wearing an Elsa dress. Cosima lowered her voice to a hiss. "You've never driven in Paris traffic, and certainly not on France's highways."

Edie rolled her eyes. "In Wisconsin, they hand you a permit the summer after your freshman year of high school after you take a computer test that a goldfish could ace. Then you bomb around on county roads until you think you can pass the practical. I learned to drive shuttling my littler brothers to Boy Scouts day camp, dodging horse and carriages from the Amish community, long-haul truckers, and farm equipment. I'm not scared of a highway in a country with less people than Ohio at ten o'clock at night. You can lean the seat back, and I'll play something soothing while you finish your nap."

Cosima shook her head. "My father was a *Formula One race car driver*."

"I'm sorry, did you learn to drive when you were three? If so, I'm happy to step aside."

"My point is that I *inherited* a driving style both immaculate and aggressive that is faster than a Midwestern farm tractor and will get us to Rouen before the sun is already coming up."

Edie put her hand over her mouth. "Immaculate and aggressive, princess?"

"That's what I said."

"How about this? We agreed to arbitrate our impossible disagreements, so we'll let the attendant decide. Whatever this guy in the orange blazer says when we get up there goes."

"Fine." Cosima could've stomped her foot, but the kid sitting on the luggage was shooting her daggers.

The minute the man in front of them was done, they both raced to the counter, Cosima immediately spilling out her request in what she hoped was adequate French. "J'ai besoin de louer une voiture, quelle qu'elle soit, pour une durée indéterminée."

The man raised his eyebrow and started typing. "Oui."

Edie leaned forward, the high counter hitting her at sternum height. "Excuse my friend. She ate bad cheese on the train. *I* need to rent a car."

He stopped typing. "Who's the driver?" He spoke English with a strong Caribbean accent.

"I am," Edie said, at the same time Cosima replied, "Moi."

He stared at them both, his hands hovering over the keyboard. "Who is renting this car?" He looked on the counter at the stack of passports, driver's licenses, and credit cards they had both provided.

"We want you to decide," Edie said, breathlessly. "She and I have a deal, and you have to settle it."

He raised his eyebrows again, looking first at Edie, then at Cosima, who held her breath. He began typing again. "I pick this short American. All I have left is the Fiat 500. The tall American will hit her chin with her knees if she tries to drive it."

"*Yesssss!*" Edie actually pumped her fist. "How do you like that, Legs?"

Cosima tried to give Edie an imperious look, but she couldn't help it—she started laughing.

They laughed the whole time Edie ground the gears of the cramped car on the way out of Paris while Cosima tried and failed to get her phone to pair with the onboard navigation, and when they finally found the road to Rouen and the lights of the city had faded behind them, Cosima did, in fact, fall asleep, the heater blasting, listening to Edie's husky voice singing along with the radio.

Her most fun in Paris yet.

Chapter Fourteen

Edie squinted, opening one eye. The sun lasered through a gap in the curtains.

She was mad about it, because the sheets against her bare legs were divine. She rubbed her feet along the smooth fabric experimentally and gave herself goose bumps.

The mattress was a cloud. The pillow, unlike Morag's, did not smell like bleach, but lavender. When she stretched her arms over her head, arching her back, it was as if the previous day of treasure hunting and travel and late-night driving had been whisked away by the magic of Normandy and the amenities of this hotel, with its steep off-season discount.

The twin beds were side by side in the small balcony room, not quite touching. With their thick, white, square-cornered duvets, they had looked to Edie like perfectly proofed, matched Pullman loaves. She and Cosima hadn't even turned the lights on, only waited on each other to use the miniscule but expertly appointed en suite, grateful for the provided toothbrushes, toothpaste, and soap. They'd stripped down in the dark, backs to each other—though Edie had never been more aware of someone undressing in her proximity—and slid under the covers.

Edie hadn't meant to draw a line that meant they'd leave behind the intimacy of the train entirely. But in the room last night, she'd found herself too shy to avoid the uncomfortable series of moments when they were both awake and aware of each other but politely silent, and then she'd heard Cosima's breathing slow and deepen.

She remembered nothing after that.

She rolled over to look at the other bed. The only sign of Cosima was a bouquet of curly, frizzy hair sticking out of the top of her duvet.

Edie slid carefully out of the bed, gasping when the cold air hit her bare legs. She'd give a lot for one of her oversized sweatshirts right now. Her button-up barely reached her ass, and because she'd taken off her bra from underneath, she'd had to undo the top several buttons. She pulled a throw off the end of the bed and wrapped it around herself, creeping to French doors—French doors in France!—that led to what she assumed was the balcony.

The curtains pulled back silently, the pale silver February sun only partially filling the suite. *God. The view.*

She turned the handle of the door slowly, as quietly as she could, and opened it just enough to step out onto the balcony, wrapped in her blanket, with the storybook of medieval Normandy laid open at her feet.

Her perch gave her a vantage in both directions along a lane of half-timbered buildings. Their mullioned windows glinted against plaster and dark beams. At the end of the lane, there was a perfect, faceted, breathtaking slice of Rouen Cathedral—

unbelievably tall, taking in all of the sunlight that couldn't penetrate the crowded lane.

It was a dream. A good dream—one where Edie could be from any time in the past or future, because this view had always been here, and it was impossible to believe it would ever be gone.

And *she* was here, a part of it.

"Pretty."

Edie startled, making a noise that scared away a pair of pigeons on the neighboring roof.

"Sorry." Cosima was also wrapped in a throw, her hair felted on one side and enormous on the other. She yawned, and when she finished, the light caught her sleep-blue eyes and turned them aquamarine.

"Good morning." Edie didn't know why she was whispering.

Cosima sat down on a small wrought-iron bistro chair, wrinkling her nose. "It's so cold out here."

Edie laughed. "You're not a morning person, are you, princess?"

"Who is? Morning is the coldest, darkest, most disorienting part of the day. Except in the summer, when it's too bright, too soon. Everyone expects you to be cheerful. It's when they schedule the most important meetings, even though you're either starving or vaguely nauseated, and there's no predicting which. There's an entire period of time, right away, that you have to go through a tedious series of rituals to make yourself presentable, and at least one thing always goes wrong. You didn't pick up the dry cleaning. You smash the mascara wand into your eye and set your eyeball on fire. You realize that you got into bed too soon after you painted your nails and now they all have sheet prints on them. Morning is hateful." Cosima yawned again.

"I love getting up early." Edie sat down on the other chair. It was so cold that her hips began to ache. "In the morning, nothing bad has happened yet."

Cosima looked at Edie, a long look that started out considering and then got disconcertingly soft.

"What?"

She shrugged. "We slept together."

"We did not!"

"There's so much that's no longer a mystery. For example, you snore. Not a lot, not very loud, just a low purr. You yank all the bedding out from where it's tucked into the end of the mattress."

"It's literally evil that they do that. Who wants their toes bound in place?"

"You only use one pillow. Maybe that's why you snore. I stole your second one so I could stack my upper body up properly."

Edie smiled at the view, pleased to have been introduced to grouchy morning Cosima. Pleased with everything, despite the cold. "So how do we do this?" she asked. "I'm thinking we find some kind of drugstore for a brush for me and whatever you need to tame your hair, then food, then serviceable clothes real quick, and then we get down to business."

Cosima raised one barn-swallow-wing eyebrow. "First we talk about yesterday. On the train."

Edie bit the inside of her cheek to keep her heart from leaping into her throat. "We did. We have, two times. Very mature of us."

"We achieved understanding, and we were both reasonable. But how are we supposed to keep sleeping together and traveling through Europe if we don't talk about the elephant in the room?"

"Pink marble elephant." Edie giggled, possibly nervously. "We didn't *sleep* together."

"Edie."

We're in international waters. That was what Cosima had said. As though there might be places in the world where they could do whatever they liked without consequence.

Edie had been very decidedly *not* thinking about Cosima saying that—the tone of her voice, the challenging arch to her eyebrow, the heat and tenderness and vulnerability in her expression—since nearly the moment she'd said it.

Instead, Edie had reminded herself of a joke her brothers liked to make. They said that she was the frog who a thousand princesses kissed without any one of them finding their prince.

Edie had never been able to figure out if this joke was mainly about her lesbianism, queers and their fond affinity for frogs, or more about her general failure to be an attractive adult companion, but it did have a way of drowning her desire for someone new in the wash of shame for the ways her previous relationships had crashed and burned.

All of them. Every one. With variations, cruel twists, some humiliation, but no exceptions.

"I don't wake up with my body wrapped around someone else's body," Cosima said, in her new, velvety voice that was for saying sweet things Edie couldn't figure out how to deflect. "I don't want to kiss people. I don't fall asleep thinking about how close my bed is to the other bed someone is sleeping in, and I once shared a room in Park City during Sundance with Kristen Stewart."

Edie had done all of those things, too, except for the part with Kristen Stewart, unless she counted the number of times she'd fallen asleep with one of the *Twilight* movies playing, which was innumerable.

But she had never had anyone fall asleep on her shoulder, guileless and sweet, and then, with a sleepy inhale, curl themselves around her, fitting every part against her body, breath on her neck, hand in her hair sending unending washes of pleasure over her skin. Not in any of her relationships or hookups or with any woman she was "hanging out with."

She'd never been turned on by both the heat of a woman's body and her boneless trust.

She'd never turned down the kiss of a woman who wanted to kiss her.

She'd never been afraid a kiss would break her heart.

Her poor, senseless heart. When had it wriggled its way out of the cage she'd tried to trap it in, burst through the bars, and thrown its bloody little self at the feet of Cosima Frank?

The first day, probably. The first moment she laid eyes on her.

No. Sooner. She'd heard this woman's name—*Cosima*, which meant the universe, which meant everything—and Edie had been done for. The eyebrows were just a bonus. Their charming banter. The fact that such a glorious creature didn't know how to pet a cat and would never call her "Frog."

Watching her zest a lemon for the first time. Seeing her careen down a grassy slope without hesitation because Edie had fallen down it. Witnessing the way the flashing strobe of lights in a tunnel beneath the ocean on a train going a hundred miles an hour revealed the desire in her seawater eyes—what the actual fuck was Edie supposed to do, *not* fall in love with her?

"I don't live in Los Angeles," she said.

Cosima smiled. "Currently, I don't have an address in Los Angeles myself."

"You"—Edie pointed at her—"aren't allowed to suddenly adopt such an attitude."

"Attitude?" She smiled again, one of her new smiles that was knowing and terrible. "Describe my attitude."

"I won't." Edie pulled the blanket around herself tighter. "You know what you're doing with the smiles and the devastating Chunnel come-ons and this seductive comportment."

Cosima let her blanket fall from her shoulder, revealing a thin silk strap.

"Like that." Edie pointed again, this time at her shoulder.

"Which is why we have to talk about it."

"I will, but it has to be talking. No innuendo or looking at me with your eyes all Bette Davis'ed. I'm nervous."

"That's fair." Cosima pulled up her blanket and looked out at the view. "From a certain viewpoint, I know that it does look like I've always had everything I've ever wanted. And knowing that *theoretically* I could set you up in Los Angeles does make part of me want to throw a tantrum. But, Edie, I respect what you need to do after this trip to build your life back. I do understand that you will want to be the one to build it back. I can't try to white knight you. I get it, even though I kind of hate it." She turned, and their eyes met. "But the other side of all that is that I understand you *because* I've worked my whole adult life with a woman who wanted to build something of her own. And the *other* other side of it is that I have no idea what my life is going to look like next."

"So no kissing, then." Only a small part of Edie was relieved.

"I didn't say that."

"But you did say I'm not moving to Los Angeles. Are you moving to Green Bay?"

"I don't know, are you asking me to?"

Edie closed her eyes. Her impulse to say *yes* told her this conversation had gotten away from her. Her determination to be sensible was not working.

No. It *had* not worked. Very much past tense.

She couldn't protect herself from her own worst impulses, but she'd hoped she could protect Cosima.

"That's what I thought." Cosima didn't sound hurt.

"I won't lie and tell you I can handle a vacation fling." Edie opened her eyes to the sight of medieval buildings and towering spires and a movie star's daughter with bedhead, which did nothing to slow her heartbeat. "I'm not going to pretend that I won't want to convince you to do just that. To come home with me. To be with me. I've done it, you know. I've leaned into the stereotypes and rented the van after a long weekend that convinced me everything would be perfect forever. I've also had to call my brothers to move me out before I'd gotten my boxes unpacked."

"I wish you would beg me to move to Wisconsin. I'm angry that if you did, I couldn't say yes. I've scheduled two years of work for myself to begin the moment my mother died. I'm angry about it, and that tells me how much this very strange runaway vacation has restored me to myself. It's been good for me."

"For me, too."

"Yes, exactly. For both of us. I have hope now that someday I can think for myself. Duncan wasn't wrong—I *do* want to make something important, and it *has* to be important. Because that's me. But Duncan was, *is*, always trying to make everything okay. He has a way of asking for what he wants that no one can say no to, but I can never get angry with him because whatever he's asking for, he doesn't want it for himself. He wants it for the higher purpose of nothing ever going wrong. Ever."

"The impossible dream." Edie smiled at her small joke.

Cosima smiled back with a shake of her head. "I don't want perfect, Edie. My mother never settled for anything but perfect, and I think that broke Duncan a little, and it killed her."

"Cosima?" Edie pulled the throw more tightly around her legs, unsure. She took a deep breath. "Did your mom have a problem with alcohol? Or substances? Something like that?"

Cosima's expression didn't register anger, shock, or sadness. She didn't protest. She only leaned back as her body seemed to untie. "My mother was an alcoholic. It killed her. How did you guess?"

Edie made herself drop her shoulders from her ears. "I think one of the reasons so many people struggle with admitting they're an alcoholic is because of what we think an alcoholic *is*. We think of mean drunks and people who get in trouble at work and with the law. We think of out-of-control people who are violent and get thrown out of places. But most of the alcoholics I've known aren't like that. Remember I mentioned the guy my mom left Mike for, who she met at work?"

"I do." Cosima gave her a very kind smile.

"Scott. He was a decent guy. Very hard worker. He'd worked at the factory where my mom met him since he was fifteen, and no one who ever worked with him had a bad thing to say about him. Very . . . hygienic."

Cosima laughed. "Hygienic?"

"Maybe I mean barbered. Groomed. Always smelled like Zest soap and breath mints. Shaved twice a day. Our entire household revolved around him, but not because he was the sun. Because knowing how Scott felt, what kind of day he'd had, if he was going to need my mom so I would have to help my brothers with homework and put them to bed, was the way to keep everything as nice as he looked."

"Oh." Cosima put her fingers to her lips. "Oh."

"He never hit us. He didn't miss a day of work, never got a DUI, never yelled. But my mom did have to go to Al-Anon for five years after he left because she would have panic attacks trying to decide what to make for dinner. She learned about codependency. Sometimes, loving an alcoholic means living a life where you're always trying to get ahead of disaster, until you feel like everything is a potential disaster. Like making ordinary conversation. Or your too-much daughter being too much."

"Thank you," Cosima said. After a long moment, she gave her shoulders a little shake and leaned toward Edie. "Whatever it is that I manage to claw back from Phoebe Frank Studios, and from Phoebe Frank"—she raised an eyebrow to acknowledge Edie's preference for her mother's full name—"and even from lovely, kind Duncan, it will be messy. Unruly. Thank you for giving me the understanding I need to be messy. Or try to be messy."

"No problem, princess. I'm so sorry about your mom." Edie stretched her foot across the balcony, into the cold air, and touched Cosima's shin.

Cosima reached down and squeezed Edie's foot, her hand warm. "So I want you to tell me," she said, "is ignoring what we want going to keep us safe? Safe from hurt or heartache?" She met Edie's eyes and held them. "I know that no matter what, I'm going back to LA thinking about nothing but you, and it will make everything that much worse and that much better."

"Worse, huh?"

"Worse because you can't be with me. Better because I'd rather know you and miss you and think about you than not. Both of us already ran away to feel *better*, and we both know life's a lot more complicated than that. However far away you are from the problem, the feelings come with you, no matter how much you wish they didn't."

She ran her thumb down the inside of Edie's arch, over her instep, and then eased back again.

Edie's body buzzed and ached. Her bones were warm with Cosima's words. Cosima was right. Ignoring what she wanted had never made her feel better. Getting what she wanted, losing it, and then ignoring it some more hadn't made her feel better either.

Messy.

When Edie stood, her feet hit the cold tile of the balcony. The blanket was soft around her body. She could smell damp brick and lavender and then, when she sat on the small, low table that put her knee to knee with Cosima, she could smell Cosima, too, and she knew the smell came from Cosima's hair because she'd buried her face in it on the train. Like vanilla, but deeper. More complicated.

Cosima leaned forward. She put her hands on Edie's knees, and liquid fire raced up her thighs.

Edie reached for her, her hands finding her nape, hot under the blanket, and Cosima's hands fully parted the blanket over Edie's legs and found the back of her knees. With a screech of the table legs on tile, she pulled Edie between her thighs.

The rough, sudden jerk of it, the knots and ringlets at Cosima's nape, her parted lips, turned Edie on so fast, her middle swooped with desire. Cosima slid her hands from the backs of Edie's knees, over her arms, and then she felt Cosima's thumb against her bottom lip, pressing the middle of it, so when Edie moved to kiss her, Cosima's thumb was between their lips for a moment—was against Edie's tongue for just a second—a sensation more explicit than anything she had ever felt.

"Edie." Cosima whispered her name. It sounded good the way she said it. Her lips were soft, parting easily, her teeth slick, her tongue rough, the kiss pouring over Edie like hot honey, pooling between her legs. She traced the round muscle of

Cosima's shoulder beneath cold-prickled skin, the taut strap of her silky bra, the warm dip at her waist. She swept her tongue into Cosima's mouth and swallowed the sound she made, a moan of surrender. Edie smiled.

"What?" Cosima asked against her mouth. Edie's hair had somehow been gathered up into the tight grip of Cosima's fist.

"You like kissing me. It's like I never once exasperated you."

Her scalp burst into hot prickles as Cosima pulled the ponytail she'd made of Edie's hair. "You're exasperating me right now. Although it's possible *that's* what I like."

"Lemme see." Edie dropped her mouth to Cosima's neck and scraped her teeth against skin so soft, it made her throb and soften to a kiss, then a kiss with tongue, tasting her skin, lavender-scented from the sheets.

This time, Cosima's moan broke, and her hand left Edie's hair, traveled down her throat, and found where Edie had unbuttoned her shirt. "Can I touch you?"

Edie tried to suck in a breath, pressing her mouth against Cosima's shoulder. She was wet, her heart was bursting, she couldn't *breathe*. One taste of Cosima's mouth, and then her skin, had made her mind go blissfully dark. She didn't have words, so she took Cosima's hand and moved it over the top swell of her breast, and even that contact made Edie's hips lift.

She was kissing the bow of Cosima's lip when she felt her fingertips brush over her nipple, inciting her to bite. "Sorry."

"Fucking bite me again," Cosima breathed, thumbing Edie's nipple as firmly as Edie assumed she wanted her teeth.

Well, shit. It was going to be like that—white-hot sparks from Cosima's slow pinches and incautious kisses feeding into an unending upward spiral of lust that held Edie in a tortured grip of not-quite-enough, winding toward some completely new kind of coming that would definitely kill her.

Both of Cosima's hands slid around Edie's ribs and tugged her shirt.

"What do you want?" Edie asked.

Cosima stood, pulling Edie with her. "To keep kissing you, but with warm toes."

Edie laughed and let herself be towed back inside, where the hush of the dim room amplified the sounds Cosima made in her throat when she kissed her, backing her up against the bed, and then they were sprawled across the wrinkled duvet, Edie half out of her shirt, Cosima so unbelievably hot in a criminal, tiny bra and panties that Edie couldn't look hard enough.

The pillowy, lavender-scented mattress took her down.

Cosima's hair brushed against her cheek when she kissed Edie's jawline, behind her ear, down her neck.

Her firm grip trapped Edie's wrist above her head as she moved above her, as if Edie would get away, as if Cosima knew second thoughts were the threat.

It was the determined furrow to her eyebrows, the way she kissed Edie like she wanted to acquire this—to learn and master and memorize the slide of her tongue against Edie's and the way it sped up the rolling movement of her hips—that made Edie's boundaries dissolve like sparkling dust, blowing away the last of her sensible thoughts and every inhibition.

She slid down the bed, letting Cosima keep hold of her trapped wrist but adjusting and readjusting until the palm of her free hand laid across the top of Cosima's ass, her fingertips pushing past elastic to splay over firm flesh. Their kiss got slower and deeper, the thrust of Edie's tongue keeping time with her hand guiding Cosima's hips to ride Edie's thigh.

Cosima's arms came down, and she framed Edie's face with her forearms, breathing broken, her cheeks red, and when Edie dragged her heel over the bed to flatten her foot against it and push her thigh harder, Cosima smashed her cheek against Edie's, the movement of her hips tighter, unambiguous.

"Is this okay?" It wasn't a whisper, but it wasn't Cosima's crystalline, precise voice, either. It was needy. Edie's free hand snuck down to play along the soft skin of her own inner thigh, helpless not to tease herself.

"Is this how you want it, princess?" Edie's fingertips had found the wet gusset of her own panties, and just that small bit of contact had made her eyes roll.

"Yeah. Yeah." Cosima's cheek pressed harder, her skin burning hot.

Edie moved the hand on Cosima's hips lower, dipping past the band of her panties. Finding her soft and wet and pushing up against Edie's sliding fingers wasted her, ruined her with a fast, hard pulse between her legs, and then Cosima's rough shout was forced against Edie's temple. For the first time, she came while hardly touching herself, came only from how turned on she was, how hard Cosima came and the sounds she was making, and it was good—so good.

But as she started to breathe again she could feel her aching heart, like crushed velvet, and knew this wasn't only sex.

It wouldn't have happened if it was only sex. Cosima had already told her that.

Edie brought her arms around Cosima, who was trembling.

God.

She thought of the line from a poem her sister-in-law had painted on a barn board and hung over her mantle. *Don't be a merchant who won't risk the ocean.* It had made her wonder if her twenty-one-year-old sister-in-law ran a little deeper than

Edie ever guessed, and remembering the words now, she felt equally terrified and exhilarated. *Risk the ocean.*

Cosima sank away from Edie's body onto the space beside her on the narrow mattress, and they both moved to their sides to look at each other. Edie's heart picked up again, amazed when Cosima's eyes met hers and neither of them looked away. Her experience with heedless lust involved a lot of hurry and chagrin in the aftermath. Cosima's steady, soft eye contact and relaxed smile were different.

This was different.

Cosima's hand wiggled up between them, and then her index finger traced along Edie's forehead. "Cassiopeia," she said.

"Who is that?" Edie closed her eyes as Cosima traced over her face.

"Queen of Ethiopia. Her daughter was saved from a sea monster, but in this case, the constellation. Your freckles make it, here." She touched Edie's forehead again, then her temple. "Orion's Belt." Her fingers brushed under her eye. "Ursa Major."

"Not frog polka dots," Edie said.

Cosima kissed her nose. Had any woman kissed her nose? Even her mother? "Certainly not."

Edie lifted a coiled strand off Cosima's flushed neck. "Your hair's lighter, curlier, and your eyes are bigger." Edie touched her fingertips to Cosima's lips. "And this is not at all the same. Or this." She cupped Cosima's square jaw. "You're entirely you. I think you always have been."

Cosima sunk the heels of her hands into her eyes. "You stop. If you start with that kind of thing, I'll lose my edge." She smiled and rolled on her back and turned her head to Edie. "You know, the only time anyone ever tells me I look like her is when I'm with her. On my own, I'm just me." Her stomach gurgled. "Oh, no."

They'd left the door to the balcony open a crack, and Edie could hear noise from the street—traffic, someone shouting, faraway church bells. The city waking up.

It made her wish for a different life. For real magic that would let her stay in this moment, where they could pull the covers up over them and she could fall back asleep with her head on this woman's shoulder, breathing in the scent of her, wrapped in her arms.

But she didn't resent the busy day ahead of them, any more than she could regret what they'd done. For the first time in weeks, Edie found herself looking forward to whatever came next.

"We're hungry," she said. "We need to buy a couple of sweatshirts with Joan of Arc on them. The bathroom is stocked with a pharmacy's worth of toiletries that look better than anything I've ever paid for, so we're set there and only need to shower. Should we get ready, then take the map to a café to figure out where we might go?"

"Yes, let's do that." Cosima moved to a sitting position, giving Edie aftershocks between her legs. This woman's beauty was a lot to take in at once. "But I might have already figured it out."

"Really? When?"

"You fell asleep first." She gathered her hair in her hands.

"I'm absolutely positive that *you* fell asleep first."

"I had a nap in the car that took the edge off. You were snoring almost as soon as your head hit your single, sad pillow." Cosima had begun sifting her fingertips through her hair, searching out tangles and gently pulling them apart.

"I heard your breathing change!"

Her shoulders dropped, and even in a cross-legged position

on the bed, Cosima appeared to gain a few inches in height. Imperious again, but not intimidating. Not in the least. She tugged at a particularly stubborn tangle. "I was probably just relaxed, because you one hundred percent fell asleep first, and I got bored. Then I got out the map and my phone."

With a sigh, Edie sat up, too. "Well, I don't remember that, so you must be right," she grumbled.

Cosima leaned over to grab the hotel notepad and pen that was on Edie's bedside, giving Edie a glorious glimpse down the cup of her bra, which Edie now regretted having failed to remove.

"I'm going to write that down," she said, tapping the pen against the notepad. "'Cosima is right.' I'll put the date and time, and you can sign it for me."

"I take it back. You fell asleep first and then got out the map in a fugue state of sleepwalking."

"Shush." Cosima flashed her a killing smile, one filigreed eyebrow arched. "I used one of *your* methods of research."

"What's that?"

"A tourist brochure. I'd grabbed one from the front desk when we got the room. And it turns out there's a one-for-one connection between a location in Rouen and one of Agatha's illustrations on the map."

"Tell me." Edie felt her brain spinning back up to its usual state of hyper-awareness. It made her notice again how *good* she felt, like Cosima had poured syrupy light over her body.

"The illustration looks like a skull and crossbones, which we had both thought was very treasure-hunting pirate-like. But when I was looking at it more closely, I realized it's not a human skull. I'm fairly sure it's a cat's skull. I took a picture and reverse image searched it."

"What does a *cat* skull mean?"

"Right, so, Rouen was hit by the plague hard, twice. The first time, in the thirteen hundreds, at least half the people died. They couldn't give them all proper burials. They dug a mass grave near the church of Saint Maclou."

"Grim."

"Very. Over the years, the area around the pit was built up, but they didn't disturb the pit itself because the church said those people were going to need their full set of bones in the resurrection. But then, two hundred years later, the plague came back. Time to dig another pit."

"Bam!" Edie was getting too excited. She had done a fourth-grade project on the Black Plague.

"Again, more than half the population's dead. They wanted to put the bodies in the same spot, but they couldn't destroy the old bones, so they dug them up first and put them in an ossuary that circles around the pit in the middle."

Edie rubbed her hands together. "Here is where I confess that I love stories that explain how something completely out of pocket happened like it's normal. Yes, of course, the two plagues killing basically everyone meant the survivors had to make an enormous warehouse to store thousands of bones in. Perfectly regular."

One of her knees had begun to bounce. Cosima smiled at it. "Unlike a lot of medieval landmarks, this one survived the centuries and even the blitzes of World War II. It's been archaeologically studied and excavated. There are fascinating examples of medieval carving and statuary."

"Which sounds amazing, but you were telling me something about a cat skull."

"So I was. Around the time Agatha was here, a cat mummy

was excavated from one of the walls. It would have been a big deal that everyone was talking about."

"Cat skull, cat mummy!"

"Yes. I think we're meant to start there, at the Aître Saint-Maclou."

Edie pulled up her legs and wrapped her arms around them, needing a way to contain her feelings about an adventure that involved both the Plague and a cat mummy. "I don't know if I can wait until we track down matching Joan of Arc sweatshirts before we go."

"I'm not wearing a tourist sweatshirt, but yes. Let's hurry. I think it will be so interesting."

She sounded like she meant it, and her eyes were warm. Cosima's bra strap slid down in time with her grin.

Risk the ocean.

Edie wanted to kiss her again.

Chapter Fifteen

"I can hear you." Cosima pressed the cool glass of her phone against her ear and stepped back into the long, stony passage of Aître Saint-Maclou to stand in front of a pair of wooden doors. The interpretive signage said the doors led to the original chapel.

She could really use some divine intervention right now.

"Excellent. As I said, I've been reluctant to interfere with your vacation, but there's a bit of friction we should discuss."

Vacation. A bit of friction. Duncan's tone didn't hold recrimination or passive aggression, but Cosima nonetheless had to squeeze her eyes shut against the pain of the knives, twisting around the plate of pastries she'd devoured from Patisserie Julliene.

They'd had a delicious breakfast at the concierge's recommendation. Edie had surprised Cosima by asking the counter server a few questions about the bread in a slow but serviceable hybrid of culinary French and English, which drew one of the bakers out of the kitchen. By the time they left, Edie and the baker had exchanged vegan pastry recipes, and Cosima had been replete with sweetness of every kind.

Whatever she had thought it would be to make love to Edie, she hadn't understood it would involve every cell of her body and all of her feelings.

She hadn't known it would balance her life on the edge of heartbreak, and that she wouldn't care.

She'd been trying to hang on to the morning since she saw Duncan's name on the screen of her phone, but she could feel it slipping away.

A bit of friction—it wasn't what Duncan meant. She settled in to translate from Duncan to English what level of crisis had precipitated his calling her. She knew it had to be a crisis, because he would have avoided reaching out otherwise. He wouldn't want her to have *feelings*.

"Friction?"

"Indeed. It's been requested by the board that you appoint an interim CEO. They've voted on this request, I should say. Keep in mind, there was a majority of only one vote. Nearly half the board isn't *as* anxious to see the matter resolved. There may be some room for finesse. Options they would be willing to consider."

Cosima unbuttoned her coat, feeling constricted by its fit over the sweater she'd purchased in the hotel shop. She translated Duncan to mean that half the board was angry and wanted an interim CEO appointed. The other half was angry and couldn't agree enough on what to do about it to form the coalition required for a majority vote.

"Options?"

"Of course, I'm not sure. It may be easier to suss out the resolution they'd settle for if you had a short window to return.

No more than forty-eight hours. Your office could make the arrangements."

Like a spike between her eyes, she had a sudden vision of the PFS studio building in Burbank with the California sun bouncing off its mirrored windows and heating the concrete pathways to its ultra-modern lobby.

Here, now, the wood she laid her palm against was nearly black with age. She could hear Edie talking to a docent, his French-accented English amused with whatever Edie was telling him.

She couldn't do Burbank. She *couldn't.* She had to claw back, wherever she could. Here was where the messy hit the road. "I'm not able to return to LA."

Duncan was quiet.

Cosima watched her finger trace the wood carvings, softened to indistinct shapes with time. Her stomach cramped, forcing her to silently suck in a breath.

"Perhaps we could arrange a teleconference?"

His voice was so familiar, so easy and reasonable. He'd been patient with her. His diplomacy was legendary. He'd doubtless covered for her generously, such that the board members had no choice but to believe that Cosima's departure had been planned, her trip providing time away for her to recover and return ready to work.

She wasn't ready for anything but the next time she could kiss Edie and the next clue on the map.

"I don't think a teleconference is possible." Cosima tried to relax her shoulders, her lower back, searching for a path to a deep breath. Anything to loosen the sickening knot in her middle that told her that a teleconference wouldn't be a big deal, and she should just go ahead and arrange it. The knot was so certain that a fifty-year-old company would implode unless she, Cosima Frank, was pleasant to Duncan and deferential to the wishes of its board.

It wouldn't, though. It really *wouldn't.* Cosima knew for a fact that her mother had left the board in a spitting fit more than once while she did what she needed or wanted to do. It had been enough, always, that she didn't want to.

Well. Cosima didn't want to.

"I *can't,*" she told Duncan, this time with princessly authority. "I will, of course, do what needs to be done, but I've earned the right to take my time to decide what that is and to remind the board I'm not fourteen or their secretary."

"What's the matter, love?" She could hear the creak of Duncan's leather desk chair as he sat down. She imagined him removing his reading glasses and reaching for his tea, which had probably gotten cold as he worked. It was the end of the day in California, a day in which Duncan had gone to an unscheduled emergency board meeting, likely after putting out fires for *An American Castle's Garden* and making excuses for her, and then been unable to prevent the board from passing this resolution that obligated him to call her. A long and difficult day. He sounded tired.

Cosima couldn't answer his question, and she was surprised to realize it was because here, right where she was, there wasn't anything wrong.

There always had been, before.

"I don't have an excuse," she said. "I don't believe I need one."

Duncan went quiet again. Twice in the same call, he'd let what she said stand without trying to say it back to her a slightly different way. He cleared his throat. "Since you've been gone—actually even before you left—I've felt increasingly ashamed that I didn't speak to you about your mother. Her illness. Her.

You. Us. We should have talked with honesty a long time ago, or at least talked about what was actually happening instead of what I dearly wished was happening. I must sound to you like I'm not making any sense at all."

Cosima wondered if the kiss she'd given Edie on the cheek was enchanted, and it was opening every previously closed box that held feelings. Her heart. Her sexual awareness. The real story of her family. Edie's insights.

Her mother had said Gregory Place was magic, but she had not said what kind.

"Duncan."

"No, please listen. I did try, Cosima. I tried not to enable Phoebe. Her habits. I encouraged her to get help."

Cosima studied the wood beneath her fingertips. She could hear Edie laughing with the docent, and she wished she were in the sunlight beside her. "Did you?"

"Several times over the years. Probably not as many as I should have, although I've joined a group, a support group, online, and I've learned it's common for the family and friends of someone with a problem like your mother's to assign blame to themselves."

Cosima let go of the post and crossed to where the light slanted across the covered walkway. She stepped into it so she could look out into the courtyard at Edie in her green jacket, her hair shining. From the hotel shop, Edie had picked out a black T-shirt with an image of Joan of Arc above the word NORMANDIE in old-fashioned lettering.

When Cosima talked to Edie, she never had to translate. Edie had witnessed so many of her *emotions*, which meant Cosima had the experience of her emotions being generously received instead of shushed. Redirected. Oppressed.

She *liked* feeling. She liked knowing she was safe to express herself. It meant she was expressing herself more, and reacquainting herself with the girl she'd been before she had grown old enough to step into the role of her mother's silent everything.

Whatever happened between them, her time with Edie would be the most generous gift anyone had given her in her very privileged life.

"Al-Anon? Is that your support group?"

"It is. Have you found them as well? I have to say that there's nothing like having your completely unique, secret, and impossible problem turn out to be the same problem thirty other people in your group have been going through. Humbling."

"A friend told me there's a lot to get into there. So maybe, since we're working on this, let's call what we're talking about 'Phoebe's alcoholism.'" Cosima couldn't spend the rest of her life *not* saying it while it stabbed her in the stomach. "You asked her to get help with her *alcoholism*, and she refused. You tried not to enable her drinking, but you weren't even able to join a group to get help for yourself until she was gone, which means she wouldn't let you when she was alive. She wouldn't permit anyone to help her. She wouldn't admit to the doctors or the nurses at the hospital that the problem with her liver was the consequence of her drinking. That was the secret she made us keep."

"Yes." Duncan's agreement came much more quickly than Cosima might have expected. He'd probably believed that she was as unwilling to break the seal of silence as he was.

"Her list, with the museum sleepover and the skydiving?" Cosima asked. "She was trying to show me the mother she would've been if she hadn't drank. She was trying to fit everything in before she died."

"Yes," Duncan said again.

"If she'd asked me, I would have told her she didn't have to do that. I loved the mother I had. I still love her. I love you." Cosima took a deep breath. "The father you are to me."

"I love you, too." Duncan was not holding it together. Neither was she. "And I hope you know I have always loved you as my daughter."

"I do know. Mom—" Cosima stopped. She hadn't ever called Phoebe "mom." Not because Phoebe hadn't wanted her to, but because even when she was young, Cosima had known that "mom" was a term of endearment, and there was always a part of her too angry with Phoebe to call her *mom*. "Part of the reason *Mom* loved you is because she loved me so much, she wanted me to have a dad."

"I think so. Yes."

Cosima pinched the bridge of her nose so she wouldn't cry. "I should've had a mom for a lot longer than I did. I'm barely thirty. I have so much ahead of me that I'll need a mom for, and she won't be there. She's turning our Castle, our home, into a performing arts center! We're being evicted, Duncan!"

He laughed, a sound stuck midway between resignation and gratitude. "I'll always be nearby if you need me."

"And I'm grateful, but neither of us got quite what we wanted, did we? Even though we always knew what *Mom* wanted."

Duncan laughed again, watery now. "We did. Like it was our job."

"Well, I don't have that job anymore, and neither do you. For years, I've had this terrible pain, and I haven't known what caused it. I couldn't find a doctor to help me with it. I didn't know if it would go away or if it would kill me. When she died, I thought I would know. I think I secretly thought the pain was *her*, or her drinking. But now I think the pain must have been secrets. You know, Duncan, I would rather have a great big bleeding wound on the outside, where I could take care of it and help it heal, than an ache inside that I'm afraid might kill me."

Cosima heard his chair creak again. "I want you to know that I don't regret my life with Phoebe. I would have married her. Even at the end, I would have."

Cosima had never doubted it. "I think she thought she was keeping us safe from the worst of herself, but she didn't ask us if we agreed with her plan."

"Codependent, as you and my group have enlightened me."

"I should go to one of these groups." Cosima's face felt hot against the glass of her phone.

"I think you should, yes." Duncan cleared his throat again. "Cosima, darling?"

She knew he meant that he needed to know what to tell the PFS board. They were still good at having a full conversation without saying a word. But Cosima could look forward, now, to a future when they didn't rely on silence and shorthand. Maybe someday they would even learn how to bicker.

She sighed, long and gusty. "I'd like to activate the board policy that deals with what to do in the event of incapacitation. I'm not keen on appointing an interim directly. That will invite power struggles later."

She heard Duncan tapping on his keyboard. "In the section about CEO duty."

"Yes. Wouldn't that be Reggie?"

"The policy is that the most senior board member under the chair would serve as interim CEO, with certain limitations to powers . . . blah, blah, blah. Yes, Reggie. I think the only other time this was used was when Phoebe was quarantined in Romania after scouting locations with Gerwig and getting exposed to the measles."

"I remember. Let's get that started. Have the paperwork directed to my FileJoin account, and I'll sign."

"This only buys you ten business days. And you should know there are three new negotiated contracts on the table from the union, delivered yesterday. I'm sure you wouldn't want to cause any panic about those jobs. Reggie won't be able to touch those contracts, and you wouldn't want him to. And the CFO's office has concerns."

"The stock price." Cosima's stomach buckled again.

"Perhaps if you could authorize your assistant to—"

"I know. I'll send a soothing memo."

"And do you suppose an additional, revised version of that soothing memo could be shared for me to circulate to the executive producer of our show? I've been stalling by authorizing a great deal of B-roll of the garden waving in the breeze and silhouetted by the sunset."

"Yes." Cosima forced her jaw to unclench. She *meant* this yes, if only so there wouldn't be a whiff of concern coming from the top to worry the people who needed their checks. The union would, rightfully, step in on their behalf as well if any concern went on too long.

The chair creaked. "Good. Good. I love you, Cosima."

"I love you, too."

After disconnecting, she closed her eyes, trying to focus on how Edie smiled when it was just for her. She wouldn't think yet about how fast ten days would go by, or about the employees of PFS who depended on her presence and her decisions.

She put her hot phone in her back pocket and walked across the courtyard to where the plague burial pit had once been, now occupied by a patch of dormant grass shaded beneath a knobbly collection of lime trees.

"This is it, huh?" She stood as close as she could to Edie, who was gazing at a mummified cat displayed vertically on bright silk, glassed in from the elements. The cat appeared to be leaping into the air, a bit of rope having trapped its front paw to hold it in place. The shapes of its bones were visible through its skin, and a mummified rat sat at its feet. "That is a grim spectacle."

"It really looks like if you gave it some food and water, or wrapped it in a towel and took it to one of those rescue places, it would wake up and be okay."

Cosima did not agree, but she saw no reason to say so. "I have to assume that if it was interred here, it was a loved cat, so there's that."

"According to the docent, it might have been someone's idea of a joke. Because this place gets dug up so often, relatively speaking. A cat mummy might've been a way to freak out a priest or archaeologist." She wrinkled her nose. "Or, another theory, it's a black cat, so it might be here to ward off evil. They gave a dead cat a job."

When Cosima put her arm around her, Edie leaned into the nook of her shoulder. It happened without hesitation or effort, easing away the last of the worry from Cosima's stomach. She indulged the impulse to lean down and kiss Edie on the temple, which earned her a quick smile.

"Well, this cat is loved now," Cosima said. "You talked to the docent. Where do you think we should look for Agatha's clue?"

"Not here." Edie turned around under Cosima's arm and put her own arms up on Cosima's shoulders.

"No? Is there another bony cat somewhere?" Edie's eyes were new-leaf green in the sunny courtyard.

"There could be. Turns out that Rouen has at least half a dozen old, amazing churches. But no." She smiled again, the way the cat might have, once, with the rat caught beneath the points of its claws.

"What did the docent tell you?"

"First, the bad news. He said there isn't anywhere *here* that a visitor almost fifty years ago could have hid something that wouldn't have been found already. It's a gallery and artists' space now, but before that it was an art school, crawling with children."

"Disappointing."

"Yes. However, when Agatha would have been around in the seventies, the cat mummy was still big news. There's a café a short walk away that's been around forever. Back when the cat mummy was recent, the daughter of the café owner took over management. Mostly as a joke, she had a sign painted with a cat skeleton on it and hung it up over the café doors. Ever since, it's been known as 'The Dead Cat.'"

"And you think Agatha might have left something there?"

Edie picked up a strand of Cosima's hair and twirled it around her finger. The gentle tugging sensation made Cosima's knees go weak.

"I really *do* think so, because the other thing the docent told me is that ever since the German occupation of France, people have been pinning letters to one of the walls of that same café."

"Oh." Now Cosima could feel Edie's same excitement quickening her pulse, because pinning a letter to the wall of a French café sounded like something Agatha would do. And wasn't that surprising—that in the short time they'd been following her clues, Cosima had started to get a sense of what made Agatha Llewellyn tick?

"That's right," Edie said, nodding her head. "I'm talking about letters they hoped loved ones would find on their way over the channel, or letters to their future selves, or—"

"—to a treasure hunter."

"Right. The café never takes anything down. Only the person who a letter is meant for can claim it."

Cosima picked up one of Edie's long braids and smoothed it over her chest—a touch with no purpose but to reassure herself of Edie's aliveness. "Let's go, then."

Edie stepped next to Cosima and wrapped two arms around her elbow, and they ambled the few blocks to the café, a low building straddling a street corner whose forest-green awning sheltered bistro tables. The upper story was half-timbered, and over the awning was a gilded wooden sign, Le Chat Mort, showing a cat skeleton chasing a ball of string. The café's double glass doors emitted a pleasant smell of coffee, wine, baking bread, and cooking onions as people came in and out.

"Let's sit by the wall." Edie slipped off her coat in the warm room. Her snug black T-shirt looked effortlessly cool with her braids, jeans, and Converse, and it put her lush body on display, turning the heads of more than one of the people seated around the glossy wooden tables.

"The docent wasn't exaggerating about this place never taking the letters down."

The eight-foot-tall wall ran uninterrupted by windows along the entire back of the café. There had to be thousands of letters tacked up, folded into thirds or tucked into envelopes and layered like shingles. A wooden ladder leaned against the wall, presumably so that customers could climb it to post their writings higher up or study what they found there. Some of the letters were new, the paper stiff and the ink vivid, while others were brittle with age. Each of them had a name written large along its margin to identify the intended recipient, making the wall look like a giant illustration made up of names in different inks on every color of paper—though the overall effect was not of chaos, but a Gallic tidiness.

"I'm hoping it will be easy to find the general era that Agatha wrote her letter in." Edie sat down at a table next to the wall, her eyes on its contents. "All of these look like they could've been left yesterday. The names are in Sharpie and glitter pen."

A server came around. Cosima informed her that Edie was vegan so the server could tell her Edie's options and Cosima could translate.

"I'll have the potato gratin and sparkling mineral water," Edie said. "Can you also ask her about the letters and where we might find one from the seventies?"

Cosima ordered for herself, then asked, "Pourriez-vous m'indiquer où je pourrais trouver une lettre rédigée dans les années soixante-dix? Une dame plus âgée de notre entourage nous a demandé de la chercher." It wasn't strictly true that Morag had sent them here to get Agatha's letter, but true enough.

"Je demanderai à la propriétaire de venir à votre table dès que possible. Elle saura vous aider." The server set down utensils and wove back to the bar through the tables.

"The owner is going to help us when she gets a chance." Cosima pushed her chair away from the table to make more room for her legs.

"It isn't terrible watching you speak French *in* France," Edie said with a smile. "Although if you didn't speak French, I would be absolutely scandalized by the quality of Swiss boarding schools." Edie put her elbows on the table and leaned closer. "Speaking not at all of Swiss boarding schools, I have a feeling the phone call you took wasn't the kind that was great, and then I started thinking about what time it is in California, and now I'm worried. This is actually a reason I may never have a phone again by choice. It means I'm unable to look up news about Phoebe Frank or you, and so I can't blow a fan on my mental spirals until they're spinning so fast I can't think. I'm serene now, I'm sure you've noticed. Anyway, you don't have to share with me what may or may not be going on, but I'm interested to listen if you want me to."

Cosima surveyed the letters on the wall, thinking about her mother's note that she and Edie had found in the wallpaper.

You're impossible, her mother had written, *and right now, made only of stars and hopes I didn't know I had.*

Sitting in a French café with the side of her boot touching Edie's black Converse sneaker gave her a glimmer of what her mother had been trying to express. All of this—Edie, and Cosima's feelings, and the wall full of wishes and dreams and broken hopes beside them—had been, just a few short weeks ago, impossible.

A petite woman with a steel-gray pixie and heavy horn-rimmed glasses came to their table. "Vous cherchez une lettre?"

Cosima turned and smiled, grateful to be saved by the bell, so to speak. "Oui," she said. "Nous recherchons une lettre que nous pensons être de 1977 ayant été, laissée par une femme. Une écrivaine."

The woman's dark eyebrows lifted to her hairline, and she pulled a chair from a neighboring table and sat down. "You're looking for a letter from a writer you think wrote one in seventy-seven." Her English was clipped, only slightly blurred by her accent.

"We are." Edie leaned forward. "A mystery writer. Agatha—"

"—Llewellyn," the woman finished. "Of course. But a lot of people ask me to read that letter. Especially English people. Australians. Americans."

"They do?" Edie scooted closer. The café was getting loud. "Why? None of these letters have the letter-writer's name written on them. How would anyone know she wrote one? Is there a name connected to Agatha on the letter?"

"You ask a lot of questions at once."

"I like to get them out before I forget I thought of them."

The owner's appreciative smirk made Cosima reach for Edie's hand, a reaction that should have embarrassed her, theoretically, but was the only way she could think of to unlock her back teeth, clenched in unnecessary jealousy.

"I wouldn't have done it," the woman said. "It was my aunt, who owned this café before I did. She recognized Madame Llewellyn when she asked to pin up the letter. My aunt pinned it up under Madame Llewellyn's supervision, but as soon as she left, she took it down and framed it. She displayed it in the hall on the way to the toilets."

"Holy fuck, that's bold," Edie breathed. "Is that where it still is?"

"No. I did not like that she did that. Tacky, and the kind of thing that may discourage someone who does have a profile from leaving a letter." She raised an eyebrow at Cosima. "I am very sorry for the loss of your mother."

Cosima swallowed. "Thank you."

The woman nodded. "I took down the letter. I tried to remove it from the frame, but the glass had adhered to the envelope, to the ink, so I decided to keep it framed until the rightful recipient came. Then we could, as they say, break the glass in the event of an emergency." She looked at Edie. "If you are the rightful recipient, you can tell me now, who is the letter for?"

Cosima got out her phone. "It's intended as a clue, we believe, for whoever is searching for a treasure in a hunt that Agatha devised. If you look here, you can see the pictures from where it began, in this guest book, and where it took us in England. We found the treasure map in the church."

Edie turned around and fished the map from her jacket

pocket, spreading it out on the table while Cosima showed the café owner her pictures.

"Then we went to a manor house, a castle, and finally here." She finished flipping through the album, ending on the picture of the mummified cat. "We have reason to believe she left the next clue in that letter."

The woman looked at the map, tracing over the details. "This is fantastic. But what gave you the right to start the hunt?"

"The owner of the inn, where the guest book is kept. Morag. She's known about the hunt since Agatha stayed at the inn back in the seventies, but she hasn't let anyone look for the treasure until us, though I have no idea why."

The café owner stared at Edie for a long moment. Then she looked at Edie and Cosima's joined hands. Uncertainty prickled along Cosima's hairline.

"You don't?" the woman asked.

"No," Edie said. "Morag keeps her own counsel."

The woman shook her head, letting out a chuckle, and Cosima couldn't work out the source of her amusement *or* her wry knowledge. Annoying. "Could we read the letter, then?" She hadn't meant for the question to come out so sharp, but she rarely did.

"I will allow this. One moment." She stood up and disappeared into the crowded café.

"She is *so cool*," Edie whispered. "Might also be a witch."

"I think she was a little dramatic."

"Hmm." Edie nodded. "You, of course, would know."

"Says the woman who considered finishing off her outfit with a child's sword and sheath that was printed with 'Sainte Jeanne d'Arc' in neon pink."

"I might still buy that. My niece would love it, and in the meantime, I'd have a *sword*."

"Voila." The woman appeared in front of them again, startling them both. She held an outsize dark wooden frame, which she set on the table. Its sticky, yellowed glass held an envelope, which read, "For the seeker from Gregory Place."

"That's us!" Edie pointed at the phrase. "And this is definitely Agatha's handwriting." She started to lift the frame, but the woman put her finger up to stop her. She grabbed Edie's water carafe, held it over the glass, then brought it down sharply. The glass dissolved into thousands of sparkling cigarette-smoked amber pieces, contained by the frame.

"Jesus!" Edie laughed. "No turning back now. Cosima, do you want to do the honors?"

Cosima picked up a corner of the heavy white envelope, the same as the envelope the map had been sealed into, and gently shook off the pieces of glass. She turned it over, broke what was left of the dry glue holding the seal, and pulled out the paper, which held several lines of Agatha's bold, stylized cursive.

> Minnie,
>
> If you've made it all the way here again and you're reading this letter, maybe you've already walked through the city, searching out the dark corners and cobbled alleyways we found to steal kisses, to sigh into the other's neck, and to otherwise believe in the magic of someplace far away from any other place you've been, where any kind of love is possible.
>
> Isn't it possible? Isn't it? If you're reading this, I have to think you've decided that it is.
>
> Minnie, my darling girl, I don't care if you didn't know right when I wanted you to, and I don't believe I ever will. I believe I will only ever care that you eventually decided to

come to me. I hope you know that. I hope you never thought that I left you. I didn't, I didn't.

I'm crying writing this, half-afraid you'll never read it, sick with excitement that you will. Love is not impossible. Not in any place, any language, and not any kind of love, even ours. If you're not yet convinced, go back to the sacred family, go back to the Gaudí, and I'll try again.

I'll never stop trying.

Yours yours yours,
Bronwyn A. Llewellyn

Cosima looked at Edie, who was so excited, so expectant. She had no way of knowing that this letter had given Cosima a glimpse of their future, and it looked a lot like the pile of broken glass inside the frame.

Chapter Sixteen

Edie pulled off her work gloves and waved at the man whose truck had just lifted the full skip onto its bed. He waved back, hopped into the truck, and drove away.

Morag had gone to visit a sister she'd heretofore never mentioned. This had happened almost the moment Edie and Cosima returned from Rouen in the wee hours of the morning the day after they found the letter at the café. She'd stuck around just long enough to give Edie a list of where she had accounts and to warn her not to break her Aga, and then she was gone, leaving only a number to call and let her know when "the dust had settled."

Edie wasn't sure what dust Morag meant. The dust from the hundreds of square feet of mauve carpet that Edie had pulled up tack by tack? Or the dust between Edie and Cosima that had kicked up in the aftermath of reading Agatha's letter to the mysterious Minnie?

"Wow." Cosima emerged through a temporary plastic flap

that Edie had hung on the landing, then minced down the stairs on the protective paper Edie had taped down in order to cover the wool runner that didn't need replacing because it was actually quite nice. "Who would have thought?"

Edie looked over the lounge—the only room Morag's deal gave her dominion over. Its furniture now sat beneath a cheap yard shelter on the lawn next to the garden gate. She had put furniture broken beyond repair in the skip and saved the rest, most of which needed only polishing or reupholstering. "How old do you think this floor is?"

Cosima tipped her head at the foot-wide, buttery-smooth planks of the wood floor Edie had revealed by pulling up the carpet, removing tacks, and running a rented buffer for several hours. "If it's not original, it's nearly."

"That would make it almost three hundred years old."

"I think this must be Victorian, though." Cosima walked across the empty room to the fireplace Edie had found under a more modern box and a mantle made from drywall and pine. The elaborate cast iron fireplace beneath had survived Edie's inexpert attention with steel wool and beeswax to take on a dark glow. Under the carpet, a glossy tile hearth was hiding, with handmade tiles in a relief pattern that matched the one on the fireplace—oak leaves and ivy.

"I called someone on Morag's list to come have a look at the chimney."

Cosima nodded. "Did you call someone for the plaster?"

Edie had stripped the mauve-and-brown flocked wallpaper to reveal lime plaster that needed some repair. The reception had never been wallpapered, its plaster kept up with a creamy mineral paint Edie had found a few cans of in the inn's shed, and she thought the best plan would be to make them match. "I did. I'm hoping it's mostly sound."

Cosima shoved her hands into the pockets of the green coveralls she'd been wearing in the garden. Her hair was schooled into a tight braid, and she wore socks, ready to step into her wellies by the kitchen door.

Ready to avoid Edie some more.

It was the third day of this. Seven left before Cosima would have to leave. Then Edie would be here another week with only Morag to cry on before she scraped herself into a plane. On the other side, her mother would be waiting in her Dodge Ram in the pickup line at the Green Bay airport.

"Do you think we could have tea before you went into the garden?" She tried to make her voice sound casual and not like she was pleading for her life.

Cosima shook her head. "Okay."

"No? Or okay?"

Cosima looked at her pink socks. "Okay. I will have tea."

"I won't poison it." Edie made her way to the kitchen, glancing back at Cosima to make sure she was following.

"I know that." The other woman sighed and then disappeared into the pantry. She emerged with Edie's bourbon creams and her own Jammie Dodgers. "But I've been assiduously avoiding you, and your offer of tea is an affront to my project." She smiled, barely, sitting down on a stool around the work table.

"Why, though?" Edie started the kettle. When Cosima opened her mouth to speak, she lifted her hand. "No, I know. The letter spooked you. Clearly, my kisses pledged your heart to mine forever, they were that good—"

"Don't joke."

Edie's stomach sank at the deserved reprimand. She had paused by Cosima's door and by the garden gate so many times, desperate to talk to her. To figure this out. "I'm sorry. That wasn't fair. But why do we have to avoid each other? What is it that you think I want?" Edie leaned on the table, looking into Cosima's sky-blue eyes for the first time in hours and hours.

"If we avoid each other, we can pretend like our kissing is without consequences. If we go to Barcelona, find out who Minnie is, and learn just how bad the ending to this story is, we'll be piling sad onto sad."

"We don't know it's bad!" Edie yanked a stool under her butt, annoyed. This was the same argument they'd had several times now, whenever they *tried* to talk, eating their meals or having tea. Even when they pledged to keep things light and not talk about it. It was the argument that had started right after Edie read the letter and continued the whole way home on the train. "Maybe Minnie didn't follow Agatha's clues in the guest book, but that doesn't mean we can be sure they didn't end up together. There's lots and lots of ways two people can end up together." Edie knew her voice had gone husky, but she had finally captured Cosima out of the garden, and they had to find a way to resolve this. Her heart felt like she'd spent three days ripping carpet tacks out of it.

Cosima studied the biscuit packets. "I know that."

"You do?"

"Obviously, I do. Obviously, I've been trying to think of any way that we can just . . . not go back to California and Wisconsin." Cosima had deftly switched from Minnie and Agatha to her and Edie. That was how their argument went. "But, as I explained, I am on a do-or-die timeline right now that is going to turn into a black hole of obligation and work the moment—"

"Yes, you told me all of that."

"And you told *me* that you have a job waiting." Cosima put both of her palms flat on the table. "That you have to rebound, at least financially. That you're not sure what your new goals are, and, to be honest, I don't know what mine are either. Have

I known for some time, for many years, that I'm not interested in the life of a studio mogul? Yes. Again, *obviously*, because when my mother offered me that life, I turned it down. You've not met my mother, so you cannot know what a difficult thing that was to do. But how do I make a decision about my whole future when the only things I can think about are the David Austin Roses catalog and the freckles on your thighs?"

Cosima near-shouted this last part, just as the kettle whistled. The air whooshed out of Edie's lungs.

Every muscle she possessed was ruined from the physical work she had been throwing herself at for the last seventy-two hours. Her hands smelled like buffing wax. At night, when she sank her body into hot water in the enormous tub in the bathroom, she hissed as the water stung new blisters. But none of this in any way impeded her response to Cosima. The way her heart wobbled. How every nerve filled with horny longing.

She pulled the kettle off the hob with a clumsy clatter.

"Don't come over to my side of the table," Cosima warned.

Edie hadn't been headed toward Cosima. Now she wanted to. "I *am* coming over to your side of the table." Edie did.

Cosima stood up and started moving around the table, away from Edie. "You can't. We have an agreement."

"We don't. If we'd come to an agreement of any kind since Rouen, I would definitely remember." Edie made it to Cosima's side just as Cosima slid in her socks to the end. "We haven't even agreed to disagree. What *I* want is you, no matter how bad an idea it is. I don't really see that we have a choice. We decided that on the balcony in Rouen. Nothing has changed except that now I also want to go to Barcelona, because I can't leave this story the way it was left in France."

Cosima held on to the edge of the table, her knuckles white and her eyes huge. "Edie."

Suddenly, she felt bad. What was she doing, *chasing* Cosima around an enormous table, talking about wanting her?

"I'm sorry. Please." Edie didn't know what she was asking for. "It's just, I've thought a lot about this, too. I've tried to talk myself out of it, to tell myself that it's just a proximity thing. Isolation. But I don't think that even *I* could fall for just anyone who I found myself holed up with in an end-of-the-world English inn. I wasn't counting on you. I can't believe how brave you are. I can't believe how we're neck and neck in the worst game about who has the worst life, and your chin still points that high into the air."

I can't believe how much I love you. That was what she was trying to say without taking the risk of saying it. *I can't believe how much I want you.*

"Stay there. Don't chase me." Cosima made her way to Edie until she stood directly in front of her, pink-cheeked and tall.

"What are you doing?" she asked.

"I have no idea what I'm doing." Cosima stepped even closer, until the canvas of their coveralls was nearly touching. "I should think that would be obvious."

"What do you want?" Edie raised her eyebrows, desperate to tease Cosima into giving her one of her smile kisses, but also afraid she would scare her off like a bird she held out a cupped palm full of seed to.

"Sit on the table." Cosima's blush was so red-hot, Edie was afraid she'd set her curly hair on fire.

"You want me to sit on the table." Edie put the heels of her palms behind her, on the smooth wood, ready to hop up. "Then what's going to happen?"

"Maybe I'm just going to make your tea and feed you bourbon creams."

Edie hopped up on the table, her eyes right on Cosima's.

Seawater blue. *Risk the ocean.* "You can feed me if that's what you want."

Cosima rolled her eyes, but she smiled, and then Edie heard the underwater whoosh of Cosima's hands holding both sides of her head, covering her ears, before her palms slid down to either side of her neck. She opened her legs so Cosima could step as close as possible, and she did, her hips fitting between Edie's legs so well that Edie wrapped her thighs around Cosima's hips, her arms over her shoulders.

Her entire body sighed in relief.

"Call me princess," Cosima breathed against Edie's mouth.

Edie used her tongue to pull the bow of Cosima's upper lip into her mouth, and when she sucked it against her teeth and Cosima made a rough noise, Edie slid her hands over Cosima's front and unzipped her coveralls to the waist, revealing Edie's familiar Green Bay Packers T-shirt. "You stole my shirt."

Cosima kissed Edie's lower lip. "You left it in the bathroom. It smelled like you. Call me princess."

She didn't. She snuck her hands into the coveralls and onto Cosima's waist, pulling up the hem of the tee until she felt her bare skin, soft, so soft, and hot. "I like that you stole my shirt. You should know that I'm not wearing a shirt under my coveralls."

Cosima kissed Edie's lower lip again, and Edie used her legs and hands on Cosima's waist to pull her closer and deepen the kiss, and then, impossibly, the kiss slowed—impossible because it was clear neither one of them could get enough of each other, enough closeness, enough touch, enough breath, and this should've meant a kiss that was heated, frantic.

But this was a kiss with an iron anchor, pulling them both under, reassuring them of the perfect vastness of their want. Edie felt the melting sensation again, her pulse a naked throb, and as if she had said out loud, *I want you*, Cosima's hips pressed into her, and they found a rhythm of their bodies against each other that echoed their kiss.

Cosima slowly bit her way over Edie's jaw, her earlobe, her neck. It was preposterous that they hadn't been doing this since they came back from France. They could've been doing this *while* they argued about going to Spain.

"Cosima."

"Hmm." She softly bit her way back up again, stopping to pull Edie's earlobe into her mouth.

"*Fuck*." Cosima sighed with pleasure.

"What *are* you wearing under this?" Cosima tugged down Edie's zipper as Edie kissed her forehead, her temple. She ran her hands up Cosima's sides under the Packers tee, and there wasn't a bra, but Edie edged herself with the velvety bare skin of Cosima's sides, her armpits, letting herself fully fantasize about her breasts.

"Ah, god." Edie pushed her hips forward as Cosima pulled down one of the cups of her bra, which was the one printed with apples housing smiling green worms.

"Edie," Cosima whispered.

She opened her eyes. Cosima was brushing her fingertips over one of Edie's breasts. Edie had big breasts, something that had never not been a very mixed experience, and revealing them could be vulnerable for her. She tried to see the same thing Cosima did—her heavy breast spilled over the shoved-down cup, the bunched nipple almost disappearing among the freckles, pure eroticism—but it was hard not to notice the red welts from her bra, how her breast hung from her chest, and she felt herself stiffen involuntarily.

Cosima eased her hand away. "Not okay?"

Edie took a deep breath, turned on and shy at once. "It's okay. I'm self-conscious about them, but you feel good."

Cosima pulled back a little, and Edie had to move her hands to give her room. She grabbed the hem of the green and gold T-shirt and yanked it up to her neck, exposing her entire naked torso to Edie's delighted inspection. "I feel that way, too. They're so small, except for the one that is trying to be bigger than the other. One of my nipples is inverted." She touched the nipple, its edges tight, its tip pulled inward. Edie was so wet, it was hard to focus on how sexy Cosima was with the shirt ruched under her chin, her naked tits as flushed as her chest, their asymmetry somehow making her seem more naked, more exquisitely fuckable, which then turned her own self-consciousness on itself and made Edie want to strip her clothes off in front of this woman and let her examine every part of her, put her mouth on every part of her, and then return the privilege.

"Okay, fuck," Cosima said with a wet kiss to the side of Edie's mouth, "you're so hot, can we—"

"We can, princess," Edie whispered into Cosima's smile, finally giving her what she wanted.

They could. They pressed their breasts together, moaned into a sloppy kiss, and then their hands were everywhere, their mouths. They were going to fuck right on this five-thousand-year-old table with the Aga looking on, and it was going to be the best sex of Edie's life when she had already had the best sex of her life with this woman in France, but that was how it was with them, wasn't it?

That was why they were in so much trouble.

Cosima had Edie's coveralls partway off one shoulder and Edie had just placed a kiss that would leave a mark on one of Cosima's breasts when the kitchen door banged open, making both of them yelp and grab at their coveralls. Edie nearly fell off the table in her haste to leap off it. Their zippers were hardly up before Morag burst in, a hulking man behind her who had to be seven feet tall.

"Jesus Christ, Morag! I only have the one heart! You have a phone! I've seen you text!"

Morag hung up her handbag on the hook by the door and shrugged out of her coat. "Doesn't look like you would've paid any attention to a text, does it?"

Edie checked her zipper, died a little, and zipped it up the last three inches. "You didn't say you were coming back from your sister's!"

Morag crossed her arms. "And why would I have to? This is my inn, isn't it? Better question is what the two of you are doing here when you should be on a plane to Barcelona already. You take a lot of tea breaks clearing out a single room? Were you too busy making my inn look like a boot sale with the furniture spread out under a tent in the front garden?"

The heat of Edie's lust transformed into anger at this string of uncalled-for criticism. "What is your deal? Ever since we've come back from France, you've grown more spikes than a hedgehog. *You* wanted me to redo the lounge. *You* gave me free rein. We told you we hit a snag in France. Do you want us to find the treasure or not? Do you want to update this inn or not?" Her ears were hot. Never a good sign.

"I'm just looking for a bit of follow-through! Who's young with all their wits about them, rich"—she tossed her head in Cosima's direction—"and at least partly clever"—she flicked her wrist at Edie—"and gives up a treasure hunt across Europe because of an old letter? I thought Americans were supposed to be tough, but you're both soft as trifle. Come back here pitching and mooning over each other and not talking, knowing there's more in Spain, and instead Cosima's making a mess of the garden and you're throwing away quality furniture!"

Morag's voice didn't shake, but there was more than anger in it. What was going on here? What didn't Edie know?

They stared at each other, and the tension meant Edie couldn't decide if she should offer Morag a chair and a cup of tea or if she should scream.

Her inclination was to scream. She felt like it might get them somewhere faster.

"Ma'am." The giant who'd come in with Morag cleared his throat. "If you could just point me to the lounge, I'll get on."

"Who are you?" Edie demanded.

Morag hooked her thumb over her shoulder. "He's come for the plaster. Did you even phone around? Everyone knows the Whippledurn brothers charge a king's ransom for a slap of patch."

The man looked at the ceiling. "If I should go on, then—"

"No," Edie said. St. John Whippledurn was who she'd called to fix the plaster. Morag's list didn't have a name for plaster repair on it. "Follow me to the lounge, and I'll get you started."

She shot Morag one last look that made her scowl, and then the man followed Edie into the lounge, where he seemed relieved to be surrounded by cracked plaster and relative silence.

"You know my granddad plastered this place. Back in the sixties, it would've been. Since he did the job, I doubt there's anything needed more than a few repairs and a smoothin' out to get ready for paint." He looked around appreciatively. "He always said it would be satisfying to see this inn back to bones. Never understood why Morag put in wallpaper and wall-to-wall. Shame, that. Looks a treat now."

"Morag was the one who made the shrine to mauve?"

"That's right."

Edie considered the room—now so much brighter, objectively more beautiful, and, what's more, definitely more to Morag's taste, given her preference for sturdy linen aprons, good leather boots, and her walnut rocker.

Morag had spent a lot of money to make this room pink, so she must have thought it would bring in many more modern guests. Based on the guest book, she hadn't been wrong. What was strange was how long it had taken her to remodel once the look became tired.

"Listen, I know you came in today to do an estimate and give me your opinion," Edie said. "But since you're familiar, if you're able, I think you could get started."

St. John rubbed his hands together. "Right. Good. I'll just prop open the lounge door then and load in my gear."

He disappeared as Morag came in.

"You hired the Whippledurn boy?"

"That man is at least fifty."

"Hmpf." Morag stepped around Edie and looked at the lounge for a long time. It was golden hour, and spring had been racing into this part of England all week. The "bones" did look good. The light showed it off, while a breeze kicked up the smell of beeswax and cleanser. "Seems you got on fine here."

"That's all you have to say?"

Morag turned around. "I can supervise one Whippledurn. I'd have expected you away by now."

Edie couldn't figure out Morag's urgency around the treasure hunt after so many years. Her eyes were still all laser, without even a trace of fondness in them. Her posture was straight, but she held her shoulders tight. Something was wrong.

"After the letter in France, it didn't feel like our business," Edie said, trying once more to pick her way through this conversational minefield. "It seemed like this may be not so much of a treasure hunt as a trail of breadcrumbs left behind after a bad breakup between Agatha and somebody else. But I have to believe you would know more about that than I would."

"Who knows anything about any of that?" Morag huffed. "I keep well and away from the business of my guests."

"Lies!" Now Edie could feel lasers coming out of her own eyes. So much for careful. "I haven't had even one moment in this inn without you bossing me."

"Go to Barcelona, or you won't polish one more stick of my inn." Morag turned on her heel and walked out of the lounge, across reception, and disappeared into the kitchen.

Edie passed by Cosima on her way out. "Is everything all right?"

She took a breath to consider. Was everything all right? Was this particular situation she'd gotten herself into *good*? When she booked this trip—this time out for her broken heart—she hadn't had the slightest inkling that she would be fighting with the village witch, tearing apart an inn, hunting down a treasure across Europe that turned out to be an old and sad love story, and doing it with a woman more likely to step out of one of her dreams than be real.

"I don't know," she said honestly. It felt good to give up on being careful and simply tell Cosima the truth. "It's not a state of being I'm used to. Most of the time, I switch back and forth between wild hope and black dejection. More than not knowing anything, I'm worried about the aftermath of fighting a mythical creature disguising herself as an old woman."

"You two have been getting into it since the moment you arrived, but I think that's just how you're friends. I wouldn't worry."

Maybe Cosima wasn't worried, but Edie was. She liked Morag. She'd thought they had a special connection, but it wasn't enough of a connection to tell her what to do next. "If I can't worry about Morag, should I worry about what we managed to get up to on the prep table?"

"Whoa. Do not bring your angst into those absolutely perfect five minutes on that prep table, which we both very much enjoyed and wanted and, I'm certain, would be happy to repeat." Cosima slapped her hands on her garden-dirty coveralls thighs. "I think we should let the map show us what to do. We should let this hunt make our decisions. I admit that I freaked out when I read the letter, but you're right. We need to know what happened to this couple, Agatha and her Minnie, and if it's really as bad as I decided to believe."

Edie looked through the dining room at the doorway to the kitchen. Morag had financed this treasure hunt after years of hiding its first clues from anyone interested. She'd been cagey about what they discovered in Rouen, and now she was angry they weren't going to Barcelona. But her motives weren't financial. Edie and Cosima had agreed on the train back from France that it seemed unlikely there was a treasure to find. Only a story.

Morag was Edie's friend. And Morag cared about this story. In any event, there would be no making up with Morag until she was willing, so she could cool off while Edie and Cosima were in Spain.

"I think you're right that I'm right. But no matter what, you *are* going back to California, and we *are* a train flying a hundred miles an hour down a track toward a bridge that's gone out."

Cosima straightened, and somehow her coveralls arranged themselves into crisp lines. The two tails of the scarf she'd knotted to tie her hair back in were precisely the same length, its gold picking up the green and gold of Edie's Packer's T-shirt. "I don't believe I'm wrong about how I feel about you right now," she said. "Or about how much this treasure hunt has already disrupted my life in a good way. And I don't want you to tell me what to do, ever, any more than I want fear to tell me what to do. I'm willing to go where the map tells me, and I want you with me. In fact, I insist."

The vase on the reception desk held Morag's week-old arrangement, its ferns and blood-dark flowers unwilted, the bird tied to its stick as alive-looking as ever, watching Edie to see if she would take another chance on what she wanted or if she would let a Green Bay vegan cheese shop be the only risk she ever allowed herself.

I want you with me. In fact, I insist. Had anyone ever said such a thing to her?

No. No one ever had.

She hadn't believed anyone ever would.

"I assume everything I'm excited about will end in failure," she said, "so you will have to continue to remind me how right about everything we both are."

"I will."

"And, to be clear, I'm *very* excited to go to Barcelona, but I'm deliriously excited about you."

The princess of Gregory Place pulled herself away from the reception desk to stand in front of Edie. "Do you want to get on a plane to Barcelona with me and see what happens?"

"More than anything," she admitted. "More than anything, ever, I want to."

Cosima reached for Edie's hand and laced their fingers together, pulling Edie close. "This is why Morag didn't let anyone look at that guest book," she said, her voice husky. "She knew it was dangerous."

Edie leaned up on her tiptoes, and Cosima met her mouth halfway.

"Pardon me, ladies."

They pulled apart, startled, as St. John Whippledurn nodded at them both, holding a ladder and pushing a hand truck stacked with supplies. "I'll squeeze myself through. No worries at all."

He brushed past them, and Edie slapped her hand over her mouth to stop the laugh. "Truly nothing goes unwitnessed in this village."

Cosima shook her head. "I'll call Tam to have Killian take us to the train. We'll go to London. You buy the next available plane tickets."

They left the room to the sound of St. John's cheerful whistling.

Chapter Seventeen

"It's not cheating!" Cosima tried not to be exasperated with Edie as she put her bag down by a ten-foot-long curved white sofa. It faced a bank of windows that looked out over a pool set into a stone patio in such a way that it appeared faceted out of the rock. Steam rose from the water.

She collapsed onto the sofa like a teenager, reaching for a slice of pocket-sized muskmelon that had been arranged with champagne grapes and what looked like almond cookies on a tray. A globe of glass filled with crystalline water held an arrangement of miniature yellow orchids on long stems.

The staff had done a beautiful job.

"Why did Phoebe Frank have a seven-bedroom villa in Barcelona? How did this never come up? Why didn't you mention it, perhaps, at some point after we figured out the dead cat letter led us to Spain on Agatha's map?"

Cosima raised an eyebrow at Edie, who'd been asking these questions while unlacing her shoes in preparation to shove them off onto the flat woven white carpet. "Sometimes she worked in Barcelona."

"Sometimes I cater in Appleton, but I don't have a seven-bedroom villa there."

Edie sounded as though she was enjoying this argument. She'd been in a good mood throughout their journey on the express train from Grantham to Heathrow and over the pond on a budget flight. Cosima had made arrangements by text for the villa to be prepared for their arrival, and Spain still had proper taxis, so Edie hadn't figured out where they were staying until Cosima tapped the code into the keypad at the entry.

Her protests had started up immediately thereafter.

"Sometimes we took a short vacation here," Cosima explained. "Or lent it out to friends."

Edie crossed her arms over her red sweatshirt. It was another item of clothing that was obviously just hers, like the shirt with mice. It fit her body perfectly and was made from a drapey material that bared one shoulder and a black bra strap. So far, Cosima had refrained from fondling that rounded, freckled shoulder, but she had little restraint left. Edie's hair was loose, falling nearly to her waist. She looked edible.

"And I thought you got a C in Spanish," Cosima shot back. "What was that display of perfect Spanish with the taxi driver?"

Edie sat down gingerly on a leather sling chair that she would be horrified to learn was an antique and probably five times more expensive than the sofa. "I got a C in *school* Spanish. But I live in Green Bay, and despite its reputation for being whiter than white, in fact my hometown is *also* home to Mexican immigrants and their children and grandchildren. You want to eat conchas in the snow? Come to Green Bay. I worked as a server at my closest friend's family's Mexican restaurant on and off for years. It would be shameful if I didn't speak a little Spanish. You know what *I* didn't know, other than that you were going to shamelessly break the rules of our agreement and lure me into this palace? That Spanish isn't the main language in Barcelona. It's Catalan. The taxi driver gave me a whole lecture to correct my ignorance."

"In Spanish."

"In Catalan, mostly. But he switched back and forth, so I got the gist of it."

"Come here." They'd had to sit in separate seats on the plane. She'd been torturing herself thinking about what they'd gotten up to before Morag burst in on them and what they might have gotten up to if she hadn't. "You know, this is a home, my family's home. Our staying here is actually a frugal decision."

"I still think it's cheating," Edie said as she stood up and took a step toward Cosima. "There's a significant element of overhead. Whatever it costs to heat up a pool for two people. That melon you ate in two bites that I happen to know costs eight dollars a pound wholesale."

Edie was definitely fake-protesting at this point. Which meant she was real-flirting.

"On the other hand," Cosima said, willing Edie closer with her mind, "you might consider that Phoebe *wanted* me to stay at the Gregory Inn. I promise you she would have insisted that we follow this map and, when the map led us here, been insulted if we didn't stay. We have to do this in her memory."

"In memory of Phoebe Frank? Utter takedown." Edie carefully toed off her Converse onto the wood part of the floor while maintaining eye contact, giving Cosima hope she planned to crawl onto the sofa next.

"This place isn't precious." Cosima looked around at the pale woods and pale stone, as much evidence of Duncan's influence as the pink marble, gilt, and dark wood of Phoebe's Old

Hollywood Beverly Hills castle were of hers. "We could relax here. There have been a lot of deals made, but only between meals and siesta."

Edie took the final few steps and sunk into the sofa beside her. Cosima inwardly rejoiced. She turned her body to face Edie and scootched to get as close as she could.

"You've been happy in this place." Edie was searching Cosima's face, her green eyes serious. She bit her lip. "Your mom?"

It was a direct question, not careful, but full of empathy for a difficult subject. Edie wouldn't make any demands, and her question didn't make Cosima's stomach hurt. Even if it did make her heart hurt.

"I never saw her drunk, you know?" She inhaled, sharp, surprised at her audacity, though of course Phoebe wasn't about to walk into the room. She was gone. Cosima waited until her heart steadied. "What that means is that I *did*, all the time, but I never saw that she was impaired. I grew to understand that her biggest problem was secrets. When her liver started to fail, I learned from her doctor she had checked herself into discreet rehabs more than once. I didn't know. Duncan only knew about one time. But with something like rehab, you're supposed to trust the people that love you to get you through. I had a nurse tell me that when you keep your problems to yourself, you stop having perspective. You start to believe everything is your fault. Then you drink more. Hurt yourself more."

"We both know that's true."

Cosima picked up a hank of Edie's silky hair and ran it through her fingers. "Is *this* the part of our game where the discomfort and social embarrassment settles over us like a black cloud?" She smiled.

"What a terrible game. I'm sorry I subjected you to it. But

at the time, you would only open up to me if I let you be miserable."

She laughed. "We are not sad stories," Cosima said. She leaned forward and settled her lips against Edie's temple.

Edie slipped her leg over Cosima's hip, making her shiver. "What time does La Sagrada Família open tomorrow?" The letter had referred to Gaudí and the "Sacred Family," which Cosima had known could only be the architect's world-renowned basilica in Barcelona.

"I made tickets for a ten-thirty tour." Cosima traced her finger around Edie's kneecap. "I can hire a car or we can call a taxi—"

"A taxi." Edie's jaw was stubborn. "I would never hire a car."

"What else would you never do?" Cosima didn't quite recognize her own low, teasing voice, but the woman asking this daring question wasn't entirely unfamiliar. She'd been inside Cosima, patient, waiting for Edie Whitelock.

Edie picked up a slice of melon. "Hmm." She licked melon juice off her thumb, then took a bite. "Generally, I have a never-say-never philosophy, though I would grant that it's narrowed a bit as I've gotten older. I'm twenty-nine next month, so I feel the wisdom of age coming over me."

Cosima snorted as Edie smiled at her around her last bite of melon. "You know I was giving you a line, right?"

Edie turned to Cosima, tightening the leg around her hips, then ran her finger over Cosima's bottom lip until she opened her mouth and pulled in Edie's finger, sticky with melon juice, and sucked it, making everything clench in a wave that felt like almost coming.

"*Fuck.*" Edie's green eyes had gotten so dark, they matched her hair. She gently pulled her finger out, then put it in her own mouth, pressing it against her tongue.

Then, Cosima couldn't get her lips to Edie's fast enough. Her body was trying too hard to rush it, to seduce her to come or make Edie come. But Cosima wanted to savor these heartbeats *before,* with her upper lip against Edie's teeth, their tongues sliding past each other, the way a moan vibrated against her neck. She dreamed about kissing Edie. She woke up touching her mouth, feeling her there. Most of her brand-new fantasies were replays of kissing Edie, sometimes of one moment that couldn't have lasted even a second, like the first time their lips touched and she'd understood so much about herself at once.

"Cosima." Edie was kissing the underside of her jaw, and she was pretty sure that somehow this kissing had unknotted the tie at her waist. Her jersey dress felt slack.

"Yes?"

Edie eased back. Her freckles were connected by little blooms of flush. Cosima admired how much she'd messed up her hair. "We're alone?"

"We are."

"No one has a reason to let themselves in? Or interrupt us with a hulking monster of a plasterer? It's just us until ten-thirty tomorrow morning, and right now it's—"

"Nine forty-five at night." Cosima read the time off the sleek, midcentury Cartier desk clock at the end of the stone mantel.

"There are seven bedrooms."

"Yes. The one I use is on this floor. When I shot up in height at seventeen, we came here for part of the summer, and I threw a tantrum over my feet hanging off the end of my antique bed. Duncan had a comically huge mattress delivered. It requires custom sheets."

Edie quirked an eyebrow. "Do you want—"

"Yes."

"You have no idea what I was going to say!"

"You confirmed the existence of bedrooms and then started to ask a question, so the answer's yes." Cosima brushed her hand down Edie's arm. "I want to. But also, I want whatever *you* want to happen. I don't know how to explain it, but that's how it works for me."

Edie traced a finger along every one of Cosima's fingers on Edie's thigh.

She tried to steady her heart. She focused on Edie's expressive face, her pretty eyes, the cleavage that had revealed itself in their kissing and touching.

"I want this, too," Edie said. "So much. But I'm afraid of what I'm always afraid of. That I want the wrong thing. That I've set myself up for disappointment. I worry about getting into my head. I worry about getting *out of* my head and becoming someone's weird sex story at the bar." Edie frowned.

"Have any of those things happened? In France? In the inn's kitchen? Right now?"

"No. God. I haven't . . . it's never been like it is with you. And I never thought I'd even say something like that out loud, because I would've thought it was corny. But it's so true. Everything feels good. Everything is what I want."

Cosima moved herself closer. "Do you want to go down the hall and into my bedroom?" The question sent heat over Cosima's skin. It made her middle disappear. Her mouth needed Edie's mouth.

"Yes." Edie pulled in a breath that hollowed out her throat. "What if I told you what else I wanted?"

Cosima closed her eyes, happiness flooding into her system like hot sun. "Tell me." She wanted to laugh, she was so excited. "Do you want to go to the screening room and watch a movie?"

Edie kissed her. She would never get over how good that felt. "No."

"We could find something to eat. I told the staff you were vegan, and they said something about vegan tapas." She put her tongue in Edie's ear, which was burning hot and made her more desperately horny than she already was.

"I'm not hungry." Edie's hands slipped into her open dress to grip her waist. She ran her thumbs over Cosima's navel, making her wet.

Cosima smiled. "I ordered some things that I brought with me that could give us some ideas."

Edie let go of Cosima's bottom lip, which she had just sucked between her teeth, and sat back. "Excuse me? Roll that one back."

Cosima put both her hands over her mouth, feeling her blush in her hairline, but that was mostly due to her excitement. "Do you want to see?"

"You, in the period between hitting the brakes in France and getting on a plane to Barcelona, 'ordered a few things'"—Edie made air quotes, adorable—"for us? To bring on this trip? Adult items, to be clear."

"I would love to show them to you. I've never thought I was interested in the creative kinds of things people get up to, but lately I've found out that if it's you and me in a depraved setting, my imagination is absolutely unfettered."

"I want to see what you've got. You're good at shopping."

Cosima scooted out of the deep sofa and turned around and pulled Edie up. Her dress was falling open. Edie's sweatshirt slipped lower off her shoulder. Cosima ran to the foyer and grabbed her wheelie, then ran back with it, took Edie's hand, and pulled her toward the hallway to her room.

She wanted to tell her that she loved her. It turned everything on high instead of her body. Maybe she *would* say it, but first she would at least show Edie the toys she'd ordered in her room at the inn in the middle of the night, yearning for Edie down the hall.

She opened the door to her room, which smelled like lilacs and glowed blue from its close-up view of the pool.

"Fuck me, Cosima. You weren't kidding. The whole room is bed."

With a coy look over her shoulder, she let her dress fall the rest of the way off, leaving her in only her black tights and a black wisp of a bra. "What do you want *now*?"

Edie closed her eyes. "I want to get my jeans off. Crawl into this bed with you. See what you have in your suitcase with the fancy logos all over it."

"Can I help with the jeans part?" Cosima bit her finger, looking at Edie's tight jeans.

She laughed. "Yes."

"Sit on the bed."

Edie sat, and Cosima immediately kneeled in front of her. Edie put a hand through Cosima's hair. She pulled off Edie's socks, delighted with the red polish on her toes. She grabbed her foot and kissed the arch.

"Whoa," Edie choked. "I've had those socks on all day."

Cosima stuck her tongue out at Edie. "I don't care. I've had a lot of thoughts about your toes in my mouth."

"Okay, fuck." Edie wiggled restlessly. "God help me."

Cosima laughed and held her foot for another moment, watching Edie watch her before she licked between Edie's toes, making Edie bite her bottom lip and turning herself on more than she thought possible.

"Lay back." Cosima ran her hands up Edie's legs as she laid back, and then she made short work of Edie's button and zipper, fisting the waistband and peeling the denim down. Her small white bikini panties had little hearts on them. They started to come along for the ride, and Cosima pulled slower. She watched the panties start to roll off with the jeans, exposing Edie's bare hips and a few curls of dark hair below the freckled swell of her belly. Edie had navel jewelry that centered a polished tigereye in her belly button, a bright gold bead pierced through the rim. Once Cosima got the waistband of the jeans to her thighs, the panties stayed where they were, half-off, half-on, and there was something so painfully erotic about that—how it looked, how it must feel for Edie, her bare skin on the duvet, her panties cutting into her hips—that Cosima had to rest her cheek against Edie's knee as she got the jeans the rest of the way off.

She was throbbing and breathless. She wanted to touch herself, or to touch Edie. "Whatcha doing?" Edie asked.

Cosima rubbed her nose against the soft skin of her inner knee. "Give me a minute."

"For?"

"I don't want to burst into flames before we're even both on the bed."

"That will be hard, because I'm already smoking up here."

Cosima kissed Edie's knee, tasting her soft skin, making Edie's legs rub against the duvet. She liked that. She liked seeing Edie's reactions to everything she did and knowing that Edie would tell her what she felt, what she thought, because she always did. Cosima stood up, a little sad to be leaving behind such an interesting position until she saw what Edie looked like laid out on the mattress, her hair everywhere, her sweatshirt up under her breasts, her panties pulled halfway down. "Oh."

"Oh?"

Cosima climbed up, and Edie slid back so they were both fully on the bed, Cosima over her on her forearms. "*Oh*, as in horny awe at how you look."

Edie kissed her slow, soft, wet, and it was just right for turning everything up, but slow enough Cosima felt like she could enjoy the ride and notice everything. Like how, when Edie's leg hitched over hers to get closer, to kiss deeper, Cosima felt the precariousness of those panties at the same time she felt Edie's hand toy with the waistband of her tights, and then they were trying to kiss and to get her tights off at the same time. They managed. Edie kissed her neck while running her finger under the back of her thong, and it didn't take much of that before Cosima had her hands up under Edie's sweatshirt and was fondling her breasts over what felt like a thin, tight camisole.

"What next?" Cosima panted, taking luxurious handfuls of Edie's breasts, already riding her thigh.

Edie rolled away a little, pulling her legs up, and ran her hands over her scalp looking at Cosima. "If there's more, I won't survive it."

"So you don't want to see what I bought?" Cosima got close to Edie again, kissed her mouth, kissed her cleavage, kissed the tigereye centered in her navel, making her jump, so she experimented and kissed a bit lower than that, breathing Edie in.

Edie went still, her thighs pressed together, but then she relaxed. Cosima looked up at Edie from between her legs. "Okay?"

"It's so, so okay. It's . . . the number-one thing I think about."

"When you touch yourself. The number-one thing you think about is getting eaten out." Cosima studied Edie's face. Stroked down Edie's thighs.

"Yeah."

"But."

"But it's also the number-one thing in real life that's sent me straight to overthinking. So then I switch gears and focus on the other person, and sometimes they seem relieved they don't have to, and my worry feelings and overthinking build, and sometimes I feel like I've rejected them, but I don't know what to say or do to make it better."

Cosima had thought about it, too. She'd thought about her tongue licking through Edie, everything as soft and wet as she was herself. She'd thought about putting her own slick fingers in her mouth, wondering how Edie tasted. But in all of her fantasies, she'd also imagined Edie begging for Cosima to eat her. She'd thought of how Edie would say her name, or say *please, princess.*

"So maybe for now we set that aside," Cosima said, kissing Edie's soft stomach. "You should know that I would like nothing more than for you to come against my face."

Edie put her head back on the bed and laughed. "God, Cosima. Where did you come from?"

"A castle." Cosima smiled, then slid to the edge of her bed, grabbed her suitcase, and unzipped the top enough to rummage around and find the two cloth bags she'd packed. She pulled them out. They were bright pink with the name of a London adult toy store printed on them. She got herself back to Edie, kissing her and putting the bags between them. She started to grab one, and then Edie put her hand over the opening.

"Before we take a look." Edie laid her palm against Cosima's face. Her upper lip had swollen. Her freckles made starlight across her cheekbones. "It hasn't been like this, with anyone. You're taking care of me. You're sexy. There isn't going to be anyone else like you."

No, there isn't, Cosima thought. *Because you're mine, mine, mine.* She didn't say it, not yet, but she would. "I'm so glad you asked me for that walk."

It was the best thing that's ever happened to me.

Edie pulled Cosima to her, and her mouth was so perfectly sweet. "All right, princess. Let's see it."

Cosima grinned and sat up, and Edie sat up, too, her shirt doing nothing to be a proper shirt and instead revealing new parts of Edie every time she moved. Cosima wasn't complaining. She undid the drawstring of the first bag and grabbed the two items, pulling them both out at the same time and holding them up.

"Cosima *Frank*. I would have never." Edie's eyebrows were at her hairline as she took the hot pink harness and dildo from Cosima's hands.

"I would have never, either, but you make me think about a lot of new things." Cosima took the strap set back. "But unless you tell me different, these are mine."

"Is that right?"

"It *might* be right. Obviously, you would need to agree, but the harness *is* my size, so there's that. I'm perfectly willing to slide these back in their bag." Cosima picked up the cotton drawstring.

"Um. Don't do that." Edie ran her finger down the dildo's strategic bumps. "I know I have a kind of tomboyish presentation, and I struggle with expressing myself in bed. Probably that's why I'm usually the one tagged in for this, even though . . ." Edie shrugged, then looked at the set again in a way that made Cosima wet.

"I want to fuck you," she said, and the pulse throbbed in her wrists as vulnerability sluiced over her in goose bumps. "Tonight, or anytime."

Edie looked away, but smiled. "What's in the other bag?"

Cosima uncinched the bag and pulled out the white, cordless wand. "My favorite. I intimidated myself buying the strap set and then impulse-bought my old faithful. Plus, I wasn't sure we'd get here, and I wanted a backup plan."

Edie laughed. "Should we see where we get to?"

Cosima met Edie's mouth and reached for the hem of Edie's sweatshirt, and Edie helped her pull it off, then reached around to the hook in Cosima's bra, which she shrugged off with a moan as soon as it was undone. She gently pushed Edie to the bed, and they yanked her cami-bra off between kisses, and didn't stop kissing even when they struggled to shove off their panties.

God, the feel of Edie everywhere, soft and right and so good and unlawful and forbidden—it took her apart. They'd settled on their sides, their legs entwined, their hands everywhere, when she felt Edie against her thigh, so wet. Cosima gasped. It was a moment that shot through her, hot and sudden and so erotic, tears came to her eyes.

"You okay?" Edie panted.

"Better than okay." Cosima loved how Edie's flush made her pale freckles recede and her darker freckles rise up in new patterns. She loved how the strands of her long hair clinging to her neck made her look like a mermaid. She loved how her full breasts made Cosima feel wild and dirty with them pressed against her chest. She loved that she had never felt so good, so *right* that it hurt.

It was okay if this love broke her apart. Cosima was starting to believe that was what love, true love, might be for.

"Princess." Edie said it on an inhale as Cosima kissed her temple and pressed her thigh against Edie.

"Yeah."

Edie's hands skated up from where they had been on Cosima's hip and nape and captured her face. "I don't know how this works when it's been weeks and not months or years, but I should tell you that I love you, because we *have* made it to here, and I can't go farther if I don't say."

Cosima couldn't breathe. She hadn't hoped, hadn't let herself wonder. "Edie."

"I love you," she said again. "And I know it's not just the moment, because I've been heading toward this since at least Gregory Gregory's manor, or maybe since you threw that rock that knocked my boot down the hill. I tried to be smart and think through everything first, but it turns out I can't be naked with the woman I love and not talk about it. I understand if this means we should take a minute and heat up some vegan tapas and watch a movie. That would be one of many reasonable responses."

"I love you." Cosima gripped Edie's shoulders between her hands. "This would not be happening if I didn't, I'm perfectly sure. For me, there isn't where *this* begins and where my love begins, as two separate things. It's all the same, though I'd love you even if we weren't naked right now. There would just be more yearning. I was ready to love you and yearn for you until I withered away."

Edie laughed, a too-happy-not-to-laugh sound. "What are we going to do about this?"

"I don't know." Cosima kissed the corner of Edie's mouth. "It's a state of being."

Edie's thumb found the corner of her mouth, and then they were kissing, and it was even better, because Edie loved her, and Edie wasn't diplomatic, wasn't careful, didn't make silent rules. When Cosima's heart broke, she could tell this woman. When Edie's heart broke, she would say.

There were worse things than heartbreak. Worse than humiliation, worse than loss, worse than death, was never saying the things you needed to say. Never allowing yourself to feel the way you truly felt, to be the person you truly were.

If she'd never come here, never met Edie, she wouldn't know that.

It was why Cosima couldn't kiss Edie Whitelock and *not* believe in magic.

She slipped out of Edie's kiss and kissed her neck, lifted her breast in her hand and kissed it everywhere, licked the rough nipple, turned herself on more, felt Edie arch against her body. She brushed her hand over Edie's hip, then her thigh. Her inner thigh. "Can I taste you?" she asked. "I want to. You'll have to tell me what you like, because I want to be the best at giving you head. Better than anyone else could ever be for the rest of your life."

Edie choked, then laughed. "Yes, Jesus, Cosima."

She smiled as she kissed her way down Edie's body, grabbing hold of her wand along the way, cataloging every single inch of Edie while her legs refused to settle, and then she had Edie to herself—her inner thighs, the arrow of her dark curls, the way she looked, familiar and illicit at once. Cosima put the head of her wand into the cup of her high inner thigh and turned it on low, and even at an indirect hum, it made her clit pinch dangerously. But she wanted to come when Edie did, once she figured out how to make that happen.

She didn't know she wouldn't be able to hold on to her thoughts, or a technique, or a conquering plan, as soon as she tasted her—the moment Edie's fingers were in her hair, the very second that nothing was theoretical, or a fantasy. But she couldn't. It was only how Edie felt against her mouth, how her body moved, the prickle of Edie's hands tightening in her hair, the threatening orgasm from her rumbling wand. Every sense was an ungrounded wire, and Cosima was humping, touching, tasting, gone.

"There," Edie whispered on an inhale, her thighs going still when the flat of Cosima's tongue pressed alongside her clit. "Oh, god."

Cosima focused, then lost focus as Edie pressed herself against her mouth, her face, and she felt Edie letting go and had to yank the wand away from between her thighs so she wouldn't go over too soon. But then she realized Edie's hands were on her shoulders, her arms, trying to move her.

"Should I stop?" She closed her eyes tight, hoping she didn't have to stop, but also only wanting to give Edie everything she wanted.

"No, turn around. Let me—" Edie touched the side of Cosima's face, and Cosima looked at her. "Turn around."

Cosima had to breathe to keep herself from losing it right there. *Jesus.* She turned around, she wrapped her arms around Edie's thighs, and she almost died when she felt Edie's hands come around her hips, stroke up her inner thighs, tug her closer. Then her breath. Cosima was hot, all feeling, then Edie's mouth, the first touch, made her brain tunnel to one goal, the biggest orgasm of her life, which would take moments, a few moments and every day she'd been alive. She found the spot Edie had guided her to and kissed it again, licked, recovering her attention, testing until she hit the pressure and rhythm that made Edie's mouth pause and her hips buck, creating a feedback loop that made Cosima press herself against Edie's tongue.

Edie became her whole world, everything she wanted or needed, and too soon, too soon, she was pushing herself against Edie's face what had to be too hard, except she couldn't get enough of how Edie was pressing up, grinding, how breath had become superfluous and her body gorgeous and full of light.

She came in a long, hard shudder, her thighs shaking, and Edie was coming, she'd gone silent, her hips pressed up and still but for small movements, and she was wetter suddenly. Cosima didn't want it to end, didn't know she was still chasing aftershocks until they both went slack and she collapsed to Edie's side, her eyes closed, kissing the side of Edie's leg absently.

She loved her. She loved her.

"Come here," Edie whispered. Her voice was hoarse. Cosima turned and fit herself in her love's arms, her head in the nook of her shoulder, her leg over both of Edie's legs, just like she'd dreamed. She wasn't surprised when her throat closed and she felt tears spill over her cheek and against Edie's chin.

That was how she fell asleep, their skin cooling, her heart permanently spoken for, and Gregory Place's spellwork done.

Now it was up to them.

Chapter Eighteen

The young tour guide, whose name was Nerea, came to the end of her speech about the architect Gaudí, who had worked on this church for forty-three years but died before the project was complete. Tidy in her below-the-knee dark skirt and cabled sweater, she was washed in color from the stained-glass windows fit into hundreds of feet of white towers. When she frowned at Edie, it spoiled the dreamy effect.

Edie slapped her hand over her yawn. "Por favor, discúlpeme. Su tour es maravilloso. Me temo que tengo jet lag."

The tour guide nodded tightly.

Edie did not have jet lag, but she had good reason to be exhausted, even in the unbelievable hulking collection of stone-crystal towers that was Gaudí's La Sagrada Família, the Sacred Family basilica, growing up from the sun-washed, golden-roofed neighborhood of the same name like a cluster of smoky quartz.

It was gorgeous and weird, like nothing she'd ever seen, and it made her feel both rapturous and small. But Edie could not stop yawning because the woman to her right, prim in a chocolate brown sleeveless jumpsuit paired with another one of her silky full-coverage blouses, had kept her up all night. With sex. Sex like no sex she had ever had before. Orgasms upon orgasms. Feelings upon feelings. Rhapsodic, sacred eye contact and utter debauchery.

When Cosima looked at Edie, her expression was as stern as the tour guide's. But her eloquent eyes were smiling.

After she'd made Cosima show her how she liked to use her wand, they had shivered their way into the pool, which was as warm as bathwater, and told each other stories about themselves. This time, they weren't stories that revealed how their hearts had been broken or proved whose life was the worst. They were stories about where a scar had come from, and one of Cosima's fantastical trips with her mother, what a particular celebrity was like, how Edie cultured nut milk and built a cedar cooler to develop a perfect rind on vegan brie. They'd devoured the tray of tapas the villa's staff had left, each bite an ambassador for the produce of Spain. Edie had made Cosima open her notes app to write down what had gone into a skewer with ripe olive frito and thin pieces of preserved lemon.

They'd dozed between food and stories and kissing and patient orgasms until they realized the light coming into the villa was the pale gray that meant they had to shower and dress. Over vegan bocadillos with layers of thin-sliced roasted vegetables and peppery oil, they consulted the map. Its rendering of Spain indeed had a sketch of the basilica, this one accompanied by a nun with a ring of keys.

The tour guide began walking over the ochre floor, and Edie stifled another yawn. "How are you so perky?" she asked. "You look like you got eight hours and had a massage."

Cosima patted her smooth curls. "I didn't turn down a triple espresso."

"I can't have caffeine if I haven't slept." Edie tugged on the hem of her jacket. "It makes me see colors that don't exist."

When the guide stopped at a contemporary-looking nave, Cosima stepped them to the back of their tour group. "Can you ask Nerea if any nuns work here? I may not *look* tired, but I don't know if I can stand up for as long as this tour is going to last."

"We'll get in trouble. Remember Barnabus? He didn't like it when we ditched the group at Tattershall, and the tickets to this one were three times pricier. Nerea would string us up on a tower so the seagulls could peck out our eyeballs."

Cosima raised her hand.

"What are you doing!?"

The tour guide stopped mid-lecture, and every single person in their group turned around and stared at them. "Si?"

Cosima looked at Edie. "Translate for me. Ask her where the nuns work."

"What? No. Absolutely not."

"Señorita," Cosima began.

"Señora," the tour guide bit off. Edie looked under her feet for a handy trapdoor.

"Lo siento." Cosima cleared her throat. "Where could we find, um, la religiosa?"

Edie yanked her elbow from Cosima's grip. "Por favor, disculpe a mi amiga. Necesitamos consejo y nos gustaría hablar con una hermana. ¿Podría indicarnos dónde ir? No lo pediríamos si no fuera urgente. Gracias."

"Thank you," Cosima whispered. Edie glared at her.

The tour guide and the group had gone quiet, but an older woman who had come in with a young man smiled at Edie.

"There are some offices behind the crypt. If you're looking for a nun who works here, that's probably where to go, but I can't promise you'll be able to get back there. The sisters also present a meditation of singing at noon." Her Mexican accent was thick, but her English was perfect.

"Gracias, Señora." Edie smiled at the woman, feeling a little homesick for kind Mexican matriarchs who had been bossing her at her jobs for years. She looked at the tour guide for permission to depart. Nerea nodded once in irritation.

"Let's go." Cosima took her elbow again.

Edie gave another apologetic smile to the rest of the group before she followed behind Cosima's clicking heels, looking up at the fractal patterns the interior buttresses made, the windows, the carved and sculpted art everywhere, meant to create a feeling of golden satisfaction with the heavens. It took her breath away, although she couldn't be sure how much of that was due to Cosima's pace.

The crypt chapel was likewise a jewel, with rounded ceilings and artworks that would take decades to appreciate. "Where would the offices be? I haven't seen a door or an ordinary hallway in this place. I guess it's so we won't think of mortal life and mundane concerns when we're here. I'd probably have a better idea if my guess is correct if you hadn't made us leave the tour group." Edie was struggling to keep up now.

"Don't get distracted," Cosima said.

"I'm not." She was. She'd never been so distracted in her life. Her fatigue, her ecstatic bliss, the tender shoots of love bursting into bloom in her heart every time Cosima did something mundane like cut her breakfast sandwich in half before she ate it—all of it smashing into the visual feast of what was the single most beautiful edifice Edie had ever seen, an artwork so vast that it still wasn't complete nearly two hundred years since construction began—meant that she could not attend to anything in particular because she was trying to feel every feeling she'd ever had.

Then, Cosima lifted her arm for the second time in five minutes and *hailed* someone. A priest. Oh, god, she'd hailed a priest. "Padre, if you could spare a moment."

Other than the day they'd met, when Edie recognized her familiar eyes, this was the first time Cosima had reminded Edie of Phoebe Frank. Acutely. Killingly. Edie was willing to bet that Phoebe Frank would hail a priest *just like that*, and probably had, and Cosima had learned it from her.

This actually outrageous behavior told Edie a great deal about what it had been like for Cosima to spend her life with one of the most famous women in the world for a mother.

The priest blinked at Cosima for a long moment, then seemed to startle. He broke in their direction at a rapid walk that soon turned into a jog. He was in late middle age, his temples streaked white against dark hair that swooped over his forehead and curled behind his ears. His beaky nose made him interesting to look at. "Miss Frank, is it not?" he asked. "I remember when you were here with Señora Phoebe. Years ago." He extended both hands and, when Cosima gave hers to him, clasped it between them. "What can I help you with?"

"We're trying to solve a puzzle," Cosima said. "We have a map with a series of clues we've been following. It's led us here. The basilica is represented on this map with a drawing of a nun holding keys. Do you have any idea of the significance?"

Edie watched, fascinated, as the priest's face broke into a wide smile.

"I do," he said, nearly laughing. "I can't quite believe this day has come, but I do. I can't believe it is you at the end of this journey. If you'll follow me?"

Cosima did, of course, and kept up a polite conversation with the good-looking priest that Edie couldn't attend to as she trailed behind. If she burst into tears, would it be from the colors, from gratitude for vista after vista of beauty, or would it be from the sight of the woman she loved coming into her full princess powers right before her eyes?

They'd ducked into a less ornamented area, not quite a corridor. There were no straight lines here, which meant where they'd ended up felt more like a place Edie might discover beneath the canopy of a willow tree, if such a place could be built from pale stone. The priest knocked once outside a room and leaned into it, gripping the room's opening in strong fingers.

"Imagine this," he said to someone Edie could not see. "I have a woman here who's followed a map and is looking for the nun with the keys."

"If you're lying," a woman's voice said, her English more strongly accented than the priest's, "I'll make you pay for it."

The priest disappeared into the office, the sound of his laughter drifting out. Cosima stopped at the threshold, turning to spear Edie with a look. "Well, hustle yourself in here," she said. "You think I'm doing this without you?"

Edie hustled. She found herself settled into a sturdy wooden chair beside Cosima, before the desk of Sister Ona, if the nameplate was correct. The nun had short-cropped gray hair, a dark sweater, a silver chain around her neck with a bright silver cross, and a lit cigarette between her lips. She looked older than Morag. She pushed a tin of cookies in Cosima and Edie's direction. "Have one," she demanded. "The cloistered sisters make them. They're hard to find, but I have a source."

Edie peered into the tin. She took a crumbly cookie out and smelled anise. "Are these baked on bricks? Butter or olive oil?"

The nun's head disappeared below the edge of her desk,

where she'd opened a drawer with a screech of metal on metal. The priest stood behind her chair, his arms crossed, beaming. "I didn't think I'd be here to see this," he said. "I wasn't here for the beginning, of course, but I believed it would go on long past my time."

Sister Ona snorted. "Things come to an end, José Antonio. I knew *I* would live long enough for this day. I plan to live to see the building of this basilica to an end." The top of her head rose back into view, and she looked at Edie. "Bricks, yes. Olive oil." Then she dropped something white onto the desktop. It was a stack of envelopes. It immediately toppled, sending the one on top skating toward Cosima, who snatched it just as it was about to drop to the floor.

Edie took a bite of her cookie. "Did you know that cloistered nuns invented marzipan?" The question was mostly for herself, to help her focus. "They used to make cakes and pastries for the rich in exchange for donations."

Cosima opened the envelope and extracted a letter written on cream stationery. Edie wasn't sure she wanted to know what it said. She focused on the sandy cookie melting against her teeth with coarse sugar, the tang of anise both familiar and different from how it tasted back home.

"She sends a new letter every year." Sister Ona patted the pile of letters. "I've read all of her books. They are . . ." She looked at the priest. "Sobre gustos no hi ha res escrit?"

"There's no accounting for taste," he said.

Edie watched Cosima read the letter, her expression revealing nothing. After a moment, she passed it to Edie.

Agatha's handwriting was still strong, but the lines were slightly uneven. The handwriting showed the age of the author, and this made Edie's heart squeeze.

Darling Minnie,

If you're reading this, you've come to Barcelona. Love has triumphed over fear, or maybe you've become curious. I don't care which.

You told me you didn't know how to find the way to be with me, and I told you I would make you a map. I said it would be there when you were ready, and so would I.

Come to One Tree Cottage in Tintern. You said you wanted to see it someday. Is today someday?

I love you still.

Bronwyn A. Llewellyn

Edie's tears fell through the fingers of her hand she'd clasped over her mouth. She looked at Sister Ona. "How many?"

Ona put her hand on top of the stack. "Not quite fifty. The first one was handed to me in 1977. The others have come each year around Epiphany."

"And we're the first to ask for them?"

She nodded. "Agatha told me the person who claimed them would have a map. That was your ticket, though I suspect you're not who she's expecting."

Edie shook her head. Cosima and the priest were quiet.

"May I?" Sister Ona asked, holding out her hand.

Edie watched Ona read the letter, then shake her head much like Edie had. At last, she handed the letter to Father José Antonio, who read it and then solemnly kissed the top of the paper. He looked at Edie and Cosima. "What will you do? The messengers?"

"We'll go to Tintern, in Wales," Cosima said. "It's the only thing to do. Agatha has to know that Minnie never came back to the inn to start the hunt. She should know that Morag, the innkeeper in Harlaxton, had us go, I assume because Morag knows it's a lost cause or suspects it is. Or, at least, she knows something."

Edie felt lost. This evidence that Agatha had never stopped loving Minnie was unexpectedly devastating. Ever since Rouen, she'd hoped it wasn't the case—that the map was an old chase made by a romantic girl during a time when few queer people would have felt they could love who they loved no matter what. Cosima had told Edie about Tam and Killian, and about Tam's father. That was Minnie and Agatha's world, too. But now it was clear—Agatha had never stopped hoping. Never. The torch she held for Minnie was as bright as this paper, sent at Epiphany, which was in early January. Only last month.

"We have to go back to Gregory Place," she said. "Morag knew this treasure hunt wasn't to find gold or jewels, but she acted like it was. Negotiated a split. Even after the Rouen letter, she insisted we get back to it. I think she made us keep going so that she could settle her guest book. Or, I guess, get word to Agatha that whatever happened at the inn all those years ago wasn't happening? I don't know. But I don't think that's something we should do. What if Minnie's passed away? Or what if she's a grandmother or great-grandmother somewhere, and she doesn't want anything to do with this? We need to go back and sit Morag down and make a plan that's kind. We can't just show up on Agatha's doorstep and relieve her of her hope with no chance of closure. It's cruel."

The stack of letters on Sister Ona's desk felt like a sacred trust, an archive of one woman's most cherished dream. As much as she enjoyed reading about sapphic romance and queer history, Edie couldn't play tourist with someone else's heartbreak.

Not when her own was bearing down on her.

Cosima turned in her chair and took Edie's hand between both of hers, the same way the priest had clasped her hand in his. "I hear you, I do, but I still think we need to go to Agatha. Today. It's been too long. It's none of our business. It wasn't Morag's business either. If it were me, if this were *us*, Edie, I'd want some evidence that I hadn't been writing into a void all this time. I'd want some kind of permission to grieve. Maybe that's why we're both here. Because we can understand, can't we?"

Edie pulled her hand away to wipe her tears again. "I don't know. I don't think this is for us. It may be that we brought it to light, but I can't imagine we're supposed to finish this? Once and for all? That feels awful. I came to England in the first place with a broken heart. Now I don't know how you and me will end. I can't deliver heartbreak to this woman."

"Then who can?" Cosima argued. "Morag calls her? *Morag?* She's not known for her sensitivity."

"We said at the beginning if we didn't know what to do, we had to ask a third party."

"You picked last time. The Sixt clerk."

Edie nodded. Cosima looked between the priest and the nun, then back to Sister Ona. "You've been part of this since the beginning. What should we do?"

She folded her hands on the desk in front of her. "Father José Antonio will drive you to the airport. You can take a car to Tintern from Cardiff."

Edie's belly sank, but she reached for Cosima's hand anyway. Because if you couldn't reach for the woman you loved when you felt the worst, when could you?

She hoped Agatha hadn't been sad this whole time. She hoped her life had been good, even without Minnie.

Cosima squeezed her hand. “I know it seems impossible, but I think it’s going to be okay.” She said this in her most imperious voice, so Edie chose to believe it.

It would be okay. She couldn’t remember the last time she’d thought so. Even when she had tried to make a legacy and was running entirely on hope.

“So goes my princess, so goes my nation.”

Edie smiled and hoped that this time, everything would turn out different.

Chapter Nineteen

Twilight in the Welsh countryside wasn't something that Edie would soon forget.

The light was a scrim of purple-gray over everything. The bright spring flush on the trees and hedgerows glowed against the suppertime light. The gearshift of the Mini felt strange in her left hand, but the A466 from Cardiff was a forgiving route to learn UK rules of the road. She'd expected more pushback from Cosima about driving. Instead, she gave in quickly and fell asleep within minutes of beginning the drive. Edie was pretty sure she was a secret passenger princess.

At times, the A466 rose up to reveal the slow sparkle of the River Wye, which wound through this part of Wales. According to the map, One Tree Cottage overlooked the river. Agatha lived away from Tintern village, which sat on the main road. She was within walking distance of the famous Tintern Abbey.

When Edie was a sophomore in high school, she had an English teacher who read them the Wordsworth poem about the abbey. Edie remembered the stormy day her teacher had read it and how it sounded. There was a single line that she'd collected like a crow sitting in the classroom. It came to her every once in a while when she ran into a particularly pretty view driving around Wisconsin. *Connect the landscape with the quiet of the sky.*

She hadn't thought that someday she would be remembering that line in the place it had been written, far from home, and understand it deep inside her body.

Cosima's phone navigation indicated that the turn for the lane that led to One Tree Cottage was a half mile away. Edie downshifted and slowed. There were no other cars around. Slowing down was enough to wake up Cosima, who sat up and stretched her arms along the top of the car.

"Hello." She smiled at Edie, looking no worse for wear than she had this morning, except that the back of her hair where it had rubbed against plane seats and the car seat was having a party.

"Hi there." Edie grabbed the phone and gave it to Cosima. "Tell me where to turn."

She studied the navigation and the road until they came on the right-hand turn that would narrow into Agatha's lane. Edie made it and then stopped and put the car in park. "What's our plan?"

"Knock?"

"After that?"

"After that, we tell her who we are," Cosima said.

Edie thumbed the gearshift, looking out at the darkening twilight.

Telling Agatha who they were sounded harder than an introduction. In the same way the landscape was starting to look formless, there was a way Edie *felt* formless. Who was she now?

She wasn't the same person who'd checked in with Morag the first day she arrived, wet, oversharing, and sad. She was in love. She knew that Cosima was it for her, no matter what happened—and given that their future together was the definition of uncertain, this told her that the heartbreak of Fauxmage hadn't broken her.

Maybe heartbreak could teach someone to risk more, not less, because of how much it was possible to learn about love every time a heart started to heal.

"Tell me who you are," Edie said.

Cosima turned to the side, her long legs folded awkwardly in the small seat. She was so beautiful in the blue-purple light. "I forgot to ask myself who I was," she said. "I ran away. I shut myself up in my room at the inn and turned into primordial ooze. I slept, and when I woke up, I knew I was hungry. I ate, and then I knew I wanted to soak in the hot bath. I drank Morag's juice and decided I'd like to read a book. When you came to my door and asked me to take a walk with you, I did, because I discovered I wanted to."

"You *only* ever do what you want to do."

"That started when I came here." Cosima looked out the windshield at the cottage. "I needed to find her. Find me. It made sense to start from ooze and do only what I wanted, one thing at a time."

"You were following the clues."

Cosima turned back toward Edie in time to catch her smile and return it. "I was following the clues. I started with my body's clues, then I followed my mother's clues, and now we're following our clues, which are Agatha's clues."

"Did you find her? Did you find Cosima?"

She clasped her hands in her lap and leaned closer, her eyebrows lifting into an elegant configuration that promised Edie,

I'm going to tell you a secret. "When you were pulling tacks out of the lounge, I was in the garden. I wanted to clear out a pile of leaves that were mounded over some marginal plants by the pond. I uncovered a glorious border of hostas—they'd died back over the winter, but I could see the potential. I wanted to cut back last year's leaves that had frozen and rotted to give the new shoots an easier time of it, and so I could get a better look, and that was when I discovered an enormous infestation of slugs."

"I hate that you said 'enormous' so close to the word 'slugs.' It makes my hindbrain shudder."

Cosima gave her a broad grin. "I picked them off one by one, slime trails thick as mozzarella pulling from a slice of pizza. I was merciless, Edie. I gave those slugs no quarter, and as I was doing that, my fingers frozen and stinging, slime all over me, I thought, *There you are, Cosima. There you are.*"

"I love that your self-discovery story could double as a villain origin story. It's hot in a way that's just wrong enough."

Cosima laughed. "I'm a gardener. And because I'm also Phoebe Frank's daughter, this means I love everything about it, even the disgusting parts. It means I want to make devastatingly ambitious gardens. I want roses named after me and for people to be jealous. I want to know everything and be someone who gets name-dropped. That's who I am. I love the Castle's garden, but it feels like it was my sandbox."

Edie rubbed her hand over her chest. Her heart felt overfull. "Do you want to know who I am?"

"More than anything."

"Who I am, I think, is someone who's not ready to give up on having a legacy."

"I never thought you were, or ever would be."

But then Cosima went quiet. Edie held her breath, because

she could tell Cosima was thinking, and she wanted to know what she had to say.

"Okay. Here is what I want to tell you," Cosima said. "Next time, you can't do it by yourself. Phoebe surrounded herself with people. PFS has thousands of employees. But at the end of the day, she didn't have anyone to give her legacy to but me. I think legacy has to be a group project."

Edie nodded. She couldn't say aloud what her heart wanted.

"Let's drive to the end of this lane, Edie."

She put the car in gear, and they drove down the narrowing lane until it turned to gravel and wound around an enormous oak not unlike the one in the field in Harlaxton. As soon as they cleared the shadows of the oak tree, a low-roofed stone cottage came into view, sitting on its own with nothing but grass and scattered rocks around it. There were lights on inside. "One Tree Cottage," Edie said.

"Very apt. Whoever's inside must know they have visitors. You should park."

They hadn't even gotten out of the car when the Dutch door to the cottage opened and a woman stepped out. She was short, thin, but her posture was ramrod straight, and Edie could see her lean muscles where the sleeves of her chambray shirt were pushed up. She wore a knitted vest and loose pants with wellies. Her hair was cut in a short style reminiscent of an old movie star like Cary Grant. She wore dark-framed glasses. An enormous dog sat at her feet, its huge, square head looking up at her, obviously waiting for her instructions regarding whether or not to eat them.

"Hello! Very sorry to bother you," Cosima said. "We didn't have a way to call ahead. I'm Cosima, and this is Edie. We're here from Harlaxton. We've been staying at Gregory Place, and we followed your clues in the guest book."

The woman stood at the door of her cottage for a long, long moment. "Is Minnie gone?"

The anguish in this question carried across the space between them. Her dog whined at her feet.

Edie swallowed over a throat sore with empathy. "Ms. Llewellyn, we don't know. We were hoping you could help us."

Agatha put her hand on her dog's head. A freezing-cold blast of wind from the river made both Edie and Cosima wrap their arms around themselves in defense.

"Come in, then." She disappeared inside with her dog.

Edie looked at Cosima. "You first," she said.

"Me first?" Cosima lifted her chin. "Why me?"

"You were the one who wanted to race here from Barcelona. We could be in the lounge at Gregory Place, interrogating Morag so we didn't walk into a situation with a masc fae and her massive hound in the middle of Wales, in the dark, yards away from a deep, cold river, but no."

Frowning fiercely, Cosima started walking. Edie followed her a couple paces behind, her ragged breath making her feelings-sore throat worse.

They scuttled to the door, and Cosima disappeared inside the cottage.

Edie stepped over the stone threshold and toed off her Converse, leaving them on a rubber mat next to Cosima's. Then she looked up and froze.

Mauve.

Mauve everywhere. Mauve-painted plaster walls. Mauve rugs. Pink or pink-and-white or pink-and-blush upholstery on every stick of furniture. The room glowed like the inside of a conch shell.

"Edie!" Cosima whispered. Agatha must have stepped into another room, or she was hovering against the ceiling above them, her spidery wings spread, poison dripping from her fangs.

"What?"

"The mantle."

Edie looked. There were two porcelain shepherdesses. "What the fuck."

"What the fuck, indeed." Agatha stood at the entrance to the room with a tray. "The clues were not meant for you, and you don't seem to know Minnie, so what are you doing here? Sit down. This is tea. There's Hobnobs there, but I'm on my last packet, so don't be greedy. Plenty of cream and sugar." Agatha smashed the tray down on an ottoman in the middle of the room.

Edie quickly filled a mug from the Brown Betty teapot and grabbed two Hobnobs, another variety of accidentally vegan English biscuit that she'd enjoyed. She planted herself in a pink chair. Cosima followed suit, if a little more elegantly, perching on the edge of a settee.

"Ms. Llewellyn," Edie started.

"Agatha. I use she and her. This is Sherlock. He uses he and him, though I imagine he's actually beyond the binary." She put her hand on the dog's cement-block-like head, and his mouth dropped into a panting smile. He was some kind of pit bull mix, but Edie was beginning to suspect he must be all for looks, given his wagging tail and constant side-eyes at Agatha asking for permission to slobber on her guests. "You're Phoebe Frank's daughter," she said to Cosima. "I recognize you. Didn't want to act like I don't. I hate it when people do that."

"Me, too," Cosima said.

"My condolences for your mother. Her studio produced *The Clock Stopped at Midnight* years ago. Very nicely done. I still receive residuals. Didn't get to meet her, though. She didn't come to Wales, and I don't leave."

Agatha had taken command of the room. Though Edie knew from her biography she was north of eighty, she seemed much younger. Her hair was a smooth blend of gold, blond, and white. Her navy eyes were large and sharp.

But Sherlock had moved closer to her, and when she put her hand on his neck, stroking him softly, it trembled. She was nervous. Upset.

Edie felt a thought like a sharp needle stabbing her in the back of the neck—a thought she couldn't quite form. There was the business of the mauve-explosion decorating. The similarities between this room and the Gregory Place lounge, including the shepherdesses, were too strong to be coincidences, but when Agatha had been at Gregory Place, it was 1977. The inn had been newly decorated in all of its mauvy glory years later. So the mauve here could not be a result of Agatha, heartbroken, redecorating in memory of Minnie.

"You never leave Wales, but you went to Harlaxton in 1977," Edie said.

Agatha's eyes narrowed. "And you are?"

"Edie Whitelock. Of Green Bay, Wisconsin. My mother never produced any of your books into movies, but she did have a copy of *The Bones of Kildeer* when I was growing up that I read in middle school. It gave me nightmares for weeks, so well done."

"Edie, yes. I was in Harlaxton in 1977."

"No other time."

"I was not." Agatha seemed composed, but her hand had drifted again to the smooth spot on top of Sherlock's square head.

"Do you get a lot of visitors here?"

"One Tree Cottage is my sanctuary. The only invitation I ever issued was through the guest book. Officially, Agatha Llewellyn doesn't have an address. In the village, I'm called Bronwyn. Does that answer your question?"

Edie's brain was racing, trying to find the source of her neck prickle. "Agatha's your middle name."

"Yes, but—"

The prickle became a stab as the pieces finally fit together and she remembered the photograph of Morag in the guest book, a striking young woman with dark braids and a cigarette. Morag Tourmaline Beveridge.

Tourmaline.

Minnie?

"Oh my god, that *witch*, how dare she?" Edie asked.

"What?" Cosima put down her tea mug. "What is it?"

"She used us as her minions. Her familiars. We're nothing more than girls who she's ensorceled and turned into bats to fly over the countryside and do her bidding."

"What the hell are you talking about?" Agatha demanded.

Edie frowned at Agatha, riding the wave of her anger so she didn't have to feel any of the sorrow beneath it. For heaven's *sake*. "Your one and only is perfectly healthy, I can tell you that much. Your *Minnie*, aka Tourmaline, aka *Morag*, who until recently had Miss Havisham'ed herself into a pink travesty of an inn, moping around, waiting for what? Maybe you can tell me. And nothing funny. I've had enough of getting pushed around by octogenarians who can't get their shit together. As a twenty-genarian, I am perfectly capable of not getting my own shit together without assistance. 'Are you girls going to find the treasure?' she asks. 'Oh, I'll be waiting for you forever,' you say, in a letter you have to know *Cistercian numbers* to find."

"Oh! The Cistercian monks were the ones who built Tintern Abbey, where we are," Cosima interjected. "So that makes sense."

Edie turned to Cosima. "You"—she pointed at her—"have to be on *my* side."

"Noted. It's just that if this is going where I think it's going, I thought it was quite interesting to mention."

Edie sighed. "Out with it, *Bronwyn*. This instant. Have you been stalking Morag in this ridiculous and invisible way for fifty years? Who has the broken heart? Are *you* seriously the treasure? Would Morag even think so?"

"Only her mother called her Morag," Agatha said.

"*Everyone* calls her Morag!" Edie shouted, discovering to her dismay that there was a vein of fierce protective feeling beneath her incandescent anger. Damn it all to hell, she loved *Morag*. Lose one vegan cheese shop and apparently a vacuum opened in the center of your heart. "Every single person! Morag. Of Gregory Place. Probably since before I was born."

Agatha nodded. Then she put down her tea mug and leaned back in her chair. For the first time, she looked her age.

She stared into the fireplace, which had a flickering gas insert. After a long moment, she spoke.

"I was so full of myself then. I had just written my fourth bestseller. I was traveling the world, calling it research for my books, but really doing a lot of sunbathing and drinking and chasing pretty women. I finished a signing at Foyles in Charing Cross, and my new American literary agent was there. I had a trunk full of clothes tailored for me in Mayfair—you know, the Savile Row places. *Annie Hall* had made my look popular that year, and I was riding it into every bedroom in Great Britain."

"All right. I get it, Dream Butch." Edie didn't want to know where this was going. She wasn't interested in crying over a love story. Morag's doomed love story, especially.

Agatha laughed. "I deserve that. I had decided I wanted to write a murder mystery set at a small Lincolnshire or Herefordshire vicarage. I went to the library, and the Harlaxton church was on the registry of historic places. I wrote the vicar at the time. A woman, which was still new. She advised me to take a room at Gregory Place. Convenient, she said, and it came with meals. I rang up Gregory Place and reserved my room for three months. I had my things shipped ahead. I anticipated a rural idyll, rusticating with locals to infuse my book with flavor."

Edie crossed her arms. "Harlaxton is not a bouquet garni."

"No, it's not. I figured this out almost right away. First of all, the services at the church were . . . more than research. They were beautiful. The people were charming, for the most part, but mainly they were hardworking and honest, with themselves and with me. I figured out that my parties and traveling and women had been a way to avoid a lot of things. A lot of hurt."

Edie wanted to lash out at Agatha again, but she understood what she was describing. There was something about Harlaxton. Maybe magic. Maybe just who Edie had been there.

Who Agatha had been, it sounded like.

"Gregory Place was another surprise. Minnie had only just taken it over from her parents, who'd run it a bit to ground. She'd gotten the place back together with nothing more than her two hands, working all the time. Not a few folks would stop by to help out, but she wouldn't let them, because she couldn't pay them, she said. I thought she seemed to have a lot of pride, a lot of things to prove to her family, but this first impression of her wasn't fair because her very existence, her embodiment of hard work, called my own existence to task. So I mostly avoided her except for meals. Her food was too heavenly to avoid."

There were painful truths already beginning to be sketched out in Agatha's story, but Edie would have to mull them over later. She hated this, which made her antsy for it to be over. "It's getting late," Cosima said, and the ice in her tone filled Edie with gratitude. They were Team Morag, the two of them.

They would settle up with Morag after they finished defending her.

"I had trouble sleeping, so I was going for walks late at night. One night, I noticed the red glow of a cigarette at the back of the inn. It was Minnie. I discovered this was her only break of the day—a late cigarette by the kitchen door. I bummed one from her. We started talking. It became my favorite part of the day."

Sherlock put his head on Agatha's knee.

Edie tried not to notice, but then she couldn't keep herself from imagining what it would be like when she went back to Green Bay, trying to keep her mind occupied with work while she thought about Cosima in Barcelona with a love bite on her shoulder, putting her hair up to get into the pool. Cosima's sad blue eyes when she read Agatha's letter in the dead cat café. Cosima enraged after Edie scared her in the dark during the storm. Cosima looking down at her from the hill at Hermione's Stile, her intimate appreciation making an expression Edie hadn't seen yet.

How had Agatha stayed here in this cottage? How had she walked past someone smoking on the street, smelling the sharp burn, without bursting into tears? Why hadn't she gone to Morag?

"We fell in love," Agatha said. "It surprised both of us. Me, because I had thought I was beyond things like love and commitment, and Minnie because she had grown up in a restrictive and difficult family and hadn't been given a margin to think about anything more than work. I think she had come to a place where she didn't believe there was anything but work. Her parents hadn't had the gift of innkeeping like her grandparents did, and their marriage was troubled, besides. They had three boys when they were young, quite a bit older than Minnie, and lost them in the war. Then they lost themselves. Minnie and her sister, Maisie, were late-in-life babies. I can't imagine they had real childhoods."

"But Morag loved the inn?" Edie needed Morag to have had a chance to love something other than a woman who left her fifty years ago.

"Yes. She had the gift. Even in the beginning when she was still shoveling out from under the pile her parents had left, Gregory Place was a charming spot for young people and students. And of course she loves Lincolnshire. She'd shown me some of her favorite places. The church, the manor, the castles. After I'd gone, there was a time, a long time, when Gregory Place was one of those secret hideaways for the rich and famous."

"My mother never forgot her visit," Cosima said. "It changed her life, I think."

"I have no doubt. It did mine."

"But you just said you were never there to see it in its prime." Edie was frustrated. "You're rich and famous! Why would you stay away? Did Morag come here?"

The novelist shook her head.

"Agatha!" Edie stomped her foot, making Sherlock look at her balefully.

"We fought. I came to understand in Harlaxton, from how I was accepted there, from the friends I made and the little church community, that I should give my mother another chance. I couldn't ever hide who I was. My mother had been made single by the war, and she despaired over me. It got worse until I left and we didn't speak. I decided to write her. I wrote her to tell her I missed her, because I did, and I hoped we could have another chance, and of course that I was in love, so I believed in it again. She called the inn. She wanted me home. She was dying."

Edie turned toward the strangled noise Cosima made in her throat. She reached across and held out her hand, and Cosima took it, shaking her head. "I'm fine."

"I'm sorry," Agatha said, looking at their joined hands. "I talked to Minnie. I knew, of course, she was in a precarious place with the inn. Her parents were selling it to her, making her pay in installments directly to them. It's not my story to tell beyond that, but this and other obligations meant her life was limited."

"You fought, and that was it?"

Agatha looked away at the fire again. "We tried the best that we were able to at the time. We ran away for a few precious days. Her sister covered for her so we could go to Rouen. She wanted to see where Joan of Arc was burned and Richard the Lionheart left his heart. Barcelona, because I wanted to show her the basilica. We hired a car, both of us pretending we could find a way to make it work."

Agatha was gazing toward their clasped hands, her eyes unfocused and bright with tears she was holding back.

"But after we'd returned, when I went to give her my address, how to write me, how to visit, she told me she didn't want to know. She said she didn't see a way for us to be together. It would hurt too much to pretend. Again, not my part of the story to tell. I couldn't leave it like that, so I made the hunt. I put it in the guest book for her to find me. Every year, I wrote my letter for the nun in Barcelona to keep. I've settled for knowing

I'm giving the woman I love what she wanted. I don't really expect anyone to understand."

Edie did understand, and she hated it. Hated it, hated it, *hated* it. It made her want to burn everything to the ground, this story. It made her want to cry. It made her want to tear up the guest book into pieces and feed it to the restored Victorian fireplace in the lounge.

Fuck this story. This was not the story that belonged at the end of the map.

"She sent us on this hunt," Cosima said. "Everyone in the village knows about it, too. That you left a treasure hunt, but everyone also believes it's treasure. They think Morag's been guarding it. But she sent us to find you. What do you think we're supposed to do with that?"

Agatha shook her head again. "I can't hope to know."

"Well." Edie got to her feet. Leapt to her feet, maybe, spilling over with too much energy. "You *will* know. In deference to your great age, I won't make us set off right now. I assume you have a room or can point us to the entrance to the land of the fae where you are king to sleep for the night. Then I'm driving us to Harlaxton first thing. Sherlock's welcome to come."

"I don't leave Wales." Agatha said it without much force.

"And before all of this, I had basically never left Wisconsin," Edie said. "But it turns out it was never that hard. Pack snacks. I'm not stopping on the way unless we run out of petrol."

"There's a guest room at the end of the hall. Make the bed up yourself. Linens in the wardrobe." Agatha sat up straight, and Edie thought that maybe she seemed a little excited. Maybe. "I'm taking Sherlock outside."

With that, the famous Welsh novelist got up, stepped into her boots, and disappeared into the dark with her dog.

Edie grabbed the rest of the Hobnobs and Cosima's hand. She was starting to pull her down the hall when Cosima drew her close instead.

"Edie." She put her hands around Edie's face. Her eyes were blue, blue, but Edie was afraid to look at them in case they told her yet another story she did not want to hear.

"Yeah?" she croaked.

"We're not Agatha and Morag."

She turned to kiss Cosima's palm. Closed her eyes. "I know that. But I also know I'm perfectly capable of behaving like a wankhammer for at least fifty years, and I'm scared."

She tried to keep her voice light. Tried to keep her faith intact, and to remember that it, and her optimism, was a gift. Not a curse. Edie wasn't cursed. The greatest love of her life was not doomed. Even if she couldn't see the path in front of them, it didn't mean they wouldn't find one.

Edie wrapped her arms around Cosima.

Her treasure.

Chapter Twenty

"Morag Tourmaline Beveridge!"

Cosima scrambled to stay with Edie as she burst through the back door of the inn and shouted into the kitchen. They found Morag at the prep table, putting a tea towel over a bowl of dough to proof.

They had left Agatha with Tam at the Gregory Arms. He and Killian would drive her up when they got the all clear. Edie was determined this would be the only grace they extended to Morag.

Cosima didn't think it was going to be so cut-and-dried.

"You're back from Spain already?" Morag wiped her hands on her apron and started cleaning the table.

"Correction." Edie pointed at her. "We're back from Wales."

Morag stopped cleaning. She didn't look at them. "I see."

"Otherwise known as the end of the trail. 'X' marks the spot. But you probably already knew that." Edie hung her coat up on the hook, rounded the table, sat down on a stool, and folded her arms, glaring at Morag. Cosima sat next to her, with much less theater.

"The Whippledurn finished with the plastering," Morag said slowly. "I brought in the paint from the shed and ordered another two cans. Turns out Slate and Thatch roofing isn't in business anymore, but I was directed to an outfit called LeLand's, and they've taken a look at the roof. That will be next week. Jenny from the manor came, Cosima."

"Oh." She blinked. Jenny was the head gardener at the manor, and Cosima had asked her to come over for a garden consult days ago. "I didn't know she'd be here when I was gone."

"No trouble. She left you notes. I have them at the reception desk." Morag folded the rag she had been cleaning with.

"What was your plan, Morag?" Edie leaned forward. "You sent us on this journey, knowing what was on the other end, aware of my preference to get over-involved, and here we are, not a velvet bag of rubies or golden chalice between us. But you knew we wouldn't find that kind of treasure, didn't you? Don't worry, though. We brought the spoils back. We've got her stashed at the Gregory Arms, with Tam keeping guard. We'll figure out how to carve off your seventeen and a half percent."

"Bronwyn's here?" Morag didn't say this to Edie or to Cosima. It looked like she said it to the rising bread dough, but Cosima suspected she was saying it to herself.

A little bit of the bluster seemed to escape from Edie. "She's here, Morag. She gave us her part of the story, but what's yours?"

Morag reached for the kettle, banging it against the stovetop in an uncoordinated lurch. After she'd filled it and placed it on the hob, she pulled down the tea tin and mugs. Cosima waited patiently. The inability of British people to talk about anything difficult without first making a cup of tea did not surprise or bother her.

It seemed, however, that the act of making tea was itself soothing enough to allow Morag to speak. "I was sleeping on my feet to make this place go," she said. "My goal was to make enough to hire my sister, Maisie. She was still at home with our parents, and it was a right nightmare, I'll say that. When Bronwyn came, I was almost there. The advance payment she sent meant I could make Maisie's room ready. Then Maisie told me she was pregnant."

"Fuck," Edie whispered.

Morag shook her head. "She was grown. It was 1977! Not the Dark Ages, believe it or not. I begged her to come anyway. I knew she didn't have good memories about growing up in the inn. I didn't either, but I was trying to make it over into something different. But she said our parents would take the place from me if she came. Long story short, I found out she was right." Morag put tea bags into the mugs. "Because the universe has a good sense of humor, this was also the first time in my life I fell in love."

Sitting on the kitchen stool, her feet on the rungs, Cosima had a sense memory of being on the plane to England, feeling as though the floor of the plane had dropped out and she was hung over the clouds, rushing past at six hundred miles per hour. Her mother was gone, Cosima tapped with the immaculate maintenance of her legacy, needing more from Duncan than they had learned to give each other, and then, yes, she fell in love.

It amazed her, *amazed* her, that everything that had driven her here in a breathless, stomach-twisting compulsion to escape was still true. It amazed her because all of those things felt smaller. Loving Edie hadn't *distracted* her. Loving Edie had made her more capable of tackling these problems.

They *were* problems. They would take time. She would be surprised by low moments. She might need help. But she couldn't believe there was a bad time to fall in love with someone who only wanted the best for you.

"Why did loving her make things harder?" Cosima asked.

Morag grimaced. "It didn't. It made things beautiful. It gave me ways to stand up to my parents that I hadn't had before. I nearly had Maisie convinced we could do it, and I could keep the inn. Bronwyn gave me so much. She even reached out to her mother, did she tell you that?"

"Yes," Edie said. "She did."

"It was a problem we could have solved." There was a trace of Morag's usual edge in her tone. "I might not have been able to grow the inn as quickly. My family difficulties and Maisie's pregnancy would only have been made worse by my openly being with Bronwyn, but I didn't care about that. I was scared, you understand. I'd been scared my whole life."

"Me, too," Edie said to Morag. "But Cosima said something that made me think in the car ride here, and you know what I figured out? I could've saved Fauxmage. I thought that if I couldn't do it all by myself, I couldn't do it. I tried to take on the ocean without a crew. Exactly how long, Morag, have you been running this inn without help?"

Morag sighed and took the whistling kettle off the hob. She poured water over the tea bags into the mugs. "Always, I'd say."

"And what happened?" Edie gestured generally toward the lounge. "I did not find this inn in the UK special edition of *Condé Nast Traveler*."

"At some point, the denial set in."

"The pink," Cosima said. "That happened some years after Agatha left."

Morag smiled. "That's because your mother happened."

"Phoebe Frank?" Edie dumped sugar and soy creamer into her tea.

"She fell in love while she was here. Not unlike I had, years before. We got on. I told her about Bronwyn, and she said I needed to set the scene. I needed to be able to visualize exactly what I wanted and what magic I required to make it happen. She helped me paper her room while she was still here."

"That does sound like my mother."

"I wasn't brave enough to get into the clues Bronwyn had left behind, but I had piles of money by then, and so I hired a designer and told her that Bronwyn's favorite color was pink. She'd always complained about how cold the wood floors were. It was the eighties, and the designer was delighted. Bronwyn had bought those shepherdesses in town. She thought they were funny. I'd kept them in the room she used, but I brought them down here."

"Then what happened?" Edie raised her eyebrows. "Because I am here to tell you that there is a much better-maintained twin to the former mauvetastic lounge in Tintern, Wales, right down to the shepherdesses, and you can imagine my shock."

Cosima didn't expect Morag to cry, and Edie obviously didn't, either, because she looked horrified when it started. Morag waved her hand at them and blew her nose in her napkin. "Bah. I wasn't expecting to know that, was I? After so many years, you can imagine why I would think that she never thought of me again. It's why I chickened out after the lounge was done."

Edie clucked her tongue, but not unkindly. "The final clue, in Barcelona, required her to write a letter to a nun every year. We met this woman. Sister Ona. She might have been a ghost. It was hard to tell. She had a desk drawer full of mash notes from your ex-girlfriend, which she wanted me to take, but I made Cosima give her two hundred euros as a donation and to cover whatever it's going to cost to post them to you instead." Edie handed Morag her untouched napkin. "Agatha spent three hours this morning in a very small car with the two of us and her dog, who I think needs to reevaluate his diet based on the ratio of gas to clean air, and I have heard more heartwarming stories about you than I ever would have thought possible considering that you once literally slapped my hand away when I tried to look in your recipe box. *Slapped.* It stung."

"She hasn't seen me in fifty years." Morag reached up and touched one of her long white braids in a show of vanity that made Cosima suddenly appreciate how fond she had become of this woman. Morag had given her a place to collapse, to rebuild and recover, and then she'd sent Edie to her.

"She knows you're not immortal," Edie said. "I'd say you're holding up."

Morag rolled her eyes, but Cosima could see that she was pleased.

"Should I give Tam a call?" Cosima asked. "Invite Agatha to the inn?"

"No." Morag untied her apron. "I'll go down to the Arms myself. I think I'd feel better if we started on neutral ground. Also, I need to give Edie a chance to carry on without my having to bear witness to dramatics after I leave her with one last thing."

"What's that?" Edie said this around a bite of bourbon cream. "Are you going to give me your carrot raisin quick bread recipe and let me try it out in your Aga for the last week I'm here?"

"You can use the Aga and more," Morag said. "I'm giving you Gregory Place."

Cosima's stomach dropped away, leaving behind a whirling hollow. Edie had frozen with a biscuit halfway to her mouth. The look in her eyes was how Cosima would have felt if she'd been the right person to take charge of her mother's company.

Morag came around the table as Edie watched, her face pale. The older woman sat down on a stool and leaned toward Edie.

"I've known I ought to sell for a long time, but I've been resistant, because as much as I've let this place go, I can't let it *go*. My sister won't have anything to do with it, and she's as old as I am. My niece works in the C-suite of Tesco and shows miniature dachshunds. She doesn't have children. When I saw Cosima's reservation come through, well, I don't believe in fairy tales, but it felt like a sign that something was coming. Imagine my surprise when the something was you."

Edie shook her head. The tip of her nose had gone red, and her lips were clenched so tight that a dimple appeared on her chin.

It was the kind of moment Phoebe Frank would've loved. The kind she would have hired John Williams to score.

And, for once, Cosima was right at the center of it.

She moved her stool closer and put her hand at Edie's hip. This one was hers. And, if Cosima could make it happen, so was the two-acre garden of Gregory Place that deserved Grade I registration after a jaw-dropping restoration.

"Your phone may not work, but I can do research," Morag said. "Fauxmage was good. But I'm not convinced this Wisconsin is the right place for you. Don't you have dual citizenship? Because of your worthless father?"

"Yes," Edie said. Her voice was almost a whisper.

"Maybe you don't want it," Morag told her. "But you understand this place, and you've learned the lessons I never did."

"I have negative money," Edie said. "I don't know anything about running an English inn. I have a job already. I went to the factory and had a meeting with HR to fill out all my paperwork."

Morag stood up. "This is the part I mentioned that I don't plan to be here for." She set her mug down on the drainboard and looked at Cosima. "Be a duck and let Tam know I'm on my way. I don't know what the state of Bronwyn's heart might be, but I'd hate to be the reason it stopped in shock."

"There are still some Lenten roses in the garden," Cosima said. "If you'd like to take her flowers."

"No, I would not." Morag took her coat. "Can you imagine giving that woman flowers? I'll give her a new silk necktie if she doesn't turn around and run back to Wales when she sees me."

And then she was gone.

"Edie." Cosima shifted over to Morag's stool to be closer. "How are you doing?"

"What is that woman's long game, Cosima? Is this the first temptation in a gauntlet of torture? Or, more likely, I take her devil's bargain, and then I'm doomed to run this inn for eternity, my skin bursting into flames if I walk more than ten yards from the threshold."

"I think she just wants you to have the inn," Cosima said, as gently as she could. She knew Edie was making jokes because her fear and overthinking were taking over. "I don't think there's anything behind her offer but her belief that you're the right person to carry on a legacy. And she's right. Edie, look around! This inn is *already* a legacy. You can be the next person in an unbroken line of people, some of whom were very damaged, who have taken care of it. Someday, you'll pass it on, probably in better shape than you received it. This building, I am absolutely certain, will be here a hundred years after you're gone. That's the goddamned dream, isn't it?"

Edie closed her eyes, her cheeks flushed, and when she

opened them, they were tide pools. Forest ponds. "But where will you be?"

"Come with me." Cosima slid off her stool and waited.

When Edie rose, she led her out the back door and along the path to the garden gate. It didn't squeak when she opened it, because Cosima had repaired and oiled it. She'd had to watch six YouTube videos, but she'd managed it. Then she stepped aside, hoping Edie could see not what she'd done, but what it would become.

"Oh, shit," Edie said. "It doesn't look like a place the cops should bring ground-penetrating radar to and look for bodies anymore."

Cosima laughed. It was the earliest part of the spring in England, but she could see where the roses would come in and make a path to the step-over apple trees she had just started to retrain. Beyond that, there was the pond to clean out and replant, more marginal plants to edge it with. There were the box hedges that needed to be looked at for blight. She'd found the remains of a sunny dry garden, and the greenhouse was a disaster, but it would be gorgeous when it was repaired.

It was a kingdom, and she had laid claim to it as its queen. And king, if she were being honest about her ambition.

"This is where you want to begin your takeover of the world of gardening? Here?"

Edie's face was still too pale. Cosima could see that the brokenhearted part of her hadn't caught up to the part that was already running the inn. Kissing Cosima every day. Making everybody in town her new best friend.

"This is a two-acre garden, the oldest parts of which date to the beginning of the eighteenth century, even before the inn. It's older than the gardens at Gregory Gregory's manor. There are important artifacts of pre-Victorian pleasure gardening around every corner, some of which would be the first of their kind to be restored. There is stained glass in the greenhouse by an English artist whose pieces are in the British Museum. So yes. Here."

Edie wrapped her arms around herself, scanning the muddy garden. "I suppose no other garden in the world has me—*might* have me—if you're cataloging its features."

Cosima bit her lip to keep from scaring Edie off with her excitement. "Nope. No other one."

"Do you think we could charge twelve pounds to tour it?"

"Let's say eighteen. It would be Cosima Frank's, after all."

Edie stepped farther into the garden, looking at a table where Cosima had been keeping tools organized and the pile where she was putting good pots where she found them, when Cosima's phone buzzed in her back pocket.

It was Duncan.

She held up a finger to Edie and walked away, taking the call to a private space by the garden wall.

"I'm glad I got you right away."

The air in Cosima's lungs went cold. Duncan never forgot his polite greetings.

"Duncan? What is it?"

As she listened to what he said, the cold reached every vein in her body. When he was done, she told him what she would do.

What she *had* to do.

"Edie." Cosima found her, still by the table with the tools. She'd rearranged them by size. Some of the color had started coming back into her face.

Cosima hated that she didn't have any time. That she couldn't be with Edie in this moment—one of the most challenging in her life, given Edie's history. As it was, she would be pressed to get to Los Angeles by five o'clock. She reran the time-zone calculations in her head, the same ones Duncan had patiently explained to her even though it was so late in California. It was morning here. Harlaxton was eight hours ahead. Cosima would be on a plane for twelve hours if all went to plan, and she had to get to the airport, check in, go through security, board. "I need to leave. I'm so sorry. In fact, I think I have to break whatever rental agreements we signed and take the Mini."

"You have to go back." Edie's voice was low. She didn't sound like herself, which made Cosima think she must have been able to hear at least part of the phone call.

"Burbank. I have to leave right away so I can make it before the end of the day. Not the end of the day here. The end of the day there. I'll take the bag I packed for Spain." Cosima tried to calm her racing brain, her stomach cramping already.

She had no means and no time to wipe the confusion from Edie's face. She had to hope that showing Edie the garden was enough. Telling her that *this* was where she wanted to be. Showing her that she trusted her decisions, her ideas, her ambitions.

She went to Edie and put her hands around her beautiful face. "This is my garden. I won't let anyone else have it. You have to keep it for me. Don't go anywhere, okay? Even if you don't hear from me. This is not good-bye."

She kissed Edie's forehead, hoping she could beam her feelings right into Edie's brain so that she wouldn't lose faith.

Maybe she could call her from the plane. Or on the drive, if she had a moment when she wasn't focused on traffic. "I'm so sorry. I wish I could be a part of this for you."

And then, just like before, she ran away, with no idea when she would return.

Chapter Twenty-One

Edie cut her paintbrush along the baseboard, a perfect line without painter's tape.

She'd learned that from Mike. How to cut in with a brush. How much paint to load to avoid dripping or leaving brush marks. It was a task that, if you didn't do it every day, required attention and not a little concentration.

That was good.

Paying attention to anything but the brush in her hand and the line of the lounge's baseboard made Edie want to curl up inside one of the cedar hedgehog garden houses that Baroness Rachel had brought over for Cosima, who was not here, who would not be finding the perfect shady corner for a theoretical hedgehog to live in the inn's garden, though the baroness was nice about it when Edie took the houses from her and then burst into tears.

It was exactly three days before her job at the pizza crust factory started, and two *weeks* since Cosima left, and two days since Edie was supposed to have gotten on a plane to Wisconsin.

That meant that so far she had managed two days of her theoretical new life with her imaginary inn and her girlfriend who lived in California. Two days had been enough to become exhausted and dizzy from the speed of her own spiraling thoughts.

When Morag had returned from the pub late the day Cosima left, flushed and looking so much younger that Edie accused her of having an enchanted painting in the attic, Edie had to tell her that Cosima was gone.

Instead of making her a snack and feeling sorry for her, Morag had *called Cosima*, then sat on her rocking chair for fifteen minutes, nodding and only saying yes or no. Then she'd hung up and told Edie that it was too soon to know the scope of Cosima's trip to Los Angeles, but that Edie should "keep herself busy."

The next morning, Edie went into the village, to the mobile phone kiosk in the gift shop, and purchased a phone from a teenage boy with what was left of the money Morag had given her to travel for the treasure hunt. She'd charged up the phone. Then it occurred to her that she didn't know Cosima's phone number, so she dug through everything at the reception desk until she found it, and because she had no idea what time it was in California, she texted so she wouldn't wake her up.

new number who this? it's edie. Tam brought me an extra large basket of chips a little while ago so i knew i wasn't the only one who felt sorry for me

Cosima texted back right away.

I'm so sorry. The interim CEO of the board took advantage of the depressed price of PFS stock, as well as insider knowledge from an internal report, to buy a controlling stake in the company, initiating hostile takeover. No one found out until he rejected all of the union contracts, which froze the work of about eighty-five percent of our projects, and no work means our people are preparing to strike, as they should. It's a mess, it's messy, and I'm largely responsible.

The blood froze in Edie's veins.

JESUS HC Cosima!

The text bubble went up and down multiple times before Cosima told Edie she had to go. That was one week and six days ago, and since then, all of Edie's messages had been left sitting on delivered.

Morag, who turned out to be a crack hand at googling, hadn't been able to track down what was happening with PFS. It likely wasn't public yet.

Where there had been Cosima, there was now a black hole. The inn seemed huge without her. Edie's heart was literally plinking and plonking as it drifted around her rib cage.

She couldn't think up anything soothing and reasonable to

tell herself. She could only think about how Cosima's skin felt against hers, and how her voice sounded when she was half-asleep—a yearning that came from the center of her body and gathered all of her nerves to pull on them at once.

Without thoughts she could trust, Edie didn't have actions, and without actions, it turned out that she was one of the garden's quivering slugs creeping around the inn, sliming sadly and hiding from Morag.

"Edie!"

She jumped, swiping paint onto the dark wood of the baseboard. She pulled out her rag to scrub it off. "What the hell, woman!" She spun around on her butt.

Morag stood in reception, clasping hands with Agatha, who wore an honest-to-god driving cap and was looking at Morag like she'd invented oxygen. "I'd already said your name twice."

"When you yell, you call down the spirit world. My soul is in tatters." Edie stood up. "Agatha."

"Good morning, Edie." Agatha took off her hat and kissed Morag's cheek. "I'll take myself to the kitchen and make us tea."

"Oh, so *Agatha* can use your kitchen." Edie wrinkled her nose at Morag. "But I'm back behind the velvet ropes."

"You created the menu. You haven't accepted my offer. No kitchen for you." Morag looked around at the lounge. "The paint looks good. You'll need a second coat."

"I am *aware*."

Morag gave her a long look, and Edie did her best to vibe her into walking away. It didn't work. She came closer. She didn't have her apron on, which made Edie uncomfortable.

"You have canceled three meetings with my solicitor to discuss the terms of my offer. You do nothing around here but invent a new mess to make every day. You didn't go home, nor have you paid me to extend your stay, and you haven't tried to talk to Cosima."

"I have tried!"

"What? You've *texted* her? I text the greengrocer to cancel cress for the week. I text my sister to ask her if she wants mince or beans in the burritos I'm ordering for our movie night. I don't text women I've changed my entire life for, and who are likely dealing with the biggest catastrophe I can imagine!" Morag's hands were on her hips.

Edie thought of half a dozen insulting ways to point out that Morag had not texted, called, written to, or driven to Wales to find her lost love, but she kept them in her mouth, where they belonged. "I don't know what to do," she said. Whispered, actually.

"Well, then! Someone needs to alert the press! When is the neon sign in Times Square going up, *Edie Whitelock Doesn't Know What to Do*?" Morag used air quotes. Unhelpful. "You're not the first person in this situation. This isn't even the first time you haven't known what to do."

"But I think it *is*!" Now Edie's hands were on her hips. "I have always just *done*. I haven't stopped to think about it. I do, and then it works or it doesn't, but look where that got me!"

"Look where that got you? What part are you referring to? The part where you opened a cheese shop that sold a cheese you made of nothing that usually goes into a cheese but nonetheless won 'best bloomed rind cheese' in the world cheese awards? The part where you fell in love with someone who would move heaven and earth for you? The part where a foolish old woman handed you a turnkey inn without strings?"

Edie pressed the heels of her hands to her eyes. "All of those parts, Morag!"

"You need to stop thinking and figure it out."

"Oh, well, that sounds like something a person can do." Edie hated how petulant she had become.

"It's not," Morag said. "It's not something *a* person can do."

And with that, she left.

Edie collapsed onto the step stool. She wished she could take a break from being Edie Whitelock for just one minute. She adjusted her position, then realized her phone was getting sat on and pulled it out.

Figure it out, but don't think about it.

She didn't let herself second-guess, she just dialed a number she'd been avoiding for weeks. The least helpful person she knew.

"Frog!" Her mother's voice was loud against the background noise of her truck and the road. "Color me shocked."

"Hi, Mom." Edie scratched a drop of paint on her coveralls.

"How's it going? Wait, hold on. Merge or be killed, jackass! Some of us have places to be!" Two long honks of her mom's horn blared through the phone.

"Should I call back?"

"What? No! This is a good time, Froggie. I'm just driving. Not doing anything."

Edie rolled her eyes. "So, you may have noticed that I'm not there."

"That's good, because I don't have time to get you from the airport. I picked up another shift. I'm trying to double up so I can buy a Jet Ski for the lake before my vacation in June. But when *are* you coming? The jet lag's not going to be your friend for your first week."

"When I'm coming is kind of why I'm calling. I mean, not to decide when. To talk about why I'm not there yet? And the job. I should talk about that, too, but I'm not sure what to say.

It's not that I don't appreciate how many strings you pulled for me, and those culinary science jobs with the nice benefits are hard to get, I know. Really, it should be a dream. Maybe I should call HR and talk to them? I can get the start date moved, or—who was the woman you're talking to?"

"Frog," her mom cut in. Edie realized she didn't hear the road anymore. "I've pulled into the Pamperin Park lot. Remember when I'd take you and your brothers here? And the time Ethan fell into Duck Creek and you went after him and grabbed him by the diaper and hauled him right up?"

"I remember," Edie said. She would not cry. She was not calling her mom from camp, homesick. She hadn't actually been sent to camp unless you counted the Parks and Rec city program that was drop-in childcare, which she did not. "I don't know what to do."

It was the only thing left to say.

It was the first time, maybe—the first time she could remember—that she'd ever said it to her mom.

"What about?" her mom asked softly. "About the inn, or about this girl?"

"About the—what?" Edie held the phone out and looked at it, then brought it back to her ear. "How do you know about the inn *or* the girl?"

"Morag called me days ago." She heard her mom's truck door open and the familiar sound of her zipping open the compartment in her purse where she kept her cigarettes, then the flick of her lighter and a short inhale. "She reminds me of your great aunt, my mom's sister. I wish you could have met her. I mean, obviously Morag is the British version. Auntie Sheila was born in Manitowoc. Remember when we went to the maritime museum there? I think you were fourteen or so. The boys were a handful."

Edie remembered. "Morag *called* you? On the phone? And the two of you talked about me?"

"We FaceTimed, actually. Why wouldn't we talk about you? What else do we have in common?"

"Why?" Edie closed her eyes.

"I assume because she's worried. I did have her send over the papers with the terms for the inn, and I gave them to your cousin Amber to look over the legal stuff."

"Amber's a paralegal. If I got that far, I was going to talk to Meadow. She went to law school."

"Paralegals are the same thing as lawyers. Amber went to school for two years to get qualified. Law school takes three. What could be in that last year, how to talk to the Supreme Court? I don't need that. I just wanted to know you weren't being scammed by an old English woman. Anyway, Amber said she didn't know a lot about property transfer in the UK, but nothing looked fishy to her. So there you go."

"I'm relieved that my cousin Amber, paralegal, didn't find anything fishy in paperwork she admits she knows nothing about."

"You're welcome." Her mom took another inhale of her cigarette. "But I'm picking up that it's not the nuts and bolts that have got you hung up."

"No." Edie could see, in her mind's eye, exactly where her mom's truck would be parked, and her mom next to it on the bench in the patch of white cedars by the picnic shelter. Pamperin Park was as familiar to her as the freckles on the back of her hand. Her mom liked to park her truck in the last space in any lot if she could, so at least one side wouldn't have a car next to it. It was the beginning of March, still cold in Green Bay, with snow on the ground covering the pine needles, and her mom was on the way to second shift. It was probably getting dark. There wouldn't be anybody at the park but maybe a few dog walkers.

She *knew* that place.

"You ever think there was a reason I told you to go to England?" her mom asked.

"Because that's where Greg's from." Edie meant her dad, Greg Whitelock.

"Sure. Good enough. But that's not all of it. The truth is, Frog, you don't belong here."

Edie sucked in a breath, hurt.

"It's not that I don't *want* you to go to work with me every day. I've had to hold myself back from buying us matching lunch sets at Target and fantasizing about doing meal prep with you—I mean, add meat to mine, but you can really cook! It's the dream, working alongside your kids, knowing they're going to be all right, watching them get what you had to work so hard for. Especially if it was you. You're my daughter. You and I both know your brothers are knuckleheads. I can hold a conversation with you." Her mother sighed. "But the truth is, I've hated the light that's gone out in your face since you lost Fauxmage. That place was cool as shit, Frog. I couldn't believe you'd done that, all by yourself. But it wasn't a Green Bay kind of thing."

Edie's heart skipped hearing her mom praise her. *That place was cool as shit.* For Tanya, it was the equivalent of throwing a party at a thirty-dollar-a-plate supper club. "How can someone from Green Bay not be able to make a Green Bay kind of thing?" she asked.

"Why didn't I stay with your dad when I met him in London while following the greatest jam band in the whole world, Phish?"

"I don't know." Edie was a little surprised to realize she didn't. There was a way that she'd always thought of the story of her mom and dad as fated not to work out. Her mom had been so far from home, and the fling with Greg Whitelock must have been a passing thing, Edie's resulting birth the kind of music festival event that happened to Tanya Hoberg back then. Not a plan. Not a future she'd truly considered.

"Because," her mom said, "even though there were things that I loved about your dad and England, it wasn't me. It was important for me to grow, and I got you out of it, but it wasn't me. I knew that the moment your dad proposed. So tell me, when Morag offered you the inn, what did *you* know?"

Edie gripped her knee. That moment was crystalline. She remembered it in high definition. "That I could make the inn so special."

"And then what?"

"I told myself I was on vacation and this wasn't real, it wasn't mine, I'm not even English, I would mess it up, it was too big, too much, too hard, that Harlaxton was a lot farther away from Los Angeles than Green Bay, and it was already impossible."

Her mom exhaled. Edie could picture her, blowing smoke. "But did you think, 'I can't leave home, I'm gonna miss it so much,' or 'I was really looking forward to my job at the factory,' or 'I can't wait to be my brother's last-minute-no-pay babysitter again'? Did a montage of the Fox River and the Walnut Street Bridge and the coal piles flash through your mind with a pang of longing?"

"No."

"No! That's not you. That's what *I* thought, twenty-nine years ago, right down to the coal piles, but *your* first thought was that you were the right person for this. All the other thoughts that came after were either bullshit or giving up on a girl before you've even begun with her."

I haven't given up on her.

"I'll tell you what *I* think you should do." Her mom lit another cigarette.

"What do you think I should do, Mom?"

"Let Morag be your fairy godmother. Go rescue the princess."

Edie laughed, and maybe there were a few tears. "If I do, will you come visit?"

And then, only then, after she'd given in to fate and asked for help, could Edie see it—her mom here in the lounge, talking about when she was in England following Phish, her niece and nephew eating biscuits and milky tea at the dining room table, and her knucklehead brothers being scolded by—

Cosima.

"Of course I'll visit," her mom said. "No one's going to throw away a free lodging overseas vacation. There's airfare specials all the time. I'll get one of those miles credit cards and use it for my groceries at Woodman's. And once I'm vested in my pension, watch out. I'll be speaking the Queen's English, I'll be there so much."

Edie ignored her mother's atrocious English accent. She had to, because her heart felt like it was going to burst. She thought of the letter Phoebe Frank had left for Cosima in the wallpaper, the letters Agatha had mailed to Barcelona from her cottage in Wales every year like a sacrament, the library full of romance novels Morag had read and kept. She thought of the castle-shaped play equipment at Pamperin Park that her mom had always taken her to play on, even though it wasn't the closest to their house, because Edie liked it best, and of a birthday cake she'd begged for with roses made of frosting, fit for a princess.

Edie had spent most of her life believing that castles and frosting roses and magic were for other people. But she didn't believe that anymore.

"Mom?"

"Yeah, Frog?"

"I love you. I've gotta go."

"You bet. I better get a fire under myself. Call me later." Her mom made two kissing noises. "I love you."

"I love you, too."

It took her a few minutes in the empty lounge to pull herself together. The sun was coming in a beam from the reception area, cutting a golden line across the polished floor, making motes of dust dance in the light. She slid her phone back into her pocket and wrapped up her paintbrush and looked over the whole room, bit by bit, before she was ready to get to her feet.

Then, she found Morag—to her horror, kissing Agatha in the corner by the pantry—and asked her for help.

"I hate heels." Cosima shoved off her stilettos and sank into her favorite Eames chair in her mother's study. Duncan had already taken his customary wingback by the fireplace. "I hate Reggie Rierson and his dirty, smug, white-man schemes. I hate ten-hour meetings. I'm becoming fond of the SEC and the FBI, if I'm being honest, but I hate their patience for asking the same question thirty times."

"Forty." Duncan sighed. "At least."

"Do you think he'll take the bait?"

Cosima had come home to a castle under siege. When she'd walked into the executive conference room in Burbank, there were people around the table in two layers, and more people standing in the corners holding laptops with one hand and typing with the other. They went silent at the sight of her.

As she'd listened to the executives and board members one

by one, Cosima had waited for her stomach to twist with the familiar knives.

It never did.

She'd experienced a lot of feelings over the last two weeks. Boredom. Rage. Guilt. Fear. Confusion. And, under all of them, over all of them, through all of them, her unending craving to be with Edie.

Her unending determination to get back to her.

She'd been frustrated that after she talked to Morag, she was needed and couldn't explain to Edie. Then Edie texted—the relief in Cosima's body utter—but before she could answer more than a few lines, a young man in a bad suit with an FBI badge held his hand out for her phone and then slid it into a paper bag and sealed it shut.

From that moment, her calls were monitored and—after Cosima attempted to get a call through to England when they didn't yet know if she was a conspirator attempting to flee the country or an ally to the investigation—restricted to a landline.

It was only Duncan's diplomatic intervention that had prevented her from getting herself arrested at that point, so outraged had she been by the barriers between her and the woman she loved.

She was on a better footing now with the authorities, who had come to understand that Cosima was definitely on whatever side was against Reggie Rierson.

There were two problems, it seemed, both bad. One, Reggie was an inside trader to a degree that guaranteed he'd spend several Christmases exchanging presents with his grandchildren over a Formica lunch table in a minimum-security prison, and, two, wresting back PFS nonetheless had to be accomplished well before government agencies could possibly get their ducks in a row to file charges and prosecute.

It meant that Cosima's job was to cooperate with a multiagency investigation without *yet* cluing in Reggie or certain members of the board who supported his coup. In addition, Cosima's job was arranging to purchase a great deal of stock from major shareholders—many of whom had known her since she was a baby—in order to shore up her stake in the company. And, finally, it meant getting a golden parachute approved by the board and other stakeholders to bait the turncoat into selling back his controlling shares of the company.

"I do think he'll take the bait," Duncan said. "I've known Reggie for decades. This was a fun time for him, but I don't really think he meant it to be a long time. He's been talking about buying an island in Dubai. What we're offering means he could buy three."

Cosima leaned back in the chair, closing her eyes. When she shifted, she could still smell the faintest hint of her mother's perfume. "In any event, whatever comes next is out of our hands."

She'd thought it would bother her to see the changes at the Castle. Here in the study, for example, Phoebe's things had been packed away, the papers nestled into acid-free boxes, pictures wrapped in tissue paper, art appraised and crated. Cosima's chair was still here, and Duncan's, but soon Duncan would move into the house Cosima had always liked in Thousand Oaks.

Without Phoebe, the Castle really wasn't the Castle anymore. Not Phoebe's, but also not Cosima's.

She wasn't sure she'd miss it. Cosima had grown up with Phoebe and Duncan. She'd grown up with all of the people in suits and tennis whites who she'd been talking to every day for hours, asking for what she needed and having it provided with hugs and smiles and recollections about her mother. It was with these people that Cosima had cried about her mother's death for the first time in company, and grieved. People who knew her.

She'd laughed a lot, too.

"You know what I've been thinking?" she said after a long, comfortable silence.

"What's that?"

"How much Phoebe would have loved this. What a drama! A villain emerges in the wake of a death, the succession uncertain, a daughter's betrayal, then the parade of badges and interrogations, and finally a trap. It's the best memorial we could have contrived for her. It makes up for the reading of her will being so relentlessly dull."

Duncan laughed. "Good lord, I believe you're right."

"Also," Cosima said, "don't you think she would have liked where we ended up?"

Between the marathon meetings, the tearful lunches, and the tense consultations with law enforcement, Cosima had found herself at the end of two weeks' worth of long days curled up on the leather sofa in Duncan's room, with Duncan lounging in his favorite recliner opposite her, the two of them talking until one or both of them were too tired to continue.

One of the topics of conversation was *An American Castle's Garden*.

It turned out that Duncan himself had been noodling on the topic for a long time. When he met Phoebe, he was a somewhat rootless Scottish minor aristocrat who hadn't found his passion beyond new women in new places. But at heart he was someone who loved to learn, to see how something worked from every angle. He'd learned more about the inner workings of Hollywood than most studio executives in his time with

Phoebe, and in the end he was doing as much as Cosima, if not more.

Duncan had thought about what he'd like to do after losing the love of his life, and his thought was that he'd love to work in the land of make-believe that Phoebe had ruled. He'd sacrificed his own dream to make Phoebe feel better by pulling in Cosima and changing up his *original* vision, which had been to start at the Castle and then travel the world, showing his audiences a new garden every season. Like a Scottish Monty Don.

It felt so good to give Duncan back his dream.

They'd learned in one of the group meetings they went to together that for many people whose loved ones struggled with addiction, grief could be complicated. It often took longer, following paths into feelings and experiences that had been suppressed. Cosima could feel that it would be true for her. So many of her feelings about her mother were bundled together, thatched into layers of resentment and anger and guilt and love. But she had discovered that she and Duncan, together, could tell each other the story of their family. They could admit how they'd felt and say what they hadn't been able to say.

Duncan had always been there for Cosima, from the moment he buckled her into her life vest in the French Riviera, and he'd been there for Phoebe, too. She'd built PFS with him, asking his opinion on ambitious projects and sticky situations. There was nothing about Cosima's mother that Duncan didn't know. No detail he didn't remember.

If the trap they'd set worked the way they planned and Reggie left the board, it would be Duncan who stepped in as interim chair. He'd agreed to steer the ship and find a replacement for Phoebe. He'd even told Cosima, smiling with just a hint of irony, that he believed it would be "an entertaining project."

She took a deep breath. "I wanted to tell you that my last meeting of today went well."

"Which was?"

"With the lead investigators. I needed their clearance to leave the country tonight."

Duncan sat up, took off his readers, and raised one of his eyebrows. "Headed to a certain English village?"

"I've been trying to reach Edie, and I'm not getting through. I can't imagine what she must be thinking. I left her with almost no explanation. She hasn't heard from me, despite my multiple tantrums to our friends in law enforcement these last two weeks, who are less receptive to their part in a sapphic love story than you might imagine. If I get there and I've lost this beautiful Midwestern girl, I am going to personally *Macbeth* Reggie."

Duncan laughed, then cleared his throat. "You're in love."

"I'm in love, Duncan! And I know I may be needed here more than I want to be, at least for the next couple of years, but every single other minute, if everything isn't royally fucked, I'll be at Gregory Place."

He smiled. "I didn't hesitate when I met your mother. I knew from the moment I talked to her on the beach. And I know I surprised her. She thought she couldn't love anyone again the way she'd loved your father, but I don't think she understood that she wouldn't have to love me like your father. She only had to love me. Wouldn't trade a minute." He looked at his watch. "Get the hell out of here."

Shocked into laughter, Cosima stood up, and the hug she and Duncan shared reminded her of hugs he'd given her when she was a kid. Her eyes filled with tears. "I'm going to have to insist you come down and see me once you've trundled over your estate in the countryside. And, fair warning, I'm also going to have to insist you find a place in the village so you can come for long visits, often. There's a good church, a lovely pub, the most outrageous manor to tour, and I have a lot of people I want you to meet. Especially Edie."

"I'll look forward to that. As a Scot, I've always wanted to lay claim to a bit of English property."

"Soon, then." She squeezed his elbows. "Keep me posted."

"If you do the same."

"I will."

Then Cosima ran.

This time, she wasn't running away.

Chapter Twenty-Two

"Where is it?" Edie looked down the tracks at Grantham station, bouncing on her toes, enraged.

"It'll come," Killian said. "You've got some padding in the itinerary, so you'll make the plane."

"I'm a bit worried about that, to be honest." Tam looked at his phone. "We're cutting it close."

"We should've dashed for the earlier train." Morag was craning her head to look down the tracks, too. "Avoided this drama." Agatha picked up and patted her hand.

"Well, friends, I just got word." Bert held up her phone as she walked up to the group from her position at the other end of the platform, which she'd claimed had superior cell service. "It'll be twenty-five minutes still."

Everyone groaned. Edie bit the inside of her cheek so she wouldn't scream. She pulled out her own phone. Twenty-five minutes was impossible. What had she been *doing* for the last two weeks? She read the last text Cosima had sent her for the one hundred thousandth time, making herself take in the gravity of what was happening to Cosima's whole life. There was no question that Edie should've followed her the moment she left. She should have gone with her *when* she left. Instead of understanding what Cosima was trying to tell her by showing her the inn's garden, she'd decided to dive headfirst into what she was determined to ensure was the last great wallow of her life.

She was glad she'd called her mom.

"Maybe someone should drive me to Heathrow."

"Oh, you'd never make it," Bert said cheerfully. "The traffic."

Edie bit the inside of her cheek again, and then she heard a train. *Thank god.*

Morag shook her head. Agatha adjusted her cap. "That's the one up from London. On the other side of the tracks."

The group watched the train slow to a stop opposite them, its engines hissing. Edie got out her phone and texted Cosima again. The bubble settled on "delivered." She thought about the last two hours of activity that Morag had mobilized. The driver Agatha had arranged for her at LAX, and the Hollywood friend Tam had called, an actor who'd taught workshops at the community theater years ago, who had agreed to escort Edie to the Castle—or to wherever Cosima was.

Killian had driven her here. Bert had pulled some kind of strings with the stationmaster to get an express ticket to London when the train was already oversold. Morag had purchased Edie's plane tickets.

"This flight isn't the end-all," Morag said. "She'll still be there tomorrow."

Edie shook her head. "If you had known you could have what you have now if you'd only gone to Wales at any time in the last fifty years?"

Morag looked at Agatha. "I would have climbed into the luggage compartment of the next train out."

The London-to-Grantham train started to pull away, belching diesel exhaust over the tracks, and Edie watched it pick up speed with the pressure of what felt like years of impatience pushing against every bone of her body.

She knew what she wanted. She understood what she could do. And Cosima believed that she, Edie Ashlynn Whitelock, was singular. The one for her.

Now that Edie had all of the pieces to make her legacy, she wanted it to start. She felt like she hadn't kissed Cosima in a thousand years. She hadn't shown Cosima even a fraction of the ways she could love her. She wanted to tell her that she was having new mantles, sills, and corbels made for the lounge. Pink marble, in homage to Phoebe. She wanted to show her the replacement shepherdess she'd ordered on eBay.

She wanted Cosima.

The train sped down the tracks, and Edie looked across to the other side of the platform, defeated, watching the passengers make their way over the track bridge to the car park, going home.

A family with a set of double strollers moved down the platform, revealing a woman who had just picked up her bag. A tall woman.

A tall woman with messy, curly hair in a big bun, and tweed slacks with red-bottomed heels and a silky pink shirt.

Edie's heart *flew*.

"Cosima!" she shouted with everything she'd ever learned about projection in the stands of a Packers game. "Cosima Frank!"

Her group turned to look, and then they were yelling Cosima's name, and Cosima looked up and saw Edie.

The biggest, most beautiful smile lit up her face—at the

exact same moment the Grantham-to-London train barreled into the station, on time after all, hiding the other platform, and Edie's beloved, from view.

"Jesus HC on the mount!" Edie shouted. "*Come* on!"

"Go over the bridge to the other side!" Tam shouted. "Go!"

Edie shoved her bag at Tam and ran, dodging and weaving between a full crowd's worth of Grantham passengers jockeying to board the express to London, then stomping up the stairs around the people coming down from the train Cosima had been on. She made it to the part of the pedestrian bridge suspended over the tracks, and there she was, right in the middle.

Her princess.

"Cosima!" Edie tripped over her Converse and practically fell into Cosima's arms. She smelled deep-vanilla hair wash. Edie buried her face into her neck, inhaling, kissing, and grinning.

"Oh my god, Edie. Were you about to get on a train?" Cosima pulled back, her glorious eyebrows very stern. "I was coming! I told you to stay put! Why were you going to take a train?"

"To go to Los Angeles!"

"What for?"

Edie bent backward to emphasize her full-body eye roll. "To be with you! To support you! Because I love you!"

"I know that you love me, but I was always coming back to you. I said so. Did you know that I love *you*?"

"Yes." Edie narrowed her eyes at Cosima. "Of course I do."

"For how long, Edie, have you known that?" Cosima crossed her arms. "You have not heard even a single word from me for two weeks."

"One week and six days since your text that your mother's company was burning down. So not really two whole weeks to get worried or wallow or anything like that."

"Hmpf." Cosima raised an eyebrow. "And I thought I was coming *here* to grovel. To apologize for how much you must have worried and wallowed. How much faith you might have lost, given the tender newness of our relationship. But nothing like that went on. Turns out, according to you, you're brimming over with confidence."

Edie's heart leapt. "We're in a relationship?"

Cosima fisted Edie's jacket lapels and yanked her toward her. "Yes, of course we're in a relationship!"

The pedestrian bridge had emptied, and the train to London let out a hydraulic brake noise and began to slowly move away from the station beneath them. Edie noticed a teeny-tiny tendril of desire growing to test Cosima. A little. With full knowledge she *would* pass Edie's tests, but also would have to take them. "But you live in Los Angeles. And I live here."

"Oh." Cosima bit down on her excited grin to keep up their pretense of an argument. "So you live here now, do you? In England. That is very far from Los Angeles. A whole ocean *and* a continent away."

"That's what I'm saying. I don't really do long-distance relationships." Edie ran her hands up the arms of Cosima's silky pink blouse. To help her. She wasn't dressed for England. It was breezy. She had to be cold.

"Tell me about your other long-distance relationships." Cosima kissed Edie's temple.

"I can't, because, like I said, I don't do them." Edie went up on her tiptoes and got her hand around Cosima's nape. She kissed her, and their mouths were soft already, their tongues rubbing together slowly. Edie could've actually died from it. She could feel herself dying from it. Her pulse was externalizing into her wrists and the insides of her elbows, between her legs, and it was too loud with the train pulling away to hear it, but she could *feel* Cosima's moan.

"What are we going to do?" Cosima bit Edie's bottom lip.

"You tell me. You're the one who came here to grovel."

"I only have one idea." Cosima's hands found their way into both of Edie's back jeans pockets. It was a tight fit, but she managed to get in a good squeeze.

"Does your idea involve a guest book and a medieval numbering system? Because, if so, I refuse to wait fifty years for you." The wind was whipping long, curly pieces of hair from Cosima's bun into her face. Her eyes were the same color as the gray-blue Lincolnshire sky.

"My idea is that we go to Gregory Place right this minute, I fuck you with a pink strap-on, and then I never, ever leave." Cosima gave Edie an imperious look to see where that landed.

It landed where Cosima meant for it to land. Edie had to squeeze her thighs together to survive the impact, then take Cosima's hand to drag her off the pedestrian bridge.

"Fair warning," she gasped. "So many folks are here who are going to want to involve themselves in this reunion. We've accidentally been taken into a family of English villagers. I didn't see it coming, but it's good on the whole. Not so much right this second. Follow my lead."

They made it down to the platform filled with old people who Edie and Cosima would have to deal with for the rest of their lives, none of whom called her Frog. Really living the dream. "Morag, give me the keys to your van. Stay at the Gregory Arms tonight. None of you are permitted to do anything more than wave at Cosima. No chitchat. No stories. Morag"—Edie held out her palm—"the keys."

Morag huffed, and it took her long enough to extract the

keys from her coat pocket that Tam managed to side-hug Cosima while Killian beamed and Bert elbowed him in the side. "Harlaxton Pride is going to be lit this year, eh?"

Then Morag gave over the keys with a secret smile, and as they ran to the car park, all of Edie's new old people clapped and cheered, and she and Cosima laughed as Cosima attempted to jog in stilettos. Edie ground the gears of Morag's van getting out of the car park. She pushed its limits through the roundabout and down the road to Harlaxton to the front door of the inn, which barely got closed before Cosima was pulling at Edie's jacket and kissing her.

"Take off all your clothes," Cosima demanded between kisses.

"I'm not taking off my clothes in the lounge." Edie grabbed Cosima by the waist to pull her toward the stairs. "I don't want to scandalize the ghosts."

They tripped their way up, Cosima disregarding the prudish feelings of the ghosts by stripping her clothes off as she went and dropping them on the stairs.

"I sanded these down," Edie pointed out. "Took the runner up to do it."

"You're a marvel. The wood is glowing. Take off your jacket."

Edie did, but she carried it with her, her eyes on Cosima's delicate blouse as it dropped to the floor, followed by her shoes on the landing. Edie hung her jacket over the railing, memorizing the shape of Cosima's back, her waist, her silken shoulder, the slight flare of her hips as she smoothed her tweedy trousers down her legs. She wore a phantasm of a bra, panties that barely deserved the name. Nothing else.

"Where are my things?" Cosima asked, turning to look at Edie over her shoulder. "Why are you still wearing that?" She gestured at Edie's apparently offensive clothes.

Edie began unbuttoning her mouse shirt from the bottom. "In your room. I didn't touch anything."

"You didn't. That's interesting." She lifted her arms and began pulling the pins out of her hair, letting them fall to the carpet as she ambled down the hallway. "Considering how confident you were in my return, and the security of our love, I might have thought you would have packed the room up. Put it to service, since I would be sleeping with you when I returned."

Edie had considered moving her own things to Cosima's room so she could sleep among the shades of her lost love, but she'd thought better of it. "No, lucky for you, I didn't doubt you in any way, and I haven't had time to start ripping out the pink wallpaper yet. Morag doesn't have another guest booked until May."

Cosima flung the door open and sat on the edge of the bed, smoothly crossing her legs. Edie picked up the last of the hairpins from the carpet and fanned them out between her fingers. "You dropped these," she said.

"And you picked them up." Cosima held out her palm.

She settled the hairpins into Cosima's hand. "Now what?"

"Now we settle out the game. I tallied up our points on the plane. We have an equal number." She put the hairpins down on the table beside the bed.

Edie smiled. "What a twist of fate. Do we do a tiebreaker round now?"

"We do not. I've decided to divest myself of my points and whatever glory I could potentially lay claim to. Even if my life were worse than yours, everything I won a point for was an experience that led me to you."

"That's unbearably romantic." She meant it. Her heart ached. "I divest, too. Consider the game renounced."

"I will." Cosima smiled. "Take off your shirt."

Edie shrugged out of the shirt she had unbuttoned. Because she'd been in the middle of racing halfway across the globe in a romantic gesture, she had her best bra on, a black, strappy number that visibly strained against the weight of her breasts, but in a sexy way.

Cosima cleared her throat. "Um."

"Hmm?"

"I've run out of bossy. It's—" She gestured at Edie's rack.

"That's good, because the way I have to shimmy out of these pants didn't really go with the atmosphere you were trying to create." Edie unbuttoned her very tight, very stretchy jeans and wiggled out of them while she tried not to pant, taking her socks with them.

Cosima looked at her and let out a long, happy sigh. "I'm so glad to be here. I'm so glad to be here with *you*. I never want to miss you again. Let's be the kind of couple who only ever does everything together."

"I'm not sure they have other kinds in Harlaxton. Morag and Agatha have been a lot to behold. I keep beholding them by accident, which is a lot to bear up against without you here."

"Poor Edie," Cosima said. "Get the pink bag from my closet. Then I'll make you forget you've ever felt anything but blissful and satisfied." She bit her fingernail and flopped back on the bed.

Laughing, Edie found the bag easily, locked the bedroom door, and crawled onto the coverlet beside Cosima. "Your mattress is more comfortable than mine. Tell me how long you're really staying so I can brace my heart up against disappointment. I'm not going to admit I lost faith for one week and five and three-quarters days, but I will say that I've had a hard time stringing together coherent thoughts, and I'm still shaky. And tell me if everything is okay back home. Are you and Duncan good? Did you save the company, or will I have to boycott PFS movies and merchandise for the rest of my life? That could be difficult. My niece is really into the new animated series of *Ship of the Cosmos.*" She curled against Cosima's side and stroked her fingertips across her bare stomach. "I have a lot of questions."

"I feel confident that Duncan and I saved the company. He and I are good, really good. I think you may meet him soon. There is a long road I'll tell you about when I don't want to lick every inch of your body, but I don't believe it will take me back to California for a while, and definitely not without a few days' warning."

Edie played her fingertips over Cosima's skin, watching her expression. Her eyes were half-mast—not sleepy, but loved and aroused. Every part of her was soft. Every part of her was *here*, right here.

She kissed her favorite place behind Cosima's ear, taking her fingers under the waistband of her panties, then back out again, then a little lower. Every time Cosima's breathing got deeper, or she moved restlessly, or her hips rolled, Edie slowed down. Had it ever been this way? Had she ever felt, with a partner, with a lover, like she had all the time she needed and nothing to prove? That the goal of pleasure was achieved just by being together, and there was no beginning and no end to it?

She had not.

But that was how it was with Cosima.

"Tell me what you want." Edie kissed under her chin.

"I want to try my strap set. I'm glad we forgot about it in favor of other things in Barcelona, because now we'll remember this forever."

Edie reached over her body and opened the bag, pulling out the harness and the dildo, testing the shiny rose-gold bullet that fit into the harness for Cosima and peeling the seal off the little bottle of lube. "Can I put it on you?"

"You can."

Cosima watched as Edie slid her panties down and fitted the dildo and bullet into the harness. She was glad for her own experience with this so she could share it with Cosima and make this first time—this experiment with a fantasy—go easy. The harness slid up and over her legs, then her waist, and tightened from there. Edie spent time fastening every buckle, drawing it out, turning herself on, listening to Cosima breathe and watching her skin flush.

"How does it feel?" Edie asked. "Because it looks like I'm going to die six kinds of erotic deaths."

Cosima came up on her elbows, then reached down and traced the straps. She ran a finger down the dildo and under its base, her eyes fluttering. "Turn on the bullet."

Edie leaned over and kissed Cosima's thigh and pressed the base of the bullet, tight in its pocket. Cosima's knees came up, and she rolled her hips.

Well, that looked good.

"Yeah?" Edie reached behind her and unhooked her bra, pushed her panties down. Her focus on how Cosima looked in the strap set, her hair spilling over her bare breasts, had made it difficult for her to pay attention to anything else.

"God, yeah." Cosima's eyes were looking everywhere. At Edie, at the strap-on, and them together. Edie leaned over and kissed up Cosima's thigh, demanding eye contact, until she got to the dildo. Then, she grabbed it at the base and licked her way up it in one long stripe, never letting her eyes leave Cosima's, swirling her tongue at the end.

Cosima's rapid breathing hollowed the dip at the base of her throat. Her nipples were tight beneath the fabric of her bra, her pupils blown. "What do you want?" Edie reached down and felt how wet she was, forced to tease herself to take the edge off.

Cosima let out a long, shuddering breath. "Can you straddle me and take it? I want to see."

"Jesus, Cosima." But Edie smiled, coming up on her knees, then putting a leg over Cosima's middle, leaning down and kissing her until they were both starting to get impatient. The bullet probably had Cosima dangerously close. Edie's chest was tight, her throat tighter, her eyes burning and threatening soppy tears, but that seemed correct. Everything felt right.

She sat up, running her hands over Cosima's breasts in their filmy bra, and reached for the lube. She filled her hand with it and then rose up, slicking her hand down the dildo and pressing its tip along where she was wet before directing it at her entrance.

She slowly moved her hips down, down, taking it in, feeling how everything was slippery, how she and Cosima were connected, how the dildo inside her hummed a little from the bullet and made her full, very full, just as Cosima's hands reached up to cover her breasts.

Edie leaned forward, and Cosima shifted, finding an angle that pressed the bullet against her and made Edie reach down to touch her clit.

This wasn't going to be a very long experiment.

"Are you okay?" Cosima's wide eyes were on Edie's face, even as her hips found a rolling pulse that made her eyes roll back. "Is this okay?"

Edie pushed down, meeting Cosima's rising hips. "It's okay, it's so okay."

"Kiss me, Edie." Cosima used her hair to pull her close—such a demanding move that it made Edie's scalp burn, which made her eyes burn worse, and that was when the angle changed again, their hips discovering a better rhythm with every sliding, sloppy, welcoming kiss until one of them sent Cosima over, pressing her face into Edie's neck, and Edie right behind her.

"I love you, I love you," Edie breathed, letting herself fall into something that she couldn't feel the beginning or end of. It was pleasure, it was love, it was just the right amount of new and forever.

"I love you." Cosima kissed Edie's forehead, something she had grown to love so much, how this difficult woman poured tenderness through her and made whatever was happening easy.

Edie slowly rose up, coming to Cosima's side, then helping her with the buckles so they could pull off the harness and press themselves together, face-to-face.

"Was that like your fantasy?" Edie rubbed her thumb over Cosima's mouth.

"No. That was much more romantic than what I'd thought of. I didn't think about the mutuality of it. I didn't imagine how all the love would get in there. But I didn't know about love yet, how it specializes in what should be impossible. Very sneaky." Her cheeks were pink, her lips swollen. The tension was gone from her eyebrows, and the contrast to the first time Edie had seen Cosima at the door of this very room was more than stark.

"So in your fantasy you're strapped in, very hot, and fucking me to the mattress?"

Cosima closed her eyes. "Sometimes into the wall. Or over a chaise."

Edie laughed. "Plenty of time to see those through. I've already sent a chaise I found in the attic to the upholsterer."

"Edie," Cosima slurred. "Here's the thing. Two weeks of near twenty-hour days. Lots of suits. Late-night conversations with

Duncan when we should have been sleeping. Too many feelings. No you."

"You're falling asleep." Edie slid her arms under Cosima's shoulders to lift her up and grab the top of the duvet, bringing it down and then over them both.

"Oh, that's good." Cosima settled into the spot she'd claimed, the nook of Edie's shoulder, her leg over both of Edie's. "Don't move even a little. No, scratch that, you can Edie-wiggle. But make sure one part of you is always touching me. Wake me up in ninety minutes and make me Morag's carrot bread. I assume you've managed to steal, test, and improve the recipe by now."

Edie had. She kissed into the curly mass of Cosima's hair. When she adjusted to fit her cheek against the top of her head, she noticed the place on the wall where Cosima had cut her mother's letter from beneath the wallpaper—the first one of fifty years of letters that brought them here. Right here.

And most of what they found hadn't been on the map.

Acknowledgments

As we get older, we discover how affected we are, how actively changed we are, by the stories that emerge from our families—sometimes stories that are generations old. All those stories that we were too young for, or were too painful, have a way of surfacing as time goes on, and it's shocking how they explain so much, affirm and validate so much, and how something that happened to your grandma or her mother or a cousin much older than you, or even a relative or family friend you never met, can echo forward and change the trajectory of your life.

This is a book about legacy and treasure, but not in the way we usually think of those things. We often don't think about how heavy it is to carry what was important to everyone else while we try to live our own lives. We want to thank those in our lives who have made everything lighter, sweeter, and so precious we can truly believe our own lives are priceless:

Our children, August and James, always. Sharing this part of the map with you continues to be so joyful, fascinating, and a real quest of the heart. Let's never stop adjusting our character sheets for the five thousandth time.

Our agents, Tara Gelsomino and Pamela Harty, who especially in this season have exemplified what it means to foster professional relationships infused with values, conviction, and the full force of allyship. We've fought hard this round, and we know we'll all keep fighting to get stories like this into the world.

Susan and Sara, our truest friends, biggest fans, and book tour ride-alongs who remind us what it's all really about.

Our remarkable author friends, Emma Barry, Ruby Lang/Opal Wei, Charlotte Stein, Joanna Lowell, Molly O'Keefe, Becca Grischow, Mia P. Manansala, Katie Siegel, and Matthew Sullivan. You are all real ones.

Harlaxton village is a real place, with a real storybook village and castle-like manor house. Annie lived there as a student once upon a time and always wanted to return to it in a story, to thank this place for making a part of her life magical in a way she could never have imagined for herself. Here, it has been gilded with the 24K gold ink of imagination, but only to serve the plot vagaries of *The Guest Book*. As a place, a real place, it is naturally gilded with history, beauty, and many actual treasures. Magical places in our lives cast their spell forever.

Thank you to our St. Martin's Press team—our ever-incisive Alex Sehulster, who genuinely understands the heart of the story we're telling; and our assistant editor, Ashley Quintana, who is unfailingly supportive, detail-oriented, and answers anxious author questions instantly and well.

Finally, Mae Marvel readers, booksellers, reviewers, and bookish champions have given us everything you see here—a world to write our books in, to share our messiest and queerest characters, and to make our lives so much richer. You are the treasure, always.

About the Author

Alyssa Lentz-Underwood

Mae Marvel is the alias of cowriters Ruthie Knox and Annie Mare, bestselling authors of over a dozen acclaimed romance novels between them. Mae lives with two teenagers, two dogs, two cats, four hermit crabs, and a plethora of snails and fish in a witchy century home in Wisconsin whose extravagant perennial garden gives them something to look forward to in the depths of winter. In addition to romance, they also write mystery novels and cannot promise not to branch into new territories at a moment's notice. They can be found online at maemarvel.com.